Captain Brian Sloan joined the British Navy (RFA service) in 1976 and qualified as Master Mariner in 1987. He saw action in the Falklands war '82 and First Gulf War '90–91. He helped with the aftermath of hurricane Gilbert '88 and Hugh '89 while stationed in the Caribbean on UK/US anti-drug smuggling operations. His last naval job was 3 months on Operation Haven, taking Aid to the Kurds in southern Turkey in spring of '91.

He and his family joined Youth With A Mission (YWAM) in September 1991 and after their initial missionary training in Uganda and Kenya, he joined the 12,000 tonnes hospital ship "m/v Anastasis". Brian served as the chief officer, then the captain from 1996. In 1999, Brian became the first captain of what would be renamed "m/v Africa Mercy", a 16,500 tonnes replacement for "m/v Anastasis".

From 2003, Brian started pioneering ship equipped ministries for YWAM in the Amazon, Lake Tanganyika, Tanzania and the Mediterranean. Focusing initially on medical relief and aid delivery, then later on mainly training the next generation of YWAM mariners.

He married Anne in 1980, and they have two sons and six grandchildren. Studying the history of the many places he visits has been a lifelong interest.

To my ever-supportive wife, Anne, our two sons and their families, Peter and Nina, Rachel, Hannah and Nathanael, Andy and Rebecca, Finnley, Elliot and Poppy. You all bring me so much joy.

Brian Sloan

THE DAGGER AND THE ROSARY

AUSTIN MACAULEY PUBLISHERS™

LONDON * CAMBRIDGE * NEW YORK * SHARJAH

A CIP catalogue record for this title is available from the British Library.

ISBN 9781035806447 (Paperback)
ISBN 9781035806454 (ePub e-book)

www.austinmacauley.com

First Published 2023
Austin Macauley Publishers Ltd®
1 Canada Square
Canary Wharf
London
E14 5AA

Thanks to my wife, Anne, of over 40 years, whose patience with me and initial proofing helped me finish. Also, those that have given me advice from their experience, and the publishing team at Austin Macauley who turned a manuscript into a book.

Table of Contents

Historical Notes

The Spanish Inquisition

From the union of the crowns of Aragon and Castile under Ferdinand and Isabel, that would later unite the whole of Spain, the church was given the **Inquisition.** With this new force within the Roman Catholic Church, bigotry and intolerance was to reach new depths and many innocent people would suffer in the name of the church. However, without giving any excuses for the inhuman and "un-Christlike" acts carried out by the Inquisition, it must be noted that their intolerance did not represent the views of the whole church. So, although opposition to the Inquisition while they were in power was dangerous, resistance did continue throughout, from within the church as well as from outside.

Sicily and Secret Societies

Over the centuries, Sicily has been ruled by Greeks, Carthaginians, Romans, North African Muslims, Normans, and various French princes. By 1442, Alfonso V of Spain had added Sicily to his territories, but Spanish rule would not be easy for the Sicilians. In 1487, the Inquisition arrived. Expulsion of Jews and Muslims followed. Intolerance to the Eastern and Greek Orthodox Christians and any group that did not match Spain's exacting definition of Roman Catholicism ensured that Sicily missed out on much of the early Renaissance. During the 1500 and 1600s, instead of artistic development, Sicily suffered North African and Turkish pirate raids, causing depopulation of her smaller islands and terror for her coastal communities. Land-grabbing barons also had the island in their firm grip, substantially aided by the church, as both found it best to keep the population in poverty and ignorance.

The 17th century marks the low point of Sicilian history, the most noteworthy events being the natural disasters: the 1669 volcanic eruption of Etna that buried much of Catania and the earthquake of 1693, which killed at least 50,000 and devastated the southeast. Yet the richness of her diverse cultural heritage and varying landscape, along with the resilience of her people provided hope for the Sicilians. These people were to fight back, not so much in all out rebellion, but in the rise of secret societies that would come to dominate in later centuries.

Exactly how these secret societies started and why they developed the way they did in Sicily is open to conjecture. There is evidence of many secret societies that developed throughout the middle ages in Europe, some of which disappeared from history quickly and others that continued for hundreds of years. Freemasons are probably the best-known survivor as they continue today. However, in Sicily, perhaps because of the degree of oppression the ordinary people felt, the mixture of cultures and the long periods of foreign rule, these societies were to become a dominant force.

Barbary Pirates

The Barbary Pirates, sometimes are called Barbary Corsairs or Ottoman Corsairs, due to their affiliation with the Ottoman empire that was based in modern day Turkey. They were mostly Muslim pirates, and privateers who operated from North Africa from the time of the Crusades in the 11th century until the early 19th century. Operating out of North African ports such as Tunis, Tripoli, and Algiers, as well as ports in Morocco, they sailed mainly along the stretch of northern Africa known as the Barbary Coast (hence their collective name). Their reach extended throughout the Mediterranean, south along West Africa's Atlantic seaboard, and into the North Atlantic, with accounts reporting raids as far north as Iceland. However, they primarily commandeered western European ships in the western Mediterranean Sea. In addition, they engaged in *Razzias* (raids) on European coastal towns, to capture Christian slaves to sell at slave markets in places such as Algeria, and Morocco.

Pirates destroyed thousands of French, Spanish, Italian and British ships, and long stretches of coast in Spain, and Italy were almost completely abandoned by their inhabitants, discouraging settlement until the 19th century. From the 16th to 19th century, pirates captured an estimated 800,000 to 1.25 million Europeans as slaves, mainly from seaside villages in Italy, Spain, and Portugal, but also from France, Britain, the Netherlands, and Ireland. The most famous corsairs were the brothers Hayreddin Barbarossa ("Redbeard") and Oruç Reis, who took control of Algiers in the early 16th century. This began four hundred years of

Ottoman Empire presence in North Africa and establishing a centre of Mediterranean piracy.

Knights Hospitaller of St John

The Order of the Hospital was founded in the Holy Land as a hospice, and monastic community to care for the sick in 1048, if not some years earlier, by the Blessed Gerard (who was probably from southern Italy). In 1113, it received papal approval, by which time it was an Order of knights with a principal objective of assisting pilgrims travelling in the Holy land. It soon became a military as well as religious order which participated in many crusades, and military campaigns. Gerard died in 1120, succeeded by a series of grand masters beginning with Raymond du Puy.

After the fall of Jerusalem, in 1187, the knights established their seat in Cyprus and, in 1310, at Rhodes, where they remained until a bloody defeat at Ottoman Muslim hands in 1523. In 1530, the King of Sicily, who was also the Holy Roman Emperor, Charles V, gave the knights the island of Malta during a ceremony in the barons' hall in Steri Castle in what is now Piazza Marina in Palermo, Sicily. Initially the knights' Maltese dominion was a fiefdom of the Kingdom of Sicily, its Grand Master a vassal. Thus, an annual feudal tax was paid, though this was largely symbolic; it included, for example, a "Maltese falcon". The Order would remain a military dependency of the Kingdom of Sicily (by then ruled by the House of Bourbon of the "Two Sicily's") until 1798. Like the feudal tax rendered to the king, this was to be largely symbolic rather than actual practice.

Genoa

The city state of Genoa first become rich with sea trading following the first Crusades to the Holy land. With the expansion of international banking, economic growth continued with a few banking families becoming extremely wealthy and powerful. This growth was threatened with the importation of the Black Death into Europe in 1347 from a Genoese trading post at Caffa in the Crimea on the Black sea. The economic and population collapse that followed, prompted Genoa to adopt a Venetian style of government, being presided over by a Doge. These Doges were elected for two-year terms and selected exclusively from the main trading/banking families who dominated the city.

In 1407, the first chartered bank, Bank of Saint George, was founded in Genoa. By the 16th century, the international position of Genoa as a major banking and trading centre was stabilised. Much of this is thanks to the efforts of Doge Andrea Doria, who granted a new constitution in 1528 and made Genoa a satellite of the Spanish Empire.

However, plagues continued to sweep Europe periodically in 16th and 17th century killing about half the Genoese population. Then attacks from France and other states wanting to damage Spain, pushed Genoa into decline, even with a Spanish fleet coming to Genoa's defence. Despite these many setbacks, with the outpouring of wealth from the Americas via the Hapsburg empire, Genoa continued to be influential. The four, main merchant banking families, in particular, continued to dominate the city, trade and politics, even beyond Genoa, but with great and sometime bitter rivalry.

Spain

Following the establishment of colonies in the Americas, Spain's imperial ambitions grew exponentially. However, to fund rapid colonialisation and maintain armies in expanding territories, the Hapsburg monarchy borrowed extensively from Genoese banking families at high interest rates. These interest and loan repayments were made possible by the vast amount of gold and silver being extracted from the new Spanish colonies in the Americas.

These were made into coins in Spain, then regularly shipped to Genoa.

Although details of these shipments were kept a closely guarded secret, they were vulnerable to pirate attack. So, information about the route and timing of these voyages was a valuable commodity to trade.

As the 17th century comes to a close, King Charles of Spain is in poor health and has not produced an heir for his Hapsburg empire. Meanwhile, his main adversary, the Bourbon King Louis the 14th of France, looks to expand his territories and influence. All the Princes of Europe recognise war is coming and political tensions rise as alliances are negotiated and the powers of the day plot to gain advantage.

Many of the states in Europe were spending far more on wars than they had income. With famine, plagues and civic unrest reducing their tax income, while they owed huge amounts to banking families, as in Genoa. Spain survived only as it stripped her American colonies of silver and gold.

France

France, on the other hand, did not have such lucrative colonies, though they sought them. They also started to suffer overly cold springs and wet summers creating crop failures, resulting in widespread famine. The high mortalities among the peasants through 1647 to 1652, then again between 1691 and 1695, meant the population recovered slowly. So, despite successful military campaigns, they struggled to finance their empire building.

This was a period of much intrigue, leading up to the inevitable war of the Spanish Succession. Alliances between strategic principalities changed repeatedly; plots were hatched behind the veneer of polite diplomacy. Secret societies flourished whose declared pious objectives could hide alternative motives that may still, to this day, not be fully clear.

List of Major Characters

(In rough order of appearance)

Cavaliere Mateo di Boscogrande

Mateo is descended from a noble Norman family that came to Sicily during the period that the Normans ruled. The Boscogrande family also originally owned lands in France, and had been wealthy and titled. However, as various other dynasties took control of Sicily, the Boscogrande family who had come to see themselves as Sicilian, lost influence.

During Mateo's grandfather's lifetime, the family lost their lands in France due to various peace treaties between France, and Spain that gave over lands. Mateo's father, while taking sides in the many wars in Europe, lost titles, and drifted into being a "soldier of fortune". Along with his retainers, a "knight for hire" with the hope of regaining his family's former status, fortune, and lands.

Mateo had followed in his father's footsteps and gained an honourable reputation after his father's death. During his many adventures, he saves a young king's life, is knighted in his own right and is made a companion of the Order of the Golden Fleece. However, although the many conflicts he, and his men fought in, gained them income, they were not always on the winning side so never became wealthy.

Abriana di Boscogrande (nee Davide)

Abriana is the only child of a widowed wealthy merchant, trading between the middle east, and western Europe. Originally of Jewish descent, the Davide family came to live in Sicily many generations before when religious tolerance was more widespread. Her great, great grandfather had accepted Christianity, rather than being expelled from Sicily by the Spanish Inquisition. So, she had been brought up as a Sicilian Catholic, but the family still had business connections with Jewish merchants and bankers elsewhere.

She is well educated in the medical practices of the east which she uses to help Mateo recover from an infected wound when he is brought back to Sicily. During this period, while she is nursing Mateo, he is attracted to her, as she is very beautiful, and they fall in love.

Mateo asks her father for her hand in marriage which he agrees. Signior Davide treats Mateo as a son, training him to take over his business, and they are very happy. Mateo leaves his fighting days behind him, and they have a healthy son, Bernardo.

Signior Davide

A wealthy merchant, and ship owner of Jewish descent, but has been Catholic, and Sicilian since his great grandfather's expeditious conversion. He, and his beloved wife had only one child, late in life, and his wife died of complications after the birth. He dotes on his daughter Abriana and indulges her interest in eastern medicine which they feel might have saved her mother.

Although he is generally seen as a generous man with many friends, his wealth, and influence does bring jealousy from some. When his son-in-law tries to speak up in defence of some injustices he sees against small local landowners, this jealousy comes to the surface.

Father Aiello

This academic Benedictine monk is an old friend of Signior Davide, and the Boscogrande family. When Mateo is brought back from France with an infected wound, he takes Mateo to Signior Davide's house in Palermo to seek help with nursing him. He trusts Abriana's knowledge, and piety. He is delighted Abriana, and Mateo fall in love, then marry.

When Abriana gives birth to Bernardo, he christens him, and later becomes his tutor.

He tries to support Mateo when he appeals to the church council against the excesses of the Inquisition after Signior Davide dies in their cells. Then he helps Abriana, and Bernardo relocate to an isolated Boscogrande manor in the Sicanian hills. He gets himself transferred from the abbey above Palermo to Santa Martia Del Bossco abbey to be near them.

William di Giovanni

William was born in France, on former Boscogrande land, but brought up in Sicily. His mother was French, and father an English archer who was a retainer of Mateo's father. The same age as Mateo, they grow up together, and become firm friends. As he was born of bonded servants, William follows his father, to become an archer of the Boscogrande family.

However, when Mateo becomes master of the household, he makes sure William is made a freeman, but he remains steadfastly loyal to Mateo, becoming his right-hand man.

Friar Diego de Loisa

This Spanish friar of the Dominican order is haunted by his troubled childhood. His mother, according to his father, abandoned them when he was young. His distraught father drinks heavily, and abuses his only son. Later, Diego happily enters the church, to get away from his father. As a very young man he adapts to the overtly strict discipline within the Spanish Dominican Order he becomes part of. Out of this Order, the Spanish Inquisition is formed, and after years of service in Spain, he is made Chief Inquisitor in Sicily.

Bernardo di Boscogrande

Much loved only son of Mateo and Abriana, who in May 1693 turned sixteen-years old. He has been educated by Father Aiello all his life and lived in a cloistered abbey since he was nine years old. Therefore, his understanding of the world is limited to a close loving mother, a monastic life, and father who he only knew when he was very young. Since coming of age to inherit his family's lands, he has been considering entering the Benedictine Order, and his education has been focused on that.

Of Norman decent he is tall, fair haired, blue eyed, and between his father's genes and regular exercise with his long bow, he has grown up a strong skilled archer. Like his mother, he has a gentle nature, strong moral code, and firm belief in God. Prayer, as Father Aiello has taught him his whole life, has been his only comfort, and protection, so far.

Captain Benedetto di Orlando (only referred to as Capt. Orlando)

Orlando is a slightly mysterious character that we only get to know in stages. An old friend of Mateo, and once a ship's captain who partnered with the Davide family shipping business. He has become regional magistrate of the Palermo region since Diego's departure.

Agata Conti (mother was Maria Tringali)

Agata is the oldest child of a small holding farmer, who lives just inland of the port of Trabia. She has three younger brothers and is almost sixteen years old. At the time and in that society, she would be expected to marry soon. However, between her family's closeness, and limited prospective husbands in the area, she is not spoken for yet, but is blossoming into a beautiful woman.

Friar Raphael

This young Dominican brother is the loyal secretary to Diego, who both admires, and fears the Chief Inquisitor. He is a dedicated Inquisitor, and efficient intelligence gatherer.

Captain Raymond De Poincy

Knight of Saint John, of the French langue, and Captain of the Knights of Malta frigate *San Giovanni*. An old friend of both Captain Orlando, and Bernardo's father who he fought alongside at some point. He comes from a wealthy French family, as many Knights of Saint John did, and also one with a strong naval tradition. Although he has been part of the Knights of Saint John order for quite some time, he also has served in the French navy.

The Knight of Malta's fleet are the main adversaries against the Barbary pirates, as the rest of Europe are either fighting each other or not agreeing on how to mount an effective defence against the pirates. The fleet manages to increase their wealth by both protecting European merchants and confiscating Turkish ship's cargoes or capturing pirates' hoards.

Father Pepe

A Franciscan friar who is the parish priest in Gela, and friend of Captain Orlando, and Captain De Poincy. Probably only sympathetic towards the Beati Paoli, rather than being part of them but trusted by Orlando, and De Poincy.

Amad Ali ibn Majid Rayar

Amad Rayar is the amīr al-baḥr (Admiral) of the Moroccan fleet and serves the Bey of Morocco who he gives 10% of his profits, cargo, and slaves. Morocco is nominally part of the Ottoman empire, but so far from Istanbul, that it is an autonomous region. He is one of the leading Barbary pirates of the time, and arch enemy of the Knights of Saint John, who has foiled his efforts several times. No longer the swash-buckling pirate of his early years, he now runs a network of spies, and collaborators. Through them he is given advanced warning of key ship movements, such as: Spanish ships full of new world silver on route to pay the bankers in Genoa; the movement of wealthy people who would be ideal to kidnap and ransom and ideal places to raid for slaves. He sees the Knights of Malta's new acquisition of the fast frigate *San Giovanni* as a threat.

Baron Castellietti of Marsa (Malta)

A Maltese nobleman from an ancient but diminishing family, well respected by the Knights of Malta as the once Captano della Verga (Captain of the Rod)— the local right-hand man of the Grand Master of the Order, although not a knight of the order himself. He is an old gentleman by the time introduced to Agata. He and his gentle wife were sorrowful as they had lost all their children from still births, infant illnesses, and a horse-riding accident.

Baroness Castellietti of Marsa (Malta)

Wife of the Baron, ten years younger and of a much gentler character than the Baron who had spent most of his life in military service of some kind. She grieves deeply for her children, all of whom have died before reaching adulthood. She sees in Agata and Stefano as a focus for the love she would have showered on her own children.

Signior Giuseppe Beniamino (in Genoa)

Originally named Mordecai Ben Heli, he was born in Pisa to a wealthy Jewish merchant family, with international connections. He was the only surviving son (infant mortality was still high, at the time, despite developments in medicine and hygiene) and went to the university there to study law. At the time of his youth, there was a large Jewish community in Pisa that was generally allowed to live in peace as the local authorities saw the benefit of the trade they brought to the aspiring port city. However, just after he graduates, his family come under persecution which was a repeating difficulty for Jewish communities around Europe for hundreds of years. False accusations of corruption probably initiated by jealous business revivals are thrown around. These do not go far in the courts, with Mordecai brilliantly exposing the instigators. However, it gives licence to anti-Jewish sentiments among some, affecting the family business and threats of violence to Mordecai himself.

Saverik Albertini (also known as Amir Ali)

Saverik Albertini goes by many names and professions, but to Genoese society he is known as Signior Albertini. Ostensibly, a trader in fine silk, but also, quietly a supplier of narcotics and pleasure slaves for the wealthy. This illicit trade, not exactly secret, but not talked about openly, allows Saverik to gather intelligence from bankers while they are under the influence of drugs. The elite of Genoa do not question where Albertini acquires his opium, hashish or young slaves, careful not to broadcast their vices.

Stephano Conti

Stephano is the Conti's oldest son, two years younger than his sister Agata and already taller than her. He is taken captive with his other two brothers after the pirates kill his father and mother.

Commandeur Robert Blundell

Blundell comes from an educated English Roman Catholic family that has experienced times of influence and times of persecution, depending on the monarch in power. Many of his family have emigrated to the "new world", some to the Virginia colony, but Robert, who studied law at Oxford, joined the military wing of the Knights of Saint John as a young man.

He rises quickly through the ranks to Commandeur of Commandery. His intellect encourages his superiors to assign him to service in the Order's diplomatic corps and he finds himself working within the Vatican. However, he is often dispatched to various other places where the Order needs a "discreet investigator".

Archbishop Stefanu Buonaparte

Descended from a branch of a Tuscan noble trading family who moved to Corsica where Stefanu was born. His family members leant towards Corsican nationalism, at a time when Corsica was a dominion of Genoa. As a younger brother, he went into the church, while still favouring Corsica aligning with France to escape the rule of Genoa. He was eventually appointed Archbishop of Sienna. Then the Vatican's nuncio to the count of King Charles in Spain, from where he spies on behalf of a French supporting group that spans several countries.

Enrico de Silva

Enrico is a 32-year-old Castilian, born into a very poor family. He joined the army at 12 years old, partly through partialism, but mainly to have a paying occupation. He fought in many conflicts, rose to the rank of Sargento, becoming firm friends with Rodrigo who had taken him under his wing when he first enlisted. During late 1691 he helps Commandeur Blundell search for stolen army pay. He is well rewarded by King Charles when they recover it, after which, he and Rodrigo leave the army to set themselves up as merchants, trading anything that will turn a profit. With Blundell's help, they start well, but are not actually that good at trading, their skills primarily being soldiering.

Rodrigo Gorostiza

Rodrigo is a 34-year-old Castilian, and his father was in the Spanish army. When he was seven years old, his mother and siblings died of disease, along with many in their village. His father, with encouragement of his commanding officer, brought the young Rodrigo into the regiment as a drummer boy, rather than abandoning him to distant poor relatives. Seven years later, his father is killed. However, the regiment is his family by then and he continues to serve rising to the rank of Sargento primero (1st Sargent). He takes Enrico under his wing when he enlists, and both help Commandeur Blundell searching for stolen army pay. After they are well-rewarded by the King for their services, he and Enrico leave the army to set themselves up as merchants to trade whatever will turn a profit. With Blundell's help, they start well, but he is not that good at commerce; his skills and all his experience primarily being soldiering.

Rachael Levi-Cases Momigliano (nee Ben Heli)

Signior Beniamino's younger sister. She, like several females in their family, lose her husband and sons, to plague or persecution of Jews, both of which erupted periodically. Her husband and sons were all traders who would travel to major cities, which is why they were more vulnerable. As a widow, she moved back to the family estate in the Livorno hills, becoming the lady of the villa when her parents die. A very capable lady that runs the family vineyards and orchards on behalf of Beniamino and the surviving extended family.

Mateo Conti

Mateo is the youngest child in the Conti family of Trabia, Sicily. He is nine years old when he is captured by the pirates and subsequently enslaved to Albertini.

Domanic Ortega Sanchez

Sanchez was Rodrigo and Enrico's first sergeant in the Spanish army, just before their adventure with Blundell. Rodrigo was promoted and replaced him when he retired, about the same time the army pay had been stolen, depriving him of much backpay that had built up whilst he had been deployed.

The Spanish army was paid in silver and not very well, which had to be distributed over their large empire. This was a momentous task and open to much abuse, which is why this story suggests it was stolen in 1691 by French agents.

Monsignor Emmanuel Garcia

Diego Sarmiento de Valladares was the actual Grand Inquisitor at the time this story is set.

However, I wanted to have a senior Inquisitor involved that was younger and more "hands-on", so invented Emmanuel Garcia as the Inquisitor General— right-hand man to the Grand Inquisitor.

In the story, he had worked with Blundell before, when the Spanish army pay was recovered. The suggestion being that the Spanish authorities were grateful for Blundell's secretive services, aiding them in recovering a large amount of silver that had been stolen.

This is important, so he will trust Blundell. Blundell is relying on him remembering, while not 'announcing' himself to the Inquisition in general. Both men realise it is hard to know whom you can trust.

Map of Sicily with mentioned places indicated

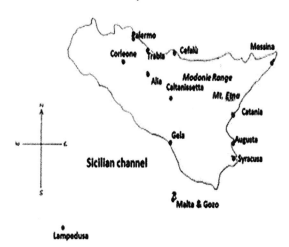

Chart of Lampedusa where pirates anchored.

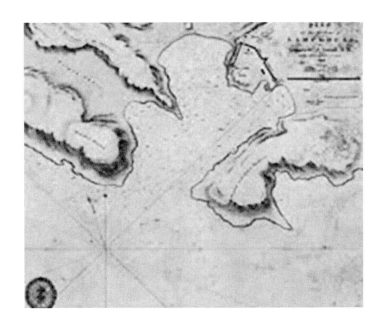

17th century engravings of Corsica and Spain

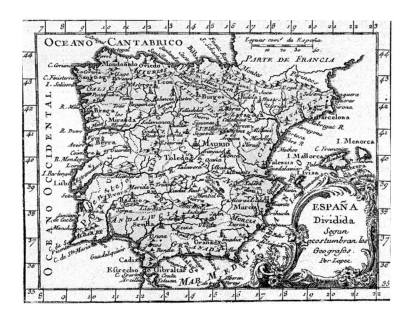

Setting for this story

Cavaliere Matteo di Boscogrande is a descendent of a Norman family that originally arrived in Sicily in the 11th century with the Norman conquest of the island. During this period, the island experienced a time of religious and cultural tolerance under King Roger 1st where Christians, Jews, and Muslims' cultures mixed freely. This helped created the unique architecture and cultural heritage of Sicily. With the later conquest of the island by the French, then Spanish, the Boscogrande family, for the sake for this story, represent the Sicilian nobility that saw their wealth declined. They became soldiers of fortune, fighting in the many disputes between rival principalities in Europe.

The 2nd half of the 17th century saw French and Spanish rivalry and expansionism, with conflicts in the Netherlands and French eastern borders. This gave good employment to Mateo di Boscogrande and his men, during which he was much honoured by the Spanish, but in 1676 he found himself on the losing side.

Years later his sixteen-year-old son finds himself on the run from the Spanish Inquisition, due to his father's conflict with a particular inquisitor. His closeted upbringing in an Abbey has not equipped him for the violent world he is to enter, as he tries to grow up fast and discover details of his family's past. Meanwhile, he rescues an innocent girl, falls in love and has multiple adventures with new friends.

A man's heart plans his way, but the Lord directs his steps.
Proverbs 16:9 NKJV

Who knows what effect the choices we make can have. Decisions that seem personal and isolated can create waves of interconnected consequences. Some impinging on people we know, and other on those we don't know. Sometimes small, seemingly inconsequential action changing world history, and even generations to come. One thing causing another, then another, making our careful planning futile, even naive.

Prologue

Palermo, Sicily
1676

Light coming through the window stung Mateo's eyes and made it hard for him to see. He closed them, trying to remember where he was. There seemed to be a dark void in his mind, fleeting images, but no sense of context or time. As he regained consciousness and his head began to clear, he became aware of a throbbing, burning sensation in his right shoulder.

He tried to move, but his muscles were stiff, and waves of nausea swept up from his stomach.

He decided to lie still and focus on his surroundings.

Movement through his blurred vision drew his attention as a graceful figure came into view. Initially just a black shape against the bright light. Then he recognised it was a petite woman as her slim frame was silhouetted by the sunlight coming through the open window. She started talking to him. A soft gentle voice but sounding very distant in his semi-conscience state. He concentrated on the image and the voice before him but was not sure if he could stay awake.

As his surroundings came into focus and his ears adjusted, he gazed upon a beautiful vision. Her long dark hair was tied up in a single, delicately braided tail running down her back. Big dark eyes looked back at him, surrounded by beautiful flawless ivory skin and a gentle smile.

'Is this a young woman or an angel?' Mateo thought. It occurred to him that he might be dead and in heaven. However, the pain from his shoulder convinced him he was still alive.

'Good to see you in the land of the living,' a voice said, but it was not the woman.

Her rosy lips were closed, and her eyes directed towards his shoulder where her hands did something to bandages. He tried to look at what she was doing, but

29

gave up quickly, as turning his neck caused shooting pains in his side. Instead, he looked beyond her to where the sound came from and to his delight a familiar face came into view.

'You are looking so much better, my son,' a smiling Father Aiello said, as he craned over Mateo, 'the colour is returning to your face.' This Benedictine monk had been his father confessor for many years and a friend of his family for as long as he could remember. He was happy to see him.

Mateo struggled to comprehend what was being said and what had happened to him.

He let his eyelids drop momentarily and images of frantic fighting flashed though his mind.

His heart pounded as he visualised swinging his sword repeatedly at the enemy, but they kept coming. More and more, pressing in around him, cries from his own men to fall back, then a burning pain in his shoulder and darkness.

'William brought you back to Sicily and sought me out, but your wound was already poisoning you and you had a bad fever. We thought we had lost you, but Abriana is a wonderful healer and has prayed by your bedside these last three days and nights.'

The old priest looked over to the young girl whose radiant face came back into Mateo's view. Abriana bent down and put her arm gently around Mateo's neck.

'Can you sit up a little?' she asked, manoeuvring a pillow behind his back. 'You need to drink this.' she gently said, holding a cup to his lips and easing warm fluid into his mouth.

It tasted mostly of honey with a bitter after flavour. Mateo found it hard to swallow as if his dry throat was closed. Abriana rubbed gently under his chin, and he gratefully swallowed the soothing liquid, even while some dribbled down his thick beard.

'The honey should mask the bitterness of the herbs and give some energy,' she was saying, but he was not sure if she was talking to him or Father Aiello.

After the drink, she brought up an earthenware bowl and attempted to spoon something aromatic into his mouth. His senses were beginning to return, and he could smell the spices rising from the bowl. He sniffed, enjoying the sensation, and became curious about what it was. Seeing his reaction, Abriana paused, the spoon hovering in mid-air.

'It is mostly chicken broth, but with some herbs and spices that will help to cool your fever and purge the poison out of your body…turmeric, ginger, garlic and such like.' The spoon pressed up to his lips again. 'You need to eat.' easing the tasty broth into his mouth, 'it will build your strength up.' Mateo did not need convincing, the flavours were wonderful, and he realised how hungry he was.

Once Abriana had emptied the cup and bowl into Mateo's mouth, she arose from beside him and without another word left the room. Mateo leaned back on the soft pillows feeling at ease. He watched her graceful movements and admired her trim figure. His heart beat strongly and although still weak, he could feel life returning to his body and a spark of desire for this young beauty. He slept peacefully, dreaming of this girl. He would have to get to know her.

Part 1 – Sicilian Inheritance

The Inquisition, Barbary pirates and a race across 17th century Sicily to rescue an innocent girl.

Chapter 1

Madrid 27 March 1693

'Enough,' shouted the Grand Inquisitor, rising unsteadily from behind his desk, carrying the latest report from Sicily, 'I am fed up with the King receiving these complaints about this…' he paused to look down at the sheet in his trembling hand, '…Beati Paoli.'

At seventy-nine, Diego Sarmiento de Valladares was one of the oldest Grand Inquisitor there had been, and he had held the post for nearly quarter of a century. He stared out of the window of his Madrid office at the setting sun turning the sky red. The colour matching his mood.

'The King and his council have more pressing things to worry about in the Empire than this back water, whose location is its main positive feature.' He walked back to his desk and slumped into his chair, clearly exhausted by the annoying correspondence of that day.

He looked around at the few gathered in his office, his loyal secretary, friar Pedro, trusted right-hand-man, Monsignor Emmanuel Garcia, his old friend Cardinal Antonio, and a diminutive Dominican friar hovering near the door. They all remained silent while he vented.

'These rebellious Sicilians need to learn obedience to the crown and respect for the church,' Valladares continued, 'secret societies with hooded assassins have thrived for too long and are clearly protected by the people who won't give them up to our interrogators.'

'I dare say God is punishing them, your Grace,' Cardinal Antonio suggested quietly, while patiently waiting for his old friend to calm down. 'The earthquake and Tsunami this January has flattened much of Catania, damaged Messina, and Syracuse, with…how many reported dead?' he asked, looking up at the secretary standing by the desk.

'Fifty thousand, your eminence,' the secretary replied.

'See,' Antonio gestured with his hand, 'with the necessary rebuilding, we will need to find a reliable and inexpensive engineer, then squeeze extra funds from the population to pay for the work. Yet, this can usher in a renewal, a time of purification once these rebels have been purged.' Cardinal Antonio felt pleased by the positive spin he had put on the situation.

'And who do we have to purify Sicily?' Valladares asked. His voice quieter and steadier now but his mood still clearly foul. His Chief Inquisitor Garcia stood, approaching the desk he beckoned the silent friar forward.

'Friar Diego here has served us well these last seven years, and before that was Chief Inquisitor in Sicily,' Garcia said, 'May I suggest we send him back with a fresh mandate.'

Friar Diego de Loisa bowed slowly to the Grand Inquisitor; he saw himself as a purifier!

Just over a month later, Friar Diego stood on the poop of a galley looking out towards Palermo, Sicily, his black cloak waving behind him in the firm offshore breeze. Already he could see the tower of the Castello al Mare silhouetted against the rising sun. The sails were being lowered and the sound of whips cracking from the rowing benches below increased, as the ship's captain began to manoeuvre the vessel into the port. He breathed deeply the salt air to mask the stench coming from the galley slaves below. He had little sympathy for them, all condemned criminals, captured Barbary pirates and heretics being righteously punished, as far as he was concerned. However, it had been ten days since they left Valencia, with stops in Mallorca and Sardinia where cargo, provisions, as well as fresh slaves, were loaded.

Now the smell from rowing benches was nauseating.

There was much noise and activity around the decks, but he ignored it. His thin frame, gaunt face, and piercing eyes covered a troubled soul. Zealous to the extreme, he observed strictly each fast day and denied himself to prove his worthiness. His philandering mother had left him with a demoralised father, who had taken to drink and beatings, when he was young.

'I need to purge the devil you inherited from your mother from you,' his drunken father would scream, as he beat him with a cane. He shuddered with the memory.

His early entry into the church was a relief. The strictness of that education made him wear his piety as a badge of honour. His god was an intolerant one, demanding recompense from sinners. He felt he had to pay for his parent's failings and the insecurities that plagued him.

He pulled his white capuce over his head, to shelter him from the morning chill, but remained on deck, lost in thought. It had been seven years since he had last been in Sicily.

Although he had left under a political cloud, being accused by the local nobility of excesses, he was returning with much more power. Now he carried letters of authority from King Charles of Spain himself and the Sicilian gentry, who had shunned him before, now needed his help. This thought filled him with confidence as they approached the wooden quay.

Despite the earliness of the hour, a welcome committee was already assembling on the shore to greet the new Chief Inquisitor. He could clearly recognise some fellow Dominican friars, by their white habits, huddled together in conversation. Further back it looked like the Archbishop of Palermo himself was being carried down in a sedan chair with a small entourage.

Archbishop Michael sat in his sedan chair and watched the galley docking. His stomach turned in disgust at having to greet this inquisitor whom he despised. However, he was a realist and these were dangerous times. He recognised that King Charles used the Inquisition as much to seal his authority as to purge heretics from challenging the church.

The King's relationship with the Pope in Rome varied as the political tides ebbed and flowed.

Yet, continuous threats from the Ottoman Turks, attacks from Barbary pirates and infighting between the princes in various parts of Europe, made for troubling times. The last thing he needed was to be at odds with the Inquisition.

This way, having Diego kiss his ring in public would cement his authority over him.

He was sure Diego would comment on his welcome in his report to the Inquisitor General and his sponsoring Cardinal. He may not like the Inquisition's methods, especially this "bloodthirsty hound" they had sent back to Palermo, but he would play the game and then avoid Diego as much as possible. He sat impatiently, wanting to get this over with and retreat before the heat of the day and from the smell of the galley slaves.

Near where they would berth, Diego could see citizens waiting for him, clutching papers that Diego assumed would be accusations against their neighbours. So, it begins…

Chapter 2

Bernardo trudged back through the thick wooded land, up the hill towards the Abbey. The sun was already going down behind the Santa Martia del Bossco Abbey's dome as he made his way along familiar paths. He had managed to kill five hares. All bucks who had been so distracted boxing for the right to mate they had quickly ignored the bodies of previous victims, allowing Bernardo to shoot another. Apart from in spring, these long eared, swift creatures were extremely hard to shoot, even with Bernardo's proficiency with his long bow.

As he approached the gate of the Abbey, the old retainer, Angelo was waiting for him as always. Previously a servant of his late mother, now serving here at the Abbey, Angelo was fond of Bernardo, who he still regarded as the "young master". As he passed Angelo, he handed him one of the hares with only a nod exchanged between them. Then clutching his bow and the other hares he made for his usual bow hiding place in the stables. He also hid the hares under some straw to fetch later. As he heard singing from compline prayers in the chapel, he suddenly felt guilty that he would be late once again.

Hoping the Abbot had been particularly stingy about the number of candles being used tonight, he prayed he could creep into the chapel stalls unnoticed and that he had not already been missed. His regular hunting trips should have got him in much more trouble.

However, the monks' pleasure in the extra meat the kitchen was "blessed" with, had everyone turning a blind eye.

He hurried along the cloisters towards the chapel trying to make as little noise as he could; confident that he would not be seen, as all the monks would be inside already.

Slipping in a side door, he tried to hide at the back behind the black-habited Benedictine monks. As he was a full head taller than everyone in the Abbey, this was not easy.

As Compline ended, Bernardo slipped out quickly. That way he did not need to face Father Aiello, his mentor, or the disapproving eyes of the Abbot. He usually wanted to recover the hares unseen and hang them in the kitchen to be "found" the next morning.

Even in the dark, he knew his way around the Abbey confines well. Despite his voluminous size, he was quick and agile, moving around silently. Although, he often felt guilty about sneaking about, even having a hunting bow and dagger, he loved to hunt. It was the only things left from his former life before the Abbey.

As Bernardo settled down to sleep that night, he hid the dagger under his mattress and set his rosary beside his bed. The dagger always reminded him of the summer that William the archer visited the small farm manor house, he and his mother lived in. Precious memories, yet also painful. It was William that brought word that his father was dead. He was only nine years old at the time and could not understand why his father was away. He did not understand all that was said, especially as both his mother and William would not tell him where his father had been or what he was doing.

'To protect him,' they said!

It was then that William had given his mother the bejewelled dagger that belonged to his father, the jewels had long since been picked off by his mother to provide for them.

Images of William and that summer he spent with them, filled his dreams. He pictured William kneeling to show him how to string the little practice bow he had made for him.

'Now draw the bow string back like this, while looking along its length at the target…' William encouraged.

He was so proud when his arrow managed to connect with the bale of hay, they had set up as a target. Then he remembered the awe he felt when William, demonstrating, let loose one of the arrows from his long bow. The speed as it flew towards the target and sound as it imbedded itself deep into the hay bale, enthralled him.

'What was my father like?' he asked William, as they retrieved the practice arrows.

'Your father was a great knight and an honourable man whom I was privileged to serve for many years.' William explained quietly, kneeling down to look Bernardo in the eye.

'We grew up together, hunting in these very hills,' he said with a smile, 'and later fought side by side in the many conflicts that raged around our neighbouring states, just like his father before him.'

William reached out and gently clasped his large hands around Bernardo's shoulders.

'Remember he loved you and your mother very much. It grieved him to not spend more time with you, but the struggles we dealt with here in Sicily endangered you too, and he wanted to keep you safe. He had no idea things would go on as long as they did.' William's gaze dropped to the ground, as he concluded, clearly distressed. Then when his mother became ill, just a few months later, his questions seemed irrelevant.

Vividly he remembered his mother calling him and cheerfully running into her open arms. The images changed to his mother's drained, sweating face as the fever took hold. Then to her growing weaker and weaker, but still trying to smile for him. Finally, images of Father Aiello's grave face entered his dream, as he left his mother's room and put his arm around him, telling him to be strong. He woke up with a start.

As on so many occasions before, he took hold of his rosary beads and started to recite the Latin prayers he knew by heart, until his spirit calmed enough for him to return to sleep.

It had been almost seven years since his mother had died and Father Aiello had convinced the Abbot to take Bernardo into the Abbey. He had known Father Aiello all of his life, having baptised him as a baby and been his tutor, even before they moved from Palermo to the Sicani hills where his family's lands where located.

'You will be of age soon, my son, to choose to join the church or seek a different path,' Father Aiello said, as their daily lesson started. 'While acting as your guardian, providing you with a home and education, the Abbey has been blessed by the income from your estates. If you choose to join the Order, you will be obliged to hand ownership of your lands to the church. However, it is your decision.'

While they looked after this orphan, his land and manor, located just beyond the woods, below Mount Genuardo which the Abbey was perched on, was rented out to provide income for the Abbey.

'How do you know your destiny, Father?' Bernardo asked, truly perplexed by the options before him. 'How can we know what the right thing to do is?'

'God has a plan for our lives, my son, you must discern what that plan is and then follow it,' Aiello encouraged Bernardo's inquisitive mind, enjoying his sharp intellect.

'God has gifted mankind with the privilege of choice, and it will be from your heart that choice will come. Will you choose to serve, to live for others, or place yourself before the welfare of those around you? How does Christ guide us?' So the lesson began.

Aiello had passed on his love of Holy Scripture and the rule of St Benedict; however, he was mostly an academic. Apart from educating Bernardo, he had spent the last eight years writing a commentary on New Testament scripture; arriving at the Abbey at the same time Bernardo and his mother moved to the area.

'What else would I do?' Bernardo almost pleaded, 'you have prepared me to be a Coenobite and I love our studies but know little else.'

Bernardo's life in the Abbey had been one of routine as dictated by the regular prayers in the chapel, his studies with Father Aiello and his many chores around the Abbey.

With the additional regular hunting trips, he had grown strong, and had become a proficient hunter, expelling much of his adolescent aggressive energies during his bow practice. Yet it had limited his experience of the outside world.

'Yes, my son, you have much to learn still about the world,' Aiello continued thoughtfully, 'perhaps we have cloistered you too much, however…' he tailed off, clearly thinking of things far off, 'at least you have been safe here.'

Over the weeks, they would return to this subject repeatedly, until Bernardo declared he wanted to join the church. After that, his clerical training had been stepped up. When completed, he would be ordained and inducted into the Order.

Chapter 3

From the upper window of Palazzo Steri, the inquisition's headquarters in Sicily, the small, lean figure of Friar Diego looked out over Palermo at the hustle and bustle of a busy port city. Fresh out of morning prayers, he was preparing his mind for all he was to hear from the many petitioners waiting for him outside his office. His arrival a few days before had caused quite a stir in the city and he guessed across the island. Anyone who knew him would have little doubt of his mission this time.

The Archbishop had, of course, received him cordially. After reading the letters he had brought, he promised to provide him with assistance to fulfil his mission. However, formalities over, they both expected to see as little of each other as was possible.

Inquisitor Diego turned his attentions to organising his team. He had spent his first few days getting to know the staff assigned him and was pleased to discover that the jailer Luigi was still alive and in their service. Many of his former assistants had fallen victim to the vengeance of the Beati Paoli, but then he remembered many of them had been weak and disorganised. If there was anything Diego loathed, more than heretics, it was poor organisation.

Luigi was always organised, laying his instruments of torture out neatly before each interrogation where both the prisoner and Inquisitor could see. He was always methodical in his approach to inflicting pain, steadily increasing it as the questions were repeated. With perverse pride in his craft, he would show no emotions or mercy, as he kept the prisoner conscious and alive for as long as possible. Diego realised Luigi would be a real asset but must remain in the shadows as he had in the past, both for his own sake and the deniability that might be needed later.

Diego heard his secretary, a young Dominican, approach him from behind and could sense his fear. It invigorated him, so he savoured the feeling for a few moments before turning to greet him with a smile.

'Good morning, brother. Shall we set about God's work?' he said, gesturing for the nervous monk to lead the way to the office.

Palazzo Steri would once more become a place of many comings and goings.

Accusers in the morning waiting to be interviewed by Friar Diego or his staff and the accused being brought in for questioning at night. Always at night when few would see them arrive and no one would see them leave.

Chapter 4

Father Aiello was often grumpy in the morning, but never more so than this morning.

Bernardo thought it might be best to avoid him. Since making it clear that he wanted to enter the Benedictine order, his disciplined existence in the Abbey had become even stricter.

Father Aiello's instructions on adherence to the Order of Saint Benedict had now been stepped up.

Over the past few days, however, Father Aiello had seemed agitated and had been seen in deep conversation with the Abbot. There seemed urgency to his manner which at first Bernardo had assumed was a keenness to finish his writings. So, when his old tutor picked up his walking staff and announced they were going for a walk, Bernardo dared not ask where or why, but just followed.

Father Aiello walked along the cloisters into the central courtyard and out of the main gates quite quickly for an old man. However, once he reached the road that led down from the Abbey, he paused, clearly out of breath. Leaning on his staff he stared past the wooded hills to the valley below and sighed.

'There is such beauty in this peaceful place, my son, far from the madness that infects so much of the world.'

Bernardo knew Father Aiello well, so remained silent, waiting for his mentor to gather his thoughts and explain what was really on his mind.

There was a large rock at the side of the road that was probably a leftover from the construction of the Abbey many years before, but now made a convenient seat for the old monk. Easing himself onto it, Father Aiello looked as though the weight of the world was on his shoulders. He stared at the ground for a moment, and then launched into a statement that left Bernardo with his mouth open and head spinning.

'Tomorrow, you and I are going to leave this Abbey and go on a long journey. My commentaries are finished and bound into two volumes. I have permission from the Abbot to take them to the great library in Rome, in way of a pilgrimage, before I die. He has also given permission for you to accompany me, as it is doubtful I will manage the journey unaided. We will continue your instructions on the way, and I hope to have you ordained into the order in the Vatican itself.'

He smiled as he finished, looking rather pleased with himself. Staring into Bernardo's eyes while he waited for a reaction, but Bernardo was speechless and stood open-mouthed.

'Shut your mouth, child, before you swallow a fly!' Father Aiello said, his mood changing rapidly. 'I thought you would be pleased. Such an adventure!' Again, he looked hopefully into his young student's eyes, 'I thought you would like to see Rome.'

Bernardo was stunned by the suddenness of this change in circumstances and could not remember a conversation with Father Aiello like this. Even after his mothers' death, Aiello had asked him '…if he would like to come and live at the Abbey?' Nearly all the conversations he had had with the old monk began with a question. Even with his studies, Father Aiello would often start with a question.

'Why did Jesus ask the cripple at the pool of Salome if he wanted to walk?' and so the lesson would begin. But this…just a statement of fact…no questions, no discussion! Yet something the old man had clearly thought through. It explained his mood of late and private conversations with the Abbot.

Bernardo looked around over the valley at his beloved hunting grounds. The woods and fields beyond were all he knew.

'It is all so sudden,' he finally exclaimed, 'such a long way!'

Yet, even as he said the words, a sense of excitement started to fill his very being.

Questions started to race through his mind.

'How will we get to Rome…what way will we go…how long will it take…?'

He started to speak very fast, and Aiello realised with relief that he was indeed excited by the prospect. The old man raised his hand to silence his charge and smiled up at him with great fondness.

'The Abbot has promised me a donkey to carry the commentaries and our provisions.

So, we will walk to Palermo where, after visiting the Abbey at Montreale to seek some funding from old friends, we will take a ship to Ostia and then follow the Tiber to Rome.'

The way Father Aiello said it, it all sounded so simple, but Bernardo had studied maps with Father Aiello and they both knew this was a long journey. He looked at his old tutor with more caring eyes and a sense of protection.

'Are you strong enough for such a journey, father?' The old monk reached out and took the young man's strong hand in his frail fingers.

'With God's help, my son and yours, I am sure we will both make it to Rome and deliver the commentaries safely, but…' Aiello said slowly getting to his feet, 'there is no time to lose.' Turning to walk back to the Abbey he continued, 'We must prepare and be on our way while the weather is fine,' and turning to Bernardo with a sly look in his eye, 'and before the Abbot changes his mind.'

As they returned to the Abbey, Bernardo sensed there was more to this situation than the old monk was sharing. Why such a rush to leave now, in early spring? Father Aiello might fear travelling in the autumn, but it was not like it was late summer. However, the chance of such an adventure and prospect of seeing places Aiello had told him about was so exciting, he brushed his concerns aside. After all, he trusted Aiello completely…he was the nearest thing Bernardo had to family.

It would not even take them long to pack up things for the journey as they did not have much. All they had belonged to the church, but then Bernardo thought about his long bow and wondered how he was going to take it without it being noticed. His mind started formulating a plan as he listened to the old monk list things to collect for the journey.

Chapter 5

It was well after dark, but Friar Diego continued to listen impassively to the reports of what had happened over the last seven years since he had last held this post and the more recent outrages of the Beati Paoli. Previously he had cracked down heavily on those that challenged the actions of the land-owning nobles and dared to question the authority of the church to judge in these matters. Even to the arrest of certain aristocratic families and wealthy merchants, which is where it was considered he had gone too far. Unfortunately, this seemed to have driven the Beati Paoli members even further underground, as well as having him recalled to Madrid and the Inquisition powers limited on the island. This time, things would be different and those that had aided the Beati Paoli, allowing them to escape or covering their identities, would themselves be brought to justice. No matter whom they were, of what rank in society or even if members of the church!

The inquisitors continued to gather evidence and it was not long before suspects were being brought in for questioning. Looking through a list of recent arrests, one name jumped out at Diego, vaguely familiar from past questioning many years before. Jailer Luigi's talents would once again be required. Friar Diego decided to send for Luigi and visit the cells personally, to see for himself whom they had managed to apprehend.

He sent a message for Luigi to join him, if he was not already in the dungeons below, for Palazzo Steri was not only the administrative head quarter of the Inquisition in Sicily, but also, an "interrogation centre". Beneath the impressive buildings, were holding and interrogation cells well away from prying eyes or ears! He descended the stairs from his office to the central courtyard and across to the entrance of the dungeons clutching some documents he had removed from old files. The guard unlocked the door immediately as he recognised the chief inquisitor and held it open for him.

The airless rooms smelled of urine, faeces, and stale sweat. Most of all Diego could sense the fear and hopelessness that oozed from the very walls of this dark place. This was exactly the atmosphere he wished to create. It all made it easier to break down the resistance of the prisoner and get them to say exactly what the inquisitor wanted to hear. Diego had learned a long time ago that physical pain was limited in its effectiveness. Fear was by far his most effective tool to manipulate people.

As Diego entered the interrogation room, his ears rang with the cry of pain from the prisoner hanging from a hook in the ceiling. He paused, just inside the door and watched as two burly jailors beat the already bleeding body with leather straps. Scanning the scene dispassionately, he noted the inquisitor standing nearby. Another younger monk was sitting on a low stool by a small table taking notes. Each occupant of the room seemed to sense his presence before seeing him. One by one, as they recognised him, they stopped and looked to him for instructions. Signalling with small movements of his hands, he motioned for the jailers to move out of the way as he talked quietly to the original inquisitor.

Then, with only a few words and gestures, they all left the room just as Luigi arrived with his tool bag. Diego waited patiently for Luigi to organise himself, reading through the notes the scribe had been taking. He was not in a hurry. He knew the silence would play on the prisoner's mind, preparing him for the questions to come.

Chapter 6

Father Aiello's progress along the mountain roads down towards Palermo was going to be slow, even if he started well, striding forward with his old staff in hand. Bernardo pulled the initially reluctant donkey behind him, listening to the old man chatter about his previous life in Palermo. Although Aiello seemed cheerful, Bernardo wished the Abbot had given them a second donkey for the old monk to ride. In the days ahead, he might not be so energetic, but at least for now the weather was fine and the path was all downhill.

The donkey had the leather-bound commentaries in waxed canvass bags on either side of a rudimentary harness, with blankets and other bags with bread, cheese, and wine for the nine-league journey to Montreale Abbey. Bernardo had also collected some long poles and wrapped them with other old blankets with which he said he would make a shelter from the mid-day sun when they took their afternoon rest. He insisted this was crucial for him to take care of Father Aiello and in truth it was an excellent idea. However, it also allowed him to hide the long bow and arrows he was determined to take with them. Although Father Aiello had always known about his bow and his hunting trips, he had never mentioned it to him. It seemed that keeping open secrets like this between them was best. He was sure that Aiello would not be surprised he had the bow with him.

This mountainous area was beautiful, but they only had narrow goat herders' paths to travel on. Although road systems had been cut through the region by various rulers in the past, mainly to extract the strong timber from the forest that once covered this whole area, the roads had not been maintained. This did not help the old academic, who was no longer used to walking such uneven paths. Much of this lush, forested hill country had, over the centuries, been deforested. In turn, this had turned the once fertile valleys into arid, rocky plains baked by the summer sun. The going would get difficult, especially as the summer heat approached.

'We should descend the mountain east to Bisacquino, then take the road north to Corleone. From there, the road continues north to Ficuzza before turning Northwest to Piana degli Albanesi, only two leagues from Monreale,' Aiello explained. 'I realise I will not be able to walk fast, however, we should make it to each settlement in a day and can seek hospitality from the locals each evening.'

Bernardo was quite prepared to camp out if necessary, even relishing the idea of sleeping under the stars. However, he was very worried about the state of Aiello's health and with each passing day his concern increased.

Aiello chatted about the beautiful artwork in the Cathedral in Montreale and explained some of the history. 'It's a mixture of Arab, Byzantine and Norman artwork that adored the Romanesque architecture.'

'…the mosaics cover most of the Cathedral's interior and…' he continued enthusiastically, '…there a few places of more grandeur.'

He was clearly excited to be returning there and to what he could show his pupil.

However, he quickly became out of breath and would have to rest regularly, so the conversations were stilted and not as informative as Bernardo would have liked. Maybe once Aiello rested at Montreale he would be able to answer some of the questions Bernardo longed to ask. For now, getting there would be the challenge.

Chapter 7

William di Giovanni's body ached all over, particularly his muscular arms which stretched above his head and were held with wrist manacles secured to a hook in the low dungeon ceiling. Between questions they had burned his chest with hot irons, then whipped and beat him. Now they left him hanging there while a discussion had gone on with others that had entered his cell.

A new jailer, small squat, and from what William could make out in the dim light, hunch backed, now laid out instruments of torture on a table opposite. He fussed over various screws and blades, making sure William could see them all neatly lined up. Then he turned to someone else in the room behind William and waited for instruction.

A vaguely familiar, steady, quiet voice, almost whispered in William's ear, 'What is your name?'

'William di Giovanni, archer to the house of Boscogrande and soldier of Christ, why have you brought me here?' William replied defiantly.

Friar Diego's memory had not failed him. He had heard of a William the Archer when trying to locate the whereabouts of the troublesome Cavaliere who had dared to challenge his authority. Boscogrande, was regarded as brave and honourable by his fellow nobles, but Diego had been certain he was a member of the Beati Paoli. Zealously tracking him down had opened so many lines of enquiry for the Inquisition. Investigations had implicated family-members from the highest echelons of Sicilian nobility until eventually the very power and methods of the Inquisition had been brought into question. In the end, Boscogrande had eluded him, and Diego had been recalled to Madrid. Now, he had a second chance and he would not let this rebel out of his clutches.

'Yes...' replied the voice, still steady, still almost a whisper, '...and where is your master, Cavaliere Mateo di Boscogrande? It has been such a long time since we last met, but I have not forgotten!' The voice became threatening, but still with a quiet, almost hypnotic rhythm as it now moved to whisper in his other ear.

'Cavaliere Mateo has been dead, these last seven years.' William replied, wondering if this new interrogator was who he thought it was.

'So, where is his wife and son and that interfering chaplain of his?' The voice hissed in his ear.

'All dead, many years ago…the plague got them,' William insisted, trying to sound convincing.

'I do not think so,' whispered the sneering voice behind him, 'let us try that question again.'

There was a pause and the jailer moved towards his instruments on the table opposite William.

Chapter 8

Bernardo was glad to have Montreale Abbey in sight. They had been walking for almost three days and he did not think Father Aiello could manage much more. Despite the good weather and reasonable food—Bernardo had provided them with meat daily and swapped some game for fresh bread and cheese from farms along the way—Father Aiello had grown weaker each day.

The climb up to the Abbey was going to be a struggle for the old Benedictine but spurred on by his enthusiasm to show Bernardo the beauty of the architecture and mosaics he pressed on. The Abbey of Monreale, from the Latin "Mons Regalis" literally means Royal Mountain, straddled a slope of Mount Caputo almost two leagues south of Palermo's Cathedral. As they approached the town it was almost deserted, as being after lunch, most people were resting and sheltering from the mid-day heat. They decided to do likewise, so entered a nearby stable to refresh their donkey. After a word with the proprietor, they retreated to a shaded area he pointed out to them for a nap.

Bernardo was too excited to sleep, so as the old monk dozed, he set off to explore this new town. Without doubt the focal point was its cathedral, "Santa Maria la Nuova" (The new Saint Mary).

'A Cathedral was founded here by William II of Sicily in 1172,' Aiello had previously explained, 'but then demolished to make room for a new castle for Charles of Anjou, who gave permission to build a new Cathedral completed in 1279…'

Aiello had so much to say about this place of worship, and Bernardo looked forward to seeing inside and the mosaics that had been described to him. Yet as he stood outside the magnificent Cathedral another sight caught his attention. Bernardo looked down over Palermo, the place of his birth, though he had little recollection of it, and stared in wonder at the city and sea beyond. Set at about a hundred and fifty cannas above sea level, the town of Montreale overlooks the "Conca d'Oro" as the valley beyond Palermo is known. This view of scattered wood and yellow stoned buildings, glowing in the sun light mesmerised Bernardo.

He stood a while daydreaming of his mother and what their life would have been like in Palermo. Noticing how hot he was becoming as the sun, high in the azure blue-sky beat down on his head, he decided to return to Father Aiello and rest.

'It would be good,' Bernardo thought to himself, 'to let his old tutor show him around the Cathedral and explain more about its history.'

Thinking of what his tutor has described on the journey, Bernardo could not imagine such a sight, but soon would see for himself. He was still entertaining these pleasant thoughts as he returned to the snoring old monk, and quietly fell asleep beside him.

Chapter 9

Although Diego had not yet obtained any useful information from William, he was convinced his old enemies were still around, making him determined to locate them and have his revenge. His spies and paid informants would have to hunt them down. He was confident that for enough silver, even their friends would betray them.

'Someone must know where that interfering old Benedictine, the Jewish witch and her offspring were,' he fumed. He would visit the Abbey of Montreale himself, where the monk had once served. With the regional magistrate's help, he would construct a web to trap those that had escaped him before. He decided to speak to the regional magistrate to ensure his assistance, then realised he had yet to meet the new magistrate.

'Odd,' he thought, 'the magistrate has not called on me since my arrival.'

He looked through some papers to see if he had information on the new magistrate and made a mental note to find out more about him, and his activities the next day.

Retiring that night, he was confident that he would find someone who would talk and hand his old enemies over to him. 'I just need to find someone close to them, then we will flush out the rest.'

His rooms at Palazzo Steri were furnished simply but were comfortable with a large four poster bed and overstuffed feather mattress. Diego normally slept peacefully, having a clear conscience about what he and his fellow inquisitors did; securely confident in his righteousness and relishing his position of power over people. However, this night he was disturbed with memories of his encounter with Father Aiello in front of the church council, almost eight years before. His failure to successfully counter the challenge from Cavaliere Mateo on his authority and methods still annoyed him. He still fumed whenever he thought about them.

His plan to silence Mateo had been to get a confession out of Senior Davide, his father in-law, that he was really a Jew and only pretended to be Christian. Several generations before, the Davide family had been forced by the Inquisition to either leave Sicily or convert to Christianity. They had supposedly converted. He intended to gain evidence that the old Jew's daughter, Mateo's wife, was practising witchcraft with her herbal healing treatments. Once he had them in his grip, he could silence the loud criticism coming from Cavaliere Mateo, but things had gone disastrously wrong.

He had not realised the old Jew was so frail. Not long after he had been arrested and brought to Palazzo Steri, he had died, even before he could start interrogating him.

'Those idiot jailors had carelessly beaten the old man even before either Luigi or I had arrived.' The thought tormented him.

As soon as Cavaliere Mateo heard of Davide's arrest he complained to both the Archbishop and magistrate, demanding a hearing. Diego was caught on the back foot having to not only explain why he had authorised the arrest of a respected local merchant, but that his prisoner had died in his custody. They should not have been able to challenge his authority, but that smart priest Aiello had made him look like a fool before the council. He already knew the Archbishop did not like him, and this was his chance to get rid of him. He had been humiliated and combined with letters complaining to King Charles, he found himself recalled to Spain to explain himself. His muscles tensed as he lay there reliving the humiliation.

'However,' he contemplated, 'there would be a reckoning now and no one would escape this time.' These thoughts comforted him, as he tried to sleep.

Chapter 10

The Abbey at Montreale, like the Cathedral, was impressive and Bernardo had spent two days exploring them both. The elaborate mosaics in the Cathedral, much of it shining with gold leaf, covered the ceilings and walls, depicting parables, the ministry of Jesus and the saints.

Even Father Aiello's detailed descriptions had not fully conveyed the majesty of the place.

On entering for the first time, Bernardo was mesmerised and with the smell of incense, and beautiful singing of the choir, he thought he could be entering heaven itself. He would never be late for offices here. Staying after, as long as was allowed, he became fascinated by the bright pictorial stories depicted in the mosaics. He could see they were clearly designed to teach and awe the people who visited the Cathedral. They were an education in themselves.

The little Abbey too was full of mixed architectural influences that delighted Bernardo as he explored every corner. He now understood clearly why Father Aiello wanted to return here and wished they could stay, enchanted as he was.

The Abbey cloister where he now waited patiently for Father Aiello was a little over twenty-three cannas on each side and boasted two hundred and twenty-eight columns.

Carved into each column were biblical figures, mythological scenes, Arabic designs, and strange little crouching men at the top of the columns. There were also carvings of Arab warriors and Norman Knights, as well as flowers and palms. Bernardo happily looked around some more but was beginning to wonder what was keeping his mentor.

After vespers in the Cathedral that first afternoon, they had moved next door to the Abbey with the monks who had presided over prayers. They were warmly received at the Abbey and Aiello immediately taken to greet the Abbot. Initially the Abbot seemed pleased to see his old friend. However, as the Abbots office door closed, and Bernardo was led away by the other younger monks, he was sure he heard the Abbot say, 'You could not have chosen a worse time to return…' in a rather grave tone.

Bernardo had wanted to ask Aiello about this the next day. However, the other young monks were keen to show Bernardo around and Father Aiello always seemed to be in deep conversation with someone.

As instructed, he now waited in Father Aiello's favourite part of the cloister. The Arab fountain in the southwest corner, surrounded by its own four-sided colonnade. Pleasant as his surrounds were, he felt oddly uneasy when Father Aiello appeared with a stranger.

Walking beside the old monk was a stern looking man, dressed all in black, including a large hat, with a feather on the side. As he came closer Bernardo noted that the man's clothes had delicate stitching in silver thread. But what really caught his eye was an elaborately engraved dagger hanging from a leather strap attached to his belt. His face was shaved clean on each side, but he had a small, pointed dark beard which, to Bernardo's eyes, made him look sinister.

Bernardo could not remember meeting a person like this before. Clearly not clergy, but seemingly a person of some importance, with a distinct air of authority, even arrogance.

Inwardly Bernardo was chastising himself for being judgemental, but also wondering why he had such negative feelings towards someone he had never met. The man did not smile as he was introduced by Father Aiello.

'Bernardo, this is Captain Orlando, now the regional magistrate and an old friend.'

Bernardo stood to greet the stranger, who surprised him by putting his hands on both of Bernardo's broad shoulders and staring with a critical look, into his eyes.

'Yes,' he said after a while, 'I can see you have your father's eyes,' and stepping back to look at Bernardo, he added, 'and build, but fortunately something of your mother in your face.' The Captain's lips turned up slightly as if to smile, but quickly returned to the frown he had started with.

Bernardo's mind raced. 'So, this man knew my parents.' He so wanted to ask questions about them, but his strong introvert personality compelled him to think through his feelings first and construct good questions. Yet, with so many questions in his head, he was finding it hard to gather coherent thoughts.

'You must learn quickly, Bernardo who you can trust and who you can't.'

Aiello said sternly, 'This will not be easy for you after your upbringing, but Captain Orlando is one of the few in Sicily you can trust.'

Bernardo was shocked at such a statement and stared at this new confidant.

'I owe your father my life,' Orlando almost whispered, leaning towards him, 'it was my idea that you all left Palermo when you did,' he continued, 'and I will help you escape once again.'

'Escape,' Bernardo thought, *'why do we need to escape?'*

More questions and an intense, unfamiliar feeling raced through Bernardo's mind. He clenched his hands and stiffened his muscles. He felt he was going to burst. So many questions, so much he needed to understand. It was all happening too quickly for him to gather this new information into coherent thoughts or analyse these unfamiliar feelings. He stood wide eyed, frozen to the spot and trying to focus on what was being said.

'You must leave Sicily right away,' Orlando said looking around to see if they were still alone.

'So, it is on to Palermo to catch a ship?' Bernardo finally blurted out.

'No,' said Aiello looking even graver, if that were possible, 'there has been a change of plans…sorry, my son, I know you were looking forward to seeing Palermo, but we might be recognised there. We will go on to the port of Cefalù where we can board a vessel leaving Sicily.'

His firm statement left no room for questions, so Bernardo did not offer one.

'Besides,' Aiello continued, trying to sound cheerful, but failing, 'there is a wonderful Cathedral there too, which would be good for you to see.'

Captain Orlando ignored the old man's attempt to lighten the mood and continued sternly, 'I will make all the arrangements for a vessel to transport you out of Sicily, but you must get to Cefalù as soon as possible and *keep out of sight.'*

Leaning in to whisper to them both, he added, 'Inquisition informers are already looking for you and Diego has not forgotten.'

Bernardo found himself silently talking to himself again, but at least kept his mouth closed this time and hopefully his face impassive. Though he felt he had been punched.

'Hide from Inquisition informers, why? Diego, who is he?'

Bernardo's mind whirled with so many questions he wondered if he was dreaming…perhaps a very vivid nightmare!

Orlando left without a goodbye, only a nod to the old monk. Aiello, immediately turned and walked towards where he had stored the manuscripts, still in deep thought.

Bernardo walked after him wanting to ask so many questions.

'There is much I have to explain to you, my son, but it will have to wait until we are on the road, again.'

Bernardo dutifully nodded and set off to the stable to retrieve the donkey, while Aiello went to collect their things. There would be no goodbyes for Bernardo and Father Aiello either, just a quick exit.

As they set off across country, as best they could, heading towards the coast, but avoiding Palermo and the main road leading there, Bernardo could no longer hold his tongue.

'Please father, tell me what this is all about. You have taught me so much, but now seem to want me to remain ignorant of something that is endangering us both.'

The old monk looked thoughtfully into the distance without breaking his pace and sighed.

'Sorry my son,' Aiello began, 'a man arrived in Palermo recently, a Dominican friar of the Inquisition to be exact. A friar I have had troubles with in the past and indeed so did your father. It was because of this friar that your family left Palermo to what was left of your father's estates in the Sicani mountains.'

He paused; the memories clearly painful for him.

'If this friar finds either of us…' Aiello stopped walking as he considered how to explain their dilemma, '…*we would probably not survive the encounter with him!*'

Over the last week, Bernardo's quiet routine existence had been shattered and he had seen and experienced more in six days than he had in the previous six years. However, the idea that someone wanted to kill them, shocked him. Meanwhile, he contemplated the news that their move from Palermo was not a casual one, but they had been effectively "on the run". He did not really know how to even process this information, having never before considered himself in any real danger or having any enemies.

As they walked along, and Bernardo considered what Father Aiello has said, he decided he could no longer accept details about his father remaining a mystery to him. For Bernardo, it was time to grow up, but his nature was to carefully think through things before speaking. With so many questions rushing into his head, he had to choose what to ask first.

However, even as he was contemplating his questions, Father Aiello, who had been preparing to reveal all to Bernardo for some time, had also decided it was now time for a family history lesson. Father Aiello took a deep breath, walked closely to Bernardo, and leaned on his arm.

In respect to his tutor, Bernardo held back his questions.

'Keeping you ignorant about your father was not easy for your mother or me, but we felt it was necessary to hide your family's experiences from everyone. Our plan was to explain things to you once you were old enough or circumstance had changed.'

The old Benedictine felt weary as he explained the bitter past, but he knew it was now essential that Bernardo understood everything.

'For you to understand about your family, I need to explain some history, the struggles on this island and about the Inquisition.' Father Aiello continued as they walk slowly along the path towards the coast road.

Aiello reverted to tutor and asked Bernardo what he remembered about his history of Spain, its unification, and empire building. He then explained about the introduction of the Inquisition and that after it was brought to Sicily, all the Jews had been expelled or forced to convert. The old monk clearly disapproved, but related details respectfully.

Father Aiello continued, 'Your father was Cavaliere Mateo di Boscogrande, a descendent of a Norman family from the time they ruled Sicily. Their lands were originally extensive all around our Abbey Santa Martia and they were very generous to the Abbey which now owns or administers most of their land. Your father, like his before him, was a…' the old monk paused trying to think of a respectful way to describe Bernardo's father, 'an adventurer, and a soldier, who fought in the many wars we were cursed with. He and his men, like William the Archer were well known and respected and although he was often rewarded with honours by grateful princes, they did not always fight on the winning side and thus he was not a particularly wealthy man.'

It was getting hot as the sun now rose high in the sky and the old monk, was clearly tired already. They stopped under an isolated tree and Aiello eased himself down onto the ground, leaning against the tree, he continued describing Bernardo's family story.

'One time your father returned to Sicily with an injury that had not healed properly and an infection had set in. I arranged for him to be nursed by a dear friend of mine, Signior Davide and his daughter, as I knew they had a better understanding of medicinal herbs than we Benedictines. It was actually his daughter Abriana, your mother, who mainly nursed him, very patiently, as the wound was quite bad, and your father took a long time to recover.'

The old man leaned back and smiled to himself as he remembered happier times, 'In the end, your father fell in love with Abriana, and asked Signior Davide for her hand. It was a good marriage—she was young, intelligent, and beautiful, and he tall, strong and devoted to her, especially after you were born. It was very much a love match, but also helpful financially as Abriana's dowry was large, Signior Davide being a very wealthy merchant and ship owner.'

'At the time, there was much land grabbing going on throughout Sicily, by greedy Barons and your father knew some of the farmers who had been thrown off their land. Being the honourable man he was, he sought to defend these farmers which brought him into conflict with some of the authorities. It was a confusing time, especially for your father, who previously had little involvement with Sicilian politics. Probably to silence your father or because of jealousy or both, some people accused Signior Davide of being a Jew and Abriana a witch for her understanding of healing herbs.'

The old monk sighed and screwed up his face.

'This led to an investigation by the local Chief Inquisitor, Friar Diego, and he was not a person any of us wanted to get involved with.'

Father Aiello sighed again, but his eyes narrowed revealing deep frustration.

'Your father was furious and challenged Diego's right to accuse them of anything. I too tried to defend them, but he had Signior Davide arrested and my old friend died under interrogation in that terrible prison of theirs.'

The old monk's face tensed in anger as he recalled these bitter memories.

'Your father was incandescent with rage and wanted to kill Diego. It was then your father became involved with a secret brotherhood that tried to defend the people from injustices, like the work of the Inquisition and greedy landowners that were throwing peasant farmers off their land…they were terrible days.' The old monk paused, reflecting back.

'This is why we took you and your mother out of Palermo and I transferred to Santa Martia del Bossco Abbey. My Abbot was keen to get me out of the Inquisition's way and this allowed me to keep an eye on you and your mother.'

The old monk's angry eyes now became sad, and he looked very drained, but reaching out to take Bernardo's hand, he continued, 'The idea was for your father to join you and at first he did visit regularly, but he also felt he should be in Palermo, as his outspokenness against the Inquisition began to win support. Some other nobles also felt threatened by the Inquisition and did not like the idea of someone of your father's social position being questioned. They joined your father in writing to the King and in the end, Diego was recalled to Madrid to explain his actions. This should have been the end of things, but by now your father had become involved in the complex politics of this island in a way he had never been before. He had learned about many more injustices and there were other forces at work that he could not control or understand.'

Tears came to Aiello's eyes as he spoke, 'As an honourable man, your father meant well, but he was fighting a different kind of foe, which he did not understand enough and so we lost him.'

Life seemed to be draining out of the old monk's face, even as he finished his story and he seemed to Bernardo to be visibly shrinking before his eyes.

'The news of your father's death broke your mother's heart. That is why William stayed to support her and help with you, but he too was by now caught up in the same struggle your father was involved in and he feared he would draw attention to you if he stayed too long. He left his bow as it identified him. Many people by this time knew of William the Archer and as the struggle for justice grew, he now had to keep a low profile.'

As Father Aiello finished and started to dose off in the afternoon heat, Bernardo leaned back to think about all he had been told. It was too much for him to take in all at once.

He felt a great sadness that the happy family life they should have had, had been lost because of a dispute he really did not understand. Over the years he had learned Latin, Greek, and even some Hebrew from Father Aiello. He had learned the rule of Benedict, about Mass and prayers. None of this now seemed of any use when faced with the threat before them.

Sitting next to the old monk, Bernardo was acutely aware of Father Aiello's weakness of body, if not of mind. The plan he had discussed with Aiello was to reach Cefalù the next day, but he estimated they were less than halfway between Palermo and Cefalù.

Probably just approaching Trabia, but it was hard to tell as they had kept off the main road and bypassed Bagheria which was between Palermo and Trabia.

He would like to get the old man, to Trabia tonight. However, he realised they might have to spend the night in the open if the old monk could not keep up a reasonable walking pace.

Finally, weariness and the confusion of emotions that flooded his mind overcame him and he too fell asleep. However, his slumber was filled with disturbing images, and it was not long before he woke. He took out his rosary, as he had done so many times before and started to pray. As his spirit settled, he asked God for wisdom and strength to face whatever was ahead. Somehow, he already knew that he was going to be severely tested, and he thought of Jesus praying in Gethsemane the night he was arrested. Jesus did not want to go through the pain ahead but surrendered his will to God. So, in the stillness of that afternoon, beside the old snoring Benedictine, Bernardo likewise surrendered his will to God and placed them both in His hands.

Chapter 11

Three heavily armed galliots and a large galley with twenty-four pairs of oars sailed around the northern coast of Sicily looking both to avoid Spanish galleys and seek out unsuspecting coastal communities. Many of the villages near the coast in the south and west had already been depopulated by previous slave gathering raids. They thought the northern coast might provide better pickings. They sailed through the Tyrrhenian Sea, as the Christians called it, steering clear of Palermo, or Bal'harm as they called it in Arabic. Keeping out of sight of the castles on the hills. These slave-gathering raids, from corsair bases in North Africa had gone on for centuries along the southern coast of Europe. In the past, they were officially endorsed by the Ottoman Empire's attempts to control the whole Mediterranean Sea and attack southern Europe, now they were mostly just for profit.

Once past Capo Zafferano, they made their way into the Gulfo di Termini Imer, but stayed under the horizon while it was still light. Then as the sun set, they started to approach the coast where they rendezvoused with a fishing boat in their pay, who led them under the cover of darkness to a settlement their spies called Trabia. As they approached the coast, the Christian slaves rowing below had their mouths gagged to stop them calling out a warning. Surprise was their best weapon, so at first light the galley ran her bows onto the shore and attacked the town. While everyone was still asleep, they kicked down doors and dragged people out of their beds. Barking dogs were killed, and they quickly located the church to silence the bells so no alert could be sounded.

They kept clear of the small fortress of Rocca della Trabia, but they already knew there were few troops stationed there. However, just in case, they positioned the galliots just off the shore with their bow cannon pointed towards the fort. If there was any reaction from the inhabitants, they would blast the fort and pin down any troops allowing the other Barbary pirates time to raid the village and escape. This was a tried and tested procedure, with speed and surprise being the most effective means of attack.

With haste and brutality, they struck the town, burning and killing as they went, but mostly they wanted people alive, the women and children for the slave markets of Algiers, as well as the men for galley slaves. They dragged the sleeping, unprepared town's folk out of their beds, tied them up and marched them down to their ships. Resistance was dealt with swiftly and severely. So, like many times below, within a few hours, a line of miserable semi-naked captives found themselves winding their way down to the shore and loaded onto the pirate ships. Any items of value were grabbed by the pirates to add to the profits for the raid.

Then, long before the authorities in Palermo could send troops to reinforce the small garrison and defend the people, the slave ships were gone. These Barbary Corsair's mid-day prayers to Allah would be made well out to sea and over the horizon.

A short distance inland of the coastal settlement was a farmhouse. It was a simple single-story building of stone and earth walls with a timber frame and thatched roof. The noise and fires from the town awoke the farmer and his wife. As the farmer looked out of a window towards the town he was not sure what he was seeing. The glow from the fires could mean that some of the buildings were on fire, but the screams that started to get closer alerted him of other dangers.

He called his three sons, asleep in the next room and checked that the front door was secured. Then looked around for something he could use as a weapon to defend them.

The boys, hearing the tone in their father's voice rose quickly and came out to join him. Then froze by the front door petrified, trying to understand what was going on. Age nine, eleven and fourteen, they had heard stories of pirate raids, but had never experienced one and had no idea how to defend themselves.

Meanwhile, his wife woke their daughter and oldest child who slept in the same room as them with only a rough curtain between them. She went to check the back door that led from the kitchen out to their vegetable plot and chicken coup, where she found her husband looking through what knives they had. Her blood ran cold as she saw him weighing one of his butchering knives in his hand.

'What exactly is going on?' she was thinking as her sleepy children arrived together in the kitchen. However, she did not have long to think about it, as at that moment there was a loud thud on their front door. Her husband and young sons went around to the door to brace it, but it was already too late. The door came crashing in on top of them followed by three armed pirates swinging axes and clubs. They instantly clubbed and whipped the stunned boys onto their knees and stabbed their father who tried to protect them.

Seeing this horrific sight, the mother pushed her daughter out of the back door.

'Run Agata, run and don't look back,' she cried, then turned to at least delay the attacker's a while, to give her daughter a chance to escape.

Agata held up her under skirt to avoid tripping and sprinted into near darkness of early morning on strong bare legs. There was a gully inland from the house, that she guessed had once been a river and she thought she could hide there.

She had obeyed her clearly terrified mother and ran but was not entirely sure what she was running from. Behind her she heard screams and instinctively turned towards the noise, losing her balance and falling on the loose earth. At that moment, to her horror she saw a turbaned clad man emerged from the same back door she had fled out of. He spotted her and immediately came running towards her.

Scrambling to her feet she frantically ran along the gully, having no idea where to go, but hoping to outrun the man chasing her. However, he was not far behind and closing fast.

Chapter 12

After their mid-day rest, Father Aiello and Bernardo continued north towards the coast.

Progress was slow, as the old man became steadily weaker. As nightfall approached Bernardo found a sheltered spot for them to spend the night, even although he realised, they were probably not far from Trabia. They had been walking along a gully for some time, probably a dried-upriver or gash in the land from a previous earthquake. Bernardo found a rock and earth outcrop which would act as a roof. He constructed a wind break with the poles and old blankets and started a small campfire close to the outcrop. Soon the heat being trapped between the outcrop and wind breaks made their sleeping area quite cosy. After some bread, cheese, and wine for supper, they both fell into a deep sleep.

As their resting place was on the west side of the gulley, the early dawn light peaked over the east side, waking Bernardo up. The fire had long since gone out, dew covered the ground, and there was not a cloud in the skies. There was only a whisper of a breeze coming down the gulley from inland, brushing against Bernardo's face.

'It will be another hot day,' he thought.

Looking north, to the coast, he could see smoke above the gulley lip convincing him they were very close to the settlement.

'People must be up early cooking breakfast or smoking fish,' he reasoned. Not that he knew anything about fishermen's lives or routines.

Father Aiello was not snoring, but seemed to be in a deep sleep, so Bernardo decided to leave him there and see how close they were to Trabia. He had only walked around the bend in the gulley when he heard screaming up ahead. Running towards the sound, he almost tripped over a sight that instantly triggered fury inside him that he did not even realise was there. A young girl was being chased by a dark skinned, turban wearing, armed man carrying a rope in his right hand. As Bernardo reached them the man had just caught the girl, and in an attempt to stop her struggling had thrown his weight on top of her. Bernardo could clearly see the terror on the girls face and was horrified. His mind raced to understand the scene before him and he opened his mouth to cry out 'stop,' but nothing came out.

The man was trying to tie the girl up, but she was thrashing around furiously and neither of them noticed Bernardo approach. Then just as the man raised his hand to strike the girl, Bernardo leapt on him, not fully thinking through what he was going to do. He brought his clench fists down hard on the back of the man's neck with much more force than he realised. Although he was only thinking of stopping the attack on the girl, he snapped the cervical vertebrae just below the atlas bone and severed the man's spinal cord. He died almost instantly and Bernardo realised what had happened as soon as he heard the bone crack.

Bernardo stood up and stared at the man's back, stunned at what he had done, while the girl now pushed and squeezed herself from under her attacker. She looked up at Bernardo taking in for a moment his size and monk's habit but turned to her now dead attacker and kicked him.

'Spawn of the devil…' she shouted among other things, but Bernardo was frozen to the spot, still shocked by his actions. Then, looking around frantically, the girl said, 'There are more, we need to run and hide!'

Grabbing Bernardo's habit, they both started running up the gulley, back the way Bernardo had come.

They had not gone far when they came to the overhang where Father Aiello was lying. Bernardo went straight to his mentor to tell him what had happened, but as he called out to Aiello and shook him, he could not wake him. The girl cautiously approached the old monk and laid her hand over his mouth. He was not breathing.

She sat back on her knees, looked up at Bernardo with large sad eyes, grief weighing her down.

'I am sorry…he is dead,' she whispered softly, but Bernardo did not respond.

He too sat back on his heels and stared at the old monk. Moments later tears streamed down both their faces as grief overtook them. They sat like this for quite some time until the tears dried up and they felt emotionally numb. It was all too much for these young innocent people. Both were realising they had to grow up immediately and no longer had the support of those they had relied on before. This was not something they were prepared for, and their young minds found it hard to comprehend the overall consequences.

The girl closed her eyes, curled up on the ground and dozed off, exhaustion and confusion overwhelming her. Bernardo stared at her dirty, but pretty face. He felt a strong sense of responsibility for her, but he did not even know her name or anything about her. He prayed as he had never prayed before, 'Lord, help us...' What to do next, he would have to decide now without his mentor. So, as the sun rose in the sky and Bernardo's pounding heart slowed down, he gathered his thoughts.

'I am Bernardo, what is your name?' he asked, as the girl's eyes opened.

'Agata,' she replied sleepily.

She looked over at the body of Father Aiello and asked, 'What are you going to do with the body?'

Bernardo was already thinking this through when he replied, 'Bury him, but not here. We need to find proper consecrated ground. Trabia should have a suitable chapel and burial ground. It will be the closest.'

The thought of returning to Trabia frightened Agata, but at the same time she wanted to know if any of her family had survived the attack. She looked up at the blue sky, the sun now well above the horizon.

'Do you think they will be gone...do you think it is safe?' she asked Bernardo.

'I have no idea,' he answered, '...but we cannot just stay here, and I assume help will come eventually.'

Bernardo got up and started to pack away the makeshift camp, securing it on the donkey that was quietly nodding off in the growing heat. He picked up the frail body of Father Aiello in his strong arms and secured him as best he could on top of the donkey.

He realised the donkey would not be able to carry all this mixed load for long, but he figured it was not far to Trabia, and he did not want to leave anything behind.

Agata helped a little but was scared about what she would find at home and therefore unenthusiastic about returning along the gulley. As Bernardo pulled the reluctant donkey along, she followed apprehensively looking all around her. Expecting any minute to see another pirate leaping out at her.

Her family's farmhouse was just inland of the coastal settlement of Trabia and the first dwelling they came to as they cleared the gulley. The external walls of stone and earth were still standing, but most of the roof had collapsed. There was smoke coming out of the centre of the building.

The back door was still open from where Agata had escaped. Initially there was no sign of anyone around or in the building. She was shaking as she followed Bernardo through the back door. Peering through the smoke at what once was familiar, now blackened and dishevelled, it seemed almost unrecognisable. Apprehension at what she might see made her feel nauseous. Yet she held on to the possibility, no matter how remote, that her family had escaped.

Bernardo, on the other hand, could not even imagine what they would find, as he had no perspective to base any assumptions on. He felt it was his duty to remain calm, both for the girl's sake and because of the teaching he had had from Father Aiello on overcoming fear.

Thinking back, it was almost as if his old tutor had been preparing him for events such as this. They inched their way through the burnt, fallen timbers, peering through the smoke that hung lazily in the still of the morning. Bernardo recalled his old tutor's voice. He tried to keep his breathing steady, but his heart was pounding so much, he thought it might jump out of his chest.

As they entered the kitchen, Bernardo stamped flames out from some of the fallen thatch. Then Agata screamed as she saw the burned shape to their right. She went over to it, but it was hard to tell exactly what they were looking at apart from charred remains of a body lying on its side.

Bernardo eased the body over so the side that had been on the ground was now upper most. Then it became clear that it was Agata's mother. She had obviously put up a fight in an attempt to save her daughter and was rewarded with a cutthroat.

Agata put her arms around what was left of her mother's body and wept. As an automatic reaction, Bernardo made the sign of the cross over himself then raised his hand and made the sign over Agata's mother. Then he knelt beside them and took out his rosary beads.

Holding the little cross in front of him, he started saying a memorised prayer for the dead in Latin.

Once he had completed the standard prayers, Bernardo started looking around the rest of the small farmhouse for more bodies. To his left was a small mostly stone and earth room with a curtain dividing part of it off. The roof here was still intact and the bedding within black, but not burned. The rest of the building was just a shell with smouldering roof timbers lying among the debris of the thatch. However, just outside what must have been the front door was the body of an older man. His head had been cut off.

Bernardo guessed this would have been Agata's father and looked around for something to cover the body, so that Agata would not need to see it like this. It was too late. As he turned to re-enter the building, she was standing at the door staring at the headless body. She did not need to see his face to know it was her father, but found she had no more tears to shed. Her face was ashen, and she slumped down on the ground. She stared out towards the sea that had brought this destruction on them.

Bernardo picked up the head of her father and place it beside the body, then went through the prayers he had been taught and knew by heart.

'Why?' Agata asked as he finished.

'I don't know, but there are so many things I do not know or understand,' he answered after a brief thought. He sat beside her and held her hand. He too was out of tears and wondered if this were a terrible nightmare from which he would awaken soon.

Chapter 13

Troops arrived from Palermo by mid-morning to reinforce the hand full of local militia cowering in the fort, but the pirates had already sailed away by then. Shortly afterwards more soldiers arrived accompanied by some Dominican monks. They began to go door to door looking for survivors and removing bodies. At the remains of the little chapel, they found one of the front doors hanging off its hinges and the local priest pinned to the other door in a crucifixion style position. He was still alive when they found him. All he said before breathing his last was, 'Under the altar.' It was there that they found the silver communion cup, plate, and crucifix which he had hidden and had clearly refused to reveal to the pirates.

It was two of the local militia that ventured up to the farmhouse just inland of the little town. They had seen some terrible sights that morning but were still stunned to find this young girl alive and with a Benedictine monk.

'Agata,' exclaimed the younger of the two, 'is that you?'

In days gone past, when they met, Agata would give this young man a coy smile.

Today she just stared past him when he knelt in front of her.

'I found her being chased by a pirate early this morning, and when we returned to her house, we found both her parents dead.' Bernardo explained as he rose to his feet.

The young militiaman looked up at him, surprised by his height and build.

'Did you chase the pirate away?' asked the older militia man to Bernardo.

'He killed him with one blow, like Samson.' Agata announced, as if pleased by some small victory.

The two men looked up at Bernardo, trying to picture the scene. Clearly impressed, if rather surprised.

'We have a total of three bodies to bury and I would appreciate some help.' Bernardo declared in an authoritative tone which ended the conversation that Bernardo did not want to continue.

After giving the house a quick inspection for other bodies, they wrapped Agata's parent's bodies up as best as they could. Then they placed them on a small hand cart and pulled them down towards the nearby chapel without another word being spoken. It was a gruesome task they would repeat through the rest of that day.

By the time Bernardo, Agata and the two militiamen arrived at the graveyard beside the little chapel, there were rows of bodies being prayed over by Dominican friars and graves being dug by the troops. Seeing the arrival of this next group, one of the friars walked over to them and asked curtly, 'Who have we got here?'

'A farmer and his wife…the parents of this girl…' Bernardo said, motioning towards Agata who continued to stare blankly into the distance, '…who were killed in the attack this morning, and Father Aiello who died in his sleep while on pilgrimage to Rome.'

'A Benedictine brother like yourself?' the Dominican enquired looking over at the black habited body on the donkey.

Bernardo nodded.

'So, are you on this pilgrimage too?'

'Yes,' Bernardo confirmed, as he caught Agata who stumbled beside him.

'She is faint and needs some food, water and rest.' he said to the Dominican, but he had already moved on to direct the men to prepare the bodies.

Bernardo sat Agata down at the side of the chapel with some left-over bread, cheese, wine and water from his supplies then went back to witness Father Aiello's burial. He was worried about Agata, so once he was certain the bodies would be properly buried, he took her back to the remains of her house on the back of the donkey.

Once they arrived back at the farmhouse, Bernardo surveyed the one room that remained intact. He shook the black soot off the bed cloths and tried to tidy up the little bedroom as best he could.

'It would be best to sleep here tonight,' he explained to Agata, 'then decide in the morning what to do next.'

His thinking was to get her to her relatives, or at least somewhere safe, before he continued to a ship leaving Sicily.

Eventually Agata started to help him, fetching water from the well, collecting basins for them to wash in and preparing candles for the night. Somehow the familiar tasks helped to steady her nerves. She even sorted out bedding for them, repining up the curtain dividing the room which was now torn in several places.

As night began to fall, they ate what was left of Bernardo's food supply, then Agata lit candles. After drawing the curtain dividing the bedroom, as best she could, she poured water into a pottery bowl to wash herself. She slipped off her torn, filthy blouse and skirt, now unrecognisable. She began to wash the blood, soot and dirt off her face and neck, only then realising exactly how dirty she was.

On the other side of the curtain, Bernardo knelt in prayer with his rosary in his hands.

However, his mind was so full of questions, he found it hard to concentrate on the set evening prayers he had been taught. He looked up and caught a glimpse of Agata's naked body through a tear in the curtain. He instantly felt guilty for seeing her nakedness but could not draw his eyes away from the vision before him.

She was so petite, with such a sweet innocent face, that he had taken her for a child.

Now he saw that although indeed young, she was a grown woman. Her smooth, unblemished skin covered a curvaceous figure, and her long slender neck gave her an elegance he had not expected. His eyes settled on her pert breasts, and he started to feel aroused which increased his embarrassment. He dropped his eyes to the floor and started to pray for forgiveness from lustful thoughts as powerful feelings of desire ran wild in his head.

After a little while, despite his feelings of guilt, he could not resist looking up to see her body again, but she had moved out of his line of sight, so he returned to his prayers, and confused adolescent emotions. Meanwhile, Agata had lain down, and fell quickly asleep, exhausted by the terrible events of that day.

Chapter 14

The young monk stood nervously before Friar Diego at the Palazzo Steri as the chief inquisitor looked through the list of those buried in Trabia the day before. Details of the Barbary pirate attack was a distraction from his main mission, but he did not want to discourage his young assistant's zeal.

'Exactly why should a burial list be of interest to me?' he asked, not looking up from the papers on his desk.

'You said you were looking for an old, heretical Benedictine, and it was slightly unusual to bury one away from his Abbey.' The young friar explained.

'His name?' Diego asked impatiently.

'Father Aiello,' he replied, pointing to his name well down on the list.

Diego sat back in his chair, staring at the name on the page, his emotions rather mixed. On one hand, he was delighted to know this troublesome monk would no longer give him any more problems but he also felt disappointed he would not have the pleasure of arresting him.

'Well done, brother,' he said to the young Dominican, whose eyes lit up with pride, 'and what of his companions?'

'A young Benedictine delivered the body of Father Aiello, along with the bodies of the parents of a local girl who was with him.' was the young friar's breathless reply, 'Agata Conti was her name, from a farm just inland of Trabia.'

'Excellent,' said Diego staring hard at his young assistant, 'now listen to me carefully.' Diego stood up and leaned on the desk as he continued, 'Take some guards and go straight to this farmhouse near Trabia. Bring both the Benedictine and this young girl Agata here.'

The young friar hesitated only a moment and Diego's temper flared.

He shouted, 'Immediately!' At which the young friar scampered out the door like a chastised dog with its tail between its legs.

As the young friar left, Diego sat back in his chair deep in thought and closed his eyes.

'Could this be the son of Boscogrande that God is giving into my hands,' he mused, 'but who is this Agata and what is her connection?'

'Raphael!' Diego shouted, 'Have you located the regional magistrate yet?' he continued as soon as his secretary's head appeared around the door.

'He has gone to Cefalù, which is why I could not find him in Palermo,' Raphael responded.

Diego contemplated this new information and considered his next move. His visit to Montreal Abbey had been fruitless, though he sensed Aiello had been there—the Abbot was evasive. If the old monk was truly buried in Trabia, the family would not be too far away.

He had not believed the whole Boscogrande family were dead despite William the Archer's insistence they were. Thinking about this family brought back memories of his humiliation, and rage slowly built up within him.

He thought he could get to the witch through her father, but the old man died so quickly after arrest, he gained no useful information, and Signior Davide's popularity had placed him in a vulnerable position. Cavaliere Mateo di Boscogrande's forceful attack on him and his authority had been outrageous, but the widespread support Mateo had from the other nobles, and the Archbishop, caught him off guard.

'The Boscogrande family slipped out of my hands before I had time to fully regroup my network and bring a credible counter charge,' he muttered to himself, 'Then, the humiliation of being recalled to Madrid to explain myself to the Inquisitor General.' He slumped in his chair and seethed!

'Obviously this Cavaliere had influential friends even in the Spanish court, so my masters lost face and blamed me…aargh!' He stood up and paced the room, trying to control his emotion.

'Times change' he said to himself, taking a deep breath. Now he was back with unquestioning authority, there were old scores to settle. The thought comforted him, and his rage subsided. He needed to control himself and follow up this new lead. They could not hide forever.

He returned to his desk and wrote a letter to the regional magistrate. Even although he had yet to meet him, he saw no reason not to give him instructions where it concerned apprehending a suspect.

Chapter 15

When Bernardo awoke from an exhausted sleep, Agata was already up and had found herself an "almost" clean dress and blouse to wear. She had brushed and tied back her long black hair automatically on waking and fetched water from the well, being comforted with following a familiar routine. It was a clear, crisp day with a gentle northerly wind freshening the air, adding to the tranquillity that was in sharp contrast with twenty-four hours before.

The charred ruins of the dwelling still smelled strongly of smoke, but trying to ignore that, Bernardo too was comforted with routines. So, he washed with the water Agata provided, then knelt by the bed and recited morning prayers, as he had been taught.

Agata had been looking around the farm's stores for something to eat. To the back of the building, just beyond the vegetable patch, there was a chicken coup, and a low sod clad building which Bernardo guessed was a storeroom when she emerged with her hands full. He could see beyond that, to the right some beehives and to the left what he guessed was a smoke house for preserving meat and fish. If these were stocked up, she would at least, not go hungry while he made arrangement to take her somewhere safe.

They sat silently on the ground outside the building, eating smoked fish and dried fruit that Agata had placed in simple pottery bowls for them. The early morning sun warmed them. At another time, this could have been a pleasant experience, but their emotions were so frail, they just felt numb.

Bernardo tried to gather his thoughts to make some plans, pushing confused feelings out of his mental focus. He knew he needed to go on to Cefalù, to at least let Captain Orlando know of Father Aiello's death. However, he also had a strong sense of responsibility for Agata, which surprised him, and he felt bad about leaving her.

'Do you have any family you could go to?' he asked, looking over at her and feeling a lump in his throat as he did so.

She did not respond right away but kept staring at the bowl in her lap. She wanted to cry but remembered her mother gently cradling her when she did and urging her to be strong, '…for the ones we love,' she would say. They were not with her anymore, but she felt she should be strong for Bernardo. He had been so brave, and she felt safe around him, but she also sensed an urge to ask him why this had happened, as her brain seemed to demand an explanation. However, she remained silent, her mother's strong, steady voice still in her head comforting her. She accepted that bad things just happened. She had seen neighbours take ill and die, storms wreck boats and kill fishermen. Until now, her immediate family seemed to have been spared such calamities.

'Together we were strong; family is everything…' her mother had said, but now they were gone.

'Family,' she thought, 'Bernardo had asked about family.'

She looked up at him, patiently waiting for her reply. He would have waited much longer, as he found great pleasure staring at her face, and found it hard to concentrate on making plans when he did.

'My mother's brother has a farm to the south near Alia, sort of west of the Modonie Mountains,' she said and stared into his eyes, intently fixed on hers.

For the first time, she noticed how blue his eyes were and she became momentarily transfixed by them, forgetting about their circumstances.

With great difficulty, Bernardo tore his focus away from Agata's face and onto the plans they had to make. He had spent much of the night thinking about what he should do next and what to do about Agata. He felt both responsible to fulfil his mentor's wishes, but also to see this girl to a place of safety. He could not just leave her, nor did he want to, but adrift on an ocean of uncertainty, as he was, he felt they were both rather lost.

'I need to go to Cefalù to meet someone and tell them that Father Aiello is dead, but I will return as soon as I can,' Bernardo said as reassuringly as he could.

He stood, feeling he had to make a move and wanting to break the enchantment he experienced when around her. She rose too and for a moment they stood next to each other rather awkwardly, wondering what to do next. He did not want to leave Agata on her own, but knew he had to continue to Cefalù and explain to Captain Orlando what had happened.

'Are you going to be all right?' he asked Agata as he stood at the wrecked farmhouse door in the early morning light. She nodded, her pretty face looking trustingly up at him.

'Hopefully, I will be back by tomorrow night. On my own, I should be able to travel quickly.'

He only had a vague plan, but this strong sense of duty, both to his old mentor, and this young girl was driving him on.

'Once I return, I will take you to your uncle's farm in the south…you will be safe there,' he stated, more confidently than he felt.

'Thank you…' Agata responded, touching his large hand with her dainty fingers.

Bernardo felt a rush of emotions unfamiliar to him, and he had to pull himself quickly away; focusing his attention on the journey ahead in order to leave.

Walking down the path towards the coast road, he had so many things on his mind he found it hard to gather his thoughts.

'What should he do when he arrived in Cefalù? How will he contact Captain Orlando? Could a ship out of Sicily be arranged for another time, another port? Perhaps after he settled Agata with her uncle's family, he could join a vessel in the south of the island?'

He so wished Father Aiello was with him to guide him, as he found himself overwhelmed with these new responsibilities and the unexpected circumstances.

He thought back to the conversations he had with the old monk on the road from Montreal. There was talk of meeting Orlando at a guest house near the harbour. It mustn't be a church property, as remaining anonymous was imperative. He was not sure how he could manage to remain inconspicuous once he arrived at the harbour but decided to head straight for this guest house. He would ask after Captain Orlando, sticking to the story that he was on church business and travelling to Rome, though people would have expected him to stay with his Order, not in a public house. What excuses could he use? He had even lost interest in looking at the Cathedral, and the large mosaic of Christ there that Father Aiello had described so vividly.

It was a long, hot journey, but Bernardo made good time, and at least the solitude gave him opportunity to gather his thoughts. So much had happened in such a short space of time. He reflected on the guilt he felt over killing the pirate that attacked Agata. He would have to confess this at the first opportunity, but could he just gain simple absolution for such a mortal sin? His heart felt heavy, and he fingered his rosary, reciting the prayers he had been taught.

It was late in the day by the time he found the guest house which turned out to be a tavern, near the harbour, with bedrooms on a second floor. The landlord did know Captain Orlando, and he had left a message for them. Bernardo explained about the old monk's death. Seeming sympathetic the landlord agreed to give him some food, and a room to rest while he waited.

Once he had eaten his first hot meal in days and drank a little more wine than he was normally rationed, he knelt by a small bed in what was no more than an attic, to pray. He laid his rosary on the bed. Beside it he laid the once bejewelled dagger he had kept concealed under the scapular that covered his habit like an apron. He stared at them. These two items representing two very different parts of his life.

The rosary, and the prayers that it brought to mind, had always been a comfort to him. Previously, he had only thought of the dagger as a hunting tool. Now, despite leaving everything else behind with Agata, he had felt it wise to bring the dagger with him, 'for protection!' Was he now going to rely on violence to save him rather than God? Things that he once felt so sure about, now seemed uncertain and these two objects seemed to symbolise all that was spinning around in his head.

His contemplation was abruptly interrupted as he heard raised voices from below talking about Benedictine monks. Rising to his feet, he grabbed the rosary and without thinking about it, concealed the dagger below his scapular.

Feeling tense and not being sure exactly what to do, he listened at the door of his small room, cracking it open to see if he could catch a glimpse of who was speaking. They could be soldiers, but it was hard for him to tell, as he only saw a part of them through the slats of the wooden stairs. Then he heard a new voice dismissing these men and talking to the landlord quietly. He thought the voice, giving the orders, could be Captain Orlando, but he quickly and quietly closed the door as there was movement towards the stairs.

Bernardo stood back from the door, as he heard footsteps approaching the room. He had to bow his head as the ceiling was so low, but he stared at the door and braced himself for whoever might enter. He found himself fingering the dagger under his scapular, then the rosary dangling from the rope belt around his waist. There was a knock and a voice calling, 'Bernardo, it is Orlando.'

He hesitated to answer, as he was embarrassed by how hard his heart was beating and how heavily his breathing was.

The door opened. Captain Orlando was not as tall as Bernardo, but he still had to stoop to enter the small bedroom. He glanced around, quickly accessing the situation by habit. Clearly a cautious man, but Father Aiello had said he could be trusted.

'Well,' he exclaimed, with a wry smile on his face, 'you have been busy.'

Sensing and probably seeing the tension in Bernardo's stance, he motioned for him to sit on the low bed, while he gingerly perched on a small stool in the corner. He stared at Bernardo for a moment silently, then sighed and placed his black leather covered arms on his knees.

'I was sorry to hear about the death of Father Aiello, he was a dear old friend, but I did wonder if he was strong enough for this journey.'

He looked down at the floor and seemed genuinely sad, but Bernardo was taken by surprise that he knew about the death already.

'How did you hear already about Father Aiello?' Bernardo asked.

Orlando looked back at Bernardo, pausing as if weighing up what he was about to say, before replying.

'As the Regional Magistrate for the Palermo area, I make it my business to keep informed of everything that goes on, but things are indeed moving faster for you than I had expected!'

He stopped to listen, as if he had heard voices from downstairs, then continued.

'Soon after the pirate raid, I and some of my men came to Trabia to see what we could do and receive a report. I was given a list of those buried and missing. The militia men that collected the bodies from the farmhouse told me about you. They were most impressed by the giant, blue-eyed Benedictine that kills pirates with one blow!'

'So, you are a pirate killer and rescuer of young maids now,' Orlando said with a sly smile. Leaning in towards Bernardo he whispered, 'You had been advised to keep a low profile, but now by morning you will be the talk of the region.'

He straightened himself up again, the smile disappearing.

'After reading the burial list, I was sure the Father Aiello on the list was our friend, but by the time I made it up to the farmhouse, thinking you would still be there, I found I was not the only one to hear news about you.'

His face turned grave, and his voice changed to a whisper again.

'Diego's men came looking for you and have taken Agata to be questioned by him.'

This news hit Bernardo like a blow to the stomach. His mouth dropped open as if he was going to say something, but no words came out. Orlando watched him with interest and waited. Father Aiello's words about Diego rang in Bernardo's ear and filled him with horror.

'If we ever met this inquisitor, we would probably not survive the encounter.'

Eventually Orlando could see Bernardo's huge hands grip his knees tightly as a passionate response burst forth.

'We have to help her…how do we get her away from the Inquisition…where did they take her?'

Orlando raised his hand and motioned for the young man to calm down. His affection for this young girl was obvious and he wondered what Bernardo had told her. Indeed, just how much did Bernardo know himself?

'Twice I have been summoned to meet with Chief Inquisitor Diego and I keep making excuses.' Orlando explained, 'Now my men and I have been ordered to find you and bring you to Palermo. I think that is exactly what I should do. However, I think we might make your visit to Palazzo Steri memorable in a different way than Diego hopes!'

Orlando rose and made to leave but turned with a wicked smile and whispered to Bernardo.

'It is time we put Diego in his place and rattle the Inquisition's cage. With the help of some friends, we will rescue this girl, and prise you both out of his grip. Gather your things quickly, I have a carriage waiting for us.'

As they began to descend the stair, Orlando turned and whispered, again.

'Do you trust me young Bernardo?'

'Father Aiello said I should,' Bernardo replied after a brief pause.

'Good,' Orlando continued, 'that is important, as appearances may be deceptive. In order to remain safe, friends have had to sometimes remain in the shadows, and many of us must wear two faces.'

There were times in the past at the Abbey that Bernardo had fantasised about adventures as all young boys do, but this "adventure" was not one he was relishing at all, and he began to wish he could return to his quiet routine life in the Abbey.

Outside there was a covered carriage, driver and two soldiers waiting for them.

'Home,' Orlando said to them all, motioning Bernardo to get into the carriage. He climbed on board after him, and they made off at speed. Sitting in the carriage opposite Orlando, as it charged towards Palermo, shaking them all over the place, Bernardo felt nauseous. He could not remember being in a carriage before, though assumed he had been as a child, but the movement was terrible and curdled his stomach already knotted with apprehension. Nevertheless, despite his feelings, and the noise of the speeding carriage, he tried to focus on what Orlando was saying, as he laid out the plan to rescue Agata.

Chapter 16

Agata sat on a filthy straw covered floor in the almost complete darkness, the only dim light coming from under the door of the cell she had been thrown in. She had never been much for praying, nor had she thought much about God in the past. The regular mass they attended as a family had been just another routine to her, and an excuse to gossip with friends afterwards.

Now she wished she could find comfort in faith, but she just felt desperately alone, and totally confused.

When the guards had come to the farm, she was in the middle of trying to clean up the surviving part of the building. They asked where the Benedictine was she had been seen with, and without hesitation, she said he had gone to Cefalù. This clearly disappointed the friar with them and seemed to make the guards angry. They tore apart what was left of the house and outbuildings looking for Bernardo.

Eventually the friar shouted at them, 'Enough...bring the girl.'

One of the biggest of the guards smiled from a semi toothless mouth at Agata. It was a lecherous look and it sent shivers down Agata's spine. He roughly grabbed Agata, dragging her out to the carriage, and pushing her inside, before climbing in after her. He smelled of stale garlic and beer, and his hands groped her as he pushed her around. She was terrified, but helpless. Without any further conversation, the friar got into the carriage, ordering it back to Palermo.

It was a very bumpy ride which made her feel sick, worse than being in one of the local fishing boats when the sea became rough. Then, she was dragged out of the carriage, into a grand looking building. Through an inner courtyard, down some stairs, and thrown into this cell. The big guard just laughed, as he slammed the door shut.

There had been no explanation, no questions, and she had no means of estimating the time she had been there, or clues to how long she would stay. She felt totally abandoned and wondered what they had done to deserve the calamities of the last few days.

She curled up into a ball in the corner, hugging her knees, drawn up against her. The cell smelled worse than the latrine at the back of their farmhouse. She stared at the door, willing it to open and set her free but dreading the large guard's return.

The outline of a rodent, scurried past the bottom of the door of the cell, disappearing in the dark corner. She did not like rats, remembering how her brothers would trap them as they tried to steal eggs from their chicken coup. She shivered, partly as she thought of being trapped in the cell with hairy things that bite, and partly as it was cold and damp. An anguished cry broke into the silence from a neighbouring cell, and fear started to work its way into her spirit.

'What was this place? What will happen to me here?'

She really did not want to dwell on these thoughts and tried to focus on something positive. Bernardo's deep blue eyes came into her mind. If only he knew where she was, he would rescue her.

Then she chastised herself, 'How could he know, and how could he help her. She would need an angel to break her out of this cell, like the one their local priest told them helped Saint Peter.'

She began to weep, the grief of the last couple of days overwhelming her, and through her tears she cried out into the darkness.

'God help me as you helped Saint Peter.'

Chapter 17

When Bernardo arrived at Palazzo Steri, it was quiet, and so dark on this moonless night, that the guards on duty had to hold up a candle lantern to his face to see who had disturbed their slumber. The guards did not recognise him, or the two soldiers, one tall and stocky, the other shorter but equally as broad, that accompanied him.

'We will just lock this one up for the night, then the inquisitors can decide what to do with him when they get up,' the shorter solider said in a weary voice.

'Mmm' was the grumpy reply from the more awake guard, but it occurred to him that this was a good plan. He did not want the responsibility of waking anyone this late into the night.

He unlocked the gate and led the way inside, through a courtyard, then down some stairs to another locked door, while the other guard locked the outer gate behind them.

Fumbling with keys, he opened the door at the bottom of the stairs. He did not have time to go in, before the taller soldier's large hand grasped his throat, pinned him to the wall, pulling him up until his feet barely touched the floor.

'Where is the girl that arrived tonight and William the Archer?' the taller soldier demanded.

'End cell and one opposite,' gasped the guard, struggling to speak.

On hearing this, Bernardo followed the plan. He walked straight through the door, down some more steps, having already taken the lantern out of the guard's hand before he dropped it. Then, with the shorter soldier following close behind him, he took out the bunch of keys in the door as he passed. They moved quickly, hoping not to encounter any other guards that could raise an alarm.

The stale, humid air from the cells hit them immediately and there was a nauseating smell that became more obvious as they descended. Bernardo was almost overcome by the sense of despair in the dungeon, but he tried to ignore it, focusing on the task before him. He could hear muffled voices from the first room they passed, then a cry of pain that sent shivers down his spine.

'Please God, do not let that be Agata,' he prayed, while unconsciously rubbing the dagger beneath his scapular, rather than the rosary.

Swiftly making it to the end cell, he fumbled with the keys as the stench made him want to retch. The sense of despair started to seep into his soul. The third key opened the door, and the dim lantern he held revealed a small, crumpled figure in the far corner.

'Agata, is that you,' he whispered.

Almost simultaneously, he handed the keys to his accomplice, who immediately proceeded to open the cell opposite. Looking furtively around, Bernardo noted the taller soldier, though only by his shadowy shape, moving a body down the stairs into an alcove.

For a moment, Agata wondered if she was dreaming, as she saw the huge figure silhouetted in the door frame and heard Bernardo's voice. Feeling weak and confused, she crawled towards the light, then felt big arms pick her up. Looking into Bernardo's face, she put her arms around his neck, burying her face in his large shoulders, she started to sob with relief.

Bernardo too was relieved to see her but did not pause to indicate it. He moved quickly to the stairs, and almost ran up them. The taller soldier he arrived with was standing guard in the shadows at the entrance, with another body near his feet which he almost tripped over. As he handled the lantern to the soldier, following him out, he momentarily wondered if the two guards were unconscious or dead. He cast the thought quickly out of his mind, focusing on getting away from the nightmarish prison.

On the street, just outside the entrance to Palazzo Steri, a carriage had pulled up.

Bernardo clambered inside, still carrying Agata. They had no sooner settled in, when a large, clearly battered body was helped in too. The shorter soldier cradled William in the seat opposite Bernardo. The taller soldier climbed up beside the carriage driver, then immediately it clattered away down the dark streets, being swallowed by the night.

Bernardo stared at the broken man he had looked up to as a child. William stared back through swollen, almost closed eyes, both barely recognising each other. No one spoke.

Relieved to be out of that hell hole, but not certain they were safe yet.

Even with the rags they had tied to the horse's hooves and carriage wheels, they clattered loudly on the cobbled streets, the noise reverberating off the building around.

Together with Bernardo's heartbeat, which seemed to fill his head, he felt certain they would be heard, but no one stopped them.

The sky was turning orange and birds were beginning to sing when they stopped near the outskirts of Palermo. The carriage doors burst open so suddenly, Bernardo initially thought they had been caught, but as those that greeted them gently helped William out of the carriage, he could see they were friends. Following them, he helped Agata out of the carriage into the arms of a small, round-faced matron who gently ushered her away inside the nearest door.

Bernardo watched her go, then looked around to see they were in a courtyard of a fine villa. Many helping hands were busy unhooking the horses and pulling the carriage out of sight. Gates were closed behind them, and evidence of their arrival cleared away, with very few words being spoken. Then Bernardo saw Orlando striding towards him.

'Well done, young Bernardo, your father would be so proud of you,' he said, putting an arm around Bernardo's broad shoulders to direct him.

'Let's go inside,' he continued, pointing towards the door Agata had disappeared into, 'We need to get you all out of sight just in case we have visitors.'

They sat at a wooden table, near a noisy kitchen. Servants were busying themselves, lighting fires in stoves and taking coals to light hearths in other rooms.

'Have something to eat and then sleep. We cannot move you again until tonight,' Orlando was explaining, as they sat opposite each other on wooden benches.

'Where are we…whose house is this?' Bernardo asked.

Orlando raised his hand in reply.

'The less you know the better, just be confident it is the home of a friend. You are among family here, but we all have to keep a very low profile.'

A plate of food was placed in front of them, and Orlando motioned him to eat as he spoke. 'Please eat a little and then sleep. You will need all your strength for the journey ahead.'

'Journey?' Bernardo questioned, with a mouth full of freshly baked bread.

'Yes,' Orlando explained, 'we need to get William, Agata and you to places of safety soon, but not necessarily the same place…preparations are already underway.'

As Bernardo finished eating, he would have liked to have asked more questions.

However, relishing the wine which he hoped would calm his nerves, he felt overcome with fatigue and decided questions could wait. He said he trusted Orlando, and so far, he had kept to his word, so sleep seemed a good idea.

As Orlando rose, Bernardo gulped another mouthful of wine and stood up too.

'Let me show you where you can sleep,' Orlando was saying as he led the way towards a large cupboard which had been pulled off the opposite wall. Behind the cupboard was an open hatch with a steep wooden stair descending into a dimly lit basement.

'There are several rooms down there and an escape tunnel, if necessary. You will be safe until we come and get you…once we are ready for the next move,' Orlando explained.

'Where is Agata, is she alright?' Bernardo asked, hesitating at the top of the stair.

'Yes,' Orlando reassured, 'she is being bathed and any wounds treated, then she too will be hidden in this basement.' He patted Bernardo on the back.

'Soon, my young friend, she will join you soon, now get some rest,' motioning him to go down the stairs.

At the bottom of the stairs, just like Orlando had stated, there were several small, low-ceilinged rooms created by wooden partitions between thick stone pillars and curtains for doors. Most seemed to have beds in them, but others had stores piled up and, at least one, had a table and chairs. With no further instructions and tiredness overtaking him, Bernardo chose a bed and collapsed onto it. He was soon fast asleep. He was asleep so quickly, he did not see Agata, a short time later, standing by the curtain at the entrance to the cubical where the bed he was sleeping in was located. She smiled at his big comatose body, hanging off the small bed and thanked God for him.

She snuggled into the bed in the next cubical, now in a clean shirt and despite the dangers she suspected lay ahead, she felt safe and at ease. She prayed that night, in a new way for her, thanking God for answering her prayers and sending an angel to rescue her. She had not expected an angel in the form of a large, young monk. However, she decided, despite everything, that God was protecting her after all, and Bernardo was her guardian angel. As she settled down between clean sheets, the intensity of her feelings for Bernardo made her heart race. The realisation that she could be in love with this young monk both excited and confused her. So many new emotions spinning around her young head, yet she slept with a contentment she had not felt in a long time.

Chapter 18

Capt. Orlando waited until just before terce prayers to reported to Palazzo Steri, by which time the place was in an uproar. The guard's bodies being found at the change of the watch and the missing prisoners shortly afterwards. He had mixed feelings about meeting with Friar Diego for the first time. Although relishing the game he was playing with him and getting the better of them all, he had lost so many friends to this Inquisitor, he was filled with hatred for him. He would have to keep his false mask firmly in place, as he had heard Diego had a sixth sense about people lying.

He entered Diego's office as soon as he was announced, not waiting to be called and waving his hat flamboyantly before him, as he bowed elegantly to the Chief Inquisitor. His dandy mask firmly in place, he looked as if he was distracted by the furnishings and flopped himself down on a chair in front of Diego's desk. Diego stared at him silently, trying to gauge if this buffoon would be useful or not.

'A thousand apologies for my tardiness in calling on you, but with so much unrest and now pirate attacks, I have been rushed off my feet.' Orlando said trying to sound weary of it all. 'Now trying to find a young Benedictine on an island full of them…huh!'

Orlando yawned and feigned boredom of the whole effort.

'However, we did apprehend a fellow, masquerading as a monk and have brought him here for you.'

Diego perked up and looked hopeful, just as Orlando had anticipated.

'Unfortunately, he did not come quietly and the rather rough fellows I have to work with killed him,' Orlando continued, 'but at least you can cross him off your list.'

'Let's see this monk, shall we, perhaps I can identify him.' Diego hissed, his eyes narrowing, but he kept his temper in check, as he stood to leave.

Orlando slowly raised himself from the chair with an air of disinterest, following Diego out of the office and down the stairs.

In the cobbled courtyard, just before the stairs going down to the cells, a body wrapped in a blanket was lying face down. Two stocky soldiers, who Diego assumed had brought the body in, promptly left as he arrived.

Pulling away the blanket revealed a naked pale young body, taller than average, with few marks and no blood. However, around his neck were distinct bruising that would indicate his neck was broken. Turning the body over, he immediately recognised the discoloured face. It was one of his inquisitors.

'This was one of my brothers, a Dominican,' Diego said through clenched teeth, 'you're supposed to be looking for a Benedictine.'

Orlando shrugged his shoulders as if this was a minor matter.

'The girl of whose services he had tasted, was not clear about the monk's Order.

When we said we were looking for a tall man, that might be posing as a monk, she thought of this one. My men found him naked, so how were they to know which Order he was?'

'We will keep looking' Orlando said over his shoulder, moving towards the exit.

'Wait!' Diego said before he could leave.

'We now have others to look for and they might be together.'

Orlando turned slowly around to face Diego, still trying to show no emotions and little interest.

'One of my inquisitors and some of my guards will go with you, I want no mistakes this time and I want them found,' Diego said forcefully.

His tone of voice made it clear his instructions were not open for discussion. He beckoned to his secretary standing nearby and whispered into his ear. The secretary scurried off, while Diego started to walk back up the stairs towards his office, indicating for Orlando to follow.

'Who do you want us to find now?' Orlando enquired, as if it was most inconvenient, while following him back to his office. Diego did not reply but carried on towards his office.

When they arrived, a nervous looking young Dominican was already standing there.

By the time Diego sat back behind his desk, two rough looking guards stopped at the door.

All stood silently waiting for instructions, while Diego shuffled some papers on his desk as he gathered his composure.

'You and these guards will accompany the magistrate,' Diego said, looking at the young Dominican. His eyes narrowed, and the young friar felt they were boring through him.

'You are looking for a tall, young Benedictine, a country girl, and a member of the Beati Paoli, known as William the Archer, or William di Giovanni, as well as any of their associates. When you find them, you will arrest them all and bring them here for questioning, alive!'

They all left immediately, without further questions or hesitation, so Orlando followed them. He tried to remain expressionless, but inside he was full of emotions.

Relieved to be leaving but his mind racing to formulate modifications to their plan. He prayed his men had followed his instructions precisely and were waiting outside but out of sight. One of them would have to update their friends on what was happening.

As Orlando and the young Dominican stood on the street at the entrance to Palazzo Steri, both deep in thought, the guards went to fetch the magistrate's carriage waiting nearby.

'Now, how do we lead these inquisitors in circles all day, while we prepare to move our friends tonight?' Orlando thought.

When his carriage pulled up, he let the Dominican and guards climb inside first, before loudly saying to the driver, 'Take us to the harbour.'

Then climbing on board, he explained that they should see if anyone was trying to leave by boat or hiding around there.

Hearing Orlando's instructions to his driver, the larger of his two soldiers, listening nearby, whispered instructions to his compatriot. He then headed off back to where they had left Bernardo, to report what was going on.

Smiling to himself he thought, 'We will lead these inquisitors on a merry dance before the sun rises again!'

Chapter 19

When Bernardo woke, he had no idea how long he had been asleep, but he felt he had slept better than he had in a long time. Through bleary eyes he focused on Agata's nimble body pouring hot water into a large basin next to his bed. The curve of her breasts were clear through the shirt she had been sleeping in and this immediately aroused him. Although this reaction troubled him, on seeing her, a smile had come to his face, and he moved only slightly to get a better view of her profile. He was surprised to see on her bottom half that she was wearing leather patched pantaloons, similar to the ones the guards had been wearing, but her slim calves and dainty feet were still bare. Catching his movement, she turned and smiled at him broadly.

'Good, I was about to wake you,' she said cheerily, 'you need a good wash and there is a fresh habit for you here.'

She gestured to some clothes on a stool, then wrinkling her nose to indicate he stank.

'I will wash the habit you are wearing,' she said.

At that, she left him and drew the curtain, closing off the cubical he was in, so he could have some privacy.

Bernardo stripped, pushing his dirty habit under the curtain and washed all over in the hot water with soap. The water became black very quickly and he realised he had not had a good wash for quite some time. As he went to put on the clean habit provided, he noted it was a white Dominican, rather than the black Benedictine habit of his Order. However, as he had nothing else to wear, he put it on. Drawing back the curtain of his cubicle he looked around.

Sitting at the table he had seen earlier, was Agata and an older gentleman. Bowls of hot food and earthenware jugs had been laid out. The smells were inviting. As he approached, Agata smiled and started serving steaming stew into a bowl and pouring him wine, while the older gentleman stood to greet him.

Feeling rather awkward, Bernardo just stared at him, not being able to think what to say.

'You certainly have your father's build, young Boscogrande,' the older gentleman said while looking Bernardo up and down.

'I am your host and an old friend of your family,' then catching himself, he said, '…but the less you know the better, eh?'

They both sat down on the benches around the table.

'You both have slept well, I hear,' the old gentleman said looking at them both for confirmation.

'Good,' he said, as they nodded, 'now eat and I will explain the plan we have concocted to evade the Inquisition and get you out of their clutches. What you are wearing is part of this plan, and now the sun is close to setting, we are near ready to make fools of them again.'

Agata and Bernardo ate hungrily while their host explained the plan, including how they should leave the city after they had duped those looking for them. It was a risky venture, but it was important that after they escaped, no one would be implicated as assisting them.

After all, the struggle against the Inquisition would continue even after they were long gone, and if there was no one to question, the Inquisition would not know where they were headed.

Bernardo listened carefully and was impressed by the cunning details of the plan, but he was still coming to terms with all that had happened and had many questions.

After remaining silent throughout the old gentleman's explanation, Bernardo took a deep breath.

'Thank you for your kindness, we are most grateful, and I pray God blesses and protects you,' he said, 'however, I have a few questions which I would appreciate clear answers to.'

He waited, while the old gentleman nodded, then continued.

'You said you were friends with my family and Father Aiello told me briefly about my mother, father, and grandfather's blighted lives and why we ran away to the Sicani mountains. However, I feel a great need to know more about my father and how he died.'

The old gentleman looked thoughtful and nodded, but before he could say anything, Bernardo added, 'Also, if possible, I would like to talk to William, both to see how he is and hear what happened to him after he left my mother and I, all those years ago?'

Standing, the old gentleman grasped Bernardo firmly on his muscular shoulder.

'Yes, you have a right to know more, and William would be the best person to talk to,' the old man said. 'Although William was a bondsman to the house of Boscogrande, he and your father grew up like brothers and fought side by side in many battles. This is a good opportunity, as I have just spoken with him and he seems much stronger, so let's visit him together.'

Bernardo and Agata both followed their host to the end cubicle, where he drew back the curtain. William was sitting upright in bed. The same woman who had taken care of Agata when she arrived at the villa, was spooning broth into his swollen mouth. On seeing them, she stopped and took the tray of food away, without a word.

Agata hovered at the entrance, unsure if she was intruding in family matters, but curious, nonetheless. Their host and Bernardo sat close to William, on either side of the bed. Bernardo took William's hand and automatically made the sign of the cross with his other hand. Raising the crucifix attached to his rosary beads, he said quietly a prayer of blessing for the sick. As he had memorised prayers for almost every situation, these actions were the first things to come into his mind. They helped him settle his thoughts, as he mostly found initiating conversations extremely difficult.

William was a bear of a man, with a thick neck, broad shoulders, and muscular arms. Even through his beard was unkempt, his strong jaw was evident. Clearly a warrior of considerable strength, it was probably this that enabled him to survive the attentions of the Inquisition. The only clue to his advancing years were white flecks and greying temples, in his thick chestnut brown hair. He sat quietly while Bernardo prayed and squeezed his hand affectionately. Tears formed in his eyes, which were only slightly visible through his bruised and swollen face.

With a hoarse voice, William addressed Bernardo.

'You have grown into the fine young man I always knew you would. Did you keep up your bow practice?'

Bernardo smiled, 'Yes,' he proudly replied, 'every day, though it took me two years before I could fully draw your longbow, I can now repeatedly shoot the eye of a hare from fifty cannas.'

'Not my longbow, Bernardo,' William insisted, 'it was yours when I gave it to you, and it sounds like you have made it truly yours now.'

He paused, staring deep into Bernardo's eyes. Patting his hand and nearly choking, he expressed how sad he had been to hear of his mother's death.

After another pause, he continued, with difficulty.

'I knew Father Aiello would look after you and teach you things of better value than I could. Now we have lost him too.' He sighed deeply as he finished.

'Please,' Bernardo pleaded, 'tell me about my father, your life together. What was he like?'

William straightened himself a little in the bed and staring into the middle distance, he began his recollections.

'My mother was French, born on land the Boscogrande family used to own, and my father was an English archer employed by your grandfather. They came to live in Sicily when the Boscogrande estates in France were lost, and I was a young child.'

'Your father and I played and learned to hunt in the same Sicani mountains you hunted in. Although your father would become my lord, we were also friends, fighting side by side in the many conflicts he enlisted us in. Saving each other's lives many times…we became sword brothers. I would have given my life for your father as I am sure he would for me.'

William tried to sit up straighter in the bed and coughed to clear his throat. He was obviously distressed in recalling the events of the past, but he also felt Bernardo should know of these things, so continued.

'Some of the earlier fighting we were involved in was for the Spanish crown and Genoa against the French. As your father and grandfather felt they had stolen their land in the treaties they had forced through, so to a degree this was personal. However, after your grandfather died, your father gave up the hope of ever regaining the previous family titles.'

'Over the years, we even fought alongside the French, when they were fighting the Protestants in Holland and to a lesser extent, crusades against heretics in southern France. Though to be honest, this troubled both your father and I, as it seemed be a war against the helpless, rather than between soldiers.'

William paused, deep in thought, and Bernardo waited patiently for him to gather his thoughts. Eventually he turned to Bernardo and continued.

'After fighting and losing against the forces of the Prince of Orange, in the low country, we had lost four of our company of eight. On our way, southwest we were ambushed just east of Lille, though I am not even sure who attacked us. Possibly unpaid soldiers thinking we had been paid and carrying a load of silver.'

He moved in the bed to make himself more comfortable and winced with the pain of his broken ribs, before continuing his story.

'If it was not for the arrival of some Knights of St John, who chased off the attackers, I think we would have all perished. As it was, two of our remaining company died and your father received a serious wound under his right arm.'

William lifted his right arm and pointed with his left hand but winced again with pain.

'A blade of some sort piercing him right through his arm pit and out of his shoulder. Praise God it was hospitallers returning from the low country that came to our rescue. They helped me patch him up and carried him into Lille, to an Abbey where we could rest and tend his wound.' William shook his head and continued.

'Over the years, I have helped patch your father up from many injuries and he helped me too, but this was the worst wound I had seen him have and I began to fear we would lose him.'

William was obviously feeling emotional about the recounting of these events, adding to his exhaustion due to his own interrogation wounds, but he continued…'However, these Knights and their accompanying brothers were wonderful healers, and your father was strong. So, within a few days, he seemed well enough to travel with these Knights to Marseille, to join a Knights of Malta vessel that would drop us off at Palermo.'

'Things started well, and although weakened by the journey to Marseille, your father seemed to be holding up. We rested at the Order's house in the port for a few days before boarding a three masted xebec, which we were assured would be fast. Throughout the voyage, your father stayed in his bunk. At first, we all assumed it was just seasickness, though it was a very calm voyage, and the six sets of oars had to be used extensively to make headway. However, a day out to sea, your father had a high fever.'

William paused, asking for some water. Agata left to get some, returning momentarily and Bernardo helped him drink a little. Once his thirst was quenched, he continued.

'By the time we arrived in Palermo, despite the hospitallers' best efforts, he was in a bad way, so I immediately rushed ashore to find our old friend Father

Aiello. He wasted no time taking your father to Signior Davide's house in Palermo, as he knew his daughter had knowledge of healing.'

William laid back more on his pillow and smiled, as he continued.

'It was there that we first met your mother, Abrianna. The closest thing I could imagine to an angel, with her beautiful, flawless face, large dark eyes, and heart-warming smile.'

William looked over at Bernardo and said, 'I am reminded of her in your smile, though you have your father's blue eyes.'

He paused, smiling, his mind focusing back to the times he was describing.

'I am not surprised your father fell in love with Abrianna, I think I did the moment I met her, but her eyes were all for your father, and I was happy for them, as well as delighted he made a full recovery. By the time, your father was well again, he had asked Signior Davide for his daughter's hand in marriage. Three months later they were married, with much rejoicing. Within a year, you were born…these were happy times,' he said, closing his eyes.

William started to drift off to sleep, but Bernardo squeezed his hand, eager to hear more about what happened to end this happy life in Palermo.

'What happened to change things for my family?' Bernardo asked.

William stirred, and with a stern look on his face, continued his recollections.

'The Inquisition had always been a nuisance, meddling in the politics of Sicily, but we had little to do with them, as we stayed away from politics, as much as we could. However, I believe there were some who were jealous of Signior Davide's successful trading company, and his business connections in many countries. It would probably be them, that put the Inquisition onto Davide, and particularly that hound Diego.'

William gnashed his teeth as he said the Chief Inquisitor's name.

'Diego accused Signior Davide, whose family had converted to Christianity generations beforehand, of secretly being a Jew, and had him arrested. They probably just intended to extort money from him, but the old man was frail and almost as soon as they got him to their "lair" at Steri, he died.' William was clearly agitated as he recalled these past events, as he continued.

'Your father had been a peaceful, happy man for nine years, slowly learning about shipping and trading as Signior Davide fully embraced him as his son and heir, his daughter having been his only surviving family. He was furious when he heard of his father-in-law's arrest and death. I thought he would explode with rage and kill Diego immediately. I know I wanted to. However, your mother was much wiser, and with Father Aiello's help protested to the Archbishop.'

'To be honest,' William continued, 'I did not understand all that went on after that…There was a hearing of the Church council, and Diego was to justify his actions, but in the midst, your mother was accused of being a witch who used magic to heal. Then Orlando, a friend of your father's, and a ship's master, had me take you and your mother out of Palermo to a manor house on your father's old estate in the mountains. You were to remain inconspicuous, as Orlando and Father Aiello, if I remember correctly, thought things could get dangerous for you both.'

William shrugged to demonstrate his credulity with the situation, but then winced with pain again.

'By the time I settled you in the manor house, arranging a couple of faithful retainers to help your mother, and returned to Palermo, Diego was in disgrace. He would be recalled to Madrid, but the damage was already done.'

William looked at Bernardo with tears in his eyes as he recounted events.

'I do not understand all that went on after that, but your father had become embroiled in Sicilian politics, which he was not well equipped for. At the same time, he was not ready to take over Signior Davide's trading business, especially now he had enemies trying to take advantage of his weaknesses and inexperience.' Clearly weary, William tried to remember details.

'Secretly your father was approached by members of the Beati Pauli to join them in their fight for justice for the people of Sicily. He was sympathetic, but even before he had agreed, rumours spread that he was involved with them, and attempts were made to arrest him. Father Aiello had by this time gone to look out for you and your mother. I tried to guard your father's back, but he sent me to Genoa to deposit a chest of money and a load of papers to banker contacts there.' William wheezed as he continued the revelations.

'Orlando took me secretly in his ship, and although we did not stay in Genoa long, by the time we returned, your father had been killed. Supposedly, he had been involved in a Beati Paoli operation to assassinate an official, but things had gone wrong, and he was trapped.' William signed and squeezed Bernardo's hand, stumbling over his words.

'Sorry, I do not know much more. It was then that I went to tell your mother about your father's death and felt I should stay to help you both. However, eventually Orlando warned me that accusations were being made about me and my presence with you drew too much attention to you both. The Beati Paoli network would help me disappear, he said, and it was then that Orlando revealed to me that he was part of this organisation.'

Bernardo sat back on his chair, considering all that he had heard. He wanted to know more but needed time to think through what he had learned so far. William's hand tightened around Bernardo's, and he smiled at him affectionately. He knew it was important Bernardo knew all the details.

'The Beati Paoli has been keeping an eye out for you secretly ever since I left you. They sent the warning to Father Aiello about Diego's return, and we have sent word to our contact in Genoa. You must get there as soon as you can.'

William reached under his pillow and pulled out a leather pouch.

'Our friends have helped me keep this for you, but I thought this would be a good time to hand it over to you.'

He put the leather pouch on the bed and removed what looked like a golden broach from the bag.

'In here,' William said, 'are letters of introduction and credit notes I brought back from the bankers in Genoa…and this,' handing Bernardo the golden medallion.

Bernardo held it in his hand and looked at it carefully. It looked like a lamb, hanging on a tree, with a ring at the top to hang from a ribbon. He had never seen anything like it before, but it reminded him of the Greek story of Jason and the Golden Fleece. Before explaining what, the emblem was, William showed Bernardo a highly decorative parchment with the Hapsburg seal. Bernardo quickly read the Latin verse, noting his father's name at the top:

"…the very great and perfect love that we have for the noble estate and order of knighthood…we desire the honour and increase, by which the true Catholic Faith, the faith of our mother, the Holy Church, and the tranquillity and prosperity of the public may be, as far as possible, defended, guarded and maintained; we, to the glory and praise of the Almighty, our Creator and Redeemer, in reverence of his glorious mother the Virgin Mary, and to the honour of my lord Saint Andrew, Apostle and Martyr…"

His head was spinning, there was so much to take in. He looked up to William to ask what this was, but William raised his hand in anticipation of his question.

'What I told you before of your father being wounded, that was in September 1676.

However, almost a year before that we had been serving King Carlo of Spain. To be more precise, his mother who was Regent at the time, as he had not yet come of age. Your father saved the young King from an assassination attempt and for that his mother honoured him, even above his station.'

He waved his hand, 'That is a story for another time,' conscious of the time he had taken to explain things to Bernardo.

'This,' he pronounced proudly, 'is the order of the Golden Fleece, normally only given to the most senior nobles by the sovereign but given to your father.'

William paused for effect and looked around at all three listeners, eager to hear more.

'It is one of the most prodigious Knightly orders in Europe and your father was made Knight Companion of the Order, despite his father losing their titles and land in the treaties that ended some long running wars. Of course, this is not yours to wear, and as a piece of gold, it is not worth that much, being mostly bronze with gold gilt. However, it's worth is to identify you as your father's son and remind important people of the debt they owe your family.' He sighed.

'I wish I had more time to tell you all about your father and our adventures. He was a remarkable man, a brave warrior, and a loyal brother in arms…but it would take me a long time to tell you everything, and you would have to understand the complex history of the struggles of the princes of Europe,' William's focus started to wane.

Bernardo thought about the history lessons that Father Aiello had given him. He realised he probably did not know enough but was filled with admiration for William. While he had read about disputes between countries, William and his father has been part of that history.

William sunk back into his pillows, now exhausted with the effort, emotions, and pains. He closed his eyes, and the old gentleman stood, motioning Bernardo to follow him out of the cubicle.

'That will have to be enough for now, Bernardo,' he said, 'let us leave William to rest.'

Bernardo, clutching the leather pouch and the medallion, followed the old gentleman and Agata back to the table they started at. Bernardo was finding it hard to take in all he had been told, when the old gentleman began to speak gently to them both.

'It would be good to give you time to think about all you have learned and perhaps talk more with William, but unfortunately we now have to focus on what is going to happen tonight. It is time to go…'

Chapter 20

As the sun was setting, Capt. Orlando was sitting, seemly lost in thought, outside of a tavern by the harbour, his slick black hair brushed back from his forehead. The young friar he had led on a merry chase all day, from the harbour, through Palermo and back again, was looking out to sea, ostensibly reciting evening prayers. However, this was more to take his mind off the dread he felt at returning to Chief Inquisitor Diego empty handed. The two guards, sent with him, were slumped over tables in the tavern, drinking too much. Thinking their work for the day was over, they felt exhausted having missed their usual afternoon nap. On a nearby table, four of the magistrate's men sat drinking. They kept one eye on their employer, wondering what his next move would be.

While they were pondering the day, a beggar walked towards them and perched himself on a nearby bollard. He laid his hat on the ground in front of him and looked over at the groups around the tavern. On seeing him, Orlando walked casually over, stood in front of him, dropping some coins into his hat. They both then stared out to sea, so no one could see their lips moving. After a short while, Orlando dropped some more money in the beggar's hat, then walked back towards the tavern.

Orlando stopped by the table his men were sitting at and gave them some instructions, as the beggar walked off. They stood immediately and walked swiftly towards the city while Orlando returned to his seat. The young Dominican, puzzled by what was going on, came to sit beside Orlando, noticing he had a smile on his face.

'We have them,' Orlando announced cheerfully to the friar, 'and you can help me set a trap.'

The young friar looked confused but listened carefully. Leaning towards him, Orlando whispered. 'One of my informers has just told me they are trying to hide in the catacombs. My men are already on their way to watch the entrance and exit. We will let the suspects go in and trap them there.'

The relief on the young friar's face was clear as he went to collect his guards, perhaps they would not need to return empty handed after all. All three eagerly followed Captain Orlando to the catacombs under the cemetery of the Capuchin monastery, near the centre of the city.

Clambering into the carriage, they dashed across Palermo. Nevertheless, by the time they reached the catacombs, there was little twilight left to see things clearly, but Orlando's men were easy to find. As instructed, two watched the south entrance and two the north exit with flaming touches already lit.

Once he had checked his men, Captain Orlando instructed the young inquisitor and his guards to follow him into the catacombs and to stay alert. It was going to be hard to see anything. The two inquisitor guards carried flaming torches giving off a limited yellow glow and the young friar followed them closely. Orlando looked prepared for action, as he carried his new Brescian flint lock pistol which he had only recently purchased in Genoa.

Meanwhile, inside the catacombs, Agata in an ill-fitting inquisitor guard's uniform, and the lager of the two soldiers that had helped rescue Agata, also in a similar outfit, waited quietly in an empty alcove. Bernardo in the white Dominican habit, crouched at the entrance to the same alcove. He had his bow in hand, an arrow already notched, his eyes now adjusting to the darkness, his instincts focusing his thoughts. He was breathing slow and steadily, just as he had during his hunting trips in the woods near his old Abbey. He knew he would hear his "prey" before he would see them and had the advantage of Orlando being part of the drama.

The catacombs were full of shadows and body shapes that seemed to move silently in the flickering torch light. The guards followed Orlando closely, but a combination of alcohol, superstition and tension had their hearts racing, pounding in their ears. They looked straight ahead at the captain, not wanting to look to their sides at the skulls staring back at them. The young inquisitor felt very uncomfortable too. Less out of fear of the dead than how sacrilegious it was to be entering hallowed ground armed and without proper respectful ceremony.

Bernardo aimed an arrow a little above and to the left of the torch light. He loosed a silent arrow which whistled just above the head of the young inquisitor and noisily struck a corpse with a thud. The friar and guards jumped with fright and ducked down.

'There,' Orlando shouted. Firing his pistol which made a loud bang, and a bright flash assaulting their senses. They did not notice that no ball actually left the barrel.

That was their signal. Bernardo and companions exited the catacombs, quickly and quietly. The pursuers, ears ringing from the noise of the pistol shot and eyes blinded by the flash, were crouched behind whatever was nearby and did not see them leave.

The two soldiers watching the exit, hearing the gunshot, and not knowing who had fired, cautiously moved towards the exit door. Out of the darkness, three figures emerged. From what they could see, it was a Dominican habited friar which they assumed was the young inquisitor and a large guard. Between them, they were dragging another guard. They guessed this was the Inquisition team and one had been shot, but where was Captain Orlando?

They approached the large guard, who did not look up, but waved at them to go into the catacombs.

'We will take care of this one, help Captain Orlando, he has them cornered,' he ordered authoritatively.

So, without questions or a second glance, they darted into the darkness of the catacombs.

With the guards out of sight, Agata, who was being dragged by Bernardo and their accomplice, straightened up. Along with Bernardo, she quickly followed the large soldier around the corner and along the Piazzo Cappuccin towards Cappuccin convent. Guided only by the soldier's local knowledge and the dim light from the carriage driver's lamps they could see ahead, they found a black, covered carriage on the road.

As they arrived at the carriage, the large soldier almost pushed Agata and Bernardo inside, signalling to the waiting driver to move off.

'Aren't you coming with us?' Agata asked the soldier with a note of concern.

He had been their guide since leaving the cellar and was much more confident about this trickery than they were.

'No,' he replied, 'I have more to do here to ensure this misdirection is complete. Your arrow shot and our observed exit from the catacombs will have convinced the Inquisition that William the Archer is travelling with you. This will help us keep William safe while he recovers. Now you must leave this region as soon as possible and be on your way to your next rendezvous…wherever that is.' Then he was gone.

Once again, they rattled through the silent streets of Palermo in the middle of the night and once again they had only a little understanding of where they were going. They had to put their lives in the hands of the Beati Paoli. They sat close together, still, and silent, deep in their own thoughts and fears for the future. They wanted to sleep, but adrenaline coursing through their veins made them hyper alert and on edge. It was going to be a long night.

Chapter 21

When they were away from the cobbled streets and their hearts had stopped racing, they tried to sleep. However, the road became increasingly uneven, jolting them awake with each large pothole. Eventually, just as the first glow of the sun could be seen ahead, they came to a stop and the driver opened the carriage door.

'Follow me,' he said and immediately headed into some trees.

Grabbing his unstrung bow, which had passed for a staff when leaving the catacombs, Bernardo helped a sleepy Agata down from the carriage. They followed the driver into the woods, almost losing him in the darkness. They did not walk far, then almost tripped over the driver when he suddenly stopped to pull a large canvas bag from the undergrowth. The shadowy sight of the bag reminded Bernardo of body bags the poor would be buried in. He briefly worried there would be a dead body inside. However, to Agata it looked like the sail bags she had seen the fishermen use, reinforced by the smell of the tar waterproofing.

The driver began to untie the cords securing it, but he had to explain what was inside. Even with the carriage lantern he carried, it was hard to recognise the dark shapes.

'Here is your Benedictine habit, clean and mended...' the driver began to remove items, '...here is suitable travelling clothes for the girl too'; trying to point with the lantern. 'There is a leather pouch with papers that I was told to take special care of, some new arrows and provisions for the journey. Also, two large books in canvas travel bags.'

The driver stood up and again tried, with only limited success, to point with the yellow light of the carriage lantern.

'There are two donkeys, tethered to that tree. They are old, but reliable and you can spread this load between them.'

He started to head off, leaving them in the dark physically and mentally. Then the directional carriage lantern swung back around to illuminate them, so they could tell the driver had paused and turned to face them as he spoke.

'Oh yes,' he said, 'as soon as it is light enough for you to see, you are to head off. Do not delay. Head initially into the sun towards the Modonie mountain range. There is a map and directions with your provisions. On the slopes of Modonie, lots of olives are grown, as well as fruit and grapes. Their trees will give you good cover to travel and stop for the night unseen. Try not to be seen together and be careful what you tell anyone you do meet.'

He paused again, perhaps to consider if he had forgotten anything.

'God be with you,' he said turning away, 'I have to go. I am running late already.'

The driver disappeared quickly, leaving Agata and Bernardo standing silently in almost complete darkness. Agata took Bernardo's hand. She was shivering, but it was not particularly cold. Bernardo wanted to comfort her but felt quite lost himself. Without the reassuring rhythm of prayer and worship, he was used to in the Abbey, time and events seemed to blend into each other.

'Kneel with me, Agata,' Bernardo whispered, not being completely sure why he was whispering, 'I think we should say morning prayers before we do anything else.'

They both knelt on the spot. He let go of her hand, took out his rosary beads, making the sign of the cross. He kissed the crucifix hanging on the rosary and began to recite the morning prayers he had been taught in Latin and had said every morning for almost eight years. This familiar act of worship calmed Bernardo's spirit and to Agata's surprise, made her feel calm too. By the time Bernardo had finished, the sun had risen sufficiently for them to see clearly.

Bernardo took Agata's hand gently and looked into her pretty face.

'Things will work out fine,' he reassured her, 'I am sure of it.'

She smiled and nodded in agreement, then picked up the clothes left for her and went behind the donkeys to change.

Once suitably dressed for the journey, they loaded one donkey with Father Aiello's Bible commentaries, blankets, poles, bow and arrows, as before. Everything else they loaded onto the other donkey, including the canvas bag, which they wrapped it all up in.

Once completed, the sun was visible through the trees, and the birds were singing loudly, on what looked like being a beautiful summer's day. They were both young and strong, so with the donkeys carrying the loads, Bernardo was confident they could travel a good distance before noon, when they would rest during the afternoon heat. However, as he looked at the map and directions, while walking along, he could see the winding track recommended to them to avoid the main roads and settlements, was a long one.

'You said your uncle's farm is west of the Modonie mountains?' Bernardo asked Agata.

'Yes,' she replied, a spring now in her step, 'near Alia...I have only visited once, as a little girl, for a family wedding. He has many fruit trees, as I remember.'

'Alia...' Bernardo said looking at the map, '...yes, I see that now, it is not far from the route we have been given.'

Folding the map over the rope around his waist, he felt the dagger under his scapular. Bernardo considered how he was going to leave Agata at her uncle's farm, then make it to Gela on the south coast, in time to rendezvous with Captain Orlando, all within a week.

He would not be able to stay with Agata's family for long but felt he could not just drop her off and leave immediately. The thought of leaving her, saddened him and as she was, despite everything, quite cheerful today, he decided not to spoil that by mentioning it to her just yet.

'Oh Lord,' he prayed silently, as he walked along, 'who am I, what am I? This is not what I thought my life would be.'

He could hear Father Aiello's voice in his head, explaining the rules of St Benedict. '...and what of this girl?' He looked over at Agata leading the other donkey. She smiled warmly at him, looking for the moment carefree.

'My feelings for her are so strong.'

He looked back along the path, deep in thought and continuing to pray.

'Forgiven me Lord for my lustful feelings, but that is not all I feel when I am around Agata...maybe the way of Saint Benedict is not the path for me after all? I need a sign...'

Bernardo sighed and started reciting psalms of thanksgiving. In the hand, he had free from leading the donkey, he held his rosary and rubbed the crucifix between his fingers.

'God is with us,' he said to Agata to reassure her.

'He is certainly with you!' she affirmed, smiling broadly at him, and laughing.

Chapter 22

The meeting with Chief Inquisitor Diego, after the episode in the catacombs, was a tense affair. Each person involved, gave their account, or at least, a sanitised version of events. There was no denying it was a first-rate fiasco. Orlando seemed to come out as the hero of the hour. Both as he had at least, located the wanted trio and seemed to have wounded one of them. An illusion Orlando was keen to encourage. As the statements were given, Orlando mused over the actual details, while keeping his face impassive. He was so tempted to laugh out loud.

After Bernardo, Agata and their accomplice had escaped from the catacombs, things had become even more chaotic. The Inquisitor guards had ducked behind the corpse resting places to avoid any more arrows, but their torches had set on fire the dry material around them. Trying to stamp the fire out, while avoiding any arrows, horrified the friar as they knocked corpses about. Then the magistrate's men, entering from the direction of the escapees, were initially mistaken for the fugitives, causing more confusion. Orlando, at least appeared, to keep his cool and take command of the situation. In reality, he was glad it was so dark, so they did not see he found the whole situation so incredibly amusing.

The first two of his men to arrive, that had been watching the exit, he sent to get water, to help dowse the flames, before the whole place went on fire. The young Inquisitor was frantic, wondering how he was going to explain setting this ancient holy crypt alight.

The other two men guarding the entrance came in shortly after the first two, when they noticed the smoke. They were the Beati Paoli men who had help rescue Agata and William. Orlando, supposedly only now realising that their prey had escaped, sent them off to try to pick up the escapees' trail. In doing so, he demonstrated he had not given up on the pursuit. Also, this gave his men all night to ensure William could be moved safely, while Agata and Bernardo's means of escape would be covered up. From the Beati Paoli's point of view, it was a very successful night, but none of this he disclosed to anyone else.

Diego listened to the various accounts seemingly impassively, but if his real feelings were revealed, it would over-shadow an Etna volcanic eruption! After the final report was made, there was some silence, while Diego gathered his thoughts and contained his anger.

'It is clear, Captain Orlando, that you have a good informant network, congratulations,' Diego said, trying to keep his voice steady.

'You will press your informants to find out where these three fugitives went to ground.' Diego did not like being duped, but he was determined not to give up.

'One maybe nearby nursing a wound, but the other two probably have fled the city,' he continued, 'so do not leave any stone unturned to find them. Good day.'

With that, Orlando guessed the meeting was over for him and wasted no time departing. He now had liberty to go wherever he wanted with the excuse he was following leads to find the fugitives. However, he suspected he would be watched, so he would have to act carefully.

The Inquisition team remained in Diego's office after Orlando left. The young friar particularly was petrified, and Diego knew it. So, he sat silently staring at him for quite some time, enjoying his discomfort.

'The girl,' he announced suddenly, making the friar jump, 'is the key to finding this Benedictine.' He paused again to consider his instructions, and the three listeners waited with bated breath.

'Go back to Trabia, find out all you can about this girl...does she have any relatives?

Does the family have any other connections to the Boscogrande family or the Beati Paoli?'

Diego stared at the three with eyes that were intense, his fury starting to come to the surface. 'They are being helped, so someone must know something,' he was almost shouting now and had leaned forward in his chair, 'report back everything.'

With one back-handed wave, he dismissed them, and sat back in his chair to consider what he knew. It was not much.

Chapter 23

Although it had been a long walk, Bernardo had enjoyed the journey with Agata much more than he had with Father Aiello. At times, the meandering path was steep and rocky, and the days had been long, hot, and dry, but being in Agata's company invigorated him. He had talked to her more than he had ever talked to anyone his whole life, even Father Aiello, who mainly talked to him!

As they camped at night amongst the trees, around a small cooking fire, they reflected together on all that had happened since they met, and what they had heard about Bernardo's family. They also talked about her family, comparing their childhood experiences, and previous expectations. What they avoided talking about was what would happen when they parted, though it was on both their minds constantly.

Unlike the beginning of Bernardo's journey, to avoid being seen, they did not visit farmsteads to buy food. However, Bernardo showed Agata his prowess with the bow and arrow. Regularly shooting some game to eat. They also picked fruit from the trees as they passed. This did mean they were alone together a great deal. Normally this would have been culturally inappropriate. However, they both felt very comfortable with each other, and were not looking forward to that ending.

One night, Bernardo shared about his mother, and their time after William left. He showed her the dagger he kept hidden under the scapular that protected his habit. He talked about his mother picking the jewels off it to sell when they were short of money, after the allowance Bernardo's father had been sending stopped. Agata weighed the blade in her hand, then slid it under the plain brown bodice she wore over her white blouse.

'I could carry this without it being noticed,' she remarked, as much to herself as Bernardo, as she withdrew it swiftly, looking at it in her hand. He was not quite sure what he thought about that. However, the moment passed, as Agata used the knife to cut off some meat from the rabbit carcass roasting over the fire.

As a consequence of not being in contact with any settlements, it soon became hard to tell exactly where they were, despite following the map they had. One morning, as they walked through an olive grove, Bernardo thought they should be near Alia, but confessed he wasn't certain.

'We are going to have to ask someone,' Agata insisted, 'I do not know exactly how to find where my uncle's farm is anyway.'

Bernardo knew she was right but remained nervous about exposing themselves.

Reaching the ridge of a hill, a small village came into view, and the smell of freshly baking bread wafted towards them on a gentle breeze. The thought of eating fresh bread, dispelled any lingering concerns, and they agreed Agata would go to buy bread on her own.

'A young girl buying some bread is not going to draw much attention,' she insisted, 'who is going to notice, and if it is Alia, I am going to be living around here anyway…'

She trailed off from her argument, as she realised how much she really didn't want to reach her uncle's farm.

For a moment, Agata cast her mind back to the one time she had visited her mother's older brother, remembering him being grumpy. Although, he had a big farmhouse with three grown sons, and two younger daughters helping, unlike her father, he was a tenant farmer. He moaned about the amount he had to give to the Baron who owned the land. She was also keenly aware that Bernardo would quickly move on, and this troubled her the most. She looked up to this hulk of a man she had grown so quickly to rely on, whose presence made her feel safe, and whose arms she longed to be enfolded in. Looking into his eyes, she raised her hand, and stroked the beard that was forming on his chin. It was rough and had a distinct red tinge.

He smiled at her, his bright blue eyes glistening. He adored her, even when she talked so fast, and change subjects in mid-sentence, so he could not follow all she said! Their discussions were not like the academic exercises, he had become accustomed to. Sometimes he would just listen to her, smile, and enjoy being near her.

To deliberately change focus, Agata took a deep breath.

'Fresh bread, mmmm,' she murmured, jumping on the spot.

She gathered up the few coins they had, then suddenly stopped. Her face became very serious, and she looked up into Bernardo's face.

'The dagger,' holding her hand out, 'just in case,' she said.

Bernardo was very uncomfortable about giving it to her, but understood her logic, so did not argue. He took the dagger from under his scapular and gave it to her hilt first. She deftly slid it under her bodice blade first. She stood looking at herself, pleased it was not noticeable. With a smile to him, she turned, and headed down the hill towards the village, almost skipping as she went.

Bernardo, trying to both keep out of sight, and an eye out for her return, hid himself among the olive trees. He strung his long bow, thinking as he waited silently, that he might just catch himself a contribution towards dinner, wherever that might be. He settled down to wait, reflecting on what a beautiful morning it was.

When Agata arrived at the baker's shop, she realised just how early in the morning it had to be, as the baker was just putting the still warm bread out. Being first there, she took the opportunity to ask if the baker knew where Luigi Tringali's farm was.

'Certainly,' the baker replied, describing a short walk from the village. '…he is popular these days…you are the second person to ask me where Tringali's farm is in two days,' the baker casually remarked.

Agata's heart skipped a beat, as her mind raced to consider what this information meant. Within minutes, other smiling ladies were there, picking loaves, and handing over coins. She tried to keep the smile on her face, as she slipped out the door, and around the corner towards the olive tree covered hill.

Her heart was pounding, and the urge to run away was rapidly over taking all other senses. As she passed behind the building, without warning she was grabbed from behind.

'Hello, little girl,' a sneering voice said, 'I thought I recognised you.'

She struggled but her attacker held her shoulder firmly. He swung her to face him and clasped a large hand around her throat.

'Now you are going to tell me where the rest of your friends are, aren't you?' he said.

Learning his face in so close to hers, she could smell last night's garlic on his breath, as he almost bent her backwards. She recognised this Inquisition guard. The one who had taken her from her home, put his hands all over her as he dragged her to those awful cells, and threw her in there alone.

'There is no way I am going back there, or giving Bernardo up to them,' she thought as fear turned to anger inside her.

In one fluid movement, she slipped the dagger from under her bodice, and brought her knee hard up into his groin. As he doubled over in pain, she thrust the dagger into his chest. It pieced his heart. He died instantly. His dead weight threatened to crush her, so she quickly slipped out from under his falling body, drawing out the dagger at the same time. For a moment, she stood there, looking at the guard's crumpled body, the dagger dripping with blood in her hand. Then she wiped the blood off onto the guards back and slipped the dagger back under her bodice again. Looking around quickly, and seeing no one, she ran back to the olive tree covered hill to warn Bernardo. Her heart pounding fit to burst and body trembling.

Near the front of the baker's shop, a second guard was tending their horses, while wondering how long they would have to watch this area. Tringali had said he had not seen Agata in years. They thought the Chief Inquisitor was grasping at straws by sending them there. Nevertheless, they had watched Tringali's farm all night. Now the young monk, with another guard had taken over the watch, so they were ready for food and sleep.

Then he saw a girl running from behind the building, up towards an olive tree covered hill. He was not sure if he recognised her immediately. However, seeing where she was running from, he half expected his colleague to come running after her.

'This could be the girl they were after,' he thought. As he could catch her easily on horseback, he mounted, and cantered after her, drawing his sword on the way. Assuming his colleague had missed her or would join in later.

Meanwhile, Bernardo was enjoying the peacefulness of the place. Watching some young rabbits, popping in and out of their burrows, while he chose one fat enough to shoot. He had just about decided that he had been over cautious about Agata going into the village and started considering what to say to her when he left her at her uncle's farm.

Halfway up the hill, Agata realised she was being followed by another guard on horseback. Desperate to warn Bernardo, she cried out a warning to him. Her call jolted Bernardo out of his musing, as when you wake suddenly from a deep sleep. In this case, from a peaceful sleep, into a nightmare! Agata was running fast through the olive trees, and the horseman was having to duck because of the low tree branches, so slowing him down. However, he was still catching up with her, and Bernardo could see his drawn sword.

At 50 cannas, Bernardo drew back the arrow on his bow, aiming straight for the chest of the guard. An easy target, coming straight towards him, but he hesitated. He did not want anything to happen to Agata, but was he prepared to kill this man? Another cry from Agata, and the horseman was almost on top of her. Bernardo loosed the arrow.

The arrow imbedded itself deep in the horse's chest, its front legs collapsed immediately. The guard flew off over the horse's head, striking the ground hard, breaking his collar bone, and mercifully for him, knocking him unconscious. Bernardo scanned the horizon for other attackers, but there were no other people in view. As Agata reached him, she grasped his arm and panted, 'They were waiting for us…we have to go!'

He knew she was right, so without any discussion, they headed, as best they could tell, south. They had to pull the donkeys, who had no intention of hurrying, as fast as they could. They did not slow down until the sun was directly above them, and their clothes were soaked with sweat.

Chapter 24

The red, eight-pointed Maltese Cross emblazoned across the white sails, ensured no one seeing it was in any doubt that this vessel was part of the Fleet of the Knights of St John. Captain Raymond De Poincy of the Knights' French langue looked up at the cross with pride. He prayed the symbol would strike fear into the Barbary pirates they chased off the southern coast of Italy. The pirate vessels were swift, and tactics well practiced, regularly allowing them to evade the Knights' patrols from Malta, and speed to their bases in north Africa. However, with this new, faster, slightly smaller galleon, referred to as a frigate, they had captured from the English, he was confident they could match the pirate vessels' speed.

The *San Giovanni*, as they had renamed her, had sixty experienced Maltese crew and twelve Knights of St John. They were finding a lucrative business escorting Genoese trading vessels to, and from, the Levant. An informal arrangement he had made, that guaranteed steady income to pay the crew well, in between capturing Barbary pirates, Ottoman Turk vessels, and their cargo.

Captain De Poincy was an experienced sea commander, from a noble French naval family. His uncle had already served with much success in the Caribbean. Close behind him stood his senior most knight, Jean Dubois, who had served with him many years.

'She is a fine vessel,' Jean remarked, seemingly reading his commanding officer's mind. 'To be honest, I am surprised we were allowed to keep her.'

De Poincy smiled, remember the night raid on the quiet Menorcan cove, a year before, where they had tricked the English crew and captured the vessel.

'If the English had known we were mostly French Knights on the raid, I think they may have accused us of taking sides with France against the Grande Alliance. Something the Knight of St John are not supposed to be involved in.' Jean continued with a broad smile, also remembering the raid with pride.

'Yes, our Grande Master did point that out to me forcefully when we returned to Malta with this prize,' De Poincy reflected, 'however, we were chasing pirates at the time, we know the English have been involved in piracy in the Mediterranean before and they could not explain what they were doing that had us mistaking them for pirates.'

'What do you think the English were up to?' Jean asked.

'I am not entirely sure; however, they certainly want more influence in these seas. A back door to Catholic Europe perhaps, or threaten Spanish treasury shipments,' De Poincy speculated, 'whatever, we have ended up with a fine ship. They certainly know how to build swift vessels, carrying impressive armaments.'

With this fast-new vessel, and his extensive connections with the merchants in the central Mediterranean, he was feeling confident about a lucrative, and productive future. Of course, opportunities for De Poincy and his crew were not in isolation to what was going on elsewhere. The conflicts between France, and the Alliance against them, distracted European navies, and the Barbary pirates were taking full advantage with ever bolder raids.

Standing on his ship's deck that fine morning, a steady southerly wind filling the vessel's sails, he reflected on the mandate of his Order, to defend Christendom. He was a powerful looking man, used to using his sword. Not tall, but well-built, smart in his appearance, with a full bushy beard, and short cropped hair on his large head.

'Once this next cargo is safely delivered to Genoa,' he said to Jean, though mostly to himself, 'and the crew well rewarded, we will focus more on catching pirates.'

He smiled to himself, relishing the idea of a sea battle in his new ship. Although a man of great compassion who had entered the Order many years before with fervour; at heart he was an adventurer. Being part of the Knights of Malta's fleet, allowed him to feel he was fulfilling his duty to God, and satisfying his taste for action.

Note: A war had raged since 1688, between France and a "Grand Alliance" made up of the Anglo-Dutch Stadtholder-King William III, the Holy Roman Emperor Leopold I, King Charles II of Spain, Victor Amadeus II of Savoy, and the major, and minor princes of the Holy Roman Empire.

Chapter 25

During the mid-day break after leaving Alia, Agata and Bernardo cooled themselves, and the donkeys in a stream, near some shade trees. They were physically and emotionally exhausted. However, they decided to only stop for the briefest of time. They wanted to put distance between them and Alia, as soon as possible. It was obvious that after the Inquisitor guard in the olive grove was found, they would be pursued again. Much of the confidence they felt before had evaporated. At the stream, Agata returned the knife to Bernardo, but did not tell him about the guard she had killed with it. On one hand, she thought, 'Confession would be a good thing, but she was not sure what Bernardo would think of her.' She noted he had shot the horse, not the rider when she was being chased. After previously observing his shooting skills, she was sure he hit what he aimed for.

The journey south from Alia was not as pleasant as the journey before. Although glad to still be together, they did not speak much. Driven by fear, not knowing where they might next encounter the Inquisition, they travelled as fast as they could during daylight. Only stopping for brief rests, then falling into an exhausted sleep at night. They skirted around the Modonie mountain range, with a plan to hide in the woods around Monte Cammartta. They decided they would avoid settlements completely. Eating only what they had with them or could forage along the way. When they arrived, they would quietly contact Captain Orlando for fresh instructions.

As they walked along through wooded valleys, avoiding the farms dotted around, Bernardo tried to make sense of what was going on, and the instructions he had from the old gentleman that had helped them. He had even lost track of what day of the week it was, which saint's feast day, and all the other things that marked his previous rhythms of life.

It was getting dark by the time they reached what Bernardo guessed was Lago Comunelli on the second day since leaving Alia. If Bernardo's navigation was correct, there were about four more hours of walking to go, before they reached Gela. They would spend the night in the woods surrounding the lake.

As they settled down that night, and ate the remaining food supplies, they were both feeling weary from the journey. So, although apprehensive as to what they would find in Gela, they also wanted a break from this part of their journey.

'It must be Sunday 31st of May,' Bernardo announced suddenly. Surprising Agata, as he had been silent for quite some time, and they had not been talking about what day it was.

'What made you think of that?' she asked. Wondering why this was important to him.

'Actually, I have been thinking about it most of the day, as I realised, I had lost track of days, and worship times.' Bernardo looked over at Agata with concern etched over his face.

'Today we should be celebrating the virgin Mary's visit to her cousin Elizabeth.' Silently he recalled the set prayers for the day.

'Tomorrow,' he almost whispered, 'we will go into Gela to look for Captain Orlando, but I suggest we are not seen together.' Agata leaned in close to Bernardo, so she could hear him clearly, 'We will approach from slightly different directions and try to find the Madonna Della Platea church. There we are to ask for Father Pepe. He will guide us to Captain Orlando.'

He reached over and took her hand, squeezing it gently. 'Sleep now,' he continued, 'tomorrow we need to be alert.' Agata felt content to be near Bernardo and slept soundly.

Chapter 26

It had been a very profitable voyage for the Captain, and crew of the *San Giovanni.* The traders in Genoa being very grateful that their precious cargo had arrived safely from the Levant.

'We thank God for your safe arrival, and look forward to future deployments,' the merchants chorused.

After stocking up on supplies, they left, feeling well rewarded for their efforts. Heading south, the *San Giovanni* called briefly at several ports on the way back from Genoa. De Poincy taking the opportunity to visit old friends to discuss future shipments to the Levant. They were horrified by the destruction they found on arrival in Catania, Sicily.

'This is awful,' De Poincy expressed to his guests, he hosted for dinner, 'is the whole region like this?'

'Unfortunately, yes,' replied Colonel Don Carlos de Grunenbergh. He had been appointed as Royal Engineer to the Spanish crown to supervise the reconstruction of Catania.

'The nineth of January earthquake was followed by aftershocks until the eleventh then came a devastating Tsunamis, many died.' The mood around the table was very solemn.

'Well, I can't think of a better person to supervise the reconstruction,' De Poincy said, toasting the Flemish Engineer, in an attempt to cheer his guests.

'I can't agree more, Captain,' echoed his other guest. The representative of the Duke of Camastra, who the Viceroy of Sicily, in Madrid, had appointed to administer the damaged regions. 'That is why we appointed your fellow Knight. Was it in Malta you two met before?'

'Yes,' De Poincy replied, 'I met Colonel Grunenbergh when he was redesigning Fort St Angelo in Valletta harbour.'

Grunenbergh told them details of the earthquake's destruction while the Captain hosted them for dinner in the grand aft cabin on board the *San Giovanni.*

He, and his officers were glad they had been far away in the eastern end of the Mediterranean at the time. To return the toast, Grunenbergh thanked De Poincy for his efforts to protect Sicily from the scourge of the Barbary pirates.

'We pledge to double our efforts, Colonel,' De Poincy assured, 'we hear the pirates have recently stepped up their raids on the coastal settlements.'

'Unfortunately, they have,' Grunenbergh confirmed, 'so where will you go next?'

'Tomorrow we will sail to Gela, where we will base ourselves, patrolling between the south of Sicily and Valletta,' De Poincy suggested, 'we should arrive there during the afternoon of Monday first June.'

Sailing from Catania at sunrise, spring weather pushing them along, Captain De Poincy felt he had the politics out of the way. Now he could focus on the practical task of patrolling the seas between Malta, and Sicily to protect against private attacks. Although, generally feeling in good spirits, he struggled with a pain in his side. He did not know it, but he had a grumbling appendix.

Also, unbeknown to De Poincy, the time of sailing and destination of *San Giovanni* was being watched carefully and reported. Other vessels were on route to Sicily, and this news would direct them specifically to Gela. However, with very different intentions than the Knights of St John.

Chapter 27

When Agata and Bernardo woke, the sun was fully up, the birds almost finished their dawn chorus and they realised they had overslept. However, as they did not need to meet Captain Orlando until the night of Monday 1 June, they were not concerned. There was very little food left over to have for breakfast, so they did not spend long eating. Apprehension about what lay ahead caused them to not say much. So, while they were packing up, they both found themselves feeling uncomfortable about travelling separately.

They secured the loads on their respective donkeys, each planning to take a slightly different route to Gela. Agata could no longer contain her emotions and with tears in her eyes she rushed over to Bernardo and threw her arms around him. Holding him tightly with her head buried in his expansive chest, she wept.

Bernardo, although enjoying the moment of intimacy with her, was not sure how to react to this unexpected display of affection. Apart from when he carried Agata out of the dungeon, the last person to embrace him affectionately had been his mother, when he was a little boy. Hesitantly he put his arms gently around her shoulders, kissing the top of her head.

'I do not want to be separated from you,' Agata sobbed, looking up at Bernardo.

'Nor I you,' he replied, 'but until we are in a safe place, we cannot be seen together.'

Agata nodded and reluctantly pulled away from Bernardo.

'You are right...' she agreed, taking a deep breath, and wiping the tears from her eyes with the sleeves of her shirt, '...I am being a silly little girl.'

'No,' insisted Bernardo, reaching back out to her, 'you are being brave enough to say what we are both thinking, but I have been too frightened to express myself.'

A broad smile came to Agata's face, as their mutual feelings were acknowledged at last. It cheered Bernardo just to see her smile. They turned to their respective donkeys and pulled the ropes around their necks firmly.

'One more day, little one,' Agata assured her donkey, 'then we will be there.'

Agata waved and smiled to Bernardo, as they headed along different paths. She made herself focus on the journey ahead. The uncertainty of her future had her emotions bouncing back, and forth like storm waves crashing on rocks. It had been a terrifying time; she was being chased like an outlaw and had fallen in love with a monk! On the other hand, she was in love, and she was sure Bernardo loved her too. With that thought in mind, her heartbeat faster, and her steps felt lighter.

'After all,' she reasoned, 'he was only a trainee monk, and had not taken his vows yet. Perhaps there was a chance for them—he had saved her so far.'

She headed through the woods, trying to travel as due south a possible until she reached the main coast road.

Bernardo would head around Lago Comunelli with the plan to approach Gela from the north as he exited the woods. Then he would go straight through Gela town centre to Madonna Della Platea church to meet with Father Pepe, as he had been instructed. Father Pepe was apparently to be trusted and Bernardo hoped he would be. He had a strong urge to seek advice from a mature monk after all that he had experienced.

Chapter 28

Friar Diego sat at his desk in his Steri office, with his hands thoughtfully cradling his narrow clean shaved chin. His face was impassive as he listened intently to updates from Alia and the latest reports on the search for the fugitives. His fellow inquisitors assured him that no one had visited Tringali's farm except them. However, the stabbing to death of one of their guards behind the bakery in Alia had to be the work of a Beati Paoli assassin. Could this be an indication that the fugitives were fleeing south? The shooting of the other guard's horse might be a sign that William the Archer had been there and was involved in these attacks. The guard that was thrown from his horse was lucky to be alive. He was in a critical condition, and so far, had not managed to give them any coherent information yet.

For some time after the reports were completed, Diego remained motionless, deep in thought. He had serious doubts about the capabilities of his fellow Inquisitors, but this was what he had to work with. He was equally unsure what their next step should be.

'Where is the Regional magistrate?' he finally asked.

His loyal secretary quickly looked through his notebook before replying.

'His last report indicated he was going to visit the Regional magistrate at Caltanissetta to seek his assistance. After the incident in Alia, and with no sign of the fugitives in the Palermo district, he reasoned they were aiming for a port in the south or east.'

This seemed logical to Diego, but he was feeling uneasy about the search, and he did not know why. Finally, he sat back in his chair, looking intently at his secretary, and the other young inquisitor.

'I think it is time I paid my respects to the Sicilian Viceroy's representative, the Duke of Camastra. He has estates near Caltanissetta if my memory serves, and then we might go on to inspect the rebuilding work in the east.'

He stood up and walked over to the nervous, younger monks, before giving his orders. 'We will leave tomorrow after Prime mass. You two will accompany me along with ten mounted, and well-armed guards. Have two carriages available, the most comfortable for us to travel in, and another suitable to secure prisoners.'

He walked back to his desk and picked up some papers. Then looked over his shoulder at the monks that were just about to leave.

'Make sure everyone knows we are going to Caltanissetta, then Catania, is that clear?' he said as an afterthought, as they reached the door.

It was time he became more directly involved. He could not let these humiliations continue or the influence of the Holy office would decrease. He was purposely taking credit for the apparent decrease in Beati Paoli activity since his arrival, so he felt the situation could still be salvaged. He had deliberately suppressed news of the escapes.

He sat back at his desk, troubled that he was not more in control of circumstances. He would fast and pray until they left for the south. In fact, he might spend the night next door in Saint Anthony's chapel in prayer. Now there was a saint worthy of petitioning. He would not be pleading to Holy Mother Mary. Although he had to keep it to himself, he regarded her as a contradiction in terms, and felt she should be seen as anathema. How could a woman, a mother, be holy? By her very nature she was a sinner. Women were not to be trusted, and certainly not revered, for they embodied betrayal.

He seethed with old bitterness, and it did not seem to matter how many witches he burned, his desire for retribution was never quenched. Yet failure terrified him even more.

He could not return to his masters a failure again. He had to ensure no challenge to the Holy office went unpunished. So, he had to extinguish this troublesome family, and their Beati Paoli friends, so no one else would dare challenge him.

'Someone,' he said to himself, 'is informing the Beati Paoli of our plans.' Frantically he shuffled through reports on his desk.

'Somewhere there is a clue to who, but to find that person, I must get ahead of them. No more waiting on reports, I will follow the leads myself. Not even my own people will know where I intend to look, until we arrive. Whoever is informing the Beati Paoli will be starved of information or misdirected. I will find them, and I will apprehend them myself. But…no one must know what I am doing, until I have them in my grasp.'

Satisfied with his deliberations, he tidied his papers, and locked them in his desk drawer. Then he heard the bell for Vespers. He looked out of the window at the azure blue sky with just a few white clouds forming.

'May is drawing to a close,' he thought, 'and so is the time of freedom of those who dare challenge us.' He locked his office and went down to the chapel.

Chapter 29

For Bernardo, the journey to Gela was relatively simple. There was a goat herder's path running around the lake, so by late morning he found himself in the outskirts of Gela. The little church was well known. Asking directions was easy and there was nothing suspicious about a monk, from out of town, looking for directions to a church.

By mid-day, Bernardo arrived at the little church of Madonna Della Platea and found Father Pepe preparing for Sext prayers. Pepe was a small man, with a bald sun-browned head, bushy white beard, and friendly smile. He welcomed Bernardo warmly and invited him to join in prayers. After quickly washing, and securing the donkey in some shade, Bernardo followed Father Pepe into the church. The familiarity of the ceremony made Bernardo feel at peace there, and it certainly helped him blend into the surroundings.

After prayers, Bernardo unloaded the things from the donkey, fed and watered him, settling him quietly behind the church in the shade. He joined Father Pepe in his small quarters at the rear of the church and was grateful to be asked to join him in a simple lunch. Pepe was a Franciscan, so identifying with the poor, meant he lived an even simpler life than the cloistered Benedictines. However, simple really suited Bernardo at that moment, and he felt comfortable with this older parish priest.

Casual conversation with strangers was difficult for Bernardo. However, over lunch Father Pepe talked freely about his congregation, how they celebrated major festivals, and the ongoing struggles with the upkeep of the building. This allowed Bernardo to just listen and helped him relax enough to prepare himself to share with the old priest about his recent experiences. However, it had already been a long day for them both. So, in the heat of the afternoon, he realised he would need to relinquish his desire to confess to his body's need for sleep. Taking his lead from the old priest he succumbed readily to their afternoon siesta.

Meanwhile, Agata headed straight south towards the coast road, with the plan to approach Gela from the west. In this way, it was hoped that anyone they met would not conclude they were travelling together or guess they had the same purpose in Gela. 'She had, at least four hours of walking to Gela,' she thought, 'as she took a slightly longer route than Bernardo.' However, as she had all day to complete the journey, she intended to find somewhere to rest during the heat of the afternoon.

Unfortunately, her navigating through the woods was not as easy as it was for Bernardo, with no clear path to follow. About the same time Bernardo was arriving in Gela, Agata emerged from the woods, and scrubland nearer the coast, onto the coastal road, as planned. However, as she turned east towards Gela, she observed, the Manfria tower, which Bernardo had shown her on the map he had been given. She remembered this was almost three leagues east of Gela and felt frustrated she had emerged onto the coast road a bit further west than they had planned.

Nevertheless, the road was straight and smooth, and so much easier than the paths through the woods, so she led the donkey along, still in good spirits. Ahead of her she could see brightly coloured fishing boats, and the smells floating on the easterly breeze reminded her of Trabia.

As the coastal road wound down nearer to the seashore, Agata could see young men sorting out nets, just in land of beached fishing boats. The nets hung between poles, waiting for repairs, and women sitting nearby were gutting fish. Seagulls, perched on the ends of the fishing boats, watched carefully for the chance to swoop down a grab scraps. Agata breathed in the salt air, tinged with the smell of dead fish. This was a scene Agata was familiar with, and the chatter of the fishwives attracted her. She approached the busy women, particularly an older, rotund, jolly looking woman, and asked for directions to the church.

Agata was greeted with a smile, and good-natured curiosity from the whole group.

'You are not from these parts, are you?' the smiling fishwife declared, more as a statement, though with the inflection of a question.

'No, I come from Trabia, east of Palermo,' was Agata's automatic reply, which she immediately regretted divulging.

She tried to cover up her discomfort at letting out where she was from by commenting on the amount of fish the women had gutted.

'Yes,' said the jolly one, rising to her feet, 'and now we need to get these baskets to the smoke house, just over there,' she continued, pointing to a low sod building on the other side of the road, about 25 cannas to the east. 'Do you think you could help us carry the baskets with your donkey?' she asked with a broad smile, and hopeful eyes.

'Of course,' Agata said, without really thinking about it.

She was in no hurry, and her donkey had been left with very little to carry, as Bernardo had suggested she could ride on him if she got tired. At that welcome reply, the women all rose and started securing two large baskets of gutted fish on either side of the donkey, using the large empty canvas bag as a sort of saddle. Pleased with their handy work, one of the women gave the donkey a slap on the rump. Agata led him along the dusty road, followed by most of the fishwives.

As they approached the smoke house, Agata noted how much larger it was than the family one they had back in Trabia, though she had seen community ones near the harbour that were of a similar size. An old, hunched-shouldered man was at the smoke house already, when the women arrived. He was spreading out the wood chips, and kindling, ready to light, and laying the beams out to attach the fish.

While the younger women unloaded the fish baskets, the round, jolly, older one, put her arm around Agata and squeezed her shoulder. 'Thank you,' she said smiling, 'it usually takes two of us to lug a basket of fish between us.'

'Happy to help,' Agata replied, 'I do not need to be at Madonna Della Platea until Vespers.' Again, regretting she had revealed her destination and timing. She was not good at this secrecy game.

'Then come with us for something to eat, and a rest,' the older woman encouraged, 'it is getting too hot to be on the road now.'

Agata happily let the women lead her a short distance further along the road towards some houses. As they came to a stream there was a straw awning erected around an area that they clearly cleaned clothes in, judging from the bleached white rocks. The awnings also covered the area facing the road, so behind there it was cooler, and gave the women some privacy.

As soon they went behind the awnings, the women started to take off their fish-stained clothes and throw then into piles near the washing stones. They started to clean themselves in the steady running stream water. Talking all the time, they were clearly very comfortable exposing their bodies to each other.

Agata let the donkey drink in the stream, and then tied him up to some poles supporting the awnings, but still in a shaded area. Encouraged by the older women, she joined them in removing her outer, dusty clothes, and cleaning herself in the water. Enjoying the cool, clear steam water, Agata took the opportunity to have a comprehensive wash, including her hair. This freshened her up greatly and reminded her that she had not had a good wash since the night she was rescued from the Inquisition. She shuddered, not with the cold, but the memory of the Steri dungeon.

Inside the shaded area some tables, and chairs where already set up. By the time Agata had washed, there was bread, cheese, smoked fish, and tomatoes on plates, with jugs of wine, and water on the tables. The older women, with broad welcoming smiles, encouraged Agata to join them at the tables, and started to introduce themselves.

'My name is Fiorlisa,' said the jolly woman, 'and that is my daughter Maria, sister Flo, her daughter, also called Maria, Cousin Assunta…' As she went around the table, Agata realised she would not remember all these names, but introduced herself when Fiorlisa had finished.

'My name is Agata, thank you for letting me join you, it is lovely to be among family.' They all started talking at once again, but Fiorlisa leaned over with concern in her face, and asked about Agata's family.

'My mother, and father were killed, and brothers I assume taken, in a pirate raid on our village.' Tears began to run down Agata's cheeks, though she made no sound, the memory of that night flooding back.

Fiorlisa put her arm around her shoulder and whispered in her ear. 'I lost my husband, and sons too,' she said, tears coming to her eyes, 'not to pirates, but the water after the earthquake in January.'

Fiorlisa's daughter Maria had come over to sit at the other side of Agata, taking her hand. 'We used to live in Syracusa where my father fished with his brothers, and their sons, my brothers, and cousins,' Maria quietly said, not wanting to disturb the other women's chatter.

'We came here to join my sister's family as we had no family left in Syracusa,' Fiorlisa continued, 'it is important to be with family.'

Agata just nodded, for although she felt immediately bonded to these women, she decided not to reveal any more details of her adventures. Instead, she yawned.

'Yes, it is time to rest,' Fiorlisa asserted loudly, taking the cue from Agata's yawn.

On hearing this, almost immediately, the chatter died down, and the women spread out to lie on their fresh clothes for siesta. Agata gratefully joined them, her emotions still tender. She started thinking over her need for family and fell asleep missing her mother terribly.

When Agata awoke, the women around her were chattering again. The younger ones were starting to clean clothes in the stream. As she listened, it was clear the married ones were leaving to start preparing meals.

'The men will sail at dusk to fish all night, and need to be fed,' Fiorlisa was saying to her, 'You are welcome to join us for dinner, but if you are to get to Madonna Della Platea by Vespers, you need to be on your way.'

A sad look came to the old lady's eyes, as if she did not want to say goodbye.

Silently Agata rose and collected her now dry outer clothes. She did not want to say goodbye either, so decided to just slip out quietly. She hugged Fiorlisa, and as they looked into each other's eyes, there seemed no need for words. A mutual understanding of the grief they both felt was shared between them as Agata left to collect her donkey.

There were some clouds in the sky which semi-blocked out the sun, blazing in the early June sky. The road was still dusty though as she, and her donkey trudged along towards Gela, which she could now see ahead. Agata's mind drifted to Bernardo, and this cheered her up, out of the melancholy that had overcome her.

While Agata walked towards Gela on the coast road, Bernardo and Father Pepe awoke from a long, peaceful siesta, for which they were both grateful. Now, just over an hour before Vespers, they sat together in the shadow of the church, and Bernardo took the opportunity to tell him about his adventures since leaving Santa Martia Del Bossco Abbey.

'Father, will you hear my confession? It has been quite some time since my last confession' Bernardo asked. He was particularly keen to confess the killing of the pirate as well as his involvement in other violent episodes. He decided, however, to omit mentioning the involvement of the Beati Paoli. He realised now how wise it was for those that had helped him, not to disclose their names. There was no way he would betray them, even accidentally.

'Forgive me father for I have sinned...' Bernardo began. Father Pepe listened quietly without comment, until Bernardo had finished, then closed his eyes in silent prayer. Bernardo felt relieved to have told his story, and confessed the pirate killing, even before Father Pepe said anything. After a short time, Father Pepe, started to recite the standard absolution, then hesitated. After few minutes, he opened sad eyes, and leaned over to put a hand on Bernardo's hands, that were clasped together on his lap.

'We live in a wicked world, my son,' the old priest said quietly, 'and your instincts to protect the innocent are commendable. Especially against the scourge of these pirates, which we have been cursed with these many years. Here too we have suffered from these raids.' He paused and thought back. 'My predecessor in this church, was killed in a pirate raid, and I remember ministering to the many families that lost loved ones...terrible!'

Shaking his head, he looked down at the ground. 'The Manfria tower, and other towers in the network, are supposed to give us some warning. I guess they have helped, but that frightful night there was no warning. I was the assistant priest then, but the tragedies of that night, and the grief afterwards, are still a burden for many.' He sighed deeply.

'Whatever happens, my son, do not let unforgiveness rule your heart, or bitterness will destroy your spirit.'

The old priest looked up at Bernardo, raised the crucifix hanging on his rosary beads, made the sign of the cross over Bernardo, and laid a hand on his head. He finished the prayer of absolution, then smiled, and rose to his feet.

'May God protect you and give you strength if you ever encounter these devils again,' then walking towards the chapel entrance he concluded, 'Let's get ready for Vespers,' reverting to his previous cheery persona.

Chapter 30

San Giovanni berthed in the small harbour of Gela just as Vespers were finishing and a small welcoming party came out to greet them. Captain De Poincy was pleased to receive an invitation to dine with fellow captains, and knights at a nearby Tavern that night.

First of all, the knights tidied themselves up to attend Compline (final prayers of the day). Leaving just a small guard of Maltese sailors on board, and a duty Hospitaller monk in charge. There were several chapels they could attend, but De Poincy decided to walk up to Madonna Della Platea, and pay his respects to Father Pepe, who was a dear old friend.

'The walk will do me good, providing this pain stays away,' he thought, rubbing his side.

The little chapel was surprisingly full at Compline, and he noted Orlando there near the front row, who also was an old friend, and he was delighted to see him. It had been a year since they had last seen each other in Palermo. As soon as the short service was over, Father Pepe greeted him warmly, and Orlando came over too, embracing his fellow captain with a wide smile.

De Poincy grabbed Orlando's trim goatee beard, 'I see you persevere with this excuse for a beard,' he teased, laughing.

Orlando grabbed the sides of De Poincy's full whiskers in reply. 'And you continue to look like a bear with this thick ruff.'

They both laughed loudly, then followed Father Pepe to his humble dwelling where he insisted, they joined him in some wine.

Upon their arrival, Agata, began pouring wine into Father Pepe's earthenware mugs, in an attempt to be helpful. Keeping busy stopped her feeling so awkward around all these imposing men. She had reunited with Bernardo and been introduced to Father Pepe just before the mass. Bernardo was also there. Although comfortable in Father Pepe's company, and please to have rendezvoused successfully with Captain Orlando, being confronted with another exotic stranger made him nervous. He found it hard to keep his eyes off Agata, who he felt was getting more beautiful every day. Their reunion, in front of Father Pepe had been somewhat cool. Pleasure at being together again left unspoken.

'Bernardo, this is Captain Raymond De Poincy, Knight of St John, and Commander of the *San Giovanni,* which just arrived this afternoon,' Orlando proudly announced.

'My dear friend Raymond, let me introduce you to the son of Mateo di Boscogrande.' Orlando said, gesturing over to Bernardo who stood to greet this imposing knight, feeling most uncomfortable, as he often was when first greeting people.

De Poincy stared at Bernardo, as if in shock. 'Young Bernardo,' he expressed dramatically, 'I think you were only five or six years old when I last saw you…my you have grown into a man resembling your father.'

De Poincy stared intensely at Bernardo, who was a full head taller than him. 'Those eyes, deep blue like your father,' he said.

Bernardo smiled slightly, and self-consciously bowed his head.

'Ah yes, but there is the look of your mother in your face,' De Poincy continued.

His mind flashing back to distant memories. 'I was at your parents' wedding,' he said, putting his hand on Bernardo's firm shoulder, 'old Signior Davide put on a lavish celebration,' he laughed, 'and when I first saw your mother coming into the cathedral, in the finest white silk gown, and delicate veil, I thought God had rewarded your father with an angel as his bride.'

Then noticing Agata looking for plates to put some olives onto, Orlando added, 'and this is Agata, who Bernardo is making a habit of rescuing from any who would dare threaten her!'

Orlando smiled knowingly at De Poincy, who had noticed the blossoming beauty serving them when he had first arrived. He smiled, and bowed to her, which made her feel even more self-conscious.

'So, here was someone else that was friends with my parents,' Bernardo thought, as he warmed to this new acquaintance.

De Poincy raised a mug of wine to toast them, then winced. 'Ohhh!' he cried and put a hand to his right side.

Father Pepe jumped up, quick for a man of his age, 'My son, what is wrong?' he said. Putting his hand on De Poincy's shoulder.

'Ahhh,' De Poincy winced, 'I have had this re-occurring pain in my right side for a few days now, I thought it had gone.' He sat down on a wooden stool and tried to catch his breath. 'I don't think I will make it to this dinner, Orlando.'

'Please,' said Father Pepe, 'have a lie down on my bed for a little while, and we will send for some help.'

Despite disliking being fussed over, De Poincy agreed and allowed Pepe to help him to his bed in the tiny adjoining room. The pain, while still there, was not as sharp as it had been, and he thought a little rest might ease the discomfort.

'See if one of our Hospitallers can have a look at me, and perhaps have a tonic they can give me,' he was saying as he lay down.

'We will send Bernardo to *San Giovanni* for help, and arrange a sedan chair to take you back, I think a carriage would be too uncomfortable,' Orlando said, looking at Father Pepe, and bringing a stool to sit by De Poincy's bed.

Father Pepe nodded, leaving to arrange things.

When they were alone, Orlando said to De Poincy. 'Sorry, my old friend, if this is not a good time to ask this, but I have an important favour to ask you.' He paused, and waited for De Poincy to nod, and look up at him. 'Diego is back and looking to settle old scores.'

This got De Poincy's attention right away, and his eyes widened.

'Bernardo has only recently found out about his father but has crossed swords with Diego already and is now being hunted.'

The pain in his side was subsiding, so De Poincy sat up in the little bed, and gave Orlando his full attention.

'He is turning out to be a hero like his father,' Orlando said smiling, 'he rescued Agata from pirates then from castle Steri's dungeons.' De Poincy looked impressed.

'Now I have to get them out of Sicily and away from Diego as soon as possible.'

De Poincy was quiet for a little while, the colour returning to his cheeks, and sparkle to his eyes.

'So, you would like me to take them to somewhere off the island?' he replied, looking straight into Orlando's eyes.

'Yes, anywhere will do for now, but eventually he should go to Genoa, and claim his inheritance…it should be enough to keep him away from the Inquisition,' Orlando concluded.

After a moment of thought, De Poincy smiled at Orlando. 'It will be my pleasure to aid the house of Boscogrande and thwarting the ambitions of that snake Diego would be sweet.'

He lay back closing his eyes, considering what he had just agreed to, and letting the pain in his side subside more.

As instructed, Bernardo walked briskly down to the harbour, glad to have Agata back safely at what he hoped was the last stage in their escape. He noted the storm clouds that were bubbling up in the south. He enjoyed the cool evening breeze that was coming in from the sea, while the setting sun tinged the clouds with red. Bernardo thought it was all beautiful.

Despite the encroaching darkness, it was not long before he saw the *San Giovanni*, being by far the biggest vessel in the small harbour.

However, unbeknown to Bernardo, his walk through the harbour, did not go unnoticed. A sharp-eyed Inquisition guard observing the comings, and goings to the vessels in the harbour, wondered what a Benedictine would be doing briefly visiting a Knights of St John's vessel? Following orders, he would report back, and later pay this vessel a visit.

Chapter 31

A large galley with twenty-four pairs of oars, and three xebecs with forward facing canon sailed towards Sicily. Their captain focused on the horizon, not wanting to get too close in daylight. The heavy bearded, rotund Amad Ali ibn Majid Rayar stood on the galley's deck looking towards the land. He was not just the captain of this Moroccan galley, but Admiral of a whole fleet of vessels, a portion of which he had brought on this raid. Also, this was no ordinary slave gathering raid. Amad Rayar's plan was specifically to steal or destroy the *San Giovanni*. In this way, he hoped to strike a blow against the fleet of the Knights of Malta, who had become a threat to the Barbary pirate's dominance of the central Mediterranean.

As the sun set, he led his men in prayer, putting their back to the setting sun. The next time they prayed together it would be sunrise, and they should be heading south. Prayers over, his squadron of vessels split up. One xebec would close and point its bow cannon at the Manfria tower to keep their soldiers busy. Another would raid the fishing settlement to gather slaves, but mainly as a distraction. The galley would lie off the west end of the harbour, to provide fire power against the harbour defences. Meanwhile the remaining xebec would, hopefully unnoticed, close Gela harbour. At the signal, being the attack on the Manfria tower, this last xebec would enter Gela harbour, and sneak up on the *San Giovanni*. The extra sailors they carried would board her.

Those in Amad Rayar's pay had informed him when *San Giovanni* had left Genoa, and when it would be arriving in Gela. With this information, he hoped to catch the knights, sailors, and citizens off guard. However, as always, much depended on stealth when approaching the coast. They had to remain undetected until the last moment. His planned diversion had to draw attention and the local militia away for their main objective to succeed.

The Christian galley slaves on the rowing benches below, five to each oar, had their mouths gagged to stop them calling out a warning. There was a good wind from the south, so the rowing was eased to reduce noise.

The stars, and moon were partly obscured by the growing clouds. So, with no lights on their vessels, the raiders approached the land silently, aiming for the lights of the town, and tower. They had the coast surveyed earlier and had even paid for the dinner in the tavern to which the captains, and knights had been invited. No one in Gela knowing or really caring who the generous benefactors were.

Small lights from two fishing boats came into view as they almost ran them over. The fishermen, so focused on laying their nets, and calling out to each other, did not notice one of the xebecs closing them until it was too late. They were unable to put up much of a fight when suddenly boarded by a large number of heavily armed pirates. Soon they were clubbed into submission and taken off as fresh galley slaves.

However, their brief cries were enough to alert two other fishing boats, a short distance to the west. They quickly dosed all lights, and raised their single sails as quietly as possible, so they could dash back to the shore ahead of the pirates. Could they warn their families in time? Could they get the attention of the troops at the Manfria tower, so they could send the warning signal? The race was on, in their swift little lateens. Fortunately for them, the pirates were unaware there was a race, and so continued to approach the coast slowly and warily.

Initially the lateens sailed close together in the same direction. Once the fishermen felt sure they were well ahead of the pirates, they called to each other a simple plan. As they closed the coastline, they split up. One trying to make a dash for their families' houses, just west of Gela, while the other headed for the tower to warn the troops there. Speed was essential.

Chapter 32

It was not long before Father Pepe returned with two strong men carrying a sedan chair, and breathlessly came into see De Poincy.

'That was easy, there was a sedan chair waiting for business just halfway to the harbour,' he announced, then stopped as he saw Orlando holding his finger to his mouth.

'Shhh,' Orlando whispered, '...he is sleeping.'

They went into the kitchen area of Pepe's small dwelling, so they did not disturb De Poincy to discuss the best thing to do.

'Bernardo has not returned yet from *San Giovanni* with a Hospitaller...he should be back soon,' Orlando whispered.

'What should we do with the sedan chair then, the men are waiting?' asked Father Pepe.

Orlando sat down at the kitchen table with Agata. She was quietly listening, chewing olives, and feeling rather apprehensive again. He looked at Bernardo's things in the corner of Father Pepe's small kitchen and thought for a moment.

Then smiling, he addressed Agata, 'I am pleased to say that Captain De Poincy has agreed to take you, and Bernardo off the island. Weather depending, you will sail tomorrow.'

A surge of excitement rippled through Agata, as she had never been on a sea voyage. Then in a commanding voice Orlando said to them both, 'As it would be best that they arrive on board separately, so not to draw too much attention to themselves, I suggest Agata goes now to *San Giovanni* in the sedan chair, with Father Aiello's commentaries that look heavy, then send the chair right back for Captain De Poincy. By the time it arrives back, we should have an assessment of his condition from the Hospitaller, and then he can return to his ship in the chair.'

This did not sound like a discussion, so Father Pepe nodded, and went into see his guest while Orlando helped Agata gather their few processions and load the commentaries into the sedan chair. He paid the men and gave them their instructions to return.

'What should happen to the donkeys?' the ever-practical Agata asked when Father Pepe came out to say goodbye to her.

'Well,' said Orlando, 'I am sure Father Pepe could use them to get more easily around to visit his parish.'

Father Pepe smiled broadly, 'How generous,' he responded looking at Agata, who nodded.

'However, Father, can I ask a favour?' she said assertively.

'Certainly, my child, whatever I can do,' Father Pepe replied.

'Could you give the smaller of the two donkeys to Fiorlisa, who with her daughter Maria lives with her sister Flo, in the fishing village between here, and the Manfria tower?'

'She lost her husband, and sons in Syracusa with the devastation there,' Agata continued, 'and it would help them carry the fish they gut to the smoke house.'

Father Pepe smiled gently and put his hand on her shoulder.

'You are a very thoughtful girl,' he said, 'I would be happy to visit them and deliver the gift tomorrow.'

He then said a prayer of blessing over her, and Agata felt content to move on. Agata climbed into the sedan chair, another new experience for her, and Father Pepe waved. The birds were silent now as she set off into the pink tinged twilight, the sun having set.

Not long after Agata left, Bernardo arrived with a monk Hospitaller. Bernardo had learned much about this brother called Antonio, on their thirty-minute walk from the harbour, and already liked him. He was a fellow Italian, thirty-two years old, but in stature looked like a young boy walking beside Bernardo. He had very alert dark eyes, olive complexion, and dark hair, apart from a little greying around the temples, and was clean shaven. Antonio was enthusiastic about his ministry and had joined the Order of St John specifically to follow a calling to treat the sick. He had served Captain De Poincy for several years, and before that worked in the Order's hospital in Valletta, where he had also trained.

'Where is Agata?' Bernardo asked concerned that Agata was not there when he returned.

'Don't worry,' Orlando reassured, 'she is on her way, with Father Aiello's commentaries, to *San Giovanni*. Captain De Poincy has agreed to take you both off the island when they sail tomorrow, and I thought it best you did not arrive onboard at the same time in case it drew too much attention. You will be reunited very soon.'

Meanwhile, Brother Antonio spoke to Captain De Poincy, with Father Pepe holding a lantern for him.

'So, I am told you are feeling unwell,' Antonio asked, laying a hand on his forehead to check for a fever. 'Tell me what symptoms you have experienced,' he continued, now looking into the colour of De Poincy's eyes.

'I had a shooting pain here,' De Poincy replied, pointing at his abdomen. 'though it has gone again, almost completely.' Antonio pushed gently with both hands on the area he indicated there was a pain, watching for De Poincy's reaction.

'Stick out your tongue' Antonio instructed, having Father Pepe bring the lantern closer. 'Mmmm,' Antonio murmured, 'you do not seem to have many symptoms, so if it is what I think it is, we could be doing with getting you back to the Sacra Infermeria in Malta.'

'Well, the pain has gone now, and I feel quite refreshed after that brief nap,' De Poincy announced, trying to get out of bed.

'Nevertheless, let's get you back to the ship in a sedan chair, rest tonight, and I will have another look at you tomorrow.' Antonio insisted. De Poincy looked reluctant, but nodded agreement, trusting Antonio's judgement, and not wanting the pain to return.

Bernardo looked through what was left of his things, retrieving his precious long bow and arrows from the poles and old blankets that had been left.

'Come on, Bernardo,' Antonio called, 'we will go back to the ship now, and get you and Agata settled onboard. Orlando wants to accompany the captain to *San Giovanni.*'

Bernardo happily set off to walk back, looking forward to the walk with Antonio, and learning more about the hospitallers.

It was dark now, and young boys were earning money by carrying torches to light people's way through the streets. Father Pepe called one he knew over for Bernardo, and Antonio, and paid him. What was earlier a busy port town, had become mostly silent as people ate together in their homes. Only the clap of the monk's sandals, and the low chatter of voices of people unseen echoed around as they walked.

Chapter 33

Enzo, Fiorlisa's brother-in-law, his brother, and their oldest sons, sailed their lateen, single masted fishing vessel, with great skill. They beached it as near to the Manfria tower as the rocks, which they knew well, would allow. As soon as the bow hit the sand, Enzo leapt out, and ran to the tower, shouting as he ran, 'pirates…barbary…light your beacon…man your canon.' Reaching the stout door, he banged on it with both his fists.

A young lieutenant, who hadn't encountered pirates before, opened a hatch in the door. 'What is this noise all about?' he asked, irritated.

'Pirates…a raid…here…now,' Enzo breathlessly exclaimed.

The young officer's eyes widened. He slammed shut the hatch and ran up the stairs calling out to his men.

By then, Enzo had been joined by his brother, and their sons, so they ran with all their strength towards their families' dwellings. Soon they could see commotion up ahead, as their comrades from the other boat, arrived ahead of them with a similar warning. The women were grabbing young children and babies into their arms and racing for the supposed safety of the town.

Within minutes, the beacon on the tower was lit and the troops started priming their canon while the lieutenant peered out into the blackness for something to shoot at. He did not need to look for long. He saw a light silently flash, followed by a bang, and then a cannon ball smashed into his vantage point, killing him instantly.

The second xebec breached near the fishermen's dwellings, and pirates leaped ashore with clubs, and ropes to gather slaves. They were met by fishermen, ill-equipped to fight armed, experienced pirates, yet determined to give their women folk time to escape. Despite their bravery, it was not long before the fishermen were either dead or captured. Led off to slavery on the rowing benches.

Quite deliberately, the pirates allowed the lanterns in the fishermen's dwellings to set the buildings alight. As hoped, the local militia, already alerted by the beacon on the Manfria tower, were attracted to the burning buildings. They rushed out of the town towards the supposed location of the attack. As planned, this allowed the third xebec to slip unnoticed into the harbour, and silently approach the *San Giovanni*. Meanwhile, the galley, sat off the breakwater, cannons ready to subdue the port defences.

Chapter 34

The sedan chair dropped off Agata at *San Giovanni* and returned for Captain De Poincy. Agata explained to the Maltese sailors on duty that she had been instructed to leave the commentaries in the captain's quarters and wait on board for him. She was surprised by their cold reception. They pointed her towards the aft cabin but made no attempt to help her into the cabin with the heavy commentaries.

The aft cabin was in darkness, and as no one showed her into it, she did not know where the lanterns where located. As she tried to look around for a lantern, and means to light it, she heard what sounded like thunder.

'A storm must have built up quickly, as it was fine this afternoon,' she thought, 'I hope it will not be rough at sea tomorrow.'

Then a different sound filled her with apprehension. There was a loud bang from just outside, unlike anything Agata had heard before. Then the clashing of steel, followed by men shouting, and crying out in pain.

'Fighting,' she thought as she crept to the door, opened it just a little, and peered out. To her horror she glimpsed men in turbans, welding curved swords, swarming onto the vessel. Soldiers were fighting with them.

'No, these are not soldiers' she realised, a horrible memory coming into her mind, 'these are guards of the Inquisition!'

Agata closed the door quietly, hoping not to be noticed. This was a nightmare situation for her. The two groups that frightened her the most, pirates, and the Inquisition, were both on board this ship. She backed into the dark cabin wondering where she could hide. Then she heard a sound behind her, and a lantern light partly illuminated the cabin.

She stood petrified, then heard a sneering voice, almost hissing. 'Hello, now who would you be…a friend of the Captain? Well, I know the Knights of Malta have abandoned their vow of poverty, but have they now forgotten their vow of celibacy too?'

She turned slowly towards the voice which was quiet and almost hypnotic. From the glow of the lantern, she could just make out the white habit of a Dominican friar. The face was hard to see, silhouetted against the lantern light, with his back towards the aft cabin windows. It was a small, lean figure, but before she could react more, a shape appeared behind the friar's head.

An arm was raised, and the shape struck the friar from behind. As he fell to the deck the shadowed shape was revealed. It was a pirate, and a second one was following him through the aft cabin window.

As the pirate came towards Agata, the adrenaline surging through her body, changed her mood from fear to fight. She was not going to be taken by these devils, she determined. Frantically she looked around for something to use as a weapon.

Dodging the pirates initial lunge towards her, she found herself backed up to the captain's desk where the lantern was secured. She glanced at the other pirate who seemed to ignore her, as he tried to set fire to the Captain's bed. Then a glint of metal caught her eye, as she saw the brass dividers the captain used to mark off distances on navigational charts.

Simultaneously, trying to deflect her attacker by putting out her left arm towards him, she reached with her right hand for the brass dividers. As the pirate lunged at her, and pinned her to the desk, she swung the dividers in a wide arch, out of his sight. She plunged the points into his neck. By chance, she cut into his carotid artery. So, despite the pirate clutching at the wound, blood sprayed out over him, Agata, the desk, and the deck around them. With the pirate writhing on the bloody deck, she tried to make a dash for the door. The other pirate caught her from behind and struck her on the temple. She blacked out, and was dragged to the open rear window, then passed down to the waiting xebec's deck.

Chapter 35

After saying their goodbyes to Father Pepe, Captain Orlando set off to the harbour walking beside Captain De Poincy who reclined in the sedan chair, carried by two strong men. The sedan carriers were getting tired by this time, but they were happy as it had been a profitable evening for them.

Realising that everything they said could be heard by the sedan carriers, and the boy carrying a torch, the two captains kept their talk to reflections on international politics, rather than the matters at hand. They were making good speed through the dark streets when they heard a low boom. Both looking west, they noticed the beacon on the Manfria tower was lit.

'A raid!' they both exclaimed simultaneously.

'The fishing village?' Orlando thought out loud fingering the dagger at his side.

Then another bang which they both recognised immediately as a musket. This sound was not coming from the west but the harbour which was close now.

'A raid on the harbour,' De Poincy exclaimed.

He leapt out of the sedan chair, grabbed his sword, and sprinted towards the sound of clashing steel which now echoed around the harbour area.

Meanwhile, Bernardo and Antonio were engrossed in a discussion on Christ's call for his church to heal the sick. Bernardo felt he was back with his mentor discussing ethics, so did not hear the cannon boom clearly, so they stopped to listen for more sounds. The musket shot, was unmistakable to brother Antonio, who had witnessed much fighting with Captain De Poincy. They both raced through the harbour, and soon saw the frantic fighting on the deck of the *San Giovanni.* Then Bernardo saw the smoke coming out of the aft cabin's windows on the frigate. Fear for Agata's safety overwhelmed him, and he wished he had not let her out of his sight.

'Agata!' he shouted.

Running as fast as he could towards the vessel he bounded up the gang plank. On reaching the top, a pirate rushed him waving a scimitar above his head. Bernardo swerved, and using his unslung long bow as a staff, he struck the pirate hard in the lower abdomen. The pirate doubled over immediately but Bernardo hardly broke his stride, rushing towards the aft cabin door.

As he entered, he coughed. Smoke was beginning to fill the cabin. By the glow of a bed-on-fire in the far corner, and the obscured lantern light, he caught sight of a turbaned figure disappearing through the aft window. He rushed towards the window but slipping on a pool of fresh blood, lost his balance, and fell over a body on the deck. He hit the deck hard, knocking the breath out of him. Recovering quickly, he saw right in front of his eyes, another body, this time a gaunt looking Dominican friar. His face was almost touching the friars nose, so he could see the friar was still breathing. Pushing himself to his feet, he glanced back to what he had tripped over. He could see it was another pirate, clearly dead with a something sticking out of his neck.

His mind raced to consider what kind of struggle had gone on here, but quickly returned to concern for Agata. He stumbled over to look out of the aft window, but there was no longer anything there. The smoke in the cabin was rapidly building up, and he was finding it hard to breath. So, he scooped up the lean body of the Dominican in his powerful arms and made for the door as quickly as he could, while holding his breath. As they hit the fresh air, Bernardo took a deep breath of clean air, and looked for somewhere to lay the friar's body. He could see Antonio was already tending the wounded on the deck. The fighting was almost over, and the surviving pirates were disappearing over the ship's side.

'But where was Agata?' he puzzled.

The fresh air momentarily revived Diego who looked up into the face of his rescuer. Then felt dizzy, and nauseous, so closed his eyes again. Bernardo laid Diego down and rushed to the outboard side of *San Giovanni.* He looked down into the xebec which was already pulling away from the ship's side. On the xebec's deck, he could see the prone body of Agata with the back of a pirate standing over her with a club.

Fury gripped Bernardo, and he quickly slung his long bow, notched an arrow, and drew it back. This time, with no hesitation, he aimed at the centre of the back of the pirate and loosed an arrow. At this short distance, the arrow went right through the pirate, who looked down to see the barbed head sticking out from his chest, before he collapsed in front of Agata.

Bernardo instantly notched another arrow, but the forecastle of *San Giovanni* obscured the xebec's deck. He ran for the *San Giovanni's* forecastle head, and loosed another arrow, killing a second pirate. By now, with cracking whips, the xebec oars were pulling hard, her speed was picking up. She disappeared into the darkness.

In frustration, Bernardo rushed ashore, running along the harbour breakwater in a feeble attempt to catch the xebec. In despair, all he could see were two faint shapes, fading into the night, the cloud-covered moon not helping. He dropped to his knees and wept as he felt his heart had been ripped from his chest. How could he rescue her now?

Moments after Bernardo rushed ashore, Orlando, and De Poincy arrived on board *San Giovanni*, swords drawn but the fighting was over. Orlando noted the uniforms of the defenders, and Diego's unconscious body near the aft cabin door. De Poincy ignored this, jumped over Diego, and into his cabin. Orlando joined him, as De Poincy frantically tried to put out the fire that engulfed his bed. Fortunately, apart from smoke damage, little else of the dense oak interior had caught fire. It only took them a few minutes to put the flames out. So, while De Poincy surveyed the damage, Orlando went out to look for Bernardo, and Agata.

As he stepped back onto the *San Giovanni's* deck, brother Antonio had already covered dead Inquisition guards, and was treating the wounds of others. A young Dominican, and another guard were helping Diego off the vessel, and Orlando decided to keep a low profile. He walked along the outboard part of the dark deck, trying to assess what had happened and considering the implications of the Inquisition guards being there.

Standing on the forecastle head, Orlando looked out into the dark night, and wondered what became of Agata, and Bernardo. He noticed an unmoving, kneeling figure at the end of the harbour breakwater. Somehow, more by intuition that evidence, he knew the figure would be Bernardo, and that he had lost Agata again.

Soon Captain De Poincy, arrived on the forecastle beside Orlando. He had quickly surveyed the rest of his ship, noted the dead Maltese sailors, and was puzzling over the dead Inquisition guards, 'At a guess, that sad retch is Bernardo, grieving he has lost Agata to the pirates.' Orlando stated to De Poincy, indicating the figure on the breakwater.

'After all they have been through, she is destined for the slave markets after all.'

'Not necessarily,' was De Poincy's surprising reply, 'I will not let this attack go unavenged.' Orlando stared at the captain's determined face, focused out to sea.

'The crew are being recalled, as we speak, and as soon as they are gathered, we will sail. They can sober up, and clean up on the way, but we will make best speed to catch those brigands.' De Poincy continued with a stern, determined voice.

'In this frigate, we can catch them, and God willing we will engage them before they reach the African coast.'

'Would there be room for a large Benedictine monk in your ship's company?' Orlando enquired, still looking at De Poincy.

'Yes,' said De Poincy, without hesitation, 'but although I pray, we can rescue Agata, my main purpose is to sink these barbary vessels.'

Orlando considered this as he left De Poincy to his preparations and walked along the breakwater towards Bernardo. This would give the boy hope, but was it cruel to allow such slim hope?

Part 2 – Knights of the Sea

Joining the Knights of Malta to chase barbary pirates, sea battles and
an innocent young girl turning into a beautiful woman and
determined warrior.

Chapter 36

Standing beside Bernardo on the end of Gela's breakwater, Orlando did not know what to say. It seemed an impossible situation, 'But then again,' he thought, 'this is a man of faith.'

'Do you want to try and get her back?' he asked the distraught figure on his knees.

'How?' was the only weak response from Bernardo.

'Well *San Giovanni* is preparing to sail and chase these pirates down. The captain says you could go with them if you want,' he replied holding out a hand to help Bernardo to his feet. A glimmer of hope came to Bernardo's tear-filled eyes.

After settling the distraught Bernardo on board *San Giovanni,* Orlando felt he was in the busy captain's way, so he said his goodbyes. Embracing him warmly, he wished his friend De Poincy every success, and hoped to see him again soon, in better circumstances.

'Bernardo may not be a sailor, but he is his father's son, and Mateo was a man you wanted by your side in a fight,' Orlando asserted to a clearly distracted captain, 'help him find his potential, and I am sure he will serve you well.'

With those parting words, Orlando left *San Giovanni* and Captain De Poincy to the task of preparing to go to sea. His crew were returning to the ship, some rather inebriated, but the returning knights urged them on, clearly agitated by the news of the attack. Despite the late hour, and darkness, there was much activity on, and around the vessel. There would be little sleep for most this night.

Orlando walked back to his lodgings in a nearby inn, wondering what his next step should be. He was not sure if any of the Inquisition had recognised him in the darkness, and confusion, but he could not be certain. He would need an excuse they would accept for being on board *San Giovanni*. It maybe that they were already suspicious of him. Their presence on board, fortuitous for *San Giovanni* as it turned out to be, might indicate he was being followed.

When he arrived at the inn, it was deserted, except for the proprietor and his wife who busied themselves clearing up from the earlier revelry. Everyone else had either gone home or to their pre-arranged posts in case of another pirate attack. On seeing his soot-covered face streaked with sweat, they were concerned, urged him to sit and brought him a jug of wine.

'Captain Orlando, sir, we wondered if you had got caught up in the troubles tonight and we can see you have been,' the Inn keeper said as his wife brought him a bowl with water to wash his hands and face.

'Are you all right, sir? Is it all over?' asked the Inn keeper's wife, with much concern.

'Yes, thank you Bella, the pirates had fled by the time I arrived at the harbour, but they had tried to set one of the vessels on fire, which is why I am covered in soot,' Orlando explained using the water to clean himself up a bit.

He was fond of this couple, who he had first got to know when he was a ship's master and regularly called into Gela.

'Oh, what a business,' Bella exclaimed pouring him some more wine, 'everyone in such a jolly mood tonight too, with so much generosity from those merchants to the sailors…are you hungry…can I bring you something to eat?'

Orlando did feel hungry and remembered he had missed dinner, so readily agreed to food. 'Thank you, Bella, I would really appreciate a plate of something.'

As she slipped into the kitchen and back, Orlando was struck by Bella's remark and puzzled over it.

When she returned, he enquired, 'Bella, what do you mean "…such generosity from those merchants to the sailors"?'

'Well, sir, on account of those merchants from Genoa, least I think it was Genoa,' she thought for a moment, '…or in might have been Pisa, exotic types anyway, leaving money with us to pay for the knights and Maltese sailors' food and drink.'

'…and the other taverns around the harbour,' her still sweeping husband, interjected.

'Oh yes, generous they were…to thank them they said…good bunch on the whole,' Bella continued as she went back and forth to the kitchen.

'That was good of them,' Orlando agreed, 'but rather unusual, won't you say?' he continued to probe, as Bella returned once again.

'Oh yes,' she said, 'never known it before…have you Enzo?' she called out to her husband.

'No, never,' he reflected, pausing his sweeping, and leaning on his broom, 'if anything merchants usually moan about sailors being lazy, damaging, or steeling cargo, not usually generous like that…' Enzo continued sweeping in mid-sentence, leaving Orlando's mind racing. Clearly there was some investigation needed, but Orlando could feel his bed beckoning him, so he finished the food and wine, then got up to go to his room, saying good night to Enzo.

As Bella came back out of the kitchen, expressing how glad she was he was all right and saying goodnight. Orlando could not resist asking some more questions, 'These generous merchants, have you seen them before? You did not happen to hear some names or where they might be staying?'

Bella and Enzo stopped and looked at one another, surprised at Orlando's interest.

'No, never seen them before and now you come to ask,' Bella replied, 'when we asked if they needed rooms to stay in, they said they were on board a cargo vessel and sailing this morning.'

'Did they mention the name of the vessel?' Orlando pressed.

'Sorry,' Bella replied, 'not that I can recall, they just emphasised they wanted to ensure that the sailors and knights had a good time their first night in Gela and how sorry they were that they could not stay to join them.'

Orlando went to bed that night, convinced there was something odd about these generous merchants and decided to visit the harbour master the next day, to find out details of the vessel the merchant men arrived and sailed on. Also, how they knew the knights would be in Gela in advance? Later, he would have to think of what to say to the Inquisition when they asked for a report.

Chapter 37

The dawn sky was a brilliant red as the sun's rays were defused through clouds that had been building all night. The wind continued to back, now increasing in force from the west.

Captain De Poincy was convinced a summer storm was on its way and the wind would soon become northerly and increase in force. Every sail on *San Giovanni* had been raised and Captain De Poincy had them adjusted to remain full, maximising the speed they achieved in the freshening abeam wind. Lookouts scanned the horizon carefully, searching for the sails of the vessels they pursued and trusting their Captain's instincts would not fail them.

It had still been dark when they sailed from Gela and most of the crew had only had a few hours' sleep. Although they had been summoned back from their revelry early, many still had sore heads. Nevertheless, adrenaline running through their veins had transformed the initial shock of seeing the aftermath of the attack on their ship into a desire for revenge. So, they had thrown themselves into preparing the frigate for sea and battle, allowing the sea air to clear their heads.

Satisfied they were sailing as efficiently as possible, De Poincy called his fellow knights, the Maltese sailing master, and Bernardo into his cabin. The smell of the smoke from the night before was still strong, but the burnt bed had been removed and scorched timbers rubbed down. By the end of the day, the carpenter would have built him a new sleeping cot and his steward was sorting out fresh bedding.

As they all gathered around the large desk in the Captain's cabin, De Poincy spread a chart of the central Mediterranean out for them to see as he stood over it. He had put a mark on the chart where they were at present, just south of Sicily, with a line running southwest towards the peninsular snaking up from Zeugitana. There was also another track line running west towards the Pelagie group of islands and particularly Lampedusa.

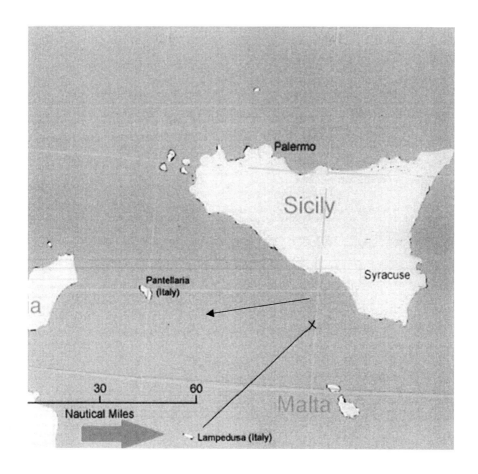

'It is my belief,' De Poincy asserted, 'that the pirates will want to head west for the relative safety of the north African coast as soon as possible. However, the wind will have been against them all night, therefore, I am guessing they will have headed further south towards the safety of an anchorage at Lampedusa.'

He ran his finger along the pencil track he had drawn to clarify his point.

'We know that slaving raids have left these islands uninhabited for years, but we also know the pirates use them as staging posts for raids into Sicily and beyond.'

There was a general murmur of agreement from his fellow knights, as De Poincy continued.

'So, I plan to head south towards Lampedusa at best speed with the hope of catching up with them there. With this gathering wind and the weather gage, we will have the advantage of speed and manoeuvrability and if they think we were damaged too much to sail, they will not be expecting us. From the multiple

161

attacks last night, what Bernardo witnessed and what we know of their raiding methods, we should expect two or three xebecs and a large galley working together. So, we must be ready for this.'

He stood up straight, satisfied with his plan.

'For now, we have done the best we can. Catching them or not, is now in God's hands. Our chaplain will lead us in our usual morning mass, and we will pray for divine intervention. By then, I expect all stations to be battle ready, any question?'

There was silence, as they all knew their captain well. Once he had decided on a course of action, it would be hard to change his mind. However, from experience, they also knew he had an innate intuition about these things and ultimately, as always, it was in God's hands. De Poincy dismissed them, and they left without a word to prepare as he had instructed. All, that is, except Bernardo.

Having no specific duties on board and all of what had been said being outside of his experience, he remained in a thoughtful stance by the desk. De Poincy looked at him with sympathy. Impressed he had gained his sea legs quickly, only throwing up once just after they left port. He guessed his mind was focused on his lost love. He wondered how he could comfort him.

'You seen worried, brother, but you must have faith,' he said as gently as he could.

'Please understand Captain, I am very grateful you are pursuing these pirates and have allowed me to accompany you, but my fear is…' Bernardo paused, feeling very out of his depth even discussing these things with the captain of the ship, '…when you engage with the pirates…will Agata have any chance of surviving a sea battle?'

Sympathetically, the captain replied, seeing so much of his father in this young man.

'Your concerns are reasonable, brother. When we engage in battle, many people will die or be injured, and all sorts of things can happen, so I can make no promises. However, wherever possible, we will board the enemy vessels and free the slaves from the rowing benches. At that point, we will have a chance to rescue your Agata, assuming we come across the right vessel, as we know there were several involved in the attack last night.'

He reached over and placed a powerful hand on Bernardo's equally powerful shoulder.

'If you are as good with your long bow, as I have been told, you will be very useful when we engage with these brigands. Find yourself a good vantage point to shoot from and keep your eyes sharp for where Agata might be. Then when we board them, you can join us and look for her but be prepared to see some awful sights and to fight for your life!'

De Poincy clapped Bernardo's shoulder, then went out on deck, leaving Bernardo standing there to think things through. He had admired the boy's father greatly and saw much potential in Bernardo but realised his cloistered upbringing had not prepared him for what he was about to witness. If he was to survive, he would have to adapt very quickly.

On deck again, De Poincy breathed deeply and with great satisfaction as he surveyed his busy ship from the quarter deck. At a hundred and twenty feet, she was the largest vessel he had commanded and with thirty-two guns, the most powerful too. Twelve, forty-six pounder, seven-inch bore cannon, lined each side of the gun deck, amongst which most of crew slept and ate. Six more four-inch bore demi-culverin, firing twelve-pound shot, were fore, aft, and mid-ships on deck, which would be most effective in closer action. His best acquisition, however, were the two powerful, eight-inch bore, English Royal cannon throwing sixty-eight pounds of iron nearly up to three miles. These, he hoped was going to surprise any attacking vessel, and would be aimed at the enemy vessel's cannons, as well as rigging. He was relishing the opportunity to even some scores with the pirates and hopefully free some retches from the rowing benches.

He listened to the Maltese petty officers shouting out orders and curses but noted the efficiency of which this experienced crew busied themselves. They had been repeatedly practised over the preceding months and he was confident they would perform well in the coming battle. The challenge was going to be subduing the pirates, perhaps crippling their vessels, without killing all the rowing slaves at the same time.

Previously, just like the Barbary pirates, the Knights' tactics had been to close an enemy vessel as quickly as possible, board her and do most of the fighting hand-to-hand.

However, naval warfare was changing and De Poincy had seen this clearly during his service in the French navy. With the developments in firepower and move away from oars to sails, warships were becoming long-range gun platforms and tactics were changing to accommodate this.

With the right winds, his new style frigate had far more firepower than the xebecs, was faster than the lumbering galleys and could sustain speed longer than any of the pirates' oared vessels. Now was the chance to put *San Giovanni*, her crew and all he had learned to the test.

Chapter 38

The southerly wind that the barbary pirate galley *El Jadida* had rowed into after the attack had soon increased and veered to westerlies, slowing them up considerably. Amad Rayar paced the poop deck of his ship trying to decide what was the best course of action as things weren't going to plan.

Slaves that were dead, dying or too weak were thrown overboard, as a standard practice, but the rate of death on the rowing benches was causing concern. It required a large number of men to pull the oars and he only had a limited supply of spares to replace the dead. It was clear that fever was running through the rowing benches, and he had seen this wipe out every oarsman before.

At first light, each of the xebecs had come close to *El Jadida* and called out brief reports on their situation. Amad Rayar had signalled that he planned to heave-to for morning prayers. After which all the qubtans (captains) were to come on board *El Jadida* for a conference and fresh galley slaves transferred.

He had *El Jadida's* bows turned into the wind and waves, and rowing stopped. As they did this, each xebec brought its bow to the galley's lee quarter. Then the respective qubtan leaped on board, going straight to the poop deck to report to their amīr al-baḥr.

'amīr, on our way to attack the Manfria tower, we captured eight fishermen from their boats. We need to keep two or three to replenish our own slaves, the rest will be transferred to you presently,' said the first qubtan.

Amad Rayar was silent but nodded his approval and turned to the second qubtan.

'amīr, the fishing settlement had some warning of our raid, the women escaped with the children while the men put up a fight. We had to kill many of them, and we were only able to capture six fishermen fit enough for the oars. We too need a couple of replacements for our rowing benches, but the rest are being transferred to you as we speak.' Again, Amad Rayar only nodded, then glowered at the last qubtan.

'amīr, a thousand apologises for not managing to capture *San Giovanni*. We must have been betrayed, as there was a large group of soldiers waiting for us as we boarded. We did manage to set her on fire and capture this girl,' he asserted pointing to Agata who had been dragged on board after him, 'who was in the captain's aft cabin with some kafir priest.'

Amad Rayar looked at Agata, who had congealed blood in her hair, and he could see bruising on her arms through her torn shirt sleeves. She stood quietly between two pirates, staring straight ahead of her. He noted she still had an air of defiance about her, rather than fear. Even though she was in a mess, he could see this was a pretty young girl. He considered for a moment if he would get a good price for her or if he should keep her for himself. However, he did not dwell on these thoughts for long. There were much more urgent matters to deal with and critical decisions to be made. He signalled for his servant, Abu, who was standing quietly at the corner of the poop deck, to approach.

Short, fat Abu was a eunuch, easily identifiable with his closely shaved head and tattoo on his forehead. Amad Rayar had purchased him as a ten-year-old boy, nearly two decades before. Initially serving as a general house servant, he had graduated to Amad's personal body servant. He approached his master, head down and ear inclined to receive instruction. Only a few words passed between them, Abu nodding to acknowledge his understanding. Then he grabbed Agata's arm in a vice like grip and pulled her towards the accommodation below where they were standing.

As Abu and Agata left the deck, Amad Rayar paced up and down deep in thought. He listened in silence while the qubtan of the xebec that had attacked the *San Giovanni* continued his report.

'amīr, we approached *San Giovanni* silently as planned and boarded what initially looked like empty decks. Then, much to our surprise, well-armed soldiers leaped out from hiding places and descended on us. However, despite this set back, my men fought them off allowing me to move quickly to our secondary plan. I manoeuvred around to the stern of the infidel's ship, sending two men through the aft cabin windows to set fire to it. There they encountered a kafir priest, who they struck down and this girl, who killed one of my men.'

He paused for effect and glanced at the other two qubtans, listening intently. At this piece of information, Amad Rayar, stopped pacing, raised an eyebrow, but remained silent.

'So, he was right to sense defiance in this girl,' he mused, 'but what was going on when his men arrived?'

He puzzled over this and how soldiers had been waiting for them.

'Had the knights been warned of their attack?'

His mind shifted from this thought, as he realised the qubtan was still continuing with his report.

'...so, as the fire had been started, we grabbed this girl as a small prize and left via the aft window, picking up our surviving men as we passed the ship's side. It was clear we were not going to be able to capture the vessel after all, as we had lost the advantage of surprise as well as many men. I trust I did the right thing, amīr.'

The qubtan finished, bowing low before his amīr al-baḥr.

Amad Rayar, stared at him for a moment. Disappointed he had failed to capture the *San Giovanni*, but more annoyed at himself, for not just opening fire on the harbour, in the hope of damaging as many vessels as he could. A splash broke his thoughtful silence, as another dead slave was thrown overboard.

'This,' Amad Rayar considered, 'was a much more urgent matter.'

Looking at the bowing qubtan before him he had reached a decision.

'It is Allah's will, Ahmed Reis, we will say no more about it.' Then he turned to address all his qubtans. 'The sickness in the rowing benches threaten to wipe out all of my slaves.'

As he spoke, he looked over the heads of all those on the poop deck at another body being carried up from the rowing benches.

'I intend to head south to the islands we know there, remove the slaves, and clean out my rowing benches with saltwater. You will send me what slaves you can, but then I want you to fan out, keep a good lookout for sails. In this condition, I do not want to engage with the Knights of Malta, but...' a sly smile lightened his black mood, '...if you see any cargo vessels, we may still bring in a profit from this trip. So, while I clean out my rowing benches, you can still patrol the area for booty. Three of you should be able to capture a lone cargo vessel without my help.'

All the qubtans grinned and bowed to their amīr al-baḥr, then returned to their vessels. They knew well the technics for entrapping even well-armed cargo vessels which tended to be slow and hard to manoeuvre. This was especially so if they attacked simultaneously with their bow canons from three different directions in their swifter, more manoeuvrable xebecs.

Back on board their own vessels, they headed east in a long line, while the galley picked up speed towards the south. The sun was now well above the horizon and the slaves naked bodies glistened with sweat.

Chapter 39

Abu pulled Agata off the poop deck, that formed a covering for accommodation below, onto the main deck and semi-open rowing benches. Although he did not seem much taller than her, this stocky, tattooed man was clearly much stronger than her. Pragmatically she decided not to resist but focused on staying upright on the moving deck. As they approached a covering, made by the overhang of the poop deck, towards a forward-facing door on the main deck, two emaciated slaves dragged another wretched captive from the rowing benches below and threw him overboard.

The sight made all hope drain out of Agata. Then as the slaves turned around from the ship's side to Agata's astonishment, she recognised, Stefano, the oldest of her three brothers. She wanted to cry out to him, but he was being pushed back down to the rowing benches and Abu simultaneously pulled her through a door into a short corridor.

Agata's mind was racing now. She had taken it for granted that she would never see her brothers again, but now wondered what destiny had brought them to the same place. She allowed herself to be led in stunned silence as she wondered if escape was possible.

Just before the door to Amad Rayar's cabin, there was another sturdy door. Abu unlocked this with his free hand, without loosening his grip on Agata. As the door swung open, Agata was surprised to see that it was no more than a cupboard. From what she could make out in the dim light, a little longer than her height and with deep shelves running the full length on both sides.

Abu pushed her inside, slammed the door shut and locked it, leaving her in almost complete darkness save for a trickle of light from a gap at the base of the door. She shivered, with memories of the Inquisition dungeon flooding her mind, though this place was hot.

Trying to control her emotions, she decided to dwell on positive thoughts.

'Thank God, I am alive and at least one of my brothers has survived, there must still be hope.' She felt around at the space she had been locked in. 'Also, this place is hot, unlike the Inquisition dungeon and does not stink of human waste. In fact, what is that smell?'

She sniffed the fragrant atmosphere. Using the shelves for support, Agata stood up and rummaged around the contents. There seemed to be jars of various sizes, wrapped with straw or rags, and secured to the shelves with wooden battens. Most seemed to be sealed with waxed over stoppers. She rubbed her fingers over the tops, then sniffed them.

She recognised the fruity scent of wine and other things she guessed were liqueurs, but there were also powerfully sweet smells of what she guessed was perfume or incense.

She had no experience of such things to refer to, though she remembered the smell of frankincense resins the priest would burn in brass holders on special festivals. She also had heard talk of scented oils the rich used to anoint their bodies.

She continued exploring down through the racks until she discovered on the deck, under the shelves, chests of various sizes. They were heavy and all, except one, locked.

Easing the unlocked one open she felt inside. Not being able to see, she had to rely on feel to discern what the many items in the chest were. As it felt like smooth stones linked together with delicate chains, she guessed it was jewellery. Then suddenly she pricked her finger.

Agata withdrew her hand quickly and sucked the blood from her finger, but while doing so, had an idea. She carefully slid her fingers back into the chest, searching apprehensively for the sharp object. On picking her finger again, she located it and she felt along a very thin shaft of metal. Carefully she withdrew it, trying to free it from chains wrapped around the shaft. Once out of the chest, she held the object carefully in both hands. She felt along its length which was about the size of her palm. It seemed to be some sort of jewellery with a longish piece of straight metal running from an ornamental end. She bit the metal rod. It was a hard metal of some sort, long and thin, but with no cutting edges.

She could feel it had a sharp point furthest from an ornament, but still had no idea what it was or if the point was deliberate or if the rod was broken.

Sitting on her hunches, in the darkness of the store cupboard, she held the object in her hands and thought for a few minutes. The feeling of hopelessness, that was trying to overwhelm her, was pushed aside, to be replaced by determination. She slipped the sharp piece of jewellery under her bodice where previously she had hidden Bernardo's dagger.

Then she knelt on the deck and closed her eyes in a defiant prayer.

'Holy God, against all hope, you have sent help to save me. Send it once again, keep my brothers alive and give me the strength to rescue them.'

In the hot, humid atmosphere of the stuffy cupboard, the trauma of the preceding hours started to catch up with her. She curled up and fell asleep with that prayer in her thoughts.

Chapter 40

As instructed, the three xebecs had spread out over the horizon in search of prey, while *El Jadida* left them behind and headed straight for the island of Lampedusa. It was about sixty nautical miles away. Amad Rayar estimated, in the present weather conditions, it would take ten hours to get there, so he hoped to anchor before dark. He knew a safe anchorage to the south of the island, where they could shelter. There they would transport the slaves ashore into a holding area they had used before. Then they would wash out the rowing benches with salt water. In this way, he hoped to clear the fever that was plaguing his rowing slaves and the slaves could rest and recover.

It was not far into the afternoon when the eastern most xebec spotted a lone sloop, on its way up the Italian coastline. Perhaps on route to Sicily, but whatever, it was a catch worth chasing. Signalling to the next xebec to his west, who in turn signalled to the third, over the horizon from the first xebec. They all turned northeast towards the sloop that was struggling against increasing head winds.

The xebec's action, however, had also been spotted by an eagle-eyed look out at the top of the main mast of *San Giovanni.*

'Sails ahoy, dead ahead and starboard bow,' he called out.

This was music to Captain De Poincy's ears, and he rushed out on deck from a mid-day nap, telescope in hand. From the deck level, all he could see was the very top of two sets of masts, hull down, as seaman refer to it. However, their position and the fact there was more than one, made him confident it would probably be the pirate vessels. He estimated the range as ten nautical miles ahead. As he watched he could see they were moving eastly.

'Sail ahoy,' the topmast lookout cried again, 'two points larboard bow.'

This time De Poincy climbed halfway up the mizzen mast larboard shroud to get a better look. Hooking his right arm around the rigging to steady himself, he peered through his telescope in the direction the lookout had indicated. Sure enough, there was a north bound sloop, tacking to try to make some headway against the increasing northerly wind.

'That is what they will be after,' De Poincy said to his sailing master, as he swung back onto the quarterdeck.

'Bring her two points to larboard, master Cardona...we will catch them downwind of us.'

'Aye, aye, captain,' the sailing master replied to his smiling commanding officer.

'Actions stations, lads,' the captain called out.

Most of his ship's company had by now come up on deck, if they had not already been on watch, to see what the excitement was.

'...we will return their visit to us lads and see what damage our guns can make.'

There was a general cheer, as sailors rushed to their stations, to adjust sails or prepare canons. Meanwhile the knights opened the armoury and started distributing weapons.

Bernardo went to collect his long bow and the new arrows the armourer had given him, while wondering where a good place to station himself would be. He did not feel confident up the rigging. The forecastle was bouncing up and down too much, so he settled on the after end of the quarterdeck. Out of the way of the helmsmen and sailing master, but a higher vantage spot than the main deck.

As they approached the pirates ahead and the inevitable fighting, Bernardo had time to contemplate what he felt about the situation. There would be more killing and here he was ready with his bow to possibly take a life. Was this right? By God's grace he had the skill, but was this what God had wanted of him?

He held the rosary hanging on his belt and rubbed the crucifix attached to it, absentmindedly. It had not been the path he would have chosen for himself. He would be far more comfortable helping Brother Antonio tend the wounded. However, his main concern was Agata and if by his actions, he could rescue her, he would do anything. He began praying but found himself intermittently distracted and confused.

In mid-contemplation, he saw the ship's chaplain come out onto the quarterdeck and start saying prayers, asking for God's protection. Hearing him, the crew only paused, crossed themselves, then carried on with their preparation. However, the dozen knights on board knelt on one knee at the aft end of the main deck. They faced the chaplain, listening to his words in silence. This was obviously their routine and Bernardo joined in, repeating the Latin phases he recognised. It was all over very quickly. The chaplain went off to his station with brother Antonio on the aft end of the gun deck. He knew from experience; he would be giving the last rites to many before the day had ended.

Captain De Poincy rose from his knee and slid his gleaming sword, he had held before him, back into its scabbard. He was already semi-armoured, with a delicately patterned breast plate covering his chest and back, and a matching helmet on his head. He looked every inch a warrior as he took up his station at the forward end of the quarterdeck. The sailing master just behind him near the great wheel. His telescope switched between the sloop, now abeam to larboard about three miles; one of the xebecs fine on the larboard bow, also about 3 miles away and the second xebecs, now two points to starboard about 5 miles away.

'Sail ahoy, three points to starboard,' the lookout cried from his high perch. De Poincy swung his telescope around to the new bearing and saw the third xebec right away.

Estimating it was at least seven miles away, he knew they had to engage the first one soon, then be ready for the next. Timing and rapid, accurate shooting were going to be crucial.

He had already briefed his knights to expect fighting on both sides, and the crew were practised in this type of fighting, knowing well the routine. They would sail between the first two xebecs, drawing them in to what they would see as their advantage. However, *San Giovanni* would surprise them with its "secret" weapon.

De Poincy knew that the pirates probably were well aware of the normal fire power at the disposal of a ship of this size. Also, like other vessels of this size, they would expect *San Giovanni* to carry her heaviest, therefore, more powerful guns, on her lower gun deck.

However, to fire these formidable weapons, she needed to open her gun ports. When turning the ship, or in heavy seas, this would risk flooding the gun deck. As she rapidly approached the xebecs, he was sure they noted her gun ports remained closed.

On her upper deck, *San Giovanni's* six demi-culverins firing twelve-pound balls, had ranges of just over one mile, similar to the xebecs forward canon. However, on the forward part of their main deck, the two-royal cannons, had a range of nearly three miles. This he hoped would catch the pirates off-guard.

The xebec on the starboard side adjusted its course towards *San Giovanni*, with its forward culverin size guns ready. The pirate vessel on the larboard side, swung around from heading towards the sloop, to come straight for *San Giovanni*. De Poincy maintained a steady course and watched the xebecs carefully, judging their ranges as they decreased.

Boarding target vessels, as quickly as possible, was the main tactic of the Barbary pirates during this period. So, their fire power was limited. De Poincy, also wanted to board the pirates' vessels. However, he planned to subdue them with cannon fire before the hand-to-hand combat started.

As the xebecs closed to within two miles, De Poincy signalled the gun crew. They stood ready by the royal cannon on the larboard side for his instructions. Simultaneously he also called to the sailing master. 'Bring her to starboard Master Cardona.' The sailing master swung *San Giovanni* round sharply until the nearest xebec was just forward of the *San Giovanni's* beam.

'Fire as she bears, Monsieur Fenech.' De Poincy called out to the Maltese leading gunner, who looked along the massive eight-inch bore barrel, aiming for the bow cannon on the xebec. Although the movement of the vessels made accurate targeting difficult, there was an art to the timing which this Maltese gunner knew well.

There was a flash of light, followed by a mighty roar, and choking smoke as sixty-eight pounds of iron shot out of the royal cannon. Bernardo found his ears ringing and smelled the sulphur, despite the wind blowing the smoke away from them towards the xebec. He rushed to the frigate's side to see if the cannon ball had hit its mark and was surprised by his mixed emotions. Shock at the ferocity of the explosion, but with morbid fascination to see what the result would be.

At just under two miles, the crash of the ball into the xebec's bow was not loud and the shouting of the gun crew, preparing for the next shot, obscured other noises.

However, as the smoke cleared, all could clearly see the mayhem on the xebec deck. The ball had fallen just short of the primary target but had ripped a chunk out of the starboard bow.

Splinters exploded over the decks, piercing the pirates bodies. Bernardo watched, mouth open in horror at the carnage, while a muted cheer rose from the frigate's decks.

'Bravo, Monsieur Fenech, again!' the captain shouted.

Bernardo watched mesmerised. The gunner looked along the barrel, then stood to the side with a long wooden staff holding a match (a piece of smouldering wick) at the end. He waited, as the vessel rose on a wave. Judging the time for the ball to launch and the angle of the cannon muzzle, then touched the match to the ignition hole at the end of the gun. There was a short pause. To Bernardo, clasping his hands over his ears in anticipation, it seemed to go on a long time. Then, the flash, roar and acrid smell as the royal belched out its fury. They all peered into the smoke in anticipation. The xebec was much closer now, so they could hear the cries of distress from on board.

This time the delay in firing was fractionally too long. The ball shot well over the bow cannon but struck the mainmast. Like a felled tree, the mast crumpled and came crashing down over the larboard bow of the xebec. The pirates manning the forward cannon were crushed. The rigging, supporting the mast snapped. A loose end decapitated one of the pirates standing mid-ship, while other lines lashed at those on deck.

Bernardo stared aghast at the pandemonium on the xebecs. At least, one pirate was knocked overboard. Others lay on the deck maimed, while their larboard-forward cannon lay on its side. Then, as he watched, more of the starboard bow disintegrated and the starboard cannon slipped into the sea.

Now there was a great cheer from the *San Giovanni* crew, but short lived, as the captain shouted out more orders.

'Prepare the gun deck larboard battery and load the upper deck guns with grape.'

Noise, shouts, frantic activity. At least, that is how it seemed to Bernardo, but the crew seemed unflustered and expecting the orders.

'On the rise, Monsieur Zammit,' the captain called out to another gunner. It was all a mystery to Bernardo he observed with trepidation. The larboard gun ports were opened, and guns run out. Then, as the *San Giovanni* rose on a wave and the cannon barrels pointed up, the twelve guns on the larboard side erupted almost simultaneously.

The xebec was rapidly closing and only about a hundred and fifty cannas away now.

It was hit with a volley of forty-six-pound iron ball that ripped their rigging and upper deck bulwarks to pieces. Between ropes thrashing around and splinters from the wood, the decks became awash with the blood of the dead and injured pirates.

As the distance between the two vessels rapidly reduced, they saw pirates emerge from the smoke choked decks. The upper deck guns on *San Giovanni* fired, spraying the xebec deck with small pellets of iron grape shot.

'Come alongside her, master Cardona,' the captain shouted above the noise.

'Prepare to board,' he called down to his knights, already with swords and axes in hand.

The xebec was close now and the impact of the *San Giovanni's* side with the oars, either ripped them out or broke them. There was loud cracking of oars splitting and the cries from the injured on the xebec. With the noise and site of the carnage on the deck, Bernardo felt traumatised and stood frozen to the spot.

There was an enormous crashing sound as the two vessels collided and they both shook violently. This stirred Bernardo out of his stupor, and he frantically started scanning the deck of the xebec for Agata. He had yet to notch an arrow to his bow string and had no interest to. He witnessed sailors throwing grappling hooks onto the xebec and the knights pouring on board, hacking at any pirate that moved. However, of those still alive there were few uninjured. All on board were in a daze, including the slaves, shocked by the ferocity of the cannon fire.

The knights quickly moved to the rowing benches and started breaking the chains securing the captives. They helped them to get up and onto the *San Giovanni*. Even in their weakened state, they looked visibly pleased they were free. Along with brother Antonio and the chaplain, Bernardo, hurried to help the emaciated slaves clamber on board. However, as they did this, shouts from the captain urged speed.

'All on board…slip the xebec…ready all starboard guns.' The captain's orders were immediately followed, with the efficiency of a well-practiced crew.

While throwing their full fire power at the first xebec, Captain De Poincy had an eye on the second xebec, struggling up wind towards the them. It was now just over a mile away. Slightly forward of the frigate's beam and her forward guns were already doing their best to hit *San Giovanni*. Large splashes from cannon balls falling nearby were throwing seawater onto the frigate's deck, but the starboard gun crew were ready.

With the last of the slaves clambering on board and the ropes securing the first xebec being cut, the captain turned his full attention to the second xebec.

'Starboard guns…fire as she bears.'

As they rose on the crest of a wave, the gun deck cannons fired. Half of them hit the xebec rigging and bulwark. Like before, the collapsing mast and splinters from the exploding bulwark wood, caused devastation. Then, just as the smoke cleared, the grape shot from *San Giovanni's* deck demi-culverin spewed forth hundreds of iron pellets. Metal fragments flew across the deck of the pirate vessel, mowing down all who had not ducked behind something substantial.

This time the xebec crashed into the side of *San Giovanni* head on, as was more their practice, protecting their oars and allowing the pirates to leap from their vessel's higher bow. However, the falling rigging and slaughter on deck had disrupted the rowing rhythm, which the slaves might have exacerbated deliberately too. One oar crashing into the next, or some stopping altogether, checking the vessel's momentum as they hung in the water.

'Repel boarders,' was the captains cry, this time, as surviving pirates rushed over their forecastle head, leaping onto the *San Giovanni's* deck. Those that made it, were met by armoured, axe welding knights. Those behind them, cut down with more grape shot from the demi-culverin on the forecastle and quarterdeck. It was not long before the knights boarded the second xebec. Held alongside with the hooks thrown by the Maltese seamen, they finished off the pirates and freed the slaves on the rowing benches.

Even while this continued, De Poincy's attention was on the third xebec which was trying to sneak up on *San Giovanni's* vulnerable stern. Close to two miles on the starboard quarter she would soon be in range with her forward-facing guns. *San Giovanni* was also not in a position to manoeuvre. One sinking xebec on her larboard quarter, another attached to her starboard beam and the reduced sail, the sailing master had ordered to aid the gunners. Yet, as the captain considered his options, cannon balls started hitting the water near the third xebec. The sloop, who had initially turned and ran as the battle commenced, now returned to help them, and was engaging, if rather weakly, the last xebec.

De Poincy smiled, 'Good for them,' he chuckled, 'that should buy us sometime.'

Looking down at the main deck, the captain could see the chaplain kneeling in prayer. A crucifix held in front of him, he was giving the last rites to an obviously dying sailor. Brother Antonio was trying to staunch the bleeding of another. Bernardo was helping frail slaves onto *San Giovanni's* deck. Seeing one of his knights at the top of the xebec's bow, passing the slaves to Bernardo, De Poincy called out to him. 'Pierre, we need to slip the xebec NOW.'

With a final glace behind him, Pierre leapt onto the *San Giovanni's* main deck and shouted orders. 'Cut the lines, push her off.'

The seaman around him wasted no time obeying. Meanwhile the captain had stepped back to instruct his sailing master, who was also looking at the sloop in his telescope.

'As soon as we are clear, increase sail and bring her about, lets close haul as best we can and head up towards the xebec while the sloop keeps her occupied.'

'Aye, aye, captain.' Cardona acknowledged, before calling out orders to the crew.

The Maltese first mate, Cassar, came up to the quarter deck to report. 'xebec clear, sir, we have some damage to the main mast starboard rigging which we are fixing now and have three dead, twelve injured, only one seriously.'

'Well done, Monsieur Cassar. You all performed well today.'

De Poincy smiled, he was gratified to witness how well his young first mate had settled into his role with enthusiasm.

'Prepare all guns, as before, but close the lower gun ports while we manoeuvre.'

'Aye, aye, sir,' replied the beaming first mate, turning to leave.

As he did so, the captain, looked down at the mass of slaves on the main deck and called after him. 'Cassar…feed, water and see if you can find room for these retches to rest…you know the routine but clear the decks before we are in action again.' The first mate nodded and hurried to carry out the orders.

With the derelict xebecs falling behind, the *San Giovanni* turned towards the northwest and approached the remaining xebec starboard quarter. The sloop was now exchanging gun fire to her larboard bow. From what De Poincy could see, both had only sustained minor damage to their rigging, so far.

No sooner had the *San Giovanni* approached the xebec and opened her gun ports, the xebec crew surrendered. Seeing how *San Giovanni* had dealt with the other two xebecs and with the sloop putting up a fight, the corsairs decided they would rather not die. So, *San Giovanni* carefully came alongside the xebec's stern. Deck guns trained on the xebec's deck continuously, the knights boarded her to free the captives. Pirates replacing them on the rowing benches in chains. The master of the sloop, now standing off near-by, was invited on board *San Giovanni* for a conference.

An hour later, a rather plump Captain Salvador di Benedetto of the sloop *Rossi*, came over to *San Giovanni* in his own vessel's gig. Full of good cheer, he expressed gratefulness for the timely intervention of the frigate and the Knights of Malta's fleet in general.

'God bless you captain,' Benedetto gushed, as he joined the knights in the captain's aft cabin. 'Thank you for your swift and decisive action today. Without the Knights of Malta, pirates would completely rule these seas and honest traders, like myself, would be at their mercy.'

De Poincy chuckled to himself, as he listened to Benedetto and wondered if he was always like this. However, keen as he was to move on, he was also grateful the sloop had engaged the third xebec and wanted to show his appreciation. So, putting on his best smile and shaking Captain Benedetto's hand warmly, he expressed his own thankfulness.

'Welcome on board, Captain, it is our honour to serve you in this way and we too are grateful that you engaged the xebec when you did. I am sure it influenced their quick surrender.'

While still talking, he guided Benedetto to a chair around a dining table that had been quickly erected in his cabin. Some other knights, the Maltese sailing master and first mate, all stood around until their guest was seated. Bernardo hung back in the shadows with the captain's steward, who was serving wine and bowls of olives, cheese, and bread. Around the table, everyone was in high spirits. However, De Poincy, aware of how low the sun now was, did not feel he had much time for congratulatory chatter. He stood up, to get their attention, and thanked God for His providence. Then he made a quick toast to the sloop's master and his own men, for a job well done. They all drained their glasses, and the steward went around filling them up again, while De Poincy stayed on his feet.

There had been no sign of Agata on the three xebecs. A few of the liberated slaves, when questioned, had said they thought they saw a girl being transferred from their boat to the accompanying galley. Interrogation of the final xebec's qubtan had revealed there was sickness on board the galley. It had headed to Lampedusa to try to clean out the rowing benches and rest the slaves ashore. This confirmed De Poincy's notion that the leader of this pirate squadron was on a large galley and solidified an idea he had to capture it. Formalities out of the way, there were arrangements to be made.

'The surviving corsairs are now in chains on the third xebec's rowing benches and *San Giovanni* is overflowing with their former captives. However, there is still, at least, one more vessel to find, and we believe the leader of this group of corsairs is on that galley, probably arriving in Lampedusa as we speak.

It is my intentions to capture this vessel and free the captives. So…' he continued leaning over the table.

'My most experienced knight, Jean Dubois, will take command of the surviving xebec, assisted by my first mate Cassar, as his sailing master with as many of the former slaves as are able to crew her. They will use the pirates to row to Valletta, which is about thirty miles east of our present position.'

There was a general murmur of approval. De Poincy took a breath, and looking at Benedetto, continued, 'Captain Benedetto, we would very much appreciate it if you could escort the xebec to Malta, where we will ensure you receive a share of the prize money.'

Benedetto smiled broadly, but before he agreed, De Poincy added, 'We would also ask, if you could lend us any seaman you could to assist on board the xebec AND take as many of the former captives, too weak to serve as delivery crew, onto your vessel for the journey to Malta, as we pursue this galley?'

Benedetto continued to smile but hesitated to reply. De Poincy was sure he was calculating the cost of feeding and watering a large number of emaciated ex-slaves and wondering what the share of the prize money would be, along with the delay in delivering his cargo. His smile weakened, as he guessed he would probably end up only breaking even, but looking around the table at expectant eyes, he agreed.

'It would be our pleasure to assist the Knights of Malta in any way we can.'

A chorus of approval was exchanged, and another glass of wine consumed, and orders given to execute the agreement. However, conscious of the hours of remaining light, De Poincy was eager to get underway again as soon as possible. So, he said hurried goodbyes and thanks, then gave orders to start the transfers of personnel between the ships. All decks were soon a hive of activities.

Chapter 41

Enquiries with the harbour master in Gela had gone on longer than Orlando would have like.

He was clearly disturbed by the previous night's attacks and was looking for reassurance that it would not happen again soon. Of course, Orlando could not give him such an assurance. However, he did comfort him with the information that the Knights of Malta went after the pirates determined to hunt them down.

As to the generous merchants' vessel, that apparently was Genoese, they left early on the 1 June, supposedly bound for Valencia in Spain. The harbour master did not remember seeing the vessel in Gela previously, nor had he met the merchants before. So, he was not much help, but his final throwaway comment made Orlando's suspicions even deeper.

'Odd thing though,' the harbour master commented, looking puzzled, 'if you are sailing from Genoa to Valencia, going via Gela…Sicily even, is a rather out of your way route. Unless you have some particular business here to make it worth the detour and as far as I know, they neither loaded nor discharged cargo here.'

Orlando considered this new information and what to do next, as he walked back through the harbour. He was so caught up in his thoughts, he did not initially notice the black carriage stopping beside him. That was, until a burly individual, with a scar running down his left cheek and dressed in an ill-fitting Inquisition uniform, stood menacingly in front of him. With an expressionless face, he held the carriage door open for Orlando, gesturing for him to get in.

Looking at this *behemoth*, he decided it was not worth arguing and climbed into the carriage which, despite the morning light, was quite dark inside. He was greeted by friar Diego with a bandaged head and his weasel looking secretary. Somehow Orlando was not entirely surprised to see them. Intimidating as it was, it did solve the question of what to do next.

He switched to his dandy persona, though he was wondering if it was still serving its purpose.

'Well good morning gentlemen, what a surprise to see you here and how kind to offer me a ride.' Orlando chirped as nonchalantly as he could, 'Have you had an accident friar Diego?'

Diego glared at him silently, weighing up the magistrate. Trying to fit him into the events of the previous twenty-four hours. It was friar Raphael, his secretary, that broke the silence.

'Chief Inquisitor Diego was attacked by pirates last night, as were the Inquisition guards with him,' he exclaimed accusingly.

Orlando raised an eyebrow and stared at Diego, who raised his hand to silence his secretary, who was huffing indignantly as he sat beside him.

'Would you like to explain to us, why you are here?' Diego almost whispered in his serpent-like manner.

'Certainly,' Orlando responded, attempting to sound jolly, 'I have been following some very interesting leads, and last night thought I had caught up with our fugitives.'

'Really,' Diego hissed, 'tell me more.'

His eyes bored into Orlando, as if he could read his mind. Orlando tried to ignore it and continued with a jovial demeanour.

'It seems that the girl was taken by the pirates last night and the Benedictine has joined the Knights of St John's vessel. So, both are off the island.'

Now Orlando took his gamble, not being sure if he had been seen on *San Giovanni* and if he had, exactly when.

'Did you encounter the same pirates; I understand they attacked more than one location?'

Again, Diego sat silently staring at Orlando, and for a moment, he thought he had revealed his duplicity.

Then Diego started to explain the night's events from his perspective.

'We suspected the fugitives would be joining the Knight's vessel and were waiting to apprehend them. However, when the pirates came on board and attacked the Maltese sailors, our guards naturally defended our Christian brother's vessel. Meanwhile, I was in the captain's cabin, and I think I met this girl, Agata, although as I did not know what she looked like, I did not know it was her. Unfortunately, I only managed to start questioning her, when I was hit from behind, by a pirate I presume. The next thing I knew I was being carried out of a smoked filled cabin by a large, young man, who I think was wearing a black habit, but I was not fully conscious and so am not sure.'

He rubbed his head which still throbbed, seething that his schemes had been thwarted.

'So, you might have been rescued by this large Benedictine you are after and met the young Agata,' Orlando said, rather amused, 'Is she beautiful…worthy of all the efforts this young man is going to?'

Diego's temper flared. 'What relevance is that? My priorities are clearly different than yours, magistrate.'

Although Orlando would have enjoyed poking fun at Diego, he decided to change tack.

'You are right friar Diego, this is irrelevant, but I think I have uncovered something far more troubling, and I am sure you will want to help me get to the bottom of it.'

Diego, cooled down as quickly as he lost his temper. Intrigued by what Orlando was saying, he said no more, leaning forward as if to better hear, as the magistrate continued.

'Yesterday morning, two Genoese merchants visited the local taverns near the harbour and gave the proprietors money to entertain the knights and crew from the *San Giovanni*, then sailed for Valencia BEFORE the *San Giovanni* arrived. They went out of their way to visit Gela for less than a day and seemed to know when *San Giovanni* was going to arrive before anyone else.' Orlando paused to let Diego take in what he was suggesting, '…and on *San Giovanni's* arrival, there was an invitation for the captain and his knights to attend a dinner ashore.'

Diego's eyes narrowed, but he remained silent, as Orlando continued.

'Someone wanted the *San Giovanni* deserted last night and you probably spoiled their plans. Could Genoese merchants be in cahoots with the pirates? Are these raids co-ordinated by our own Christian brothers? Is the enemy not just over the sea, but amongst us?'

All three stared at each other silently for a few moments. Then, to break the awkward silence, Orlando leaned towards Diego looking very serious.

'There is more to this conspiracy than we first thought!' Orlando whispered.

'Conspiracy?' Diego echoed.

'Well, who exactly is fighting who?' Orlando asked, 'this is not just about some random young monk and his love interest. There is something very odd about this pirate attack,' Orlando asserted.

Orlando had Diego's interest now and could almost see the wheels of his mind spinning, as he considered the implications of what Orlando was suggesting.

After a few moment's thought, Diego asked, 'What do you intend to do next?'

Without hesitation and completely honestly, Orlando answered.

'Try to find out more about these Genoese merchants for a start. As for the Benedictine and this girl, I think they are lost, but there are others to track down too, and I will follow the leads wherever they take me.'

'Very well,' Diego replied, leaning back, and rubbing his head again. 'Perhaps,' he thought, 'this magistrate is a better detective than I had given him credit.'

Chapter 42

Keys rattled in the door, then a weak shaft of light woke Agata as it entered the stuffy storeroom where she was confined. Through squinting eyes, she recognised the bulky silhouette of Abu shoving somethings towards her, then slam and locked the door again. She groped in the darkness to retrieve what Abu had laid on the deck. She felt a small rough clay pot with water in it. Feeling around the deck, she came across what tasted like hard flat bread. She consumed both quickly.

Sitting upright, leaning against the shelves, she reassuringly felt the sharp metal rod beneath her bodice. There was lots of shouting going on outside, much more than before and the crack of whips. Wondering what was going on she listened intently. Agata also noticed the vessel was not rocking as much, as if stationary in some sheltered place. She had no idea what time it was, and she started to fret about what would happen next. Praying again calmed her nerves.

The store cupboard was hot and airless. Agata was sweating profusely and longed to get some fresh cool air, but she sat still and tried to slow her heartbeat. After what seemed hours, she once again heard fumbling of keys in the lock and the door opened wide. Abu stood away from the door entrance this time, motioning for her to come out. She slowly stood up, feeling rather stiff, and edged her way into the light as her eyes adjusted. The door to the deck was open. She caught the sight of slaves being ushered from the rowing benches and across the deck.

Abu grabbed her arm, but more gently this time. He pointed to an open door in the opposite direction to the deck door which he guided her into. It was clearly the captain's cabin, and a cooling breeze was coming in through large open wooden shutters on the sides and rear of the cabin. Although still hot and humid, she breathed in the fresh, cooler air gratefully.

Agata scanned the cabin quickly taking in the salient details. A large comfortable looking bed, made up on the deck. Cushions around the bulkheads, a low table near the centre of the cabin and storage units built into or attached to the bulkheads on both sides. On one sideboard, food, and drink was laid out. On the opposite side, where Abu was gesturing to her, a large ceramic bowl, water pitcher and towel sat ready.

It looked like this sturdy little man, who said nothing, but grunted and gestured, wanted her to wash. She poured water from the jug into the bowl, which was sitting in a recess on the top of the sideboard. Then with pleasure she used the lukewarm water to wash the sweat off her face and neck. As she did this, she could see out of the open shutters. She took her time, enjoying the water and trying to assess what was going on. Boats, full of slaves were being ferried off the galley to the shore which was close and looked deserted.

Abu appeared beside her, motioning for her to do something. At first, she did not understand, until he started pulling the cords that fastened her bodice. It appeared, he wanted her to undress and wash all over. Agata thought of what was hidden under her bodice and fumbled clumsily with her bodice strings to give her time to think. She tried to remove the bodice while concealing the sharp rod amongst its folds.

Once off, she carefully held the bodice in her right hand with the rod hidden within, deliberately moving very slowly. This seemed to irritate Abu. He stood close, facing her, and started to remove the waist sash that held her skirts up. She submissively held her arms open, as if not to impede his actions.

While his face was inclined downwards and focused on the material tucked into itself, she thrust the sharp metal rod, with all her strength, into the back of his neck. Abu looked up at her, eyes wide and mouth open as if to scream. Only a deep gargling noise came out of his mouth, then he collapsed to the deck.

For a moment, Agata stood petrified, watching a pool of blood begin to surround Abu's body. His face frozen in shock, mouth still open and eyes glaring up at her. Staring at his body, a short, broad dagger on a leather sheath attached to his belt caught her attention, spurring her into action.

She took the whole belt off with the dagger attached and secured it around her waist, then removed and discarded her petticoat. Pulling the rear of her outer skirt through her legs, she secured it to her front waist with the belt. Turning the skirt into crude pantaloons and tucking her shirt into her waist sash, she discarded the bodice and the boy's leather boots she had been wearing for the walk to Gela.

Agata clambered up onto the food covered sideboard on the offshore side of the vessel. Grabbing and eating a mouthful of dates along the way, she eased herself out of the open shuttered porthole. Her dainty bare feet stepped gingerly onto the three-inch ledge where the cabin bulkhead was connected to the deck. Her head was just below the poop deck. She could hear voices clearly and even feel the vibration of feet moving above her.

Using the shutters and their frames to hold onto, she carefully walked around to the stern of the galley. Then she climbed onto the rubbing strake just above the top of the rudder which protruded slightly above the water line. Putting one foot carefully onto the top of the rudder and hanging off the rubbing strake, she lowered herself gently into the water. She hid under the stern overhang, holding onto the rudder top to keep her head just above water level.

The water felt lovely to her warm body, but she knew she would grow cold after a short time. Looking at the sky, she guessed the vessel was pointing west and it was already almost dark at the east orientated stern. However, she could make out a promontory of land, only about twice the length of the vessel away. She thanked God she had learned to swim, growing up in Trabia.

She decided to wait until it was completely dark before swimming to the land. Then make her way around to where she had seen the slaves being taken. She did not know how she was going to do it, but she was determined to rescue her brothers if she could find them.

Above her she could hear a commotion.

'They have probably found the body,' she guessed.

She could hear running feet on the deck above and later spotted a boat passing by with pirates looking around. However, with only her face above water, tucked under the stern of the galley and the rapidly growing darkness, she felt confident they would not see her.

After a little while, as she started to feel cold, she raised her head above the water and when her ears cleared of liquid, listened. There was much less shouting and running around.

She could no longer see any boats looking for her or running slaves ashore. Holding onto the top of the rudder, she pulled herself up, so her shoulders were out of the water. She was shivering now and eager to swim to the land and warm up. However, she decided to wait, a little longer until it was completely dark, so she climbed onto the top of the rudder and settled herself down to wait. Preparing herself mentally to swim ashore, she started to recall when she learned to swim.

Being their first child, her mother and father doted on Agata, and her father had always been very protective. Sometimes her father helped the fishermen drag their boats ashore and her mother would help the fishermen's wives gut the catch for market in exchange for some fish. While doing this, she would play on the beach and in the shallows with the other children from Trabia.

Her mother was always telling her to be careful, so her father decided to teach her to swim like the fishermen's boys, to help keep her safe. She took to the skill like a fish and later it was she who taught her younger brothers to swim. Agata loved swimming and cooling off in the summer evenings. However, from the age of seven, her mother made her cover up more, which annoyed her as her young brothers still freely swam naked.

Most of the time she looked and felt like a boy anyway, puberty coming on late.

She did not start her monthly bleeding until she was thirteen and did not show any significant signs of breasts until she was fourteen. So, her father remained protective and even her mother did not push for her to marry, seeing her as still a child. It had only really been in this last year that she suddenly filled out as an obvious woman. Her mother started fussing about her appearance and other parents started talking about a suitable husband. They were not impressed by the options in Trabia. They wondered about sending her to her uncle's farm to look for an eligible husband. However, her mother also liked her around their smallholding, finding her helpful and good company, so she was hesitant.

Agata started to feel sad as she reminisced about her childhood, remembering her dead parents and how the pirates had robbed her of their happy family life. As she thought about all that had happened, her sadness morphed into a fury which grew inside her and a desire for revenge spurred her on. Focusing back on the present, she noted it was almost completely dark now and very quiet. Letting go of the rudder, she pushed off towards the promontory of low-lying land ahead of her. At such a short distance, it did not take her long to swim. She clambered onto the shore, then hid herself among the long marram grass, just off the beach, while she warmed up and caught her breath.

Beyond the pirate galley, which was just a dull shape now, she could see the remaining glow of the sun. A nearly full moon was rising, which provided a limited amount of light, but mostly made the tops of things sliver and the shadows more intense. Agata thought for a moment while her clothes started to dry in the warm summer evening air. She tried to orient herself and picture where she was.

From what she had briefly seen, the vessel was lying in a small bay of low-lying unpopulated land. She was to the eastern end of the bay with the vessel pointing westerly from where a steady breeze was coming. The slaves seemed to have been taken to the centre of the bay, from which she could make out the glow of some fires and perhaps some buildings. It was hard to tell in the limited light.

She decided she would make her way around the bay, using the beach for directions.

Keeping to the grassy parts, just off the beach for cover. Once she was close enough to see where they were holding the slaves and how they secured them, she would decide on the next step. Agata headed off, her bare feet sinking into the soft warm sand, feeling her way in the darkness.

Chapter 43

'Land ahoy, one point to starboard,' cried the lookout. Captain De Poincy did not stir from his pondering, hunched over a chart of Lampedusa on his cabin desk with two of his most senior knights with him. It had been nearly two hours since they parted from the sloop and xebec, so he knew the island would be just a silhouette against the setting sun. He was frustrated by the time it had taken to close the island. The northerly wind he had expected, soon decreased as it backed to a steady nor'westerly. It would be dark by the time *San Giovanni* closed the island. So, trying to find a safe place to anchor and land boats was going to be a challenge. The sailing master put his head around the captain's open cabin door, as De Poincy expected he would.

'Come in Master Cardona, I heard the lookout,' he said without moving.

Cardona stood by the desk and looked at the chart but waited patiently for his Commanding officer to share his thoughts. De Poincy pointed to a bay at the south-east side of the island, 'That is where I believe the galley will anchor and land the slaves. It is well sheltered and where the original main settlement was.'

Tracing the coastline with his finger, he settled on another, more open bay, a short distance to the east. Tapping this spot, he looked up at his sailing master, 'If you can find it, that is where I would like you to drop us off. As close in as we dare. I will take the knights and a few sailors ashore under cover of darkness, but you lie off the island. Once we are ready for pick up or for you to approach the galley's bay, we will signal you by lantern from the hill. I will take a sailor ashore as a signalman. Probably at first light you will see the signal. Until then, keep close, but out of their sight.'

'Will do our best, sir, with wind continuing to back to the west, we'll lose it once in lee of island and with only a small hill between the two bays, we best whisper orders and lead line calls. That is assuming they do not have lookouts on the hill…' Cardona noted.

He scratched his head, as he thought through the details of the plan, '…but it's a clear night and should be a good moon, so that should help the boats find the beach…tricky if there are lots of rocks though.' He looked concerned.

'They are not expecting us, so I doubt they will have lookouts on the hill. At least, not alert ones, but we will be way outnumbered, so need the advantage of surprise,' the captain asserted.

De Poincy understood his sailing master's concerns and respected him for them. He knew it was a risky plan, with lots of things that could go wrong. However, unlike a sea battle, stealth was the key to this operation. He also hoped to avoid killing the slaves which a straightforward bombardment with his cannons was sure to do.

'From what we have been told of their plans, I would guess all the slaves are ashore, which means nearly all the pirates will be ashore guarding them. Leaving only a skeleton crew on board, who we can hopefully sneak up on.'

Looking around at those gathered in his cabin, he continued, 'We will split into two groups; a few knights and sailors heading straight for the galley to try and capture it, while I take the main body of knights to subdue the pirates ashore and free the slaves.'

'If all goes well, we could end up with a prize galley, as well as freeing a large number of Christian slaves and striking a massive blow to the pirates.'

He straightened up and looked very serious, as he addressed his sailing master.

'Worst case scenario, Master, you open fire on that bay, sink the galley and pound the settlement. We will find shelter wherever, then signal you for boats to pick us up. We are not going to let this galley sail, but if we can rescue the slaves and capture her, we will do.'

There was a general murmur of approval around the desk, though the sailing master still looked very concerned. De Poincy addressed him directly.

'In the absence of any other signs, at first light be off the entrance to the galley's bay. Look for the Saint John's flag on the galley, to signal we have captured it. Then you can enter the bay and assist, but if the flag has not been raised, close the galley, and destroy it.'

The sailing master nodded. 'Aye-aye, sir, we'll be there, guns ready, but praying you capture the galley and free the slaves.'

As the master and knights left his cabin, De Poincy sat at his desk considering what lay ahead. One thing he had not told his officers was the personal nature of this operation. He had his suspicions of who was behind the attack on *San Giovanni* in Gela and who was commanding this galley. If he was correct, this had been no random raid, but a deliberate action against the Knights of Malta, their new vessel and him personally.

A few years before, he had led a squadron of vessels that engaged a group of pirates' vessels. During the encounter, they had captured the pirates Amir, Amad Rayar, and De Poincy had condemned him to their rowing benches in chains.

However, they had not held him long, as a second group of pirate vessels caught up with them. During the ensuing battle, Amad Rayar had been freed and De Poincy almost lost his life. The two commanders, who had personally crossed swords, were left with a mixture of respect of each other's abilities and a desire for revenge. However, he had to keep a cool head and not let this become too personal, less it clouded his judgement.

Now he wondered, what to do with Bernardo. He would obviously want to try to rescue Agata. So, he should join the shore party, but would she be on board the galley, or ashore with the slaves? She was a pretty young girl and would fetch a good price in the slave markets, but would Amad Rayar want to sample her first? He guessed the Amir would stay with his ship, so that might mean she was still on board. He would discuss options with the young monk and see what he would prefer.

'I wonder if he can swim?' De Poincy thought, as he went out on to the deck.

Chapter 44

The sand was still warm as it enveloped Agata's bare feet, carefully feeling her way around the beach towards the torch lights of the encampment. At another time and place, it would have been pleasant and the moon light appealing. Right now, it made the world look surreal, her surroundings either glowing with silver, or in deep black shadow.

She was aware of her closeness to the pirates and slave holding area first by the smell, as she was down wind of their cooking fires. The spices they used filled the air with aromatic flavours. It made her feel hungry, but she also felt too tense to eat anything, being more lightly to throw up if she tried. Peaking up above the long dune grasses just off the shoreline, she could hear their murmuring voices and the occasional laugh of the pirates. She squeezed the dagger hilt in her hand and willed herself to stop trembling.

'I wonder how many there are of them,' she puzzled, 'can I get close enough to see without being detected and how am I going to find Stefano?'

She had a weapon and the advantage of surprise, but no idea what to do next, as she edged herself forward.

Movement by the water's edge caught her attention and she remained motionless, straining her eyes and ears to make out what was happening. Someone got out of a boat and made his way towards a group of pirates gathered around a small fire. As the figure approached the men, they rose to their feet and bowed to the portly figure.

'The Amir,' she decided, 'what had he come ashore for?'

She could not understand the Arabic, but she saw him take a torch from them and was gesturing them to stay where they were, as he walked off towards a building behind them.

She moved slowly around to her right, to a slightly higher position with a better view down into the building the Amir had walked towards. The stone or earth walls of the building were still intact, but the roof, probably originally thatch, was no longer there. As the Amir approached the door, a pirate guarding the entrance stood and held a torch up, illuminating the area more. Some more words were exchanged, and the Amir held his torch up and looked inside a roofless room.

Now in the torch light, Agata could see dozens of bodies lying on the floor and the Amir seemed to be selecting one. After a while, he gestured to the guard. She heard clanking of metal-on-metal, then saw one of the slaves being dragged out from among the prostate bodies towards the Amir at the door. After more words and gesturing, the guard sunk back onto his hunches, back against the wall. The slave and Amir walked off towards another building, slightly away from the holding area.

The Amir's torch helped Agata follow his movements, so she crawled around to her right and over a small ridge, until she was looking down onto a semi-demolished building.

This building looked badly fire damaged, but from the shape, and construction very different from the other dwellings. She guessed it had been the chapel.

Now both the Amir and slave entered what was left of the chapel and disappeared from her sight. She crept silently closer to the building, keeping what was left of its walls between her and the other pirates. She peered through the remains of a window. While the Amir held the torch above him, giving instructions, she caught sight of the slave. It was Stefano.

Her heart near burst through her chest. Surely God was orchestrating his deliverance, though she knew she could not just rush at the Amir with her dagger. She observed what was going on while thinking through what to do. She could see the large, curved scimitar hanging at the Amir's waist, deepening her concerns on how to tackle him.

The Amir was now using some Italian words, as Agata could make out a few. He was directing Stefano to move some large stone slabs from around what could have been the chapel's altar.

'What are they doing,' Agata puzzled, 'and why has the Amir brought a slave alone with him here?' She watched carefully, praying under her breath for Stefano's safety.

There was a noise behind her. Agata held her breath, not even wanting to turn around to see in case she gave her position away. Then more noise, off to her left, where the slave holding area was. Clashing of steel which it was obvious the Amir now heard too. There was fighting in the camp.

The Amir left Stefano, in the dark struggling with the large stone slap, while he moved to the entrance. A pirate with a torch came running up to him, calling out in Arabic. Agata might not speak their language, but she recognised enough words to realise the Knights of Malta were there, attacking the pirates.

Now was her chance. She slipped in the window near the rear of the chapel and crawled over to where she had seen Stefano. She tried to keep her eyes on the Amir, who was still holding the torch near the entrance. There was a flash of light and a sudden bang, as a musket was fired just outside the chapel. It illuminated the building and momentarily blinded her. She curled up into a ball on the floor, hoping to make herself invisible.

More clashing of steel and the odd bang, but much closer now. Agata pensively looked up. Fighting seemed to be near the chapel entrance. The Amir had backed into the interior, drawing his huge scimitar, and dropping the torch not far from the altar.

With the dropped torch light, Agata could make out Stefano, cowering in a hole he had revealed by moving the stone slab, behind the altar.

She crawled over to him and whispered his name, 'Stefano, it is me, Agata,' reaching out to him.

Stefano's head popped out of the hole and from what Agata could make out, his eyes were wide, and jaw dropped open. Quickly she put her hand over his mouth, so he did not cry out. She squeezed into the mouth of the hole he had made and hugged him. They both cried, but silently, terrified, confused, and elated.

They needed to avoid the fighting and then, in the confusion, make their escape she decided. She peeked out from behind the altar along the length of the small chapel. At the entrance, three shadowy figures were desperately fighting. Two were turban clad, so she assumed pirates, the other she could only guess was a knight.

The knight thrust his sword into the belly of one pirate, but at the same time the other slashed the side of the knight with his curved sword. The knight reeled around, screaming from the wound, but cut down his assailant after parrying his next strike. He staggered into the chapel and faced the Amir, who had observed the fight. Agata could see from a torch dropped near the entrance that he was out of breath and in some discomfort but preparing to face down the Amir.

The torch light made shadowy shapes dance around the walls, but as the knight moved into the chapel and faced the Amir, she could see it was Captain De Poincy. The Amir spoke to him in perfect Italian.

'We meet again…to finish what was started so long ago.'

De Poincy said nothing, panting to catch his breath and holding his side where he had been struck. The Amir rushed at him, swinging his scimitar in a broad arc. Agata was mesmerised and horrified at the same time. De Poincy parried the first swing, but the Amir, surprisingly agile for a fat man, kicked De Poincy hard near his wound, sending him tumbling into the chapel wall.

'De Poincy is going to get killed,' Agata realised with alarm, 'I have to do something.'

Slowly at first, the dagger tightly gripped in her right hand, she emerged from behind the altar. The Amir had his back to her, his whole focus on the fight as he raised his scimitar above his head. Agata's dainty bare feet sped her silently across the floor of the chapel. With heart pounding and adrenalin pumping wildly around her body, she focused entirely on the hulk of a man in front of her. With the Amir's arms above his head and back exposed, she grasped the dagger with both hands. She thrust it into the middle of his back with all the force she could muster. Letting go of the dagger, she stepped back looking at it, as it protruded grotesquely from his back, imbedded up to the hilt.

In what felt to Agata as an age, the Amir did not move. Then the scimitar tumbled from his hands, and he dropped to his knees, as if he was about to pray. His head slumped forward, and arms dropped to his side, but he remained in a kneeling position, motionless.

De Poincy looked over his foe's shoulder at the petite figure, petrified, trembling, eyes fixed on the protruding dagger. He made the sign of the cross over himself and kissed a crucifix that hung around his neck, then smiled up at Agata.

'You *are* a remarkable girl,' he declared.

His words snapped her out of the trance she was in, and she went over to help him up. The best she could do was prop him up more comfortably, with his back against the chapel wall. Then she remembered Stefano and hurried back behind the altar to where she had left him.

He was now out of the hole, under the altar, kneeling on the ground and staring at the contents of a wooden chest. There were rows of leather pouches which he had opened and was looking through the contents. Some had silver coins, some gold coins, and others large precious stones.

'So, this is what the Amir was after,' Agata realised.

She knelt beside Stefano and affectionately kissed him on the forehead. He might be enchanted by this treasure trove, but she was more pleased to see him alive. Questions about her other two brothers came to her mind. Before she could ask Stefano about them, there was noise from the chapel entrance. Fearful it might be some more pirates who would finish off De Poincy, Agata craned her slender neck around the altar to observe without being seen. From the torches, they held in their hand, she could see clearly the two newcomers, and to her relief they were Knights of St John.

Seeing their commander, the knights went straight to help him to his feet, one on each side holding him up. On witnessing this, Agata and Stefano emerged from behind the altar carrying the heavy chest between then. De Poincy introduced Agata to the knights as his saviour. An embarrassed Agata introduced her brother the them, as well as the treasure he had uncovered. There were astonished smiles all around, as they made their way out of the chapel to join the rest of the rescue party.

Chapter 45

Landing the knights by boat from *San Giovanni* on the eastern end of the island, had in the end proved straight forward. As predicted the island created a lee from the westerly winds, so the bay was calm. The shore area and rocks were illuminated by the rising moon in the east. This made the wet areas glow silver and provided enough light to disembark without torches which would have given their position away.

As the sailing master had advised, his orders and the calls from the sailors, casting the lead line to find the depth as they approached the shore, were passed man-to-man in whispers. However, there were no sign of pirates on that side of the island. As a precaution, the knights had stripped off most of their armour. They had strapped their swords to themselves with cloth sashes, for fear of metallic clinking as they moved, alerting those ashore.

Silently they looked down from the crest of the hill between the two bays. It was obvious how the pirates were distributed around the head of the main bay from their cooking fires and torches. It was, therefore, also clear where the slaves were impounded, and the galley anchored.

They split into two groups, as planned. One heading straight towards the cooking fire lights. The other following the bay shoreline around towards the ghostly shape of the galley, illuminated by only a few lanterns. This second group would swim out to the stern of the galley, and hopefully board without waking the pirates on watch, of which they thought would be very few.

It was the need to swim that had made Bernardo's mind up as to which group to be part of, as he had never learned how to. Therefore, he hoped Agata would be held with the other slaves or be freed from the galley by the other knights before dawn. There were clearly no certainties about this rescue. However, he would avoid the fighting as much as possible and focus on releasing the slaves.

While Agata was finding her brother in the little chapel, Bernardo was with a young carpenter's mate, who introduced himself as Paulo. They were peering into the western end of a roofless building at a dirt floor covered in sleeping galley slaves. He was armed with his trusty bow and arrows, which he gripped tightly. The sailor had a hammer and chisel to release the slave's manacles, as necessary. Their instructions were to wait until the fighting distracted the pirates enough for them to climb into the holding area and free the slaves.

Musket shots were heard to the east, where the chapel was, waking the captives. Clashing of steel and cries of pain, even nearer, soon drew the guards away from the door of the holding area. As this happened, Bernardo and Paulo climbed in among, the now agitated, slaves. Paulo immediately set to work releasing the leg manacles that shackled groups of slaves together. Bernardo tried to quiet the captives, reassuring them they were being rescued, but keeping an eye on the door simultaneously.

Working quickly, Paulo concentrated on breaking the chain links joining the slave groups, rather than the individual leg manacles of each slave. Meanwhile, Bernardo made his way towards the door, trying not to step on any limbs. This was not an easy task, as bodies covered most of the floor space and he did not want to take his eyes off the door opening. He already had an arrow notched onto his bow string and if a pirate appeared at the opening, he would lose a shaft at him immediately.

The noise of shuffling feet, still with leg manacles and Paulo's hammer releasing the bolts, soon became loud enough to draw attention to what was happening. So, Bernardo slipped out of the doorway ready to fend off any returning pirates. However, the slaves were no longer of interest to the pirates as they fought frantically with unknown numbers of knights in the darkness.

Skirmishes were taking place at various spots around the head of the bay, as Bernardo crept forward unnoticed. His senses sharp and bow ready, just as it had been in many hunting trips. His breathing steadied, his emotions calmed, he became one with his long bow, being an extension of his powerful arm. He noted the westerly wind had calmed to a gentle breeze. He even considered the effect of the humidity on the hemp he made the bow strings from. All moral discussions were pushed out of his mind, as he became the hunter and the foe in the darkness his prey.

Bernardo peered at the light from sporadic touches, noting the moon mixing shadows with humans in a macabre, ethereal dance. He saw to his left two knights being overwhelmed by pirates. He drew back an arrow, already notched and loosed silently, striking a scimitar-wielding pirate in the middle of his chest, the blow, at such short range, nearly lifting him off his feet. Before the first body hit the ground, he had loosed a second arrow into another attacking pirate. Then a third and fourth, until the knights had the upper hand in the fight and the pirates started to back away. Bernardo peered into the dark for more threats.

As the first rays of sun light started dancing over the eastern hills, there was a strange quiet around him, save for the low moans from the injured and dying. Bernardo could see pirates surrendering and knights rounding them up. Their destiny would be the rowing benches that they once held others captive. He turned back towards the slave holding building, where some were hesitantly coming through the open door. They scanned the carnage, but half expected a whip wielding pirate to strike them at any moment. Most were now free of leg manacles. As, he could still hear the clunks from Paulo's hammer freeing the remainder, he went inside to help those too weak to walk unadded.

Soon a rag tagged crowd was gathering on the beach and rejoicing as they saw the Knights of Malta flag flying high on the galley mast and *San Giovanni* anchored in the bay. Tales of individual bravery would be told of this night. Yet, for the slaves, it felt as if this was all part of some nightmare from which they were starting to wake.

As daylight unveiled disparate groups of human salvage, Bernardo scanned the gathering crowd for Agata. He accepted, if still alive, she might be on the galley. With that in mind, he continued to help the sick to the beach, until he saw Captain De Poincy being carried on a makeshift litter. Kneeling beside him, to see the extent of his injuries, he was surprised to be greeted with a very broad smile, despite his obvious pain.

'Good to see you're alive brother and I think you will be pleased with what is following behind me.' De Poincy beamed, waving Bernardo towards the chapel hill.

As he stood up, head above all around, he spotted Agata right away. Walking with a young man and carrying a heavy looking chest between them. Their eyes met and Agata dropped the chest to run towards him, but after a few steps hesitated, her emotions confused. He, on the other hand, did not hesitate. Running towards her he scooped her up in his powerful arms and held her so tight, she thought she would be crushed.

This unusual expression of affection surprised them both, and as he put her down, she clung onto him and wept. All the suppressed emotions of the last few weeks pouring out in a torrent. She felt safe in his arms and was grateful for that.

However, she no longer felt as content as she had before. As her emotions subsided, she reached over to her brother, now standing quietly confused by her side. Still holding onto Bernardo's hand, she put a protective arm around her brother. They all slumped into the sand, the treasure chest between them.

'Bernardo, this is my brother Stefano, the oldest of the three I told you about.'

She hugged her brother's neck and kissed him softly on the cheek.

'Stefano, this is Brother Bernardo, who God sent to save me and be my family when I lost you all,' and staring into Bernardo's eyes, she continued, 'he is very dear to me.'

'Agata,' Bernardo replied affectionately, 'I thought I had lost you and my faith has been sorely tested, but I see we are never alone. He hears our prayers, even from the depth of our despair.'

Joyfully Bernardo wanted to express his gratitude for their survival and even sing praises to God. Yet, he did not sense joy in Agata, but something quite different as she stared vacantly into his eyes without a word.

'Your other brothers,' Bernardo broke the silence, 'do you know what has become of them?'

Looking at Stefano, Agata asked him to repeat to Bernardo what he had told her when she asked after her other brothers. As he did, she let her blood-stained hands drop into her lap and stared at them, deep in her own thoughts.

'When we were first taken, we tried to stay together,' Stefano began, 'and were chained together on the deck of that galley,' he said motioning to the *El Jadida,* 'along with other women and children. Only a few grown men, who mostly were taken straight to the rowing benches.'

He paused, gathering his memories and emotions before continuing.

'After a couple of days, we arrived somewhere…an island I think, but not this one. There was a meeting of the corsairs from different vessels and among them was a man that did not look like a pirate. More like one of us and he spoke partly our language and partly in the Arab tongue. At one point, the fat Amir approached us and said in Italian to the man who did not look like a Turk, he would give our youngest brother Mateo to him as a gift for his help and picked up Mateo by the arm. Well at this, our middle brother Luciano, who was sitting right next to Mateo, jumped up, held onto Mateo, and said "no!" Stefano shuddered at the memory, 'They struck him hard on the side of his head and he slumped down on my lap.'

He paused again, thinking back to that fateful day, and started to cry, dry tears. 'The fat European man took Mateo right then and there, smiling all the time and later...Luciano just stopped breathing. I could not wake him, and they threw him overboard, like a piece of garbage.' Stefano clung to his sister and sobbed.

'I am so sorry, Agata, I could not stop them taking little Mateo or wake Luciano, I was so frightened.'

Agata rocked him in her arms, 'Shhh...' she whispered, 'it's not your fault.'

'After that, I did not care what happened to me.' Stefano continued, 'We arrived in a noisy port, the women and children left to be sold and I was kept for the rowing benches where I have been since we sailed about a week ago.'

They were quiet for a while, then Agata, stroking her brother's lice ridden hair, asked, 'Stefano, if you saw the man who took Mateo again, would you recognise him?' Stefano nodded, and Bernardo stared at Agata.

'What was she thinking?' he puzzled.

Chapter 46

It took until noon to get the pirates installed in *El Jadida's* rowing benches. Slightly longer to get the sick or weak former slaves, and all the wounded, settled onto the *San Giovanni*. They also loaded as much extra fresh water as they could. Then they divided up the knights, sailors, and healthy former slaves to form a delivery crew for the prize ship. By the time this task was finished, the gentle westerly breeze had veered to the north and increased enough to sail at a steady pace.

San Giovanni escorted their prize the ninety nautical miles to Malta, travelling slowly, taking nearly twenty hours to reach Valletta. However, this and the relatively smooth sail gave everyone time to recover. Bernardo helped Antonio with the sick and injured. The chaplain prepared the bodies of the Maltese sailors for return to their families and knights to be buried with honour in their respective langue chapels in Valletta. They had buried the dead pirates on the island.

During this voyage, De Poincy spent all the time in his bed, but they had managed to stop the bleeding while still on the island and his cuts appeared clean. Antonio was confident they could avoid infections. Nevertheless, he had Agata keep an eye on him while he was busy with other more critical patients. As the *San Giovanni* was crowded, she had a corner of the captain's cabin sectioned off with a sheet. There she could clean herself and change clothes. They also allowed Stefano to sleep there too once he had been deloused and cleaned up. This gave the siblings more time to talk about their experiences since they were separated.

They had both changed much in the short time since the pirate raid on Trabia. The once confident young man Stefano had been, was now fearful and guilt ridden. Agata suppressed her fear with anger and a determination to rescue her youngest brother. Exactly how she was going to do that remained unclear. However, they were now free, and potentially wealthy, if allowed to keep the treasure. They also had allies that wanted to track down these mysterious men who were possibly assisting the pirates. Agata realised, this was a different type of kidnapper from those she had encountered before. One she was now prepared to intentionally seek out. Therefore, she had to prepare herself to be a hunter, rather than the hunted but realised she may have to enter a completely different environment to do this.

Agata confided with De Poincy, while helping him eat the broth his steward had prepared especially for him. Once finished she helped him imbibe the tonic brother Antonio had prepared to help the healing process. She shared with him the information about the man who had been given Mateo as a gift from the pirate Amir and what that implied.

'It is as I suspected,' De Poincy told her, as Agata recounted what Stefano had told her, 'there are people passing on information to the pirates and I too would like to find out who they are.'

'No matter how long it takes, or what it costs, I am determined to rescue my baby brother,' Agata insisted, as she sat next to De Poincy, helping him eat.

'Trust me when I say, I want to help you,' De Poincy assured her, 'I am in your debt—you saved my life, and I want to repay you by helping to rescue your brother. However,…' he paused, shifting in his bed to make himself more comfortable and not lean on his bandaged side, '…this is not a case of chasing pirates at sea. We will have to seek help with careful investigations, something neither of us are prepared for. First I need to get my strength back and you need help to prepare yourself too.'

Agata was not sure what De Poincy meant but waited patiently for him to explain.

'When I make my report of all that has happened, I will urge an investigation into collaborators, though I doubt the Order will want you and I investigating this. Nevertheless, I have an idea of who will help you and Stefano to prepare, and I will write to Orlando as soon as we arrive in Valletta. Together we have a large network of contacts, I believe we can flush out who is passing information onto the pirates.'

Agata remained puzzled and realised how much she did not understand. She would have to trust these newfound friends.

'With the treasure you found,' De Poincy continued, 'normally all we recover is handed over to the Order. The rescued being nursed in our hospital and then helped to return home, only the rescuers receiving any share of prize money. However, I see you as one of the rescuers, so would like to see you keep most of the treasure Stefano found.'

Agata thought about what they had recovered on the island. As she and Stefano had looked through the contents of the chest, they found a great deal of coins and jewels.

'To appease my superiors in the Order, I suggest you give generously from the treasure to the Order. This would help pay for the former slaves stay in the hospital in Valletta, their repatriation to their homes and a little compensation for their families. Otherwise, these costs will be paid for by the Knights of Malta, though the Order would still gain the most from the prize ships and treasures onboard it' De Poincy advised.

'Apart from some you particularly want, give them the jewels. You have no knowledge in their value, so could be misled when trying to sell them. Keep the gold and silver coins that are easy for you to spend or invest. It should give you and Stefano a good start in a new life.'

'Thank you captain, I appreciate your advice,' Agata readily agreed. She thought for a moment, feeling quite teary. 'Please captain, I realise you want to find out who helped to arrange the attack on *San Giovanni*, but you will understand that my priority is to find out who has my youngest brother Mateo and rescue him. If it turns out to be the same person, then perhaps we can work together. Stefano said the pirate Amir gave Mateo to a fat man that looked European, least not like the other pirates and he talked in both our tongue and theirs. I will not be able to settle until I find my brother, and I will do whatever it takes to free him.'

De Poincy smiled at her bravery and nodded. He thought it would be wise to work together, especially as he could see Agata was determined. He considered Malta just the place to prepare Agata to enter a world she knew little about.

'Hopefully, we will arrive in Valletta early tomorrow morning and when we do, there will be much activity and reports to be made,' De Poincy told her, 'the sick, injured, corpses and treasures will leave, but I want you and Stefano to remain on board,' he advised her.

'In a day or so, a friend will come to collect you both. This friend will take you to his home, where I will visit you whenever I can.'

He gazed into her beautiful dark eyes and sweet face, holding her hand gently.

'Agata, you have many great qualities, but it is time for you to learn to be a lady of refinement. You have the wealth now and strength of character, but if you are to find your brother, you must be prepared for a very different world than you are used to. A world that is no less dangerous than the ones you have already experienced, but the dangers may not be so obvious. However, you have proved yourself a quick learner and you can start learning the skills you need to survive in that world, in Malta. My friends and I will help you, so that by the time you leave there, you will be able to pass as a rich lady. Then, together we will find this renegade and your brother.'

Content with De Poincy's plan, Agata sought out Bernardo to discuss what they would do while in Malta and ideas to find the man who had taken her brother. Although Bernardo was distracted helping the sick and learning from Brother Antonio, he listened carefully to all she had to say. He was very sympathetic towards her wish to find her younger brother, but he noticed the strong desire for revenge in her ambitions. This he struggled with but decided not to challenge her about it for now.

'It is good the captain and his friends can help you,' Bernardo agreed, 'however, I think it would be best for me to go with Brother Antonio and the sick to the great hospital in Valletta. There I will continue learning from the medical Order.' He felt sad to be parting but knew in his heart it was best. 'Once you are settled with De Poincy's friends you can send word where you are, and I will visit you there to discuss things with less distractions.'

He hoped by then, both his mind and hers would be clearer and not so dominated by the horrors they had witnessed. However, he recognised there had been some dramatic changes in Agata and this disturbed him, but he could not grasp what it was. She too recognised there was emotional space between them. She had killed three men at close range and although she felt justified in doing so, at the same time, she did not want to tell Bernardo about it and that troubled her.

Chapter 47

As expected, both vessels sailed into Valletta in the early morning of the next day and all on board who had not seen the Grand harbour before were astounded. The huge sandstone walls of the fortresses that surrounded the harbour practically glowed golden in the bright morning sun. Cannons bristled from almost every opening and flags proudly flew from the tops of towers.

San Giovanni sailed by the newly reconstructed Saint Elmo Fort. As they passed, Antonio pointed out to Bernardo the Sacra Infermeria behind it, where he worked and trained.

Sailing slowly passed many impressive buildings and fortifications, they continued through the great natural harbour to their berth in Birgu, where the knights where headquartered.

By the time they reached their berth, word had already spread about their arrival.

Crowds of locals gathered to greet loved ones and fellow knights paraded to honour returning heroes, news about their exploits already having been relayed by the xebec that arrived earlier. Reports of their sea battle had been expounded from grand halls to taverns and kitchens.

Agata and Stefano kept a low profile, as instructed, but were amazed by the bewildering extent of activity on deck and numbers of people coming and going. Sailors' families wanted to greet loved ones and officials wanted to talk to the Captain.

So many administrators wanted to register prize items, making the former neat decks looking more like a busy general goods marketplace.

Agata wanted to speak to Bernardo, before they were separated, but almost immediately upon mooring, hospitallers arrived on board and spoke to Antonio. They assessed the medical needs of the injured and arranged transportation to the Infermeria. They, along with Antonio and Bernardo were some of the first to leave *San Giovanni* late that morning. The Chaplain followed with corpses, either handed over to grieving families or the Order chaplaincy for swift burial.

Officials arrived to assess *El Jaida*, berthed behind *San Giovanni*, as a prize vessel, while others registered the treasures recovered from the island and *El Jaida*, including the former pirates now reduced to galley slaves. All these articles had value and shares of the prizes would be distributed between the Order and crew. Technically the knights had sworn an oath of poverty, giving all their worldly wealth to the Order. However, in practice the knights would benefit in other ways, and the crew were not restricted by any such oath.

Shipwrights also visited the vessel to speak to the sailing master before he had some well-earned rest with his family. They wanted to assess the repair needs to both vessels, then make arrangements for the work. With such a bounty in treasure, the Order could afford to look after these vessels. So, chandlers were keen to sell new cordage, blocks, gun powder, shot, small arms, as well as repair sails and planking damaged during the fighting. Everyone wanted to profit from this successful venture. As the stories of their sea battles and attacking the corsairs on Lampedusa spread, with much embellishment over jugs of wine, their reputation soared and interest in the vessel grew.

By mid-day, Captain De Poincy and his officers were exhausted, and his chief steward pushed everyone out of his aft cabin, so he could rest. The steward also took pity on Agata and let her help him take some food and drink to the captain. She was wanting to have a few private words with him, hoping he could reassure her that all was well, as she felt more lost than ever.

She helped him to take off his jacket and lifting his shirt, examined his wounds to see they were still healing. His steward poured some wine and laid out a light lunch. He was grateful and although in a positive mood, exhausted by the frenzy of questions and congratulations. He was also drained by the heat that was building away from the cooling sea breezes.

'Soon a carriage will arrive to take me to my quarters ashore. It will be cooler there and I will rest, clean up and then report to my Bali…head of my langue, this evening,'

De Poincy explained.

'Tomorrow night, Grand Master Wignacourt has invited me to dine with him and he will be expecting a full report by then,' he sighed, unimpressed by the honour extended to him. Agata smiled sweetly and tried to show she was happy for him, though mostly confused by all that was going on.

'However, I have already sent a message to my dear friend, Baron Castelletti di Marsa. He is the retired Capitano Della Verga (Captain of the Rod) once only second to the Grand Master.' He continued enthusiastically, but Agata had really no idea what he was talking about.

'It is my intentions to speak to this old gentleman as soon as possible and ask him and his dear wife to take you and Stefano into their home. They have no surviving children, and I am sure will make good temporary guardians for you both. From them, you can learn to be a lady of refinement. You can afford to purchase all the trappings that entails, but you need guidance.'

He finished and held her hand protectively, kind gentle concern in his eyes, despite his swashbuckling reputation.

'Whatever you say, sir, I know you mean the best for us,' Agata replied, 'but it sounds as if you are asking much from some important people.'

'Perhaps,' De Poincy reassured her, 'but I know them well and the softness of their heart. They have lost many children in infancy. Then two years ago, they lost their precious daughter to a fever, shortly after their twelve-year-old son in a riding accident. That marked the end of their family line. To help you two, I think would be a blessing for them.'

Agata could see how tired De Poincy was, so thanked him and left so he could rest before his carriage arrived. It was hot and humid in the aft cabin, so she went up onto the quarter deck were Stefano was helping the sailors erect awnings to create a shade. She stood near the aft railings, to catch a cooling breeze and saw the former pirates being taken off *El Jaida* in chains. 'How different life would have been for her if they had succeeded,' she thought. This sent a shiver down her sweat-soaked spine. She looked over at Stefano, happy to be free and busying himself. She smiled as he turned to greet her and under her breath, she vowed to do whatever it took to rescue their youngest brother.

Chapter 48

Since leaving the Abbey, Bernardo had seen many amazing places, yet the first sight of the Sacra Infermeria's great ward astounded him. The cathedral size scale of the space and tidy, orderly arrangements were truly awe inspiring.

'It is about 465 pied du roi long and 33 pied du roi wide with 554 beds in rows down each side, though more can be added,' Antonio explained proudly. Everywhere was scrubbed clean and smelled fresh. Patients of every kind, no bar to faith or class, being looked after and fed from silver plates.

'Honouring each patient as if they were Christ himself, is the very essence of the Hospitallers creed,' Antonio explained.

Once they had handed over their patients, Brother Antonio was keen to show Bernardo around; especially the School of Anatomy attached to the Infermeria where he trained.

'Grand Master Cotoner established this school over 20 years ago, and it is one of the foremost in Christendom,' Antonio pronounced with great enthusiasm, as he pointed out details to Bernardo during their tour.

After an extensive look around, he was introduced to senior brothers who welcomed him and allocated quarters. Then, before vespers, Antonio introduced Bernardo to the luxury of a bath to clean himself thoroughly, in this case, a large wooden barrel, filled with hot water for him to soak in. He was also provided with a large bar of soap to clean himself and towel to dry; cleanliness being very important to the Hospitallers. He was given a fresh clean habit to wear, a hospitallers habit, but black like his Benedictine one.

After vespers, they had dinner with the rest of the hospitallers, who were of many different nationalities, some experienced medics and others still training. A major thing they all had in common was their enthusiasm for their calling to help the sick, alongside a fascination for the science of understanding how the human body worked and therefore how to mend it.

Bernardo was very impressed by what he saw and heard, which made him want to learn more. They all made him feel very welcome. With so many hospitallers, of different ages and backgrounds, coming and going, he did not feel like a stranger for long.

By Rosary that night, he was asking God if this was his true calling, but he was also haunted by his experiences and actions. Added to this was his passion for Agata, though he had not yet managed to separate his carnal desire from the pastoral concern he had for her.

Although he had already confessed to the Chaplain on board *San Giovanni,* he sought out a father confessor. He wanted to also look for advice from a mature brother on how to recognise to difference between compassion and desire. Saving life appealed to him so much more than taking it. Yet he realised that Agata's journey would inevitably lead to more killing. He was not sure how much he wanted to be part of that, despite his strong feelings for her.

In the meantime, Agata waited impatiently on-board *San Giovanna* with equally confused emotions and desires. Her feeling for Bernardo had been somewhat overtaken by her mothering instinct for Stefano. This was compounded by an overwhelming need to rescue Mateo and a barely hidden desire for revenge. She knew Bernardo would not approve of her willingness to kill those who threatened her, or her loved ones and she found herself carving his approval. It was almost as if she had to put her relationship with Bernardo aside until she had freed Mateo and sought retribution for the death of her brother, mother, and father.

Confused about what to do next, she decided to put her trust in De Poincy and his guidance. After all, she had little choice. However, she would be on her guard from now on.

Chapter 49

After his encounter with the Inquisition in Gela, Orlando travelled back to Palermo. There the Beati Paoli had smuggled William to a place of safety, while they mostly went to ground. With much less activity, the Inquisition enquiries had dried up, and they were convinced William had travelled to the south. Orlando wanted to maintain this deception.

Before travelling, though, he wrote to a dear friend and mentor, Signior Giuseppe Beniamino, in Genoa, appraising him of his suspicions and seeking his advice. He had already decided to visit Genoa and knew he would need Signior Beniamino's assistance.

Access to his network was going to be vital in finding information about these supposed generous Genoese traders. For speed, he initially sent this letter over land by courier to Messina, to be taken on the first passing vessel going to Genoa. However, he would not wait for a reply before taking a ship himself from Palermo once he had put things in order there.

'There is much intrigue in Genoa and in-fighting between the rich merchant families,' Beniamino had previously warned him, 'Genoa can be a dangerous place if you asked the wrong questions to the wrong people.' However, Orlando knew he could trust Giuseppe Beniamino. 'I am only tolerated as a count Jew and city administrator, as the Doge, who effectively rules Genoa, changes every two years,' Beniamino continued, 'The new Doge needs a steady, long-term city administrator that is not from one of the leading families to maintain balance and continuity.'

Beniamino had proved himself a brilliant and reliable administrator, who met the city's needs admirably. However, he had not always been in such favour, or even known by that name.

Originally known as Mordecai Ben Heli he came from a wealthy, Jewish trading family in Pisa. He had just graduated from Pisa university after reading civil law when his family came under persecution. This was probably brought on by jealous competitors, but Jews were often vulnerable to persecutions at the time. As he successfully defended his family in the courts, he too had his life threatened and his family decided to sell up and flee.

It was onboard Orlando's father's ship he first met Mordecai:

Pisa, July 1663

'Captain Orlando, I can't express my thanks too much for you helping me to surreptitiously leave Pisa,' Mordecai said from onboard Orlando's cargo vessel. 'My parents and extended family are of advancing years, with few surviving children between them. They no longer have the stomach for a fight, or another purge. So, we have re-organised most of their business affairs, selling much to Christian associates, while they have retired to their estates near Livorno.' He sipped the Sicilian wine the captain had given him, while the vessel gently rocked on its voyage to Genoa. He was quite shaken from the events of the previous few days. 'However, some vindictive people still seem determined to kill me, so we have agreed I should disappear.'

'Mordecai, or perhaps we should get used to calling you Giuseppe Beniamino, it is an honour to assist you,' Captain Orlando reassured, 'Your father has been a good friend for many years, most honest and loyal. This is more than I can say for many Christian merchants I have to deal with!' He topped up his wine goblet. 'You are what, twenty-six?'

Mordecai nodded in agreement, 'I have known you since you were sixteen. The same age as my son, Benedetto here,' pointing at the young man sitting in the corner of the captain's cabin. 'My son is now apprenticed to me, and I pray one day will be a captain of his own vessel.' He smiled proudly at his son. 'Genoa should be a good place for a fresh start. They are always looking for good administrators there, as their banking and trading empire is under much strain. It is also unlikely you will encounter any merchants or bankers from Pisa there…as the two cities do not get on!' Orlando chuckled, sarcastically.

During the passage, Benedetto, although ten years younger than Mordecai, struck up a firm friendship which was to continue throughout Benedetto di Orlando's career at sea.

Despite Mordecai's family's misfortunes in Pisa, their connections with the banking families of Italy was strong. This allowed the now Giuseppe Beniamino, to start again with a good position in a bank in Genoa.

Over the years, Signior Beniamino's reputation among the bankers in Genoa grew, eventually gaining the trust of the rival Grimaldi, Spinola and Pallavicino trading families.

From these powerful families, the Doges of Genoa were usually drawn. For continuity, they needed a reliable and trustworthy administrator to serve each Doge equally. They began to rely on Signior Beniamino, increasing his influence steadily.

So, it was to Signior Giuseppe Beniamino in Genoa that William the archer had taken, what would become Bernardo's inheritance. Signior Beniamino would deposit cash, investing where best, sort out ship or cargo ownership and transfer company shares from Signior Davide to his heir Mateo Boscogrande. There was few others they could trust after the sudden death of Signior Davide, and Mateo struggling to hold things together while in conflict with the Inquisition.

Two weeks after the pirate attack in Gela, Orlando arrived in Genoa and went straight to the home of Signior Beniamino. Orlando was confident of a warm welcome from this old friend.

He had not seen him for five years, since becoming the regional magistrate of the Palermo district. However, he was not sure what he would make of an accusation of treachery within the Genoese trading community, or indeed if he could help, though if he could not, Orlando was not sure who could. It was also time to update him on Bernardo and seek his guidance in securing Bernardo's inheritance. Signior Beniamino had been a close friend of Bernardo's maternal grandfather, during a period he was responsible for defending the city.

He knew these loyalties ran deep.

Chapter 50

It was mid-morning on the third day in Birgu, and the *San Giovanni* was a hive of activity.

Sails were going off to be repaired, new spans coming on board, and carpenters replacing damaged decking and railings. In the midst of the chaos, Agata and Stefano were surprised by the smartly uniformed page that called on board for them from an elegant carriage that pulled up on the congested quay.

Most of the jewels from the treasure chest had been handed over as the suggested donation to the Order. Agata and Stefano had sewn large pockets into the jackets that they had been given by the captain, into these they placed two heavy bags each of gold and silver coins. It was not all that discreet. However, they reasoned it was the best they could do and planned to hide the bags wherever they ended up. Apart from this, they had little to pack, and few left on board to say goodbye to. So, within minutes they were bumping along a dusty road towards Baron Castelletti's estate near the town of Marsa, not far inland from the Grand Harbour.

Agata and Stefan nervously held hands, alone in the carriage, while the page sat on top with the driver. They distracted themselves by peering out of the window at the myriad of sites they were passing. Initially though busy commercial streets, then crowded housing that thinned as they passed into the countryside. Finally, they reached the land owned by Baron Castelletti which was surrounded by vineyards that provided the principle income for the estate.

The villa was impressive. Built in the same distinct golden sandstone and local traditional practical block design seen elsewhere, but with some newer baroque additions.

They were greeted by numerous uniformed servants as they were ushered inside a cavernous ornate lobby. Waiting there were an older white-haired couple, upright in stature and elegantly dressed. Their gentle eyes looked as nervous at meeting them, as Agata and Stefano felt. The Baron tried to welcome them formally but felt awkward, as he looked at their appearance, especially Agata, dressed more like a boy than a girl.

Agata and Stefano were overawed by the grandeur of the place and humbled at being welcomed in but could do no more than stand and gape. They felt so out-of-place standing in the grand entrance of this fortress-like building. However, they could immediately see the wisdom of the thick stone wall design. The effects of the baking mid-day heat was markedly reduced in the cooler interior. There continued an embarrassing silence, as all tried to come to terms with the strange circumstances. Then eventually, addressing Agata particularly, the Baron hesitantly spoke up, 'Captain De Poincy tells us he owes you his life and that you are a remarkable young lady…'

Agata blushed and did not know how to reply, so another silence continued the awkwardness. Finally, the Baroness walked towards the two siblings, standing close together.

'It is clear you both have been through much, and we will all…' she said, looking around at her husband and servants, '…try our best to make you as comfortable as possible during your stay with us.'

She smiled and Agata could feel the genuine warmth in her words.

'Louisa,' the Baroness said to a proud looking older lady, in a long charcoal grey coloured dress, styled almost like a nun but with keys attached to a rope belt, rather than a rosary, 'please show our guests to their rooms and introduce them to the household.'

At that, the Baron and Baroness, turned together towards one of many doors leading off the lobby and most of the servants dispersed in very purposeful ways. They were left with the grey lady, they now knew as Louisa, and a young woman and man, who looked in their late teens. They stood quietly, both dressed simply, but smartly, the woman in a similar long charcoal grey skirt and bodice, but with a sparkling while blouse and the man similarly in charcoal-coloured breaches, waistcoat, and clean white shirt.

'This is Maria, who will be looking after you, m' lady,' Louisa said, gesturing to the young women, who gave a short curtsy, 'and Carlo, who will be looking after your brother.'

Carlo nodded his head in way of a brief bow, his face remaining impassive.

'Please follow me to your rooms,' Louisa ordered and without hesitation turned and walked up a broad stone staircase in front of them. Agata and Stefano, followed her obediently, with Maria and Carlo taking up the rear of the little procession.

At a short landing with a large window, the broad staircase circled around to both the right and left. Finally, the stairs emerged onto another landing with corridors running in both directions, with numerous doors leading off the corridors. Away from the light of the stair window, the corridors looked dark. There were no candles lit, though there were many wall-mounted sconces running the length of the corridors. At this point, Agata was worried they would be split up. To her relief, Louisa took them both to the right and opened doors across the corridor from each other.

'This is your room,' Louisa announced, gesturing for Stefano to enter, 'it looks out to the front of the house.'

Stefano's mouth dropped open, and eyes bulged, as he entered an expansive, bright airy room. Tall windows faced towards the vineyards they had driven through on arrival.

There was a large four poster-bed and with fine drapes drawn back by thick ornate ropes. He looked around the room with amazement.

Louisa did not wait for a comment from Stefano, but left him with Carlo, patiently standing just by the open door. She took Agata across the corridor to the room opposite where Maria was already standing waiting.

Agata too was astounded by her beautiful spacious, bright room. It also had an enormous four-poster bed with pastel coloured silk drapes pulled back with ornate white cords. She stared out of the two large windows at a long, neat garden.

'There are beautiful views of the garden from here and it is a lovely quiet room, I hope you will be comfortable here,' Louisa said and breezed out of the room, leaving Agata and Maria alone.

Maria stood quietly by the door and watched Agata's every move as she explored the beautiful furnishings with her eyes, not daring to touch anything. Already convinced Louisa did not approve of them, Maria's silence and staring made Agata even more uncomfortable.

In between admiring fabrics and the collection of things on the dressing table, Agata glanced up at Maria. She wondered why she was still hanging around and how she was going to "look after her". Eventually Maria stepped forward and spoke.

'M' lady, I am here to make you as comfortable as possible and...' she hesitated, 'may I suggest I help you clean up and change into suitable clothes?'

Agata looked down at the clothes she was wearing, her dirty hands and bare feet, and comparing herself to this clean and neatly dressed maid, she felt rather ashamed. De Poincy had said they would help her become a refined lady and she realised she was far from being that. She would have to trust Maria as she knew she needed all the help she could get.

'Thank you, Maria,' Agata replied sheepishly, 'what shall we do first?' surrendering herself like an infant.

'Can I suggest you undress while I fetch water for this bath?' Maria said, pulling forward the largest copper basin Agata had ever seen, from the window side of the bed.

Agata's eyes grew at the sight, but she readily agreed, keen for Maria to leave her alone. As soon as Maria left the room, Agata looked around frantically for somewhere to hide the bags of coins. The bed drapes came down to the floor and ran along the back of the bed. She eased them back, not wanting to disturb anything and hid the bags behind the bed.

'That will have to do for now,' she thought.

Standing back, satisfied she could not see the bags, just as Maria returned with the first of many jugs of hot water.

Agata spent the rest of the afternoon with Maria, who eventually filled the bath for her to soak and wash her body in. She washed Agata's hair, scrubbed her nails and cut her toenails. Agata could not remember ever feeling as clean and once she overcame the initial embarrassment chatted to Maria comfortably. The two young women bonded quickly until Agata could see Maria was going to be more than just a maid. It seemed natural to Agata as they got to know each other so intimately and Maria seemed to be able to explain so much.

Once dry with bushed hair and a light cotton dressing gown on, Maria left Agata to rest in the afternoon heat, though Agata felt the room pleasantly cool, especially after the hot and humid ship in the noisy harbour. She was too excited to sleep anyway and had slept so much in the captain's cabin on board the *San Giovanni* over the last couple of days, she just lay there absorbing her surroundings.

As the sun started to sink lower in the sky, there was a knock on her door, and she opened it timidly. It was Stefano, also looking exceptionally clean. He was dressed in a new white cotton shirt, light blue silk breaches, white stockings and shiny black dainty-looking shoes topped with a brass buckle.

'Hey, look at me Sis,' he said prancing around her room, 'and I have a matching waistcoat and jacket to put on yet.'

Agata laughed, 'You look wonderful,' she said, 'Maria has not brought up my dress yet, apparently, it is still being made!'

'Being made for you...wow,' exclaimed Stefano, 'but it is all rather embarrassing...' looking serious for a moment.

'Carlo, tried to bath me like I was a baby,' he screwed his face up to look horrified, '...but he is not a bad fellow,' he continued, changing his expression quickly. 'Brought up near this estate, his father is a tenant farmer, and he has three older brothers and four sisters, but he did not want to work on the farm, so started training here as a pageboy five years ago. Being my valet and looking after me is apparently a promotion!' Stefano laughed.

'...but, washing me like mother used to do when I was younger, huh!'

Then he thought for a moment and became reflective.

'I miss mother...I miss our father and...' He started to cry but stopped himself.

'Sorry, that is no use, is it,' he confessed, wiping the tears away.

Agata reached out and put her arms around him and rubbed his thick, now clean, curly hair.

'I miss them too,' she said, feeling all the same emotions, but agreeing they had to be strong for each other. Then after a moment she said, 'Holy Mother, you even smell good.'

They laughed again, tears still in their eyes.

They were interrupted by a knock on the door and Maria entered. She stopped at the doorway and made her short bob of a curtsy to Stefano. He bowed back, then winked at Agata as he left the room smiling.

'He does not need to bow to me,' Maria said as she put a white petty coat, stockings, and a corset on the bed.

'Why not,' Agata asked, admiring the material of the garments, 'you curtsied to him?'

'M' lady, I am a maid in this household, proud to be one and happy with my position,'

Maria replied, 'we have heard something of your adventures—I am afraid you are the talk of the taverns and delivery boys.' She giggled. 'The household have also been told you and Master Stefano are wealthy now and to become a lady and gentleman. Carlo and I are honoured to help you, but if you are to pass for gentry you must learn your place and understand how others will act towards you.' She looked down at her feet, 'Sorry if I am being too forward, m' lady.'

Maria really liked Agata, seeing in her a genuine humility and no falsehood, so allowed her to think about what she had said, while she helped Agata to dress. Agata said nothing, feeling slightly embarrassed. On board *San Giovanni,* she had committed to do anything necessary to free her brother and seek justice, so was grateful for Maria's advice.

She realised how little she knew and contented herself for now to learn all she could. 'Not sure you really need this with your trim figure,' Maria said, as she tightened the corset around Agata's waist, 'but I guess you better get used to wearing one.'

There was a knock on the door and a middle-aged maid walked in caring a beautiful light blue silk dress over her arms. She stopped at the door and gave the now usual short bob of a curtsy.

'Good afternoon, m'lady, I am Anna, the seamstress,' the older maid said, introducing herself, 'and I have been adjusting this dress for you from the measurements Maria gave me. I hope it fits, but that is why we have given ourselves longer to dress you initially, so we can adjust things as necessary.'

The seamstress had a large chubby face and backside, but Agata thought she had kind eyes. She fussed over her, as she helped Maria with the dress, huffing and puffing.

'Your brother was easy to fit for, being almost the exact same size as the late young master, but you are smaller than the Baron's poor deceased daughter,' Anna explained as she breathlessly fastened up the dress at the back. '...at least when she last wore this dress.'

'Tell me about her,' Agata asked, while they pulled and tugged at the material.

'Oh well, m' lady, she was a little baby when I first started working here. They called her Katarina. A sweet, beautiful child, much loved, especially as the Baroness had lost so many other children,' Anna said, while kneeling on the floor adjusting a seem of the dress.

'As I recall, she was quite frail, and I remember her being sick quite a bit. However, the fever she got, took her quickly...it was awful,' Anna sighed, '...the

Baroness was in a terrible state, and I am sure the Baron too, only he does not show his emotions much, being a military man, I suppose.'

'I had not long arrived when she took sick...mmm, about two years ago, now,' Maria interjected, 'then young master Edwardu being thrown from his horse and breaking his neck...oh, both their surviving children dead within weeks of each other. The house was practically shut down for mourning for near a year!'

'How old were they?' Agata enquired.

'Lady Katarina had just turned 14 and her brother was only just 12...so sad!' Anna answered, 'You and master Stefano must be about the same age as they were?' Anna asked, fishing for information about the young siblings they were to look after like the Baron's own children.

'Stefano turned 13 in January, but I will be 16 on 5 August,' Agata replied.

Anna stood up to look at Agata in the dress.

'My...such a little thing, I would not have believed you are all grown up.' Then realised what she was saying when she caught Maria's eyes. 'Oh, sorry m' lady, I be speaking out of turn, but your 16th birthday is just under two months away!'

Agata thought for a moment, casting her mind back to Bernardo saying how he was losing track of the days before they reach Gela and telling her they would be there on 1 June. She had meant to tell him of her birthday then, but she thought it could wait until they were safely in Gela. Safe! That had become a rare state to be in. Things had turned out so differently to what she had expected. Though she was not sure what she had expected.

'M' lady if we take this dress off you, I will make a few more adjustments, then it should fit perfectly,' Anna said.

So, Agata allowed the dress to drop to the floor and stepped out of it.

'While Anna sews, let's do something with your hair, m' lady,' Maria suggested, gesturing Agata to the chair in front of the dressing table. She willingly surrendered to Maria's skills, sitting in front of a mirror on the dressing table and looking with curiosity into the ornate box on the table.

'What's in here,' Agata asked, lifting the lid carefully.

'Pins and clips for your hair, m' lady,' Maria explained.

Agata's eyes widened as she saw long metal shafts with jewels at one end. She took one out and examined it carefully, feeling the pointed end with her thumb.

'So, what do you do with these?' Agata asked Maria, holding the long shaft up.

'That secures something to your hair,' Maria explained, 'perhaps a hat, or hair decoration like feathers, bows, or just holding your hair up.'

Agata held onto the pin while Maria put her hair up, deep in thought.

'They come in many sizes and styles; some ladies have then made to particular designs just for them,' Maria continued.

'So, ladies of refinement can carry a concealed weapon easily in their hair,' Agata thought to herself. 'How useful that would be if she met the man who had her brother.' Then putting the thought out of her mind, she focused on the many new things she was learning.

Chapter 51

Although the sun was still well above the horizon on this warm summer evening, the tall buildings that crowded Strada Nova cast long shadows, darkening the cobbled street Orlando walked along. It had been several years since he was last in Genoa and nothing much seemed to have changed, except perhaps a greater feeling of tension in the atmosphere, reflected in the furtive looks from groups of young men loitering outside some of the dwellings. This was not a safe city to be walking alone at night in, but his business was highly confidential, so he had to risk it. For this reason, he wanted to get to Signior Beniamino's house before dark, concerned he would not recognise which building it was without light.

As it happened, Beniamino's house was distinctive by its modesty, compared with the opulence of the neighbouring palatial town houses. It's large black painted door was grand because of its size and simplicity, rather than being ostentatious At 5 feet 8 inches, he did not consider himself a short man, but this door was a good foot taller than him.

'Who were they expecting, giants?' he amused himself, 'Or maybe it was built with Bernardo and his father in mind? I wonder if Signior Beniamino knew many other men of that stature?'

He stepped up to the big brass knocker, lifted it and let it fall with a bang which reverberated down the cobbled street. He did it again, then once more for good measure, enjoying the sound echoing off the buildings. He felt like a little boy again and remembered visiting here as a teenager with his father.

The door opened slowly, and a frail looking servant stared at him though thickening cataracts. Holding up a three-branched silver candlestick, he squinted at him, as if that would help.

'Giacobbe, do you not remember me?' Orlando exclaimed, with a broad smile.

'Oh, Master Orlando, it that you?' the old servant's face did its best to smile, 'I do not hear that Sicilian twang very often these days.'

He opened the door wide and stepped to one side. Orlando entered the large black and white marble tiled hall, sparsely decorated, but with lots of wall mounted candles, giving off a flickering warm glow.

Giacobbe closed the door behind him, with a bang, and walked beside Orlando across the hall, the marble echoing with their footsteps, towards a double door opposite.

'He is in his study as usual, and as I remember now, expecting you.' Giacobbe mumbled through almost toothless gums. Orlando knew where he was going and did not wait for the old servant to keep up.

He paused at the study door and knocked. 'Venire,' was the only reply from within.

Orlando carefully turned the polished brass handle and opened the door, peering inside a surprisingly, well-lit room with lamps on tables, as well as hanging from wall brackets and the ceiling. Sitting at a paper-covered desk, studying a document through glasses he held with thick wooden frames, Signior Beniamino was concentrating on what he was reading.

Orlando stood quietly by the door and looked carefully at his old friend. His hair was thinning and what was left was greyer. Yet, he still exuded that same intensity that Orlando remembered. Looking up from the page, he smiled when he saw Orlando. He immediately put the documents down and rose from his chair to greet Orlando, embracing him warmly.

'Oh, it is good to see you again, Benedetto,' Beniamino said, kissing Orlando on both cheeks.

'It has been too long. I miss my Sicilian friends. Please sit,' he said, motioning towards two comfortable looking high-backed chairs by an unlit fireplace.

'Your letter brought back memories of Mateo di Boscogrande and his father Roberto, one of the greatest Conditierre this city has ever had.' Beniamino recollected, sitting back in his chair.

'However, the world has little need of brave Cavaliere anymore when anyone with a musket or cannon can slay them,' he concluded and sighed deeply. 'Now I look forward to meeting Roberto's grandson, at last.'

'Who would have known, his grandson would look so like him and his son in stature, yet follow such a different vocation?' Orlando reflected. 'He still has much to learn about his family's history and has an innocence about him.'

Beniamino nodded, but sat quietly for a moment thinking, then rose to his feet and went over to his desk. He groaned as he stooped down and picked up an old box from the floor underneath his desk, then carried it to Orlando, placing it on his lap.

'This was brought to me many years ago, by Roberto di Boscogrande,' he explained, 'your letter has had me thinking about what we should tell Bernardo and reminded me of a mystery I have yet to solve.'

'Not for the first time, Roberto had been fighting in France, and was slowly realising the art of war he knew was changing and his time was passing,' Beniamino recalled as he sat back in his chair.

'Roberto came to me with this box full of gold ducats and asked me to invest the money for him,' pointing at the carved wooden box. 'He said he wanted to prepare for retirement and contemplated retreating to his farmland in the Sicani Hills of Sicily.' The old man laughed as he recalled the conversation.

'I could not envisage Cavaliere Roberto di Boscogrande becoming a farmer, but agreed it was wise to save for his old age if he were to have one.'

Beniamino sighed as he continued, 'Alas, he did not live much longer and the next Boscogrande I saw was Mateo looking to collect some inheritance to fund his latest venture.' Orlando looked at the old box puzzled and was about to ask a question…

'Roberto had little interest in the box, you see,' Beniamino continued, 'he said he found it in the tent of a knight that had been attacked while resting. The tent was dishevelled as if the attackers had looked through it for valuables. The box was laying open and empty on the ground and Roberto took it as a useful receptacle, little else.'

Orlando looked carefully at the small chest. As long as his forearm and broader than his palm. He rubbed his hands over the neat carvings on top of the box.

'The wood is Cedar and very old,' Beniamino postulated, 'the engravings look to me as two Cherubim facing each other, wings outstretched over the top of a chest as the Ark of the Covenant is described in the Torah, so it is most likely Jewish in origin.'

'This is Amharic,' he said, leaning over to point out the inscription.

'It is mostly because of those words that I kept a hold of it all these years,' he concluded.

'So, what does it mean?' Orlando asked the old banker, intrigued.

'*For lack for fruit, the tree was cursed,*' he replied.

He leaned back in his chair, watching the younger man's reactions. Orlando continued to look puzzled.

'My guess is,' Beniamino surmised, 'it is a reference to a story in your Gospel of Luke where Jesus of Nazareth curses a fig tree for not having any fruit.'

The old banker was showing himself to be so much better read than Orlando.

'But what is more intriguing to me is the brand, burned into the inside of the lid, which I would guess was done later.'

Orlando lifted the lid and looked at a slightly faded symbol.

'It looks like a cup with a cross on it,' he exclaimed in an uncertain tone.

'Yes, a Holy Grail symbol, I believe, the Knights Templar used similar symbols,' Beniamino asserted.

'Did it come with anything else, that might shed some light of its origins?' Orlando inquired.

'Apart from the ducats, the only other thing Roberto left that visit, was a bejewelled dagger, which I would suggest was for ceremonial use, looking at the delicate design,' Beniamino replied, 'this I gave to Mateo, along with a bag of gold ducats.'

The pair sat quietly for a moment, contemplating the meaning of the words engraved on the box. Then Orlando's mind switched back to more present-day mysteries.

'Did you manage to consider the possible identity of the "generous" Genoese traders I wrote to you about, or how we could find out who they might be?' Orlando asked.

'That might not be such a great mystery.' Beniamino suggested. 'The Barbary pirates have been attacking shipping and raiding coastal communities for hundreds of years.

It is likely they have been informed that the Hapsburgs pay off their loans from the Genoese banks in gold and silver ducats at regular intervals and that these payments come by ship from Spain. If the pirates knew when the ships from Spain where making their deliveries, they could intercept them and make a large profit. Anyone in an alliance with these pirates, sharing information, would also make a good profit and do a great deal of damage to Spain and Genoa. Therefore, the question is, who would gain the most from bringing pain to Spain and Genoa? However, the Knights of Malta impede the pirates control of these seas, so an attack on them is logical preparation for further interception of ship between Spain and Genoa.'

Clearly, Beniamino had thought this through, Orlando reasoned to himself.

'There is much tension between the leading families here in Genoa, each trying to gain an advantage over the other. However, it is highly unlikely they would do anything to endanger the steady flow of funds from Spain, which they all rely on. It would not just be a rival that would suffer, but all of Genoa,' Beniamino assured.

'So, the people that might dare have an alliance with the pirates are probably not member of the Genoese trading families. Yet, they would still have to have spies in ports, reporting significant movements, and information about the dates for shipments from Spain to Genoa, knowing which shipments carried the loan repayments. They would also want to damage Spain, or Genoa, and possibly the relationship between the two. Additionally, they probably would not suffer much personally from the pirates stealing the money, rather gain from the bribes the pirates gave them for the information and approve of the damage to Genoa generally,' Orlando reasoned out loud.

'Exactly,' Beniamino agreed, nodding, as if coaching a student.

'But who would fit that description? Agents of France, the Turks?' Orlando asked.

'Damaging Spain or Genoa would certainly be something both would like to see happen. However, they would have trouble getting the information about the shipments without drawing too much attention to themselves. So there has to be an intermediary that would profit from such politics,' Beniamino insisted. 'There is one particular group that fits the profile we have discussed, and they have been agitating for some time now.'

Beniamino paused, and Orlando leaned towards him anticipating a revelation.

'For the last few years, Corsica has been attempting to break away from Genoese rule. Some of them would rather ally with France than with Genoa, and in this city, we have Corsican traders that move in high circles,' Beniamino asserted. 'It is to them we need to look for the men that are partnering with the corsairs.' Orlando nodded but looked grave.

'Will you help us, Giuseppe,' Orlando pleaded. Signior Beniamino nodded, but not enthusiastically. Orlando was relieved and immediately continued.

'There is one other, possibly connected situation,' Orlando continued, relieved to have help and not sure how to explain about Agata's brother. He took a deep breath.

'During a pirate raid of Sicily, among others, three young boys were taken. One has just been rescued and our mutual friend Captain De Poincy, back in Malta, has just written to me, including his story among other news. It appears the youngest of the three was given to a European helping the pirates in some way, and the middle boy died while trying to protect his brother. We received this report from the older one after being rescued. The boy describes a fat man, that looks European, but speaks Arabic and I wonder if he could be connected to the men we are looking for?'

Signior Beniamino sat for a moment in silence, clearly disturbed by what he had heard, though he knew pirate raids where all too common in the south.

'There is a rather rotund merchant that has a house here—maybe Corsican, I am not sure—who has a shadowy reputation. A few days ago, I saw him leaving the house of one of our premier families and he had what looked like a white page boy with him. As I have never had any dealing with the fellow myself, I could be pointing a finger erroneously. However, I will give you his name and you can keep an eye out for him.' Signior Beniamino paused and looked sternly at Orlando.

'Look for the more hidden trading that goes on in this city. Among those traders you may find the answers you are looking for. However, your investigations must be discreet, or you may not live long enough to find out anything useful,' Beniamino warned.

'Trust no-one. There are secrets that powerful people will go to great lengths to keep secret. Watch, listen and avoid drawing attention to yourself. I will help where I can.' Beniamino continued, 'For starters, I will introduce you to one of my men who keeps a discreet eye on the comings and goings in the city for me. He will be able to help you watch without being noticed.'

'Thank you so much, this is a great help,' Orlando acknowledged with relief. 'I will write to Captain De Poincy tonight to update him, and tomorrow I will pass the letter into the hands of a south-going ship master myself, and he will get a message to Bernardo.'

Chapter 52

'Antonio, I have been invited to a Ball in honour of Mademoiselle Agata's 16th birthday at Baron Castellietti di Marsa's Manor,' Bernardo called out excitedly. Antonio smiled at his young friend, as Bernardo came over to him waving the invitation.

'I have never been to a ball, what do you do there?'

'Well, you eat, dance, sometimes are entertained and talk to other guests,' Antonio explained, watching a worried look form on Bernardo's face.

Talking to strangers and dancing! This was not something Bernardo felt comfortable with or knew much about. Knowing his friend, Antonio laughed at him.

'Don't worry, you will enjoy it and get to see Agata.' That cheered Bernardo.

'I wonder if Captain De Poincy will be invited?' he thought out loud.

'I would be surprised if he was not, as he is both a friend of the Castellietti's and Agata,' Antonio reassured, 'but come with me and ask him. I have not seen him for a few days and would like to hear what his plans are, so will call on him straight after mass tomorrow. I will send him a note to let him know we will visit.'

'Are his wounds completely healed?' Bernardo asked.

'Pretty much, they were not deep, his leather jacket helping with that. It was a long scar though, which is why it caused him so much pain at the time and why there was so much blood loss. That and the pain made him feel weak and dizzy, but as we managed to stop the blood flow on the island he was not in much danger. Also, the stitches we put in on board *San Giovanni* helped speed the healing process and the rest he had, restored his strength.'

Antonio continued, 'I visited him every few days to change his bandage and check for infections, but there have been no problems and he healed rapidly. The man is as strong as an ox, and I have patched him up from far worse injuries.' Antonio laughed, 'if anything he is just bored now.'

Bernardo looked forward to seeing both Captain De Poincy and Agata again. He went to bed that evening in a very good mood, even if slightly concerned about how he would cope with being at a fancy ball. More than that, he realised how much he had missed Agata, despite trying to submerge himself in learning about anatomy and caring for the sick.

The next morning, Captain De Poincy was pleased to see Antonio and Bernardo when they called at his quarters among the other French knights and greeted them warmly.

'How are you feeling today, Captain?' Antonio asked as they greeted each other.

'Completely well and ready for sea duties as I have told my Bali. Thank you for your concern, brother, I hope you will be available for our next adventure?' he said cheerfully.

'I will ask my superiors, but I would be honoured to serve you,' Antonio replied enthusiastically. 'Where are you heading this time and is there room for my trainee here?' he continued, gesturing towards Bernardo.

As usual, Bernardo had remained silent, overawed by the presence of the larger-than-life Captain De Poincy, who now looked at him with concern.

'As it happens, I was going to come and see you Bernardo and discuss a letter I have received,' De Poincy said. 'It arrived from Genoa yesterday, from Captain Orlando. He has been busy investigating treachery since we sailed,' he continued, grabbing Bernardo's attention. 'He discovered that two merchants paid for my officer's welcome dinner and crew's drinks in the Gela taverns, BEFORE *San Giovanni* even arrived, yet did not wait to say hello. He suspects they wanted our ship deserted that night. The attacks purpose was probably to capture the vessel but was thwarted unexpectedly by the Inquisition guards waiting for you.'

Bernardo stared at De Poincy, wide eyed with his mouth open. A bad habit.

'Orlando also says, as part of his investigations, now supported by the Inquisition, he has visited Genoa to try to track down these mysterious, *generous* merchants. He thinks he has a lead,' De Poincy continued. 'What he has uncovered might be Corsican bankers, traders, or both, in league with pirates to intercept Spanish ships and help with a lucrative trade in slaves. They may be doing this for political gain, as well as financial.'

'Spanish ships?' Bernardo queried. Not seeing the connection.

'The Hapsburgs have borrowed heavily from Genoese banks to fund their wars and empire building. They repay these loans with the vast amount of gold and silver flowing from their new territories in the Americas,' De Poincy explained. 'Treasury ships sail from Spanish ports to Genoa on a schedule which is supposed to be a secret. However, if their route and timing were known in advance, pirates could be waiting to intercept them. Stealing this gold and silver would make healthy profits and damage the Spanish economy.'

He had Antonio's full attention now too.

'Are you thinking of getting involved with this…sailing to Genoa and does the Order know this?' Antonio asked.

'Well…Orlando has suggested we are already part of what is going on, even if unsuspectingly,' De Poincy clarified. 'The Order does know a little of this and of course, wants the piracy stopped. Furthermore, Orlando suggests it would be in your personal interest, Bernardo, to meet him in Genoa, as apparently, you have an inheritance to claim.'

Bernardo did not know what to say. He thought about his old mentor and his pilgrimage to Rome with his Gospel commentaries, and what William the Archer said to him about his father and his inheritance, "deposited with bankers in Genoa". Recently, he had put all this out of his mind. It was so jumbled up with the guilt he felt for the violence that had occurred. Now it all seemed mixed up in much larger dynamics that he felt sure was going to lead to more violence. There was a heavyweight in his stomach as he tried to reach a decision.

'Will you take the *San Giovanni* to Genoa soon?' Bernardo asked.

'Yes, I have suggested we sail soon to join Orlando,' De Poincy confirmed, 'my superiors are considering it as we speak.'

'Then I would ask your permission to join you for this passage and continue training with Brother Antonio,' Bernardo requested. 'Although I am unclear where my destiny lies, I know I have to face up to the past before I can clearly see a way forward.'

De Poincy stood up, with a wide smile on his face and clapped Bernardo on his broad shoulders.

'It will be great to have you with us and cheer up, we will soon see Agata again,' he chirped, 'My…a 16th birthday ball for her at a grand estate. How things have changed.'

He laughed, but Bernardo's returned smile was just for show, as he had a bad feeling about the news and how things could turn out.

Chapter 53

Captain De Poincy took Bernardo to the ball in his carriage to help him feel more comfortable. He would personally introduce him to the Baron and Baroness who would be intrigued to meet him. He knew he would be apprehensive meeting so many strangers and seeing Agata again. Typically, Bernardo remained quiet during the journey, and arriving at the Manor outwardly seemed unimpressed by its grandeur.

As they entered the ballroom, at the rear, ground floor of the Manor, it was already crowded and noisy. They paused to look around at the colourfully dressed guests, especially the ladies in flowing ball gowns. Soon a beautiful young lady in a carefully fitted, emerald coloured silk dress came gliding towards them. Agata had been eagerly looking out for them, but at first, they did not recognise her. She was clean, with her hair up and skin like a marble statue.

'Mademoiselle Agata,' De Poincy exclaimed when he recognised her, bowing formally.

She extended her hand to him, as she had been taught, and he kissed it gently.

'You look beautiful and even your skin seems to be different,' De Poincy complimented.

'Thank you, Monsieur,' she replied coyly with a small smile, 'but truthfully my skin is covered with powder, and I have not been allowed out in the sun since I arrived.'

'Apparently...' Agata said, rolling her eyes, '...my skin was too tanned! So, my days are filled with dress fittings, instructions on eating properly, dance and singing lessons, while avoiding the sun!'

Agata gushed and giggled. Then, becoming serious, she glanced over at Bernardo, hovering behind the captain.

'Hello Bernardo,' she said, putting out her daintily hand, palm down.

'He...ll...o, Aga...ta,' he stuttered and took her hand, but just stared at it, rather self-consciously.

She waited patiently for a little while, feeling quite emotional at seeing Bernardo again. Then, as it became clear he was not going to kiss her hand, she slowly withdrew it and focused her attention back on Captain De Poincy. At that moment, the music changed to something Agata recognised from her lessons and guests started to be lined up with partners to dance.

'Will you dance with me, Captain?' she asked boldly, 'I can show off what I have learned.'

De Poincy flashed her a broad smile. 'It would be an honour, Mademoiselle,' he replied, bowing to her, and taking her outstretched hand.

Meanwhile Bernardo stood frozen to the spot, awestruck by how different Agata looked, embarrassed by his inability to speak to her and the realisation that he knew nothing about the etiquette of such occasions.

He stared at her gracefully gliding across the dance floor in step with the music, enchanted by the spectacle of the whole scene and captivated by her beauty. Captain De Poincy and the other gentlemen lined-up opposite the ladies, stepping aside in unison, as the ladies circled them. However, he was not the only one in the room to be enchanted by Agata.

Several of the guests, especially the younger men, watched her carefully. Intrigued that this delicate flower was also the girl who, they were told, had killed the pirate leader. The Baron and Baroness basked in her radiance, they smiled proudly, delighting in her transformation and the attention she was receiving.

As the dance ended, De Poincy and the other gentlemen bowed to the ladies and took their hands to leave the dance floor. At that cue, several young men approached Agata to partner with her on the next dance. As De Poincy prepared to move out of the way, he leaned in closely to her.

'When you want some air, I have some news from Captain Orlando to share with you,' he whispered in her ear.

Her preference would have been to leave with De Poincy right away to hear the news.

However, she was aware how important it was, especially to her hosts, that she played the part fully tonight. She was determined she would not let them down. If she could pull this performance off, she knew she was ready to mix in high society and look for her brother.

So, without changing her expression, she nodded to De Poincy her agreement, then smiled at a handsome young man in a decorative uniform, accepting him as her next dance partner. De Poincy went off to comfort

Bernardo, who he knew would be feeling awkward on his own and to introduce him to their hosts.

The Baron and Baroness were intrigued to meet the young Benedictine they had heard so much about. They were all, however, rather distracted, keeping an eye on Agata, dazzlingly everyone in the room. Polite conversation ensued, but with no specific direction.

As the evening continued, wine flowed, and music filled the air. The guests, including Bernardo became more relaxed, all entertained by the dancing beauties. Nevertheless, after a couple of hours Bernardo needed some air and solitude, so he wandered out through the open rear, window-like doors and down some stairs into the garden. There, he looked up to the star covered sky and marvelled at its majesty.

Shortly afterwards, Captain De Poincy, noticing Agata fanning herself after a particularly vigorous dance, caught her eye, and turned towards the same rear doors Bernardo had left through. Beyond these doors was a wide porch, from which stone stairs led down to the formal gardens. Several guests were already refreshing themselves on the porch and enjoying the cooler evening air. He stood patiently on the porch, like Bernardo, admiring the multitude of stars, in the clear sky; his mariner's eye recognising many of the prominent constellations.

A few minutes later, Agata appeared beside him. Breathing deeply of the fresh air, she enjoyed the gentle cooling breeze bringing floral scents from the garden. They stood for a few minutes in silence, while most of the other guests on the porch returned to the ballroom.

'You look like you were born to this,' De Poincy remarked, continuing to stare at the stars and sip a glass of wine he had been nursing for some time.

'It is good to hear you think so, my tutors will be so pleased, but we both know it is a performance and with a specific purpose,' Agata replied in a very level tone, as she turned to face him. 'You said you received a letter?' she probed, dismissing pleasantries.

'Yes, just the other day I received a reply to the letter I sent to Captain Orlando when we arrived in Malta,' De Poincy explained. 'Two, generous merchants had visited the taverns of Gela, seemingly aware that the *San Giovanni* was just about to arrive. They paid for food and drink for my knights, ship's officers, and crew to "have a good time on their first night", thereby almost guaranteeing the vessel would be near empty that night.'

Agata listened intently but made no comment.

'Orlando made some enquiries and has travelled to Genoa to seek advice from an old friend,' De Poincy continued. 'His suspicions are that some Corsican nationals, who are displeased at Genoese rule of Corsica, perhaps working for Genoese trading houses, or at least, pretending to, are in league with the pirates. These men apparently come and go from Genoa regularly, so he has remained there in an attempt to find them. One of these Corsicans could be the one who has your brother,' he concluded.

'Then we must go to Genoa immediately,' Agata affirmed insistently, upon which De Poincy gave a slight smile.

'I thought you might say that,' he replied, 'so I have already asked permission to take *San Giovanni* to Genoa, with the aim of tracking down these conspirators. However, we must think through how we flush them out without first raising suspicions.'

As De Poincy finished, Bernardo came up the stairs from the garden.

'Suspicions about what?' he asked.

'Oh, Bernardo, you will come with us to Genoa, won't you?' Agata pleaded, grabbing Bernardo's arm, and pulling him close to her.

Bernardo was rather taken by surprise at Agata's unexpected show of affection. She had not talked to him since their initial, embarrassing greeting. He knew he should say something, but was unclear of his feelings about the situation, so typically remained silent.

'Of course, he will come with us,' De Poincy confirmed, interrupting the awkward moment. 'He has his own business in Genoa. As it happens, our friend that is advising Orlando on the hunt for the conspirators, is also the trusted banker that is looking after Bernardo's inheritance, and he has papers of his father's that he wants to discuss with him.'

Bernardo stood stiffly, uncomfortable about what could unfold when they went to Genoa. Agata did not let his arm go, suddenly feeling vulnerable and finding comfort in having him close.

Some sort of announcement was being made in the ballroom which attracted their attention. Agata collected her composure and returned to the guests with a smile on her face.

'She certainly has become a good actress,' De Poincy whispered.

Bernardo found he was thinking much the same. However, whereas De Poincy regarded the acting as admirable, Bernardo wasn't so sure he liked it. Duplicity was not something he found virtuous.

Chapter 54

As the ball came to an end, Agata thanked the Baron and Baroness profusely, while they joined forces to say goodnight to the departing guests. Then, declaring herself over tired, she excused herself and went up to her room. It had been a magical evening, that any young girl would be enthralled with. Yet, her mind was already turning to thoughts of Genoa and what they would encounter there.

Entering her room, she placed the fan she had clasped all evening on the dressing table and started to take off the dress she had worn. A movement in the corner of the room caught her eye. She realised it was Maria, uncurling from a comfortable, highbacked chair.

'Sorry m' lady, I waited for you to return, but fell asleep,' she sheepishly explained.

'You should not have stayed up, Maria, I can manage,' Agata gently reassured.

'Unlikely, m' lady, you are practically sewn into that dress and corset,' Maria insisted, 'and besides, it is my job to dress and undress you,' as she began unfastening the back of Agata's dress, her loyalty reassuring Agata more than she expected.

With her dress and corset removed, Agata sat at the dressing table looking at herself in the mirror thoughtfully. Maria unfastened her hair and started to brush it, placing the two hair pins, that had been used to hold her long hair up on the dressing table. They were fashioned in the shape of miniature daggers with bejewelled hilts. Agata had asked Stefano to commission them especially, as a birthday present. Interlocked, these hair pins held in place the lace, that in turn helped hold her hair up, but once removed, became two relatively small but extremely sharp weapons.

Agata looked down from the mirror and stared at these two dagger hair pins, contemplating how she could use them against the man who held captive her brother. Then looking up at the mirror again, she caught sight of the delicate, black beaded rosary. The Baroness had given these to her to help with her prayers. She remembered how she had thought of Bernardo when she had received them. She used them as she joined the Baroness at daily mass in their small private chapel. These two gifts she regarded as precious. Yet they represented two very different aspects of her present life and aspirations which did not seem to be compatible, to seek forgiveness and grow closer to God, or seek revenge.

She realised Maria was asking her about the ball and tried to switch her thoughts over to the present but found it hard. Reaching over her shoulder, she took Maria's hand which stopped her chatter. They looked in each other's eyes via the mirror.

'Dear Maria,' Agata said with much sadness in her voice, 'you have served me so patiently and taught me so much, I know tonight would not have been such a success without your help.' Both girls felt they were about to cry.

'The time has come for me to leave and sail for Genoa, as I knew I would sometime,' Agata continued, 'but I will miss you very much.'

Maria looked shocked. 'But m' lady, you can't go to Genoa on your own,' she pleaded.

'Of course, I will not be on my own,' Agata reassured, 'Stefano and Bernardo will come with me. Captain De Poincy will take us in his ship, and we have people waiting to help us there.'

'No,' Maria insisted, 'a fine lady can't travel with just men. You need to have a female companion or a maid,' Maria explained.

Agata looked at Maria with much affection as she put her long hair into a ponytail in preparations for going to bed.

'How will you dress yourself or do your hair?' Maria continued, 'No, I will ask the Baroness to let me go with you, I am sure she will agree you need looking after and bringing back safely.'

Agata realised with pleasure, just how protective Maria was and loved her for it. She could also see the wisdom of her assertion. So, smiling contentedly, she agreed to speak to the Baroness about it.

It was the Baroness's custom to partake in morning prayers in her private chapel each day before breakfast. Agata joined her, as did Stefano and the Baron, though they had often already had breakfast, and then they would dash off to the business of running the estate right afterwards, before the heat of the day built up.

The morning after the ball, Agata grabbed Stefano as they left the chapel. She was keen to let him know about the communications from Orlando and the plan to sail to Genoa.

'Please talk to the Baron about this as soon as you can,' Agata urged him, 'you have become close over these weeks, and I will talk to the Baroness.' Stefano agreed.

The Baron had been treating Stefano like an apprentice, teaching him about running the estate and bulk wine production. Stefano's enthusiasm to learn from the Baron and his estate manager pleased them both, as he was developing into a fine young man.

Agata knew it was going to be difficult for the Baroness to hear she had to leave, and she wanted to tell her as gently as possible. After breakfast, she asked the Baroness if they could walk together in the garden, while it was still cool. With parasols to protect their skin from the sun, they walked in the garden arm-in-arm, enjoying the scents from the many flowers.

'Thank you for the wonderful birthday party last night,' Agata began, 'it was a magical night, and we are so blessed to have you embrace us as you do.'

The Baroness smiled, pleased at how well the night had gone. It had been a long time since they hosted a ball and it had been a healing process for her. However, she did not know how to express that to anyone.

'You know how I told you about my younger brothers?' Agata asked, 'Especially our desire to find the youngest one, Mateo, who was taken by the European helping the pirates?'

The Baroness nodded, her face turning grave as they walked along slowly.

'Last night Captain De Poincy told me of a letter that has arrived from a friend, informing us of a clue in Genoa to the man who has Mateo. With the help of our friends, we would like to travel to Genoa and look for my brother with the hope of freeing him.'

Agata paused, a rush of emotion coming over her. She stopped, turned towards the Baroness, and took both her hands. Part of her did not want to leave this loving surrogate mother, though she felt compelled to and another part of her was ashamed to reveal the revenge which was boiling in her heart. How much should she tell her?

'Of course, you must look for your brother,' the Baroness responded, looking Agata in the eyes. She smiled, though she looked like she was going to cry.

'We will pretend to be looking to invest our inheritance with bankers there, while looking around, so we do not draw attention to ourselves,' Agata continued. 'It would help me a great deal if Maria could accompany me and continue to serve as my maid...I believe it would be expected to have a maid.'

'Yes, of course, a lady should not travel without her maid and Maria would look after you well,' the Baroness replied enthusiastically, 'and she can help bring you all back safely.'

Agata did not say anything about returning but embraced the Baroness and cried a little, feeling mixed emotions bubbling up inside of her. She found it hard to think about the future beyond rescuing Mateo. It was as if her mind struggled to consider the possibility of not managing to rescue Mateo. However, as that was too much for her to emotionally handle, she blocked out any such thoughts. It was a tormenting dichotomy which made thinking of the future impossible.

Meanwhile, Stefano was trying to explain to the Baron why he had to leave for Genoa. Like Agata, he found it difficult, as he was so grateful for the way the Baron had embraced him.

He had learned so much, in a short period and the activity had helped him to push his concerns for Mateo out of his immediate thoughts. This eased the all-consuming worry for his brother that had plagued him for the last two months.

The Baron seemed most understanding, immediately saying, 'Of course,' when he explained he wanted to free his brother. 'When will you leave?' the ever-practical Baron asked.

'Soon, I believe...Captain De Poincy gave Agata the impression he was preparing the *San Giovanni* already.'

'Then go now and start making whatever preparations you have to. We pray God will guide you to your brother and aid his release.' From the Baron, this sounded like an order, so Stefano turned and left immediately, relieved to have kept the conversation short with seemingly little awkwardness between them.

Stefano mounted the black mare the Baron had given him to travel around the estate.

He had been taking riding lessons and picked it up very quickly, now enjoying riding by himself the most. He had a fencing lesson later that day and he wanted to say goodbye to his fencing instructor. Francesco Antonio Marcelli had taught him much more than using a sword. A master swordsman of some renown, he had guided Stefano on matters of honour and controlling his emotions. His discussions with Marcelli, with whom he had shared the whole story of the pirate attack and aftermath, were quite philosophical.

'Justice is honourable, but revenge is not necessarily the same thing. Do not let it rule your heart,' Marcelli would say.

As well as fencing technique, Marcelli had guided his very willing and quick learning pupil to observe his opponent carefully, keeping his temper in check, no matter how provoked and his nerve when intimidated. During his almost daily lessons with Marcelli, Stefano had soaked up skills like a sponge. He had a natural control over his body, excellent spatial awareness, and a keen, quick eye. Marcelli thought the boy was the best student he had ever had and wished he had started with him when he was younger.

'Master Marcelli, we have some news from our friends that may lead us to Mateo,'

Stefano excitedly explained as soon as he saw the fencing master. 'Agata and I will sail to Genoa soon and under the guise of investing our inheritance with bankers there, we will look for the fat man I told you about.'

Marcelli did not respond immediately, continuing with his pre-lesson warming up exercises. Stefano was used to his thoughtful silences, so waited patiently whilst starting to warm up himself.

'Of course, I wish you every success in finding and freeing your brother, yet I caution you to tread carefully when making enquiries or challenging anyone,' Marcelli said while taking up his usual position to start the lesson.

'Genoa, as I remember it, is a place of large egos among young, privileged men. They will be quick to challenge, and it would be good that you do not get caught up in anything.'

After an hour of fencing, Stefano was sweaty, but exhilarated. He enjoyed sparing with his instructor and listening to his advice. As the lesson ended, Marcelli gave Stefano an old looking rapper, its cup handguard well dented.

'Please take this. It is a trusted old weapon that has served me well for many years. It may not look much, but you will find the blade of fine steel and it is very well-balanced.'

Stefano balanced the thin blade on one finger, at where he had been shown the centre of gravity of the sword should be. His hand was perfectly steady, and the sword was indeed well-balanced. Despite the dents in the hand guard, as he looked along the shaft, he could see no flaws. It was perfectly straight and unmarked. If used as much as the dented hand guard would suggest, the steel must be particularly strong.

'Thank you,' Stefano said, realising this was no small gift.

'Use it with honour, young Stefano,' Marcelli said, 'in the end, it is all a man has.'

Chapter 55

At the same time as Agata was enjoying her 16th birthday party, in the Spanish port of Valencia, a galley of the imperial armada was being loaded with gold and silver from the royal treasury. This precious cargo was bound for Genoa as part of the regular payments of bank loans. The chests of newly minted coins had arrived with a large army escort and security in the port was tight. The heavily armed galley was to be escorted by two smaller, but also well-armed vessels. Many eyes were observing the activity around these vessels and reporting what they saw.

Meanwhile, not far away, in a more modest part of the harbour, an inconspicuous sloop, called *Azahar* was being loaded with a mixed cargo, bound for several ports to the east. The captain was a very experienced sailing master who traded extensively throughout the western Mediterranean. Along with his respected merchant brother, he owned the vessel.

The cargo, so far, were iron ingots, barrels of wine, along with others smaller parcels. They waited on oranges, its regular cargo, which would be loaded last. At least, this is what the sailors were saying in the taverns. It was also true, the talkative sailors and stevedores confirmed, over a pitcher of cheap wine, that military personnel were joining her for this next voyage.

'Have another drink, my friends,' encouraged the rather drunk merchant, to the thirsty sailors from the *Azahar*. 'It is my birthday, and I am celebrating another successful cargo delivery.'

With cups raised and smiles all around, the merchant settled down besides the sailors and continued the casual conversation about the cargo they had loaded, so far.

'Was that a, *hic*, mil…itary commander, *hic*, and a detach…ment of troops I saw boarding *Azahar* this afternoon?' slurred the merchant to a young, inebriated sailor.

'Oh yes,' replied the young sailor, who had enjoyed the merchant's generosity most of the evening. 'That is because we are also carrying a large quantity of cannon balls and gunpower, cargo for the Spanish garrisons in various ports in the eastern empire.'

The merchant leaned in closely to the young sailor and topped up his mug of wine. 'The troops are responsible for delivering the armaments to the garrisons and re-enforcing them,' he continued, 'we will probably bring back the troops they relieve on our return voyage.' His head was spinning now, and he began to think he should call it a night.

'Ah yes, of course, *hic*, it has to be done. So many of our boys, stationed around the empire, needing to be looked after, *hic*.'

The merchant grinned but decided he had had enough too. It was not wise to ask too many questions at once, so he started to say his goodbyes.

As he staggered out of the tavern door, he paused and straightened up. He was not as drunk as he had appeared, only seeming to drink a great deal. Actually, only sipping slowly and pouring most of the wine into the sailor's tankards. He had learned a great deal observing the activities in the harbour during the day and chatting in the tavern that night.

Though he still needed more details of the treasury galley's route. As for the sloop, though the arrival of military personnel had peaked his interest, he reckoned it was just what they said it was. So, although the cannon balls and powder would be a useful acquisition, the presence of the troops made it more trouble than it was worth. He breathed in the smell of cooking fires from the city, as the evening sea breeze picked up. It reminded him he was hungry, and it was time to head off to meet his contact, who would courier his news to their employer.

'They could talk over a meal at his lodgings,' he thought, 'but he would have to wait until the treasury galley had sailed to make his final report. By which time, he hoped to have a clear idea of when they would pass close to the Corsican coast.'

Chapter 56

The days that followed Agata's birthday party, were full of preparation to sail to Genoa, both onboard *San Giovanni* and at the Castellietti's estate, but there were also very mixed emotions. There was excitement at the new adventure, but also sadness to be saying goodbye to people they had all grown fond of. However, with promises of a swift return after their business was concluded—their real mission was being kept confidential between only the few who already knew—sadness was pacified. In truth, Agata had no idea if or when she would return, although she knew she wanted to. She had an unnerving feeling that this journey would be more complicated than their outline plans. Nevertheless, she remained focused and determined, her priority being to rescue her youngest brother as soon as possible.

The Baroness had so enjoyed having Agata around, treating her like her own daughter and seeing the house come alive again with her disarming presence. The Baron too had rapidly grown fond of Stefano, readily seeing the likeness of his late son in the emerging young man. He had suggested Stefano learn about running the estate and the business of mass wine production, mostly to educate the boy. However, his enthusiasm to learn and quick wittedness had endeared him to everyone on the estate and renewed the old Baron's lust for life. Even although he had only known Stefano for a short time, he was beginning to look at him as an adopted son and wonder if indeed he could become just that.

Agata was excited when the Baron's carriage delivered them to the quay *San Giovanni* was moored to, putting aside any apprehension she had about the dangers ahead.

Her maid Maria, on the other hand, was visibly terrified. She was shaking, having never been on a ship before, or even contemplated what it would be like to leave Malta.

'It is going to be fine,' Agata reassured her. Holding her hand, a moment, as they left the carriage.

Excitedly, she practically skipped up the gangplank onto the vessel, leaving, Stefano, Maria, and a uniformed page to sort out their luggage. She went straight to the captain's aft cabin and almost burst in, but at the last moment, composed herself and knocked on the oak door.

The captain's steward, who had just delivered a jug of wine to the knights the captain was in serious conversation with, opened the door. He almost dropped the tray he was carrying when he recognised her.

'Mademoiselle Agata, my you look a picture,' he exclaimed.

She smiled sweetly at him, waiting patiently for him to get out of the way. After a moment of staring, he came to himself, mesmerised as he was by her transformation and opened the door for her to enter. Turning to the captain, he announced her formally, as he thought he ought, then left.

De Poincy's shallow smile was not as welcoming as Agata had expected. The three other knights standing around the captain's desk, looked too pre-occupied to be concerned with her.

'We will continue this conversation later, gentleman,' De Poincy said, dismissing them, 'keep me informed of any updates that arrive.'

Without goodbyes to De Poincy and only brief nods to Agata, they all departed, leaving Agata alone with De Poincy. He tried to smile, as he took Agata's hand gently and kissed it. Ushering her to a chair near his desk, he offered her a glass of wine. He looked apprehensive and was silent for a few moments as he gathered his thoughts.

He did not like to disappoint her, but the initial conspiracy they suspected was now clearly international espionage of a scale he had not met before. They had been warned of a possible interception of a Spanish treasury squadron bound for Genoa. The destabilising effect of the loss of such a cargo was profound. As a Frenchman, he had mixed views about the Hapsburg empire. However, the Knights of St John reported to the Pope, who approved of the Hapsburgs for now. Technically, their home of Malta was part of the Hapsburg empire. From a diplomatic point of view, he would have to tread carefully. The pirates were almost certain to field a sizable force to take this valuable cargo, there was going to be considerable danger. What could he say to Agata to explain the situation?

'The Knights of St John have consuls in many ports and agents that try to keep us informed of goings on. Today, we received word from one of these agents that necessitates a change in our plans.' De Poincy explained with a rather ominous tone. '*San Giovanni* has been given a difficult task, but one she is well suited to undertake.'

Agata was just about to asked what the "difficult task was" when there was a brief knock at the open cabin door and the captain's steward came in with his tray.

'Look who I found loitering outside on the deck,' the steward said, grinning broadly, as Bernardo's face appeared at the door.

'Come in brother, your timing is perfect,' De Poincy said.

He pointed to another chair near Agata, as the steward collected the mugs from the departed knights and immediately left again, closing the door behind him. The captain looked concerned at these two-young people he had grown so fond of. He wondered how best to help them while following his most recent orders.

'As you know, it had been my intention to sail to Genoa with you onboard, then, joining forces with our friends there, try to flush out the pirate collaborators; hopefully, rescuing Agata's brother, at the same time.'

De Poincy paused, learning back on his desk as he considered how much he could disclose to his young friends.

'However, we have just received credible information, that the Spanish treasury ships, delivering gold and silver to their bankers in Genoa, will be attacked by pirates on route. The treasury ships are, at present in Valencia, rather than their normal departure port of Barcelona. They are just about to sail, and we received word that a flotilla of pirate vessels has already sailed north from Tunis into the Tyrrhenian sea.'

He paused again, while they took in what he was saying. Agata, whose geography was not as good as Bernardo's, stood up to look at the navigation chart. She had noted it on her arrival, spread out on the captain's desk. Bernardo joined them at the desk, as the captain helpfully pointed out Valencia, Genoa, and Tunis to Agata. Ever observant, she noticed pencil marks made around the north of Corsica and asked about them.

'Oh, just thoughts I have,' De Poincy said dismissively, changing the subject quickly.

'The crux of the matter is, I think it would be safer and quicker, if you make your own way to Genoa. We are going to be one of numerous Knights of Malta vessels out looking for these pirates and I am very unsure how things will unfold.' De Poincy concluded firmly, but with an unusually worried look in his eyes.

The pair sat back down, rather surprised, both by this news and how pensive De Poincy looked. They thought he would have been thrilled to be off chasing pirates and they would have willingly joined him on this latest venture on route to Genoa. However, it was clear De Poincy had made up his mind, or others had made it up for him, so there was no point arguing.

'How do we get to Genoa, then?' Agata asked, after only a moment of thought.

'We will ask around for you, but there are ships sailing for eastern Sicily and Naples regularly from Valletta. So, I am sure you can secure a suitable berth on one of these, then find another vessel to continue on to Genoa,' De Poincy explained. 'As soon as possible, we will join you in Genoa, but we have contacts in most major ports that can assist you.'

There was another awkward silence, as they thought through the implications of the journey ahead on their own. Bernardo now had to decide if he should follow the plan to join *San Giovanni* as Brother Antonio's apprentice or accompany Agata. Suddenly, Agata energetically stood.

'Well,' she announced assertively, 'we are here now, so may as well ask around the port for a ship to take us north.'

De Poincy was relieved she had accepted the changes without adverse emotions, which he had feared.

'Naples eh!' Agata continued, looking again at the navigational chart.

Her reading ability was only rudimental and knowledge of geography equally limited, so, the navigational charts were hard for her to understand. De Poincy graciously pointed to Naples. However, she was a quick learner and very observant. She took in the orientation of the various port cities mentioned, in relation to each other, then took a snapshot of the chart in her mind, before saying her goodbyes.

'I do hope we can all join up again in Genoa soon,' Agata said formally, her gloved hand raised for De Poincy to kiss.

She had paid close attention to the Baroness's instructions of how a lady should behave. She quickly slipped into the role, even though she felt she was play-acting in front of people who knew another side of her.

De Poincy took her outstretched fingers gently and kissed them. He smiled at the performance; happy she had picked lady-like-manners up so quickly. He was confident she would be ready to blend into Genoese society.

'May God protect you little one,' he said affectionately to her, as he let her hand go.

'Well, I will not be alone…Stefano, who has taken to fencing as a duck to water and my maid Maria will accompany me,' she asserted, putting on a cheerful demeanour.

They both then looked up at Bernardo, towering above them. He was clearly deep in thought, and they waited for him to gather his thoughts.

'It would not be out of place for rich young siblings to travel with their Benedictine tutor, would it?' De Poincy suggested when Bernardo remained awkwardly silent.

To Agata's relief, Bernardo nodded and smiled, although inwardly he was still concerned about Agata's drive for revenge and the violence that would accompany that.

'My duty is clear,' Bernardo agreed, 'I will do my best to look after you on this next journey. Tutoring you and Stefano as we travel would be my honour, as well as a plausible reason for us being together.'

Despite the change in plans, there were smiles all around, mostly as the prospect of Agata and Bernardo being able to spend a considerable amount of time together, cheered them all. When they went back onto the deck, they were rather relieved to find the Baron's carriage was still on the quay. Agata gathered up her brother, Maria, and their luggage from the vessel's deck to reload into the carriage. Then, with a purposeful gait and Bernardo in tow, she left *San Giovanni* to find a shipping agent.

De Poincy was left pondering the information shared with him that morning and stood looking over his navigational charts. His most senior knight joined him, followed by his sailing master. They too stood around the navigational charts and waited patiently for their captain to gather his thoughts.

'If you were planning the passage of a Spanish treasury galley and escort vessels from Valencia to Genoa, Pierre, what route would you take?' De Poincy asked his prodigy, without looking up from the chart.

'Sticking close to the coast is always the safest plan, in case of unexpected poor weather,' Pierre replied, 'but I would want to stay clear of the French coast.

So, I would sail directly west to Majorca, then straight to the northern point of Corsica, calling at Bastia, before heading up to Genoa.'

'Why would you sail to the northern point of Corsica, rather than the southern point and up the coast to Bastia?' De Poincy pressed.

'Well, if the winds had been in my favour and all was going well onboard, I would then not stop at Bastia, but continue straight to Genoa,' Pierre concluded.

'Do you agree, Master Cardona?' De Poincy asked, as if this was some sort of a navigation lesson.

'Well, this time of year, the winds tend to be light and from a southerly direction, provided you stay clear of the French coast, where you will pick up land breezes in the morning,' the sailing master replied, puzzled why his captain was asking such a basic questions, 'sticking to the Ligurian sea seems a sensible plan.'

'Quite...' asserted De Poincy, straightening up and looking at his compatriots, 'and any experienced mariner would make the same sensible plan, which means that is exactly what the pirates will expect. So...' De Poincy continued, pointing to his pencil marks on the chart, around Cap Corse, '...if I were the pirates, I would wait in a secluded cove, towards the north of Corsica and intercept the passing treasury squadron off Cap Corse.'

He looked irritated, as he walked around from behind his desk, thinking out loud.

'Our superiors would have us scouring the open sea for a pirate flotilla,' De Poincy continued, 'when they will be holed up there, waiting for their prey.' Pierre and Cardona waited, while their captain paused, clearly making a decisive decision.

'Gentlemen,' the captain eventually announced, 'we will sail today, as soon as we can, for Cap Corse where I am sure we will find the pirates.'

Then, as the sailing master and senior knight turned to leave; the captain stopped them.

'Master Cardona, Pierre,' he added, 'my instructions to you are rather bending my orders, so keep our destination to yourselves until we are at sea, eh!' he concluded with a smile. They nodded and smiled to themselves too, confident the captain was correct and if they could make it on time, they could catch the pirate flotilla. Of course, they were only one vessel, against many. Yet, they also felt confident that their captain would have a plan for that too.

Left alone, De Poincy paced his cabin, thinking through the many uncertainties in his plan, and the frustration he was feeling about his orders. In his mind, his superiors instructions were not thought through enough, however, he could not effectively argue with them when all he had was a hunch. There was also a heaviness in his stomach as he wondered how deep this conspiracy went. Fighting an enemy you could see, was one thing, but a foe you could not identify was dangerous. He would have to tread carefully, both at sea and in port.

Chapter 57

Dawn's early rays coloured the calm sea with a purple hew, as a lone xebec rowed quietly into Golfe di'Aliso in northern Corsica. Just off Point Minerrio, at the southern edge of the Golfe, a small chalutier waited, its trawling nets stowed. The xebec was no more than a silhouette as it approached the chalutier that was signalling with a lamp to guide the xebec towards it. Orders to cease rowing were quietly given. The xebec glided gently towards the chalutier until it's bow touched the other vessel's stern, and lines were passed to hold the two vessels together. An agile, turban clad figure, jumped onto the chalutier and approached a fat older man, leaning on the siderails watching the sky's colour change.

'Salam Allium, Amir Ali,' said the turban wearer, as he respectfully greeted the fat man with his arm to his chest and a small bow.

'Allium Salam, Ibrahim,' the fat man replied, 'you are just in time,' still looking out to sea. 'I trust you have not come alone?' he continued.

'No, Amir,' assured Ibrahim, 'a galley and three more xebecs are not far behind me but keeping out of sight of the land.'

'Good, I expect the treasury vessels to pass close by here the night after next,' Amir Ali instructed, 'Take that message back to the other qubtans and have them assemble off here tomorrow at first light. When the treasury vessels are spotted by my lookouts on the hills here, they will signal you to intercept them.'

Ali turned to Ibrahim and stared at him intensely.

'Surprise is essential, so you must use the surrounding hills to shield your presence until our prey passes,' Ali continued, 'and take that bag of Genoese flags with you too,' looking down at a canvas bag at his feet, 'they will help to confuse the prey, at least, until you close them.'

Then he returned to staring out to sea. Ibrahim did not reply, but bowed and left the way he had arrived, carrying the canvas bag of flags. By the time the sun could be seen above the island, the xebec was out of sight of the coast.

Close behind Amir Ali, a young European boy stood nervously holding a tray with bowls of dried fruit. Ali picked out a plump date, tossed it into his cavernous mouth and smiled to himself. He patted the boy on the head and walked off to talk to the sailing master with the young boy in tow.

'In a few days' time, I will be rich beyond measure,' he chuckled to himself, 'but I must get back to Genoa right away.'

His own galliot, a modest, but a swift vessel he had swindled a Dutch trader out of some years before, was moored in Bastia. By noon, they could be at sea, on route to Genoa.

'It would be good to be seen around Genoa while the treasury ships are being intercepted,' he considered, 'then I can rendezvous with the pirates back here to divide the spoils.'

Chapter 58

A steady southerly breeze brought fine sand from the Sahara, that covered exposed surfaces like a lady's white face powder. Every sail was unfurled, catching the summer wind. New crew were being shown the ropes by the more experienced hands. Gunnery teams practiced preparing, loading, and running out the cannon to fire. They would do this repeatedly until it became second nature, knowing they would get it right, even under fire. Captain De Poincy should have been in a good mood; his vessel was in great shape and ready for action.

However, he paced the quarter deck, just in front of the wheel, deep in thought and feeling unusually apprehensive. He was not convinced his Grand Master's orders would work, having his own ideas of how to find the pirate vessels. However, his superiors had also warned him to curtail his lone wolf tendencies.

San Giovani had sailed from Valletta with instructions to join a Knights of Malta squadron, south off Sardinia that had left the day before. Their orders were to sail together south to Sicily and comb the southern Tyrrhenian sea in search of a pirate flotilla from Tunis.

Their agents had reported to them the date when a Spanish treasury squadron was expected to pass Cap Corse, Corsica. This information had been sent to the Doge in Genoa so some of his vessels could meet the treasury ships off the north coast of Corsica and escort them into Genoa. However, they suspected, the pirates had spies in many places, and it was likely they had acquired the same information or would do soon. So, the plan for the knight's squadron was to spread out, but keep in sight of each other, scanning as much sea area as possible, intercepting the pirate flotilla coming up from north Africa. *San Giovani* was useful, as she was faster than the other Knights of Malta vessel. Her English built hull, clad in thin copper plate, kept her free from the sea-life that attach themselves to the bottom of vessels, slowing them down.

Leaning over the chart spread out on his desk, De Poincy briefed his sailing master.

'Once clear of the straights between Malta and Gozo, head for the pre-arranged rendezvous point in the Gulf of Cagliari,' De Poincy ordered, pointing to the track on the chart. 'This should not delay us…it is essential we reach northern Corsica by the time the Spanish Treasury vessels arrive there.' However, even as De Poincy said the words, he was concerned they would not make it in time.

'We will follow our orders and rendezvous with the squadron at Cagliari. Hopefully all the other ships will already be there, and I will invite the commanding officers over for a conference. My hope is to persuade them to join us in a race to intercept the pirates off Cap Corse. As we sailed a day after them, hopefully I can convince them that our information is more up to date than theirs and my plan the wisest. A straight run there is imperative, rather than wasting our time searching the Tyrrhenian sea for the pirates.' Master Cardona nodded and left his captain thinking things through.

De Poincy realised if he were wrong and the pirates attacked elsewhere, he would be in trouble for not following orders. He had a reputation as a maverick, as well as a successful pirate catcher and his superiors had mixed feelings about him. If it was all just about fighting pirates, his exploits might go unchallenged and widely celebrated. However, the Knights of Malta's mission, was as much to do with politics as anything else. The Grand Master was very conscious that Christian Europe was far from united, even against persistent north African pirate attacks and continuing belligerence from the Ottoman empire to the east. Just as with his attack on Amad Rayar's galley, tracking down these pirate collaborators had a personal element to it too. If his superiors knew he intended to investigate international espionage and bring the culprits to justice, even take revenge, they would be very nervous. Commanding a Knight's ship was one thing, but who knows what such an investigation would uncover, or who would be exposed. Such investigations, at least in the eyes of the Grand Master, had to be conducted discreetly, then their findings kept confidential, until it was politically timely to reveal the information. This was all too complicated and slow for De Poincy. He would avoid getting embroiled in the politics and stick to direct action, as much as possible.

San Giovani arrived in the Gulf of Cagliari, less than two days after leaving Valletta. The early evening sun shone off the red dome of San Saturnino Basilica

256

and the deep-water harbour was very full. As they closed the port, they spotted three vessels, proudly flying the flag of the Knights of St John, anchored off Cagliari port. Anchoring near them, the captain sent a boat with messages for the commanding officers to join him for a dinner conference that evening onboard *San Giovani.* De Poincy's intention was to convince them to follow him up the west coast of Sardinia and Corsica in search of the pirate flotilla, leaving at first light the following morning. This turned out to not be as hard as De Poincy had expected; the other captains were already sceptical about locating the pirate's flotilla in the large search area they had been given.

'We have all spent weeks in the past, searching these seas for pirates, only to find out that they attacked a settlement in another area and got clean away before we could respond,' De Poincy reasoned with the other commanding officers over dinner. 'It is logical to narrow down the search areas, focusing where they mostly likely will be. In this case, it's the only reliable way to successfully intercept the treasury convoy.'

As it happened, logical arguments were not really necessary, as De Poincy's reputation was influencing them too. If he could at least narrow down the search area, it was worth going along with his plan. Readily they all agreed.

By the time, the sun was well up in the sky again and with a hot southerly wind filling their sails, four Knights of Malta vessels sped past the west coast of Sardinia, lookouts watching carefully. Soon they approached the coast of Corsica, where De Poincy was sure, the pirates would hide. All the knight's vessels were prepared for action, both to fire at and eventually board the pirate vessels, though they realised it was still a long coastline to search. There were many coves that could conceal vessels. However, the pirates had to come out of their hiding place if they were to engage the treasury vessels and the knights would be waiting.

Chapter 59

The harbour in Naples was busy, crowded, and dirty as far as Agata was concerned. Yet, she was relieved to get away from the hot, cramped cabin she had shared with her maid on the voyage from Malta. It had taken them five days to reach Naples with stops at Syracusa and Messina to drop off cargo and passengers along the way.

They had not ventured far into these cities during their visit. The devastation of the earthquakes some six months earlier, had made many of the building unsafe, there was reconstruction work in progress in many areas. However, this also provided a good excuse not to explore. They did not want to interact with anyone in the cities, as keeping a low profile was essential.

To pass the time, and in keeping with their cover story, Bernardo conducted some lessons for Agata and Stefano. He entertained them all with talks on history, geography, and philosophy. More awkwardly, he had them practice their reading, using the new testament commentaries he still carried around with him, and practicing their writing skills with supplies of ink and paper he had purchased in Valletta before they left. He had decided to start writing a diary himself, though where to start and how to explain all that had transpired was a challenge initially.

The Master of the ship they arrived in Naples on, introduced them to a shipping agent he said they could trust, so, it was not long before they found themselves at sea again. This time in a rather grand trader of the Genoa fleet, called the *San Giorgio.* There was one brief stop programmed on route to Genoa, that was Bastia in Corsica.

As they slowly entered Bastia harbour late one morning, a galliot of Dutch design sailed past them out of the harbour. Agata, Maria and Bernardo paid little attention to the departing galliot. Stephano initially watched her sail passed, with only limited interest. Then, he caught sight of a fat man standing near the starboard aft rails and a small boy standing beside him holding a tray.

'That is him,' Stefano cried, tugging at Agata's arm, and pointing, 'and there is Mateo.' He almost choked with shock. Agata turned in surprise, only catching a glimpse of the fat man as the vessel passed through the breakwater to the open sea.

'Are you sure,' Agata asked, grabbing hold of Stefano, 'and you saw Mateo too?' Her heart pounding so much, she thought it would burst.

'Yes, yes, it was definitely him,' Stefano insisted, 'that fat face is etched on my mind…' He clung to his sister, '…yes, yes, Mateo was standing beside him, dressed up in a fancy coat.' He was so shocked, he was panting for breath and finding it hard to get his words out.

'Alright, keep calm,' Agata said, as much to herself as to Stefano, 'at least we know Mateo is alive, praise God, so let's think.' Bernardo and Maria gather around them, trying to follow the conversation and understand what they had just seen.

'How long were we supposed to be in this port?' Agata asked, her mind racing.

'Only a few hours, I understand,' Bernardo replied, 'the captain said something about sailing over-night and arriving in Genoa tomorrow morning.'

'So, we must find out where that vessel is heading and pray it is Genoa,' Agata declared, 'if it is not going to Genoa, we must leave here and catch another ship to follow it, but first we must try and find out the name of that vessel and where it is going, which might lead us to the name of that man and where he lives…'

'What man?' Maria asked puzzled.

'Remember, I told you of my brother's experience onboard the pirate galley?' Agata said, and Maria nodded. 'Well, Stefano just caught a glimpse of our little brother with the fat man the pirates gave Mateo to, on the vessel that passed us on its way out of harbour.'

'If we can find that man, we can rescue Mateo,' Agata explained.

She thought some more, and the others waited patiently, their minds also racing to understand the implications of this sighting. They all knew the reason they were going to Genoa, but they guessed nothing would happen until they got there. Now, the enormity of the task was beginning to dawn on them, like standing at the bottom of a mountain you were determined to climb, looking up at how steep it is and urging yourself to take the first step.

'We need information but must be discreet.' Agata announced after a few moments of silence.

'Bernardo, I think you will draw the least amount of suspicion,' she continued, unsure of her own reasoning as she looked up at the imposing figure before her.

'Could you go ashore and seek out the harbour master? Ask him the name of the vessel that just left and where it is bound. If you can find out anything else, great, but we do not know who we can trust, so do not ask, or say too much.'

'Very well,' he said, turning immediately to leave, knowing how important this was to them and desperately wanting to help rescue Mateo.

'Thank you,' Agata called out as he walked away, her affection for him evident.

She prayed with Stefano and Maria that the vessel with Mateo was heading to Genoa, that Bernardo could find out the name of the vessel and owner; then, they could enquire about the identity of the fat man. It was a lot to ask, but God had answered so many of their prayers already.

Chapter 60

The Spanish sloop *Azahar* sailed a few hours after the treasury flotilla, following the same westerly course towards Palma de Mallorca. The treasury flotilla stopped only briefly in Palma. There she changed all their rowing slaves for pre-arranged fresh ones and loaded fresh water. Their next stop was scheduled to be Corsica, though if the steady southerly wind prevailed and all was well onboard, they would by-pass Corsica and head straight for Genoa.

Azahar arrived only two hours after the treasury vessels and also made this a brief stop. She unloaded some token cargo to keep up appearances but sailed right after the treasury vessels. However, unlike them, she swung on around to a small bay, just to the east of Palma that they passed as they circumnavigated the island. There she anchored, out of sight, with the decks steady, they assembled the extra cannon she supposedly carried as cargo. They mounted six, twenty-pound cannons on either side of the main deck, secured them well, then covered them with tarpaulins. With this task completed, they made best speed for the northern point of Corsica, staying in the wake of the treasury flotilla that was less than half a day ahead of them.

On the second day out of Palma, having seen no other vessels, the *Azahar* lookout spotted smoke ahead. The military commander and sailing master rushed to the deck on hearing the lookout. They were both thinking the same thing and were apprehensive.

'Was there a vessel on fire? Could this be the treasury vessels being attacked?'

Neither of them wasted anytime in discussions, but rapidly gave their respective men orders.

The troops onboard donned their armour, despite the mid-day heat. They collected their muskets, power, and ball, readying themselves to pick off pirates and board their vessel.

The gunners onboard, especially for this voyage, uncovered the cannon and brought powder and shot up from the dry storage in the lower decks. The sailors secured the vessel for battle and collected the grappling hooks, checking the stout hemp lines attached to them.

By the time battle preparations were completed onboard *Azahar,* the lookouts could see vessels, hulls down, heading away from them. Burnt wreckage was beginning to come into view too, floating in the water ahead of them. The sun was low in the sky by the time *Azahar* passed the wreckage and some bodies floating in the water. They kept a good lookout for any survivors but did not slow down. There was little hope anyway, as they saw sharks already feeding on the dead bodies.

Thiago Rodriguez de Castilla, Teniente de Navio, was a proud man. He stood by the wheel of *Azahar,* contemplating their next action. His orders were clear, to deliver his cargo safely to Genoa. Yet, he also wanted to help his comrades, and relished the chance to strike a blow to the pirates they had been expecting. The sailing master came to stand beside him, already knowing his thoughts.

'If we turn north now, we could avoid any action and proceed straight to Genoa,' the sailing master suggested without any enthusiasm and waited patiently for a decision from this young officer, the responsibility lying clearly on the Teniente's shoulders. A sly smile formed on Thiago's mouth, as he turned to the sailing master to give him instructions. They would fight.

It quickly became clear that it would be hard to catch two of the vessels they could see in the distance, but a third, trailed behind the others, most likely damaged and using half her rowing slaves to bail out the incoming water. *Azahar* headed straight for this vessel, a xebec they felt sure was a pirate vessel, no matter what, they would board her or sink her.

If it turned out to be one of the treasury vessels, they would help them, if a surrendering pirate vessel they would free the Christian slaves and take the pirates as prisoners, if a pirate vessel that put up a fight, they would still board her after subduing the pirates with their guns.

Chapter 61

The Harbour of Bastia was a busy place with lots of noise. Cargo of varying size and shapes being put on and taken off carts, along with ship supplies, both edible and technical. Bernardo found it all rather overwhelming. He scanned the throngs of sailors and stevedores for someone who looked like they might know where to find the harbour master's office.

Adding to the challenge was the dialect being spoken, which was quite different from his Sicilian brogue. However, eventually after much pointing, he found himself in a multiple roomed office, above what looked like a supply store. There was a large window looking out over the harbour that could have brought in much light if it had not been so dirty. Harassed looking clerks, reading over papers being presented to them, ignored him as he initially hovered just inside the door. He took a deep breath and decided to interrupt the one who looked the least formidable.

'Is it possible to speak to the harbour master?' Bernardo enquired over the general barrage of noise.

At first, there was no reaction, so he used his imposing size to push closer to the desk, trusting some respect for a monk might gain him an advantage and asked again, louder. The clerk paused from his inspection of the papers before him and looked up. The size of this "man of the cloth" was momentarily intimidating and he was not sure how to react. As he contemplated, a door on his left opened and a smartly dressed man came out of the office.

The clerk pointed to this door, but before he could say anything, Bernardo knocked on it and went in.

Behind a large paper-strewn desk, a small round, balding man, was reading some documents intently. He looked up as he heard the knock and was clearly surprised by the sight of Bernardo. Whether that being his size or his habit, was not clear, but it certainly gained his attention and a respectful greeting.

'Benvinuta Frate, how can I help you?' the harbour master said, indicating a seat in front of the desk.

'Thank you for your time, I realise you are a busy man, however, hopefully this is just a simple question,' Bernardo ventured.

'As the *San Giorgio* arrived this morning it passed a smaller vessel leaving. Could you tell me the name of that vessel and where it was heading?' he continued after a breath.

Without any hesitation the harbour master shuffled through some papers on his desk and looked at a list on one of them.

'That would have been Saverik Albertini's galliot *Fortuna*, on route to Genoa. He regularly sails between here and Genoa…' the harbour master replied, reading from the list.

'Why do you ask?' he concluded, looking up.

Not wanting to divulge anything, Bernardo thanked him and left without further explanation or conversation. This was exactly the news he believed Agata wanted, and he raced back to *San Giorgio* to tell her. It was only on the way through the busy harbour he started to contemplate what this chase might lead too. Certainly, the rescue of Mateo was something he could support. However, he felt, without more than suspicion, that it would also lead to more violence. Something about Agata had changed, more than just her appearance and confidence which he admired, it was something in her spirit, but he could only sense it.

Although the feeling was strong, he could not reconcile it with the conflicting emotions in him. He fingered his rosary and recited morning prayers, as he walked quickly passed the carts of cargo being moved back and forth.

Chapter 62

On the fifth day since leaving Valencia, the treasury flotilla spotted Cap Corse, the northern most point of Corsica. As they had made good time and the steady wind had allowed them to rest the rowing slaves much of the voyage, they decided to continue passed Corsica and go straight to Genoa.

Some escort vessels of the Genoese fleet were expected to be in Corsican waters, so they watched out for them. Of course, they would not be sure exactly when the flotilla would pass Corsica, though they had sent word of their estimated date to the Doge in Genoa, so they would not wait for the escort.

Around mid-morning, the lookouts reported four vessels to the south of them. Could this be the Genoese escort? Certainly, as the vessels closed them, Genoese flags could be seen flying from their masts, the three smaller ones were heading right for them. A larger galley seemed to be heading to Genoa like them. Later a fourth vessel came into view on their larboard bow, coming towards them.

Genoese flags or not, the treasury flotilla commander felt uncomfortable and ordered his ship to ready for battle. He also signalled his two treasury escorts to close his vulnerable stern and also prepare for battle. This was exactly what the pirates had expected. Like a shepherd and his dog, they would herd this flotilla into a tight group which they would encircle.

The pirate xebecs did not have the fire power of a larger Spanish galley. However, they were very manoeuvrable and used this to train their bow guns on the more vulnerable sections of the slower vessels. They would also avoid broad sides from the main enemy guns on the sides. Their techniques were well tested, fighting as a pack, to bring down larger prey.

The commander of the Spanish treasury galley had wisely stationed his escorts near his vulnerable rear, as three pirate vessels ahead came straight towards him in a line abreast.

They would fire their bow cannon at his bow and try to ram him, before boarding. The fourth pirate vessel tried to sneak around his stern, to fire on his rudder and cripple him. If he turned to starboard or larboard to use the cannons on his sides, he would still have a pirate vessel ahead of him, and also, start to expose his stern if his escort vessels could not fend the attackers off and keep in position close behind him.

The flotilla held their nerve and stayed in formation, while they exchanged cannon fire with the pirates. The fourth attacker moved north of the flotilla. Keeping out of range of their broad sides to attack the rear of the larboard escort. Then the larger vessel ahead, played her hand and turned towards them. This allowed the xebec on the starboard bow of the treasury vessel to peel off to the south and threaten the starboard escort in a similar manner as the one to the north.

Now with the larger pirate vessel blocking ahead, the treasury galley was compelled to turn to fire her side cannon with her escorts trying to manoeuvre with her, being difficult while trying to defend themselves at the same time. To maintain speed, the formation turned downwind and fired as their attackers came into range. At first, there was some success, as they damaged the pirate xebec to their north. However, the starboard rear escort had more distance to row to maintain station and risked exposing her own rear. This is where the southern xebec scored a crucial hit, sending men and broken spars tumbling into the sea from the Spanish escort and starting a fire onboard from damaging one of their cannon mid-fire. She soon started to fall behind. The pirates pressed their attacked on this wounded one, broken away from the formation. The other Spanish vessels could not help her, being fully engaged with their own attackers. However, the larboard escort continued her fire on the damaged northern attacker while still guarding the treasury galley's rear; like a macabre dance, but deadly if judged wrong.

Chapter 63

San Giovanni was well ahead of the Maltese flotilla, being the fastest and the others checking the various coves they passed on the Corsican coast.

At mid-day, the lookout cried, 'Sails ahead.'

This inspired the captain to climb the starboard aft shroud with his telescope. He could see multiple sails with what looked like Spanish and Genoese flags showing on their top masts. However, smoke between the vessels confirmed for him that this was no escort rendezvous, but a battle!

'All hands, battle stations,' he shouted down from the shrouds.

The vessel erupted in activity with men preparing for action, as they had been drilled.

Like before, initially only their upper deck cannons were made available. The lower deck ports remaining closed for manoeuvring.

Initially the pirates did not notice *San Giovanni* speeding towards them, in full sail—that was not going to last. The qubtan on the pirate galley was pressing down on the Spanish galley. He cursed as he saw the red cross of the Knights of St John emblazoned on the white sails. With only one of his xebecs disabled for one of the Spanish escorts and another occupying the other escort, he had the clear advantage over the Spanish. Now he would have to break off the attack to deal with the troubling Knights of Malta. He realised with the knight's vessel approaching from the south, it would have the advantage of the wind. His rowing ability was already reducing, as some rowers were dead or injured and all exhausted.

He signalled for all his vessels to disengage and join him in facing down this newcomer, realising that would take them time, as they each broke off their engagements and manoeuvred around to line up with him.

As soon as *San Giovanni* was within two miles of the southern-most xebec, about three miles from the pirate galley, they fired their long-range royal canon. The first few rounds mostly just wetting the decks with near misses. However, the next couple of rounds smashed into the xebec's sides and mast. Trailing sails and spars, along with broken oars and chaos onboard, spun her around and she started to list badly.

The pirate galley, rapidly closing *San Giovanni,* managed to hit one of her masts with their twenty-pounder. The falling spans and rigging disrupting activity on deck, causing several injuries. Yet the galley's qubtan's mood was only momentarily improved, as loud cannon fire from north of the melee was noticed. A sloop, with more fire power than would have been expected, was sinking the xebec that had tried to sneak up behind *San Giovanni* from the northwest. Added to this, his galley's lookouts drew his attention to new sails approaching from the northeast, flying the colours of Genoa. It was time to disengage and make a run for it.

With the wind dropping and the light fading, the pirate galley and one remaining xebec, both bearing scars from the fight, pushed their slaves to row faster and escape to the south. De Poincy, with a smile, let them go without a chase. He knew they would run straight into the approaching knight's flotilla and protecting the treasury ships seemed more of a priority.

Azahar and *San Giovanni* finished off the remaining xebecs, picking up survivors and freeing the rowing slaves as best they could. While the two remaining, but badly damaged, Spanish vessels rendezvoused with the Genoese escorts and limped towards port. Soon survivors crowded *Azahar* and *San Giovanni's* decks, a mix of sailors, exhausted former slaves, and bound pirates. By midnight, they had caught up with the treasury convoy and as dawn broke, Genoa's lighthouse could be seen on the horizon. One of the Genoese escorts raced ahead to bring the good news.

Chapter 64

As expected, the morning after their brief stop at Bastia, Corsica, *San Giorgio* arrived in Genoa. Here was a port city even more crowded than the previous ones they had visited.

Tall, elegant, and brightly coloured buildings surrounded the harbour area, as well as the usual warehouses for the cargo being traded. *San Giorgio* moored at the southern end of Porto Antico, not far from Piazza Caricamento where Palazzo San Giorgio was situated. This was the first of many "palaces" they were to see in Genoa. This one once housed the first Doge, but now this grand building was the Bank of San Giorgio. It was near Via Antonio Gramsci, where they were informed Saverik Albertini had a house. Agata looked out for his house when they later passed it in a carriage on route to the accommodation, they had been recommended, nearby on Via Turati.

Over breakfast the next morning they puzzled over how to proceed, as Maria brought in a letter for Bernardo.

'We know where Albertini lives and that he has just arrived in Genoa, but we can't just break into his house and take Mateo,' Stefano was postulating, 'so what do we do next?'

'Somehow we need to meet him socially and get an invitation back to his house,' Agata explained, 'and much to my disgust, I feel I must be the lure to hook this particular fat fish!'

She thought for a moment.

'If we can just figure out a way to meet him and find what type of bait he likes!' Agata concluded, noting Bernardo seemed to be ignoring them while reading a letter.

'Who knows to write to you here?' she asked Bernardo. Who looked up from his reading with a broad smile.

'I might just have the answer to your puzzle.' he replied. Showing he had been paying attention to the conversation after all.

'As soon as we arrived, I sent a note to Signior Beniamino, principally to arrange for a meeting to discuss my inheritance, as planned. He has replied already and…' Bernardo paused for effect, 'a few days from now there is a festival and parade in the city. This will be followed by a masquerade ball, where all the nobles and rich merchants of the city will be in attendance. Signior Beniamino will not attend himself, but he will try to secure you and Stefano an invitation. He says it is highly probable that this scoundrel Albertini will also attend this ball, so you can have someone point him out to you.'

'Thank you Holy mother, our prayers are being answered!' Agata gushed, 'A festival and ball too…how exciting!'

Agata was jumping up and down in her chair, not like the sophisticated lady she was supposed to be. Stefano, Bernardo, and Maria all had broad smiles on their faces, seeing Agata so happy.

'Oh, but Maria,' Agata exclaimed, 'I will have to ensure I have a dress that will get attention and buy some appropriate masks.'

Her happy demeanour changing to a serious frown.

'What is a masquerade ball?' Stefano asked, not following Agata's ideas at all.

'The Baroness told me about these and her experiences of attending some when she was younger,' Agata explained. 'She said they used to be popular amongst the nobles in many places and from what she described; it can give us a great opportunity to mingle anonymously, as we will be wearing masks.'

'Maria, come and help me decide what I have to wear and what I need to buy,' Agata said, jumping up and walking out with Maria chatting to her excitedly.

When they left, Bernardo and Stefano finished breakfast in good spirits. Then decided to stretch their legs and take a walk down to the harbour.

There was much excitement at the port entrance, as if the festival had already started.

Crowds were cheering and city dignitaries were out in the finery to greet a large number of vessels arriving together. As Stephano and Bernardo came closer, they could see that some of the vessels mooring to the various quays were battle scarred. They pushed closer through throngs of well-wishers. City guards were trying to clear a path for what they assumed was an official welcoming delegation, as well as helping clergy to evacuate the injured and dead.

Then, taking up the rear of this convoy, the unmistakable red cross of St John could be seen emblazoned on a white sail being furled. With delight, they recognised *San Giovanni* easing into port, but with noticeable damage to her rigging. They backed off from the press of the multitudes, to see better which quay *San Giovanni* would come alongside. Then walked past the crowds to greet her. Fortunately, the official welcome was, not unsurprisingly, focused on the Spanish treasury vessels: *Azahar* and *San Giovanni* being moored in a less prominent area. So, without fanfare, Bernardo and Stefano were able to greet Captain De Poincy as soon as *San Giovanni* was secured.

'Bernardo, Stefano it is good to see you…I trust Agata is well too?' De Poincy asked, greeting them warmly. Although clearly delighted to see them, he was also somewhat distracted. He noticed a column of soldiers and covered wagons approaching *Azahar* that was secured just ahead of them.

'That is heavy security for a cargo of oranges and ore,' De Poincy said out loud, but mostly to himself, scratching his full beard.

From *San Giovanni* forecastle, he looked ahead to *Azahar*, watching heavy cargo being discharged into the wagons, while troops sealed off the quay.

'There is something peculiar about this vessel and her cargo,' De Poincy mused.

Deciding he would make some enquiries but turning his attention for now to his ship's repairs. This was not the only investigation he would be making, as later Orlando visited him with news about what he had found out about the goings-on in Genoa.

271

Chapter 65

Two nights before the festival and masquerade ball, Agata invited Captains De Poincy and Orlando to join Stefano and Bernardo at their small, rented house for supper. By this time, she had hired a cook and housekeeper, recommended by Signior Beniamino. They had yet to meet him, but he had kept up a regular correspondence with Bernardo since they arrived.

'It is so good to see you,' Agata gushed, forgetting formality, and kissing them both on their cheeks.

She introduced Stefano, whom Orlando had not met, shepherding them into the little dining room. Maria would serve them food and drink there, with the new cook and housekeeper manning the kitchen.

'Thank you for sending the carriage for us, you seem to be well organised here,' De Poincy said, sitting down at a generously laid out table, 'but why such a late invitation?'

'The carriage, driver and guard are courtesy Signior Beniamino, who says we have to be careful who we trust in this city. Even servants. These men, as well as my cook and housekeeper, are his trusted employees.' Agata replied, 'Also going by his advice, it seemed wise to limit the number of people who know about our connection. So, inviting you here after sunset seemed wise.'

'Well done,' Orlando commented. Smiling with pride at how grown up Agata was becoming. 'Signior Beniamino knows this city well and is a good adviser...I have been getting to know much about what goes on here, since I arrived. He similarly advised me, so I have kept a low profile too.'

Agata raised her hand for silence, as Maria laid out more dishes. She invited Bernardo to say a prayer of thanks before Maria left again, and they continued.

'We know Saverik Albertini has Mateo and where he lives, we also have a plan on how to be invited to his house where we will grab Mateo and...' Agata paused, not knowing how much of her plan she should share with them.

'From what I have learned, this man is well known and dangerous with a criminal network in this city and beyond,' Orlando interjected. 'His legitimate trade is in silk and fine wine, but he also sells young slaves for the pleasure of rich clients, who want to keep their particular tastes secret. He also trades in Bangue, probably acquired from his contacts in Egypt or the Turks, and opium which I understand some of the older nobles here are dependent on to ease pain. With all of this, he has much influence, though no one will probably want to admit it. You are going to have to be very careful!' he concluded, with worrying glances around the table.

'He has to be brought to justice...' De Poincy insisted, between mouthfuls of food, '...getting to this man is what Agata has been preparing for...'

'Most importantly,' Stefano interrupted, disturbed by what he was hearing, 'we must free Mateo.'

'Of course, how can we help?' Orlando and De Poincy said in unison, recognising young Stefano's distress.

'The task is clear, and I have been thinking it through for some time, however, the aftermath is not easy and that is where we will need your help,' Agata explained and then took a breath as she laid out her plan, grateful for the friends she had.

'We know this Saverik Albertini has Mateo and where he lives, not far from here and that he is in the city now.' Agata stated, 'The festival and masquerade ball the night after next gives us an opportunity to meet him without raising suspicion,' she continued. 'Stefano and I will attend this ball and try to get an invitation back to his house. Once there, we will try to locate Mateo and get him out of there and away from here.'

Continuing she looked hopefully at Orlando. 'If you, Orlando, can ensure a carriage is waiting to take us all down to the harbour...we may need a quick getaway,' then looking at De Poincy, '...and if you sir could initially hide us then take us away from this city on your ship, we would be most grateful.'

She sat back, feeling quite relieved she had stayed calm enough to explain what she felt should happen to these much older and more experienced men.

'And grabbing this chap Albertini too,' De Poincy insisted.

'It would be justice to hand him over to the Inquisition,' Orlando chuckled, but looking at both Agata and Stefano he said, 'however, protecting you two...and your brother must be our priority and I will do all I can to assist.'

'Thank you,' Agata said, almost tearing up and reaching out her hand to Bernardo.

'What are your plans? You still have not visited Signior Beniamino, though you have written to him more than once a day since arriving.'

Listening to the conversation around the table, Bernardo had been quite concerned.

Although he fully supported the rescue of Mateo, he sensed Agata was planning more than she disclosed. The innocent young girl he rescued in Sicily, had matured rapidly into a sophisticated young woman and, he sensed, an angry, driven person too.

'I have arranged to meet up with Signior Beniamino tomorrow night. Antonio has agreed to walk with me. We already have discussed much of what I need to know, he really just wants to pass on somethings to me and I am keen to meet him,' Bernardo replied.

Maria brought in more food and wine, so there was a pause in the conversation as they all contemplated the plan with mixed emotion. Orlando particularly considered all he now knew about Albertini and his possible involvement with important people in Genoa. He sensed danger, without knowing details. There seemed to be many rumours about what went on at his house, but no one was prepared to confirm details. It made him uncomfortable about what Agata might encounter and how she would deal with it. He decided to keep an even closer eye on the coming and goings at Albertini's house. He would need to confirm with Agata that the house he had been watching was the address she understood he lived at.

He was not sure if he, or those helping him watch the house, had seen Mateo. However, Agata was right, looking inside the house was the only way to be sure.

The next morning, Agata and Maria went to pick up her ball gown from where it was being altered, with the accessories and the masks she had commissioned. She had brought with her a light summer, burgundy coloured, silk gown with gold lace detailing. This she would wear over a light white cotton shift. It was her most expensive gown. Yet, she had it adjusted to be more off the shoulders and revealing more cleavage, to attract more attention. With the cuttings from the alteration, she had the mask maker incorporate the burgundy silk into the mask. This went from her upper lip to above her head finishing there with a mock tiara. The mask was tied in place with a red ribbon. Leaving her hands and mouth free, so she could give the appearance of drinking too much wine and flirt easily while dancing. She had a fan adorned with some of the same burgundy silk cuttings. To finish the ensemble off, she would wear the ruby pendent the Duchess had given her for her birthday, the pendent now secured by a similarly coloured silk ribbon. It had to all declare opulence and so attract attention and mainly from the fat man.

Stefano was to wear similarly coloured silk breaches and jacket with gold detailing.

He had a full-face mask in the shape of a red fox, together with whiskers, long nose, and ears. It made them laugh and they hoped it would their fellow party goers too. To complete the frivolous, but masculine look, Agata had purchased him an elegant, jewel-hilted dagger.

This he would hang by his waist. However, although he agreed to wear it all, he insisted he also kept his trusty old rapier sword handy.

'Tell you what,' he had said to Agata, when she was giving him the dagger and turning her nose up at the plain looking rapier, 'I will have this rapier polished up and a little gold gilding put along the hilt edge, but only a hint for show. This sword is perfectly balanced, and I will not ruin that!' he insisted.

They agreed the compromise and planned to watch the festival parades, while scanning the crowds for the fat man and Mateo.

Meanwhile, with the help of Signior Beniamino's trusted men, Orlando noted who visited Albertini's house, wondering how far the collaboration with the pirates went. A thankless task for the most part, in the heat of the day. Yet, with a surprise as the sun set which he was keen to share with De Poincy and investigate more.

Chapter 66

As the sun set, the night before the ball, Bernardo and Antonio arrived at Signior Beniamino's house. They enjoyed the walk up from the harbour, catching each other up with all their latest adventures. Bernardo appreciated Antonio's level-headed counsel which he felt he might need after hearing from Beniamino.

Beniamino welcomed them both warmly, as the old servant led them to the brightly lit study, staring at Bernardo for quite some time as he remembered his father. They sat by the old man's desk, as he pulled out documents from drawers and an old box. The box intrigued Bernardo, sitting on the edge of the desk while the old man reminisced about his father and grandfather.

He already knew about his father's violent past and now the old man told him about his grandfather being employed by the city to defend it, he realised he had mixed feelings about this new information.

'Roberto was one of the best Conditierre this city ever had, but his kind of chivalry came from a by-gone age,' the old man recollected.

Uncomfortable with talk of fighting, Bernardo changed the subject.

'As I wrote to you, I am not sure what to do about my inheritance, it is a significant amount of money,' Bernardo stated, 'initially, I will go with your suggestion to draw some credit notes to assist with the journey ahead…wherever that might lead.'

He paused, feeling surprisingly emotional.

'Perhaps it would be good for you to give some guidance to Agata and Stefano, even if just via me as they neither understand nor trust banks,' he continued, taking a breath to control his emotions.

'For now, I appreciate your advice and hearing about my family…and what is this box?' he concluded, curiosity getting the better of him.

After the old man told the story about the box, Bernardo looked at it carefully, noting grooves in the inside base and a kind of shadow, caused by something being stored in the box over a long period. He looked at it under the desk lamp and showed it to Antonio for a second opinion.

'It looks like it could have once held something in the shape of a cross,' Antonio observed without much conviction.

Bernardo thought for a moment, then removed the dagger from under his scapular.

Both Antonio and Beniamino raised their eyebrows in surprise at the sight of the dagger, but neither said anything. Bernardo placed the dagger into the box. It fitted perfectly and roughly matched the shape of the shadow and slight indentation on the base.

'I wonder if this dagger was once stored in this box?' Bernardo probed.

Beniamino held out his hand for the box, now with the dagger inside, removing it and turning it over, to take a closer look at the blade and hilt.

'It once had jewels in the hilt, but my mother took them out to sell them,' Bernardo clarified.

Beniamino thought for a moment while Antonio now looked at the dagger and unwound the leather strapping round the hilt, covering holes where the stones had been.

'The hilt looks like silver, detailed with gold plate,' Antonio observed.

'Are there any insignia on the hilt?' the old man asked.

'Yes, there is a symbol here,' Antonio acknowledged, after a short pause to polish some grime off were the leather had been.

'It looks like a cub with a cross,' Antonio continued, rather puzzled.

He handed the dagger back to Beniamino who peered at it through his glasses.

'Actually, I think it is a symbol for the Holy Grail, the cup of your Christ, similar to the stamp inside this box,' the old man asserted, putting it back into the box.

'Your instinct is correct, Bernardo, I too think the dagger, when bejewelled, was stored in this box,' the old man agreed. 'An educated guess is the dagger was once used for ceremonial purposes…perhaps oath taking and originated in the Levant. Probably brought back by a Templar knight, which would explain the symbol and Aramaic text, if not the details of its use.'

He handed it all back to Bernardo, who was unsure of what he now thought of it.

Previously the dagger's only value was as something that had belonged to his father and its only practical use was as a strong sharp blade. Now he wondered if there was something ungodly about it.

'And you say my grandfather found the box and perhaps the dagger?' he asked.

'That is what he told me about the box, but he did not connect the dagger,' the old man replied, 'though I wonder now if there was more to it? Roberto was a secretive man.'

As the old man continued to tell stories about his family, Bernardo wrapped the leather straps back around the dagger's hilt. He wanted to restore some sort of connection to his father that he had felt before. It was clear they had all taken in as much information as they could for one night. Bernardo put the credit notes in the box and the box into a cloth shoulder bag the old man gave him to carry everything in and said goodnight. As Signior Beniamino's carriage was with Agata and Stefano, he had his servant call for a boy with a torch to guide them through to the harbour.

Their sandals made clapping noises on the almost empty cobbled streets. Dark now except for the light of the torch bearers here and there. Bernardo was deep in thought.

'You have quite a family history,' Antonio remarked. Wanting to initiate a conversation that he thought Bernardo should have. Not untypical there was a long silence.

'My family's life and that of mine, seem so…' Bernardo started to explain while analysing his emotions when they realised their young guide had gone. However, they could still see the street as two short men approached with torches, while two larger thugs stood in front of them with knives pointing at Antonio and Bernardo.

'So, the warnings about these streets being dangerous was true.' They both thought as each drew draggers from under their scapular.

Bernardo looked with surprise at the dagger in Antonio's hand. Antonio looked up at him and shrugged.

'The captain gave it to me, as he said these streets were dangerous…and he was right,' Antonio justified with a shrug. The two friends stood back-to-back ready to defend themselves.

The thug on their left lunged at Bernardo, who surprised him with his speed and agility. Side stepping and twisting his body around, exposing the side of the assailants head to a powerful blow from Bernardo's strong fist. He went sprawling onto the cobbles, hitting them hard and knocking him almost unconscious. Simultaneously, the thug on the right swung his knife at Antonio who deftly parried it with his dagger, at the same time, drawing his sharp blade over the attacker's wrist. The assailant let out a yelp, dropped his knife and grabbed his bleeding wrist with his other hand to staunch the free-flowing blood. The torch bearers decided this was not what they agreed to and fled. They were closely followed by the bleeding thug, while the one Bernardo hit staggered to his feet, still dazed.

Antonio and Bernardo were left in almost complete darkness. Noting a glow coming from the harbour area they hurried towards it, their leather sandals seeming to applaud them as they ran. Their hearts were pounding and adrenaline coursing through their bodies.

'To *San Giovanni*?' Antonio said panting.

'I guess so,' replied Bernardo who felt surprisingly exhilarated.

Chapter 67

The ball's main host this year was Eugenio Durazzo, the owner of Palazzo Real on Via Balbi.

Originally built for Stefano Balbi, Durazzo had purchased it 16 years before and was extending it into adjoining buildings. The grand ballroom, where dancing would take place, was lined with his art collection, being an avid collector. It was overpoweringly grand.

Agata and Stefano had deliberately arrived a little late. Their hope was that guests would be relaxed enough with drink and merriment to avoid asking them many questions, especially as they looked for Albertini. As they entered the grand ballroom, they scanned the room carefully. Not seeing any sign of the fat man, Agata accepted an invitation to dance from a handsome young man. It was a hot, humid night, and she was glad her dress was made of relatively light silk, and grateful she had so much bare skin.

Meanwhile, Stefano was finding his outfit uncomfortable in the heat, especially the mask, so he hovered near the open doors to catch what little breeze there was. Accepting a glass of wine from a passing waiter he took off the mask and used it as a fan, deciding to avoid dancing.

'Ha, I love your mask,' declared a young man who looked about the same age as him and equally as hot in his dark blue silk jacket.

He smiled broadly and politely bowed to him.

'My name is Marco Lomellini,' the young man said, introducing himself.

'Stefano Conti,' Stefano replied with a similar bow.

'Conti?' probed Marco, trying to think of a prominent family of that name.

'From Sicily,' Stefano interjected.

'Ah, that will be why I do not recognise the family name,' Marco conceded, 'what brings you to Genoa?'

'Your banks,' Stefano replied briefly. With the pre-planned response to the question, while keeping an eye on Agata, as she changed dance partners.

'That is something we have lots of,' Marco affirmed and gave up his questioning.

A slightly older young man stopped in front of them, taking a fresh glass of wine from a waiter.

'Benedetto, let me introduce Stefano Conti from Sicily…Stefano, this is Benedetto Giustiniani,' Marco ventured with a smile. 'Oh, and look, your delightful brother Francesco is staggering over to join us!' Marco pronounced sarcastically as Benedetto's older brother approached them.

A clearly inebriated Francesco nodded to Marco, but ignored Stefano, as he loudly questioned his brother.

'Did you see that beauty in the red?' he asked. Taking a glass of wine from a passing waiter and gesturing towards Agata. 'I bet she is up for it, if we take her home, we could probably both have her,' he slurred, laughing.

'That lady, sir, is my sister,' Stefano exclaimed indignantly, shocked by his own reaction.

All three young men stared at him with surprise and differing degrees of discomfort.

'Well surely you can confirm if she is a whore or not?' Francesco arrogantly blurted out.

Stefano immediately started to draw his rapier. A quick-thinking Marco, his mind fully alert after the verbal altercation, grabbed his arm to stop him, leaning in to speak to Stefano.

'Not here,' he whispered in Stefano's ear, 'this brute could be doing with a thrashing, but you will offend our host if you strike him here.'

He began to push Stefano out of the door into Via Balbi. Francesco and Benedetto followed, gesturing towards them as they talked loudly with each other. The brothers borrowed a sword from a guest they knew that was cooling off in the street near the Palazzo entrance. In the street, Francesco, who was a good foot taller than Stefano, squared up to him, breathing in fresh air deeply to clear his head.

'So, you are a Sicilian and think yourself better than us Genevans?' Francesco taunted.

Stefano ignored the jib and drew his rapier, taking up the relaxed posture his fencing tutor had taught him. An overconfident Francesco, goaded on by his younger brother, lunged at Stefano. He parried his blade away effortlessly, bringing the point of his sword quickly back towards his older opponent.

'Do you really want to do this?' Marco was asking Francesco, as he immediately recognised Stefano's skill, but Francesco lunged again.

Stefano parried Francesco's attack with ease, infuriating his larger opponent who began circling Stefano looking for a gap in his defence. The hours of fencing practice came clearly to Stephano's mind. He breathed steadily and deeply, keeping calm and alert. He did not initiate any attacks, partly hoping this encounter would not lead to bloodshed, but also, as he had been taught, analysing his opponent carefully, looking for his "tells".

'Watch the eyes,' his fencing instructor would say, 'your opponent's next move starts in his head and the eyes give it away.'

Francesco breathed in the fresh air, trying to clear his head and focus on this boy who was surprisingly calm. He was well known as a good swordsman, and had taken part in many duels, all of which he won. But tonight, sweat poured down his face, he could feel his frustration level rising. He was becoming dizzy as he circled this young Sicilian and was conscious that a growing audience was judging his performance. As word of the fight was spreading through the guests, more and more surrounded the pair, keen to see the spectacle.

It became clear to Stephano that he would have to draw blood to end this. If he could inflict a wound sufficient enough to immobilise his adversary without endangering his life, that would be best. It was easy enough. This fellow, for all his bravado, was not skilled enough to beat him, and he was becoming bored with the circling.

After another desperate lunge which Stephano easily parried, he brought his rapier to Francesco's right shoulder and stepped forward. The sharp point punctured the flesh and muscle resulting in sharp pain, causing him to drop his sword and cry out in anguish.

Benedetto quickly stepped in to assist his brother, staunching the blood flow and dragging him away. Almost supernaturally, out of the darkness angry men appeared and word of the fight's result travelled into the ballroom.

'We need to get you out of here,' Marco insisted, grabbing Stefano's arm, and signalling for his carriage driver among a row of carriages parked on the via Balbi.

In the ballroom, whispers of the fight circulated, and some young men rushed outside to see if the rumour was true. Agata overheard the chatter and looked around to see where Stefano was. Not seeing him, she began to follow a group outside, almost stumbling into a fat man, sweating profusely, and smelling of exotic spices. He seemed amused by the talk of a fight between two young gentlemen but transferred his attention immediately to Agata on seeing her.

'Well, my little beauty, I do not believe we have met before,' he hissed, giving a short bow without taking his eyes off Agata leering at her with some intent. He made her skin crawl, and her instinct was to avoid him.

'Could this be the man we are looking for…' she thought, '…where is Stefano now I need him to identify the man?'

'No, I do not think we have met,' she replied as calmly as she could, briefly extending her hand for him to kiss, 'and you are?' She had no time for polite chatter, wanting to identify this man quickly and then look for her brother.

'My name is Saverik Albertini, merchant of fine, rare, and exotic things,' he boosted, 'at your service,' focusing on her cleavage.

Agata felt her heart would jump through her mouth. She took a deep breath.

'Oh, I like fine and exotic things,' Agata replied, trying to sound sensual, 'perhaps you could sell me some exotic things?'

She was trying to flirt to get some information from him. However, as he started to tell her where to find him, she was distracted by the chatter around her concerning someone being injured.

'Thank you Signior, perhaps I will visit you.' She purred with a wave of her fan, hurrying outside, her heart pounding.

As she exited the main entrance, she thought she spotted Stefano and another man approaching a carriage on the opposite side of the road. As best she could in her long dress, she ran towards the semi-recognisable figure, distorted in the shifting yellow glow of the torches held aloft by many servants.

'Stefano,' she called out as she approached, guessing it was him from the clothes he was wearing.

He turned as soon as he heard her voice, and she reached out to take his hand.

'Are you alright…were you involved in this fight?' she pleaded, quite out of breath.

'I am fine…it was not that big a deal,' he assured, 'may I introduce Marco Lomellini,' turning to point towards Marco, who she realised looked much less at ease with the situation than her brother.

'Delighted to meet you, Signorina,' he responded with a stiff bow. 'I strongly suggest we all leave immediately,' he continued, pushing Stefano into the open door of his carriage, and indicating that Agata should follow.

'Home,' Marco ordered, as he clambered into the carriage after them whilst looking around to see if they were being followed.

Agata sensed his anxiety and was confused by the contrast with Stefano's mood.

'What happened?' she interrogated Marco, while gripping her brother's hand tightly.

'Your brother has just wounded one of the sons of a leading Genoese family and not one of the forgiving types.' Marco replied, sounding quite agitated.

'Oh, Stefano, what were you thinking!' Agata frustratedly exclaimed, inches from her brother face.

'I only gave him a small wound…I didn't kill him!' was Stefano's pleading reply. 'But…' Agata started to say, then found she could not think of appropriate words.

'He called you a whore!' Stefano shouted defiantly.

'What?' Agata was shouting now too.

'Signorina, please…' Marco interjected, 'Francesco is a bully and was drunk. Your brother was right to challenge him, clearly a better swordsman too. However, that does not mean there will not be retaliation…least not while they are all stirred up. Please take my advice and lay low for a few days. For now, I am sure my family could give you sanctuary.'

Agata's mind was now analysing these new circumstances. She sat quietly for a minute and took deep breaths. Could they salvage the situation and still rescue Mateo?

'Marco, it is good to meet you and kind of you to help us…' Agata said as she tried to gauge the best course of action. '…your offer of sanctuary is welcome. Do you think they will find out where we live, and attack us there?'

'Did you rent a house via a local agent?' Marco asked and Agata nodded to confirm.

'Well, it will not take long for them to find the agent and get your address if they remember your name, but they will be looking out for you, and it is easy to employ thugs in the street…there is much of this that goes on around here, which is why I always have a bodyguard with me,' Marco explained. Agata thought a moment.

'Please take us to our house on Via Turati first.' Agata requested and Marco immediately leaned out of the carriage window and gave the driver new instructions.

'It strikes me, Francesco's men won't be able to find the agent till tomorrow morning, therefore, we have this night to prepare for what's next. We must warn our household of what has happened and pack ready to leave in the morning. I suggest you take Stefano with you to your house and explain to your family what's happened. Please keep him safe. It is my guess that it is he who they will be looking for,' Agata asserted.

Marco nodded agreement without interrupting.

Stefano started to protest, but Agata gently put her finger to his mouth. 'Hush, dear brother. We will ensure that everyone is safe, but must keep you out of sight,' she said in soothing tones. 'We will warn everyone to pack up and be prepared to leave at first light.'

Then turning to Marco, 'Please keep Stefano out of the way until siesta tomorrow,' she continued to explain, '…when things seem quiet, take him to the Knights of Malta's ship *San Giovanni*. He will be safe there and we will be leaving Genoa soon, probably on her.'

Marco nodded agreement.

The carriage stopped near their house, and they all climbed out, looking around to see if there was anyone around to see or hear them. The street was silent. Marco waited with the carriage while Agata and Stefano went into the house. They were pleased to see everyone around the kitchen table, listening to a tall tale from Antonio about sea adventures.

On seeing Agata and Stefano, they all stood up. The servants curtsied, and Bernardo said a quiet prayer of thanks for their safe return under his breath. Agata stood silently for a moment at the kitchen door, enjoying the sight of this loyal group and smiled.

'Can we get you anything…?' Maria started to say, but Agata raised her hand.

'Listen carefully, we do not have much time,' she began. Worried faces listened.

'We are fine, however there has been an incident,' she paused wondering how much to tell them. 'Stefano was involved in a fight with a young gentleman over my honour,' she continued, 'Stefano bested the man, only slightly wounding him. However, we understand he may seek revenge.' She paused again to let this news sink into her listeners minds.

'Stefano is going to stay tonight with a new friend, Marco Lomellini.'

The housekeeper and cook's eyes widened on recognising the name, but they remained silent.

'We must pack up and vacate this house at first light. We will meet together on *San Giovanni* tomorrow.'

Turning to the local servants, she reassured them. 'I will pay you now for the rest of the month to give you time to find another position.' They curtsied and smiled broadly.

'Antonio,' she said, and he looked up attentively, 'Please explain to the captain what has happened. Tell him I met the man we were looking for briefly at the ball and intend to visit his house tomorrow night to carry out the plan as we discussed.'

Then without waiting for any discussions, she turned, stroking Stefano's cheek as she passed him.

'Grab yourself a change of clothes and leave with Marco now, he is waiting outside, and try to keep a low profile,' she whispered to him, kissing him on the cheek, 'everything will be fine.'

He blushed, feeling slightly ashamed to have disturbed their comfortable, safe set-up and plan to rescue Mateo.

Chapter 68

The Genoese bankers had been very grateful for *San Giovanni's* assistance in delivering the payment from the Spanish crown. As thanks, they paid for her battle damage repairs and generously restocked her provisions. Barrels and crates were piled up on the quay by the ship when the Lomellini's carriage pulled up, the day after the ball. Stefano and Marco, in good spirits, jumped out of the carriage as Stefano recounted stories of his old, but agile fencing master. Initially they ignored the many stevedores on the quay trying to find shade to rest in the mid-day heat, when a group approached them, almost surrounding the carriage.

'Are you Stefano Conti from Sicily?' a scar-faced, tall man asked, staring intently at Stefano, who put his hand to his rapier as he answered.

'Yes, what of it?' Stefano replied in a defiant tone.

Marco's bodyguard and driver jumped down from the carriage and stood beside them, looking around at the gathering group. Some held cargo hooks, while others clasped knives in their hands. All seemed to be taking a lead from this taller one with the scared face. There was a stand-off, which seemed to last several minutes, as they all stared at each other, wondering who would make the first move.

'My master has a bone to pick with you,' Scarface declared raising his arm and pointing a knife towards Stefano's face.

The defenders by Stefano and Marco drew their daggers. However, the gathering mob well outnumbered them. Even with skill, this was not going to be a fight they could win.

Scarface's eyes near popped out of his head when an arrow shaft pierced his arm, he cried out in pain and dropped his knife. The others froze, uncertain where the shot had come from. Just then, several armed knights started jumping ashore, including Captain De Poincy. The gang rapidly backed away while Scarface cursed them, but retreated, clutching his pierced arm.

'Well, I guess you will be safe here,' Marco exclaimed with a smile, as Stefano introduced him to Captain De Poincy. He looked around for Bernardo, who he was sure the arrow came from, but he was keeping out of sight.

Orlando was in a pensive mood when he visited *San Giovanni* as the sun dropped low in the clear blue sky. He was apprehensive about Agata's visit to Albertini's house that night and wanted to talk the plan through again. When he arrived, De Poincy was standing on the aft end of the quarter deck. He was enjoying the evening sea breeze; under an awning they had rigged to create some shade.

'Greetings my friend, another day comes to an end, and we must prepare for the trials of the night,' De Poincy reflected more philosophically than normal for this man of action.

'I wished we had agreed to send more men to grab Albertini tonight,' he concluded, turning to face his friend.

'Unfortunately, Agata is quite convinced he will allude us and endanger Mateo if we go in mob-handed,' Orlando conceded, 'I am afraid she has a point, and if Mateo is not there…'

There was a thought-filled pause, both men seemingly enchanted by the evening sun, lost in thought.

'Soon, Signior Beniamino will come in his carriage and take me to visit the Doge…he apparently has a favour to ask of me,' De Poincy announced, still staring at the horizon.

'Intriguing,' Orlando responded, '…have you any idea what the favour is and if it might change our plans?'

'None,' De Poincy replied, 'though Signior Beniamino did mention something about him visiting family in Livorno. About ten hours sail from here, and how much safer he would feel sailing with us.' Looking serious, he turned to face Orlando.

'I would like you to come with us to the Doge's residence.'

'What, to meet the Doge?' Orlando asked surprised.

'No, not actually to meet the Doge,' De Poincy continued, 'that discussion may be confidential. However, if I can, I would like to sound the Doge out about Archbishop Stefanu and then discuss the implications with you and Signior Beniamino.'

Orlando thought for a moment.

'I would be very careful what you say about that piece of information, especially with our plans this evening,' Orlando warned.

'Do not worry, I will not actually disclose what you observed,' De Poincy assured.

'However, since you told me you saw the Archbishop visiting Albertini's house, I have been much concerned about it.' He paused to gather his thoughts and paced the deck.

'What would the Vatican's envoy to the Spanish court be doing visiting a rogue like Albertini?' De Poincy continued. 'I just want to know from the Doge if this was an official visit to Genoa and if he has visited before.'

'Signior Beniamino tells me he was formally the Archbishop for Siena, before becoming the Pope's Nuncio to Spain,' Orlando added, 'However, Stefanu Buonapate was born in Corsica from a Tuscan noble family…could there be a connection there?'

'I do not know, my friend,' De Poincy replied, with a shrug, 'but knowledge about key shipping movements require a well-informed port network, and we need to know how well-connected this treacherous bunch are.'

A carriage pulled up alongside *San Giovanni* and Orlando recognised the driver as one of Signior Beniamino's men.

'You can stay with the carriage or wait in the Palazzo lobby for us,' De Poincy suggested, 'However, I think we need to have a talk before the encounter with Albertini tonight.' He paused thoughtfully. 'I agree rescuing Mateo is important and handing over Albertini to your Inquisition friends…' De Poincy continued with a wry smile, '…might be justice, but I think he is only part of something bigger.' Orlando raised an eyebrow at the comment, thinking through implications.

Chapter 69

Giovanni Battista Castaneo was a sombre looking man with a thin beard, moustache, and receding hair line. He had been the Doge of Genoa for almost two years and the responsibility had taken its toll. In contrast, with the opulence of the Palazzo, he was dressed almost clerically in a simple black jacket and white cotton shirt. His greeting was cordial, rather than warm and he wasted little time getting down to business.

'Thank you for meeting me here, Captain De Poincy.' The Doge began, as they stood at the end of a long table in what De Poincy guessed was the business part of the Palazzo.

'…your assistance with the safe arrival of the Spanish treasury vessels was much appreciated, as is your Order's service generally.'

De Poincy bowed in acknowledgement. The Doge motioned for them to sit, pulling a simple flat box towards his seat.

'Of course, the payment from Spain was not actually on the treasury ships, was it?' De Poincy dared to venture.

The Doge did not visibly react but gave De Poincy a cold stare.

'We live in difficult times, as you well know Captain. Sometimes we have to distract those that mean us harm with one hand, while conducting business with the other,' he replied.

'Which is partly why I am asking this favour of you,' the Doge continued, opening the box in front of them.

Inside, laid out on dark blue velvet lining, was a collection of magnificent gems.

Different colours and sizes, although all large stones, glinting as they picked up the light from the low sun coming through the large windows. They all paused to look on the sight, a king's ransom staring at them—it almost took the captain's breath away.

'These, once mounted on a gold necklace, will be a special gift for an important lady…I will say no more,' the Doge explained, 'and they need to be delivered to a particular jeweller in Livorno to cut, polish and mount.'

He closed the box and turned to face De Poincy.

'As you can imagine, safe delivery of these will require discretion. Any obvious official convoy will attract attention and so risk losing them.'

There was a pause, as the Doge let the importance of the approaching request sink in.

'Signior Beniamino intends to visit family and friends in Livorno, as he has done before. He knows the jeweller in question, so has agreed to deliver this box with its contents to the jeweller personally. If he sailed with you, it should not attract attention, neither of you being on official Genoese business, at least as far as any records will read. Few people beyond the three of us here know about this delivery. Will you help us?'

De Poincy thought for a moment. What was being suggested made perfect sense and Livorno was not even far out of their way. If they left at first light tomorrow, they could be secured in Livorno well before dark and deliver the gems that night. However, it was a great responsibility if anything did go wrong and they were intercepted…The Doge sat patiently, his face impassive, as did Signior Beniamino. He guessed Beniamino had come up with the plan and would probably go on another vessel if he said no.

'It would be our honour to serve, your Grace,' De Poincy agreed. 'We will sail at first light tomorrow and Signior Beniamino can deliver the gems to the jeweller tomorrow evening,' bowing his head politely to the Doge.

Turning to Signior Beniamino, 'I suggest you arrive onboard just before sunrise, when few will notice, and we will depart shortly afterwards,' he continued.

There were nods of agreement and De Poincy thought he detected a faint look of relief on the Doge's face, as he rose to say thank you and goodbye, the box going into a simple leather satchel carried by Signior Beniamino.

'May I ask an unconnected question about a guest you might have seen here, your Grace?' De Poincy ventured, as they stood to depart.

'Certainly,' the Doge replied looking puzzled.

'Did Archbishop Stefanu, the Pope's Nuncio to Spain, call on you recently?' De Poincy asked, watching the Doge's face intently as he replied.

'Yes, two days ago…' the Doge replied, '…now he has since left for Rome.'

'Has he called into Genoa before on his way to Rome?' De Poincy enquired.

'Actually, he has…' the Doge seemed to De Poincy to be answering without any duplicity, '…and my understanding is he briefly visits several places on his annual visit to the Vatican to report to His Holiness. He sailed for Livorno this morning and will then go over land to Siena, etc…'

De Poincy bowed again.

'Thank you, your Grace,' and without further explanation, left.

He would have to make more discrete enquiries about Archbishop Stefanu and who he visits. This might give them a clue to the network he was involved in, but they would need specialised help to track his movements further. Fortunately, the knights already had such help at hand.

Chapter 70

It was well after dark when the carriage drew up opposite Saverik Albertini's house. There were already other carriages parked nearby with drivers and guards quietly waiting.

'Are you sure you want to go in alone?' Orlando asked Agata, not feeling confident.

'Yes, it is the only way I can ensure he feels secure enough to drop his guard. I must appear to be a vulnerable innocent he has power over,' she asserted.

'But you are a vulnerable innocent, and he will have power over you,' Orlando replied with trepidation.

Agata smiled weakly, touched by his concern. She gathered her skirts up to leave.

'Just be sure to be ready when you see us appear at the front door,' she said as she stepped out of the carriage.

She took a deep breath and tried to focus her acting skills as she approached the door.

A young boy on duty near the entrance lifted a torch to light her way.

As soon as she knocked on the front door a large black man in a red turban opened it and waved her inside, taking her to the first door on the right.

'Oh, you did come, I thought you would, I was delighted to receive your note,'

Albertini gushed as he greeted her with too much enthusiasm.

Albertini's drawing room was dimly lit with several couches scattered randomly around the space, some occupied with semi-comatose figures. A small boy dressed in a formal coat approached her carrying a silver tray with goblets of wine. He did not look into anyone's faces, so did not recognise Agata, but she recognised him. Her heart jumped and she wanted to reach out to Mateo. She tried not to react and continued to listen to Albertini, however, she found it hard to concentrate on what he was saying.

The large black man wearing a bright red turban, with an elaborate open waistcoat, showing his muscular chest, approached them carrying another tray. This had clay pipes on it and a bowl of some sort of fibrous material. Albertini filled one of the pipes, lit it and offered it to Agata, encouraging her to inhale the smoke.

'This will relax you, my beauty,' he assured her with a serpent-like hiss.

Agata had been briefed on the drugs that might be on offer, so she was prepared. She inhaled enthusiastically into her mouth but was careful not to take the fumes into her lungs, immediately coughing to expunge the smoke. Albertini laughed loudly and encouraged her to persevere.

'Oh my,' she declared, 'I feel dizzy,' flopping down into an empty couch.

Albertini came over to join her but was distracted by the occupant of the neighbouring couch.

Agata did not recognise Francisco Giustiniani, having not formally met him the previous night. He leered at Agata though a drunken, drugged haze but was quickly silenced by Albertini.

'Patience Saheb, I will let you know when she is ready,' he whispered to Francisco.

Agata took the opportunity of Albertini's distraction to extinguish the burn chamber in the pipe she had been given. Then, she could pretend to be smoking and being overcome with the narcotic effect, while keeping her head clear.

Albertini sat beside Agata, leaning inappropriately close and rubbing his hands along her leg. She turned her face away from him to avoid him looking into her eyes, acting floppy and overly relaxed.

'Come with me, my beauty.'

Taking Agata's hand he led her towards the hall. Then, while she acted submissive and slightly uncoordinated, upstairs into the first bedroom at the top of the stairs. Through droopy eye lids, Agata quickly scanned the room as he shut the door.

A large four poster bed dominated the space. It was lit by two lamps, one on a bedside table and the other on a cabinet with a basin and jug, she guessed was for washing.

'Let's have a look at you, my beauty.' Albertini was saying as he swung her around to face him.

She was wearing an elegant red with gold trim silk skirt, with a matching bodice separate from the skirt. She had it tied at the back in such a way as she could reach a securing bow at the top of the lacing. She pulled on the bow loosening the bodice enough for her to wriggle out of it. Underneath she was wearing a thin, white, cotton blouse which barely covered her pert young breasts.

Albertini watched lustfully as her bodice dropped to the floor and she smiled coyly.

She raised her arms and removed the two specially made hair pins, letting her dark locks tumble over her shoulders, holding a pin in each hand by her side, concealing the long blades behind her wrists. A bead of perspiration ran down her long neck, both as the room was warm and her heart pumped frantically. Albertini reached out and put his arms around her waist, pulling her towards him forcefully, kissing her between her heaving breasts. She could smell the scented oil in his hair and feel his breath on her skin which repulsed her.

Agata let out an encouraging sign, raising both her arms slowly, as if to embrace her seducer.

Then, without warning, plunged the sharp pointed blades into each side of his neck.

All the anger and resentment she had kept inside since hearing about her youngest brother's kidnap, boiled over in that moment. She embedded the metal deep inside of him, right to the decorative hilts. The release of pent-up energy and emotion took her breath away.

Both of them momentarily froze. Probably just for a second, but to Agata it seem an age.

Albertini tried to cry out, but the blood filling his mouth made the air leaving his body sound like someone gargling. Both his chest and hers were quickly covered in sticky dark red blood. She was still holding both pins which she pulled out with a struggle and stepped away from him, as his body crumpled onto the floor in a growing pool of red.

She stood for a moment looking at this creature she loathed, as his body's twitching subsided, his eyes remaining wide in shock. A noise outside, perhaps from the bottom of the stair, snapped her out of this mesmeric state.

'Mateo,' she whispered to herself, abruptly alert.

She swung around to the basin and water, frantically trying to clean herself and the hair pins, before pulling back into place the discarded bodice over her lean body, whilst tying the laces as best she could, with the back to her front. Her hands were shaking, making it hard to tie the laces quickly in the dimly lit room. Breathing out to compress her chest, she tugged it around the right way. The bodice did not end up being exactly in the right place nor very tight, but she thought it should be enough to be cover her breasts and much of the blood.

Clutching the hair pins tightly in her left hand, she stepped around Albertini's body and the growing pool of blood. Opening the bedroom door slowly, she peaked outside along the hall to the stairs. There did not seem to be anyone around, the one mounted lamp near the stair casting a poor yellow light. She eased herself out of the door and along the hall to the stair, blowing out the mounted lamp as she passed. Crouching down at the top of the now dark stair, she peered through the wooden banister, looking down into the entrance hall and door to the drawing room, she had come from. There was no movement.

Having last seen Mateo in the drawing room, she thought she should look for him there, though did not really have a plan beyond that. She started to creep down the stair when the drawing room door suddenly opened. Agata froze, holding her breath. A small person with a tray of empty goblets was leaving the drawing room and going down the hall to what she guessed must be the kitchen.

'It must be Mateo,' she thought, but she got a better look at the tray and only caught a glimpse of the holder. Moving down a few more steps, the drawing room door opened again.

She froze, trying to make herself as inconspicuous as possible, helped as the only light came from the mounted lamp in the entrance hall. The large black man in the red turban came out carrying something. He too headed away from the front door towards what she guessed was the kitchen or some other utility area.

Again, she started down the stair, freezing as she saw a shadow cast from another room light coming down the same lower hall. This time, further down the stair, she could see clearly it was Mateo. In desperation, she rushed down the final steps to intercept him before he opened the drawing room door and grabbed his arm. He jumped with fright as this apparition appeared before him and dropped the tray in his hands. The glasses and jug of wine smashed on the floor making a racket, causing them both panic.

'Mateo, come with me,' Agata stage whispered forcefully. Pulling him towards the front door.

As she opened the door, she was more aware, rather than seeing, someone approaching from behind. She did not look back to confirm. Across the road, she could see her carriage where she left it. They both ran towards the dim carriage light, calling out to Orlando on the way.

By the time Agata and Mateo were halfway between the front door and their carriage, the large, turban wearing black man was coming out the door after them. Orlando stood by the carriage, feet apart steadying himself with his arm outstretched, his pistol aiming straight at the black man emerging from the house. Spotting him, the man stopped, put up his hands and backed away towards the door.

The carriage driver woke up the dozing horses with a slap of their reins, while the guard helped Agata and Mateo into the carriage, as Orlando kept the pistol pointing at the turbaned man. When they were safely inside, the guard climbed on beside the driver, and Orlando jumped in the carriage, as it sped off. Watching out of the window for pursuers, Orlando sat opposite the siblings in the carriage clopping through the empty streets. Mateo clung tightly to his sister who stroked his head and kissed him. His rescue was complete, but Orlando wondered how long it would take him to recover from his ordeal.

'Albertini?' Orlando asked Agata. Not being able to resist his curiosity.

'He won't be kidnaping any more children,' she replied, without looking up.

Orlando decided not to ask for details.

A noise outside stirred Francisco from his drunken slumber, impatient to set upon his long-awaited prey. He stumbled out of the drawing room and headed towards the stair and the rendezvous with Albertini in the first bedroom at the top of the stairs. The front door was open, and the black slave was standing in the doorway. He was momentarily puzzled by this, but more interested in what he had paid for upstairs.

The stairs were not steep, however, his head was fuzzy, so he was slow to ascend, especially as there was no stair light. Despite the dark and his blurred vision, he found the bedroom door handle and went in. He was disappointed to see the large four poster bed unused and initially the room appearing empty. Then, as he stepped into the room, he slipped on a pool of blood, tripping over a large body. From floor level, he recognised Albertini's bloated corpse. He was shocked by the open mouth and wide-eyed expression on his lifeless face. The adrenaline which surged through him shocked his mind out of its befuddled state.

Standing up he realised he was alone with a dead body and was now covered in blood. Panic set-in. Could he be accused of killing Albertini? What if this became public? His heart started to race; he knew he had to get out of there. He ran down the stairs to the front door, pushing past the black slave who was closing it and looked for his carriage in the dark street.

Travelling back home in his carriage, his clothes looked like he had been working in an abattoir. He wondered how he would explain this to his family— how would they avoid an investigation?

Later that night, a fire broke out at Albertini's house. The only casualty was Albertini himself. Asleep drunk in his bed the story went. Later, his slaves were freed and along with all his local servants, given positions with the generous Giustiniani family.

Chapter 71

Agata and Mateo's safe arrival at *San Giovanni* was a relief for all, though some showed it more than others. De Poincy, Bernardo and Antonio watched from the raised quarter deck as they arrived but gave the siblings time to embrace and cry as needed. De Poincy signalled Orlando to come up and talk to him.

'So, no Albertini then?' De Poincy noted as he took Orlando aside on the aft end of the quarter deck, keeping his voice low.

'No,' Orlando replied quietly, 'from the blood she is covered in, I assume he is with a higher judge now, but she clearly does not want to talk about it.'

'Mmm,' De Poincy responded thoughtfully, 'as I said to you before, he is…was, just part of a bigger conspiracy and our new guest has confirmed my suspicions.'

'New guest?' Orlando looked puzzled, but De Poincy did not see his face in the poor light.

'Yes, I would introduce you if I could see where he has gone.' De Poincy confirmed, looking around the quarter deck.

On the main deck, Stefano hugged his little brother with relief and they both wept as he led him back to the captain's cabin. Maria, overcome with relief, threw her arms around Agata, tears streaming down her face.

'Thank God you are safe,' she said through sobs. Then recovering her composure, she backed away.

'Sorry, m' lady, I forgot my place for a moment,' she whispered giving a short curtsy.

Agata reached out and took Maria's hands, touched by the love that had grown between them and also relieved to be back safely.

'No need to apologise to me, sweet Maria,' Agata assured her, 'There should be no pretence between us…that I am somehow better than you. We both know the truth and what kind of lady I really am. We may keep up appearances for others, but between us we know it is all an act, a performance and you are more like a sister to me.'

Maria smiled through her tears, then noticed the blood stains on Agata's dress.

'Oh my, are you injured?' Maria exclaimed.

Agata shook her head. 'No, no,' she reassured, but offering no explanation.

'Let's get you inside and cleaned up,' Maria urged.

But Agata hesitated, looking up at Bernardo watching her quietly from the quarter deck. He did not know what had transpired that night, save the successful rescue of Mateo. However, with no sign of Albertini, he guessed he was dead and Agata had some hand in that. It was clear that Agata would need time with her brothers, and he needed to see how this all might change her. His love for her had not diminished, yet he was not sure what kind of relationship they could or should have.

Seeing Bernardo, she wanted to go and embrace him, but not whilst covered in blood. Someone else's blood. Her feelings towards him were clouded with the sense of responsibility she felt for her brothers. She remembered her mother.

"Family is everything…" she would say.

Then she realised Maria was still in front of her, talking. She pushed thoughts of her mother and Bernardo aside, remembering where she was in that moment.

'Go ahead, I am fine,' she assured Maria, 'I will join you presently, I just need a minute…'

Maria curtsied again and left her to ensure there was plenty of water for her to wash with. Agata walked over to the ship's outboard side and listened to the water lapping on the ship's hull. She realised someone else was doing likewise nearby but could not make out who it was in the darkness. Not wanting to engage in any conversation, she decided to retreat to the captain's cabin, clean up, comfort Mateo, and get some sleep.

'Tomorrow we will leave and while at sea, we can think through what to do next,' she thought, realising how weary she was and needing some rest. Caring for her young brother was going to have to be a priority now.

As she left, the stranger, used to watching and listening quietly from the shadows, contemplated what he had overheard. Matching it with what De Poincy had told him about Agata and what she was doing that night.

'An interesting lady, I would like to get to know her,' he thought.

He remained quietly on his own, enveloped by the darkness, analysing the information that he had collected over the last few days, piecing together various clues to the investigations he had been tasked with. He would remain there for quite some time, staring out into the city. By the time he was feeling he should get some sleep, he noted the orange glow of a fire start in the city, a few streets away from them to the east.

'I wonder whose house is on fire?' he thought to himself, as he joined the others in hammocks on the quarter deck.

Part 3 – Gift for a Queen

**As peace and healing are sought, political tensions between late 17th century
European powers lead to a new mission, dangers, and the answer to the
Boscogrande family mystery.**

Chapter 72

San Giovanni slipped out of the harbour in Genoa with no fanfare just as a red dawn broke.

Agata was still asleep in the captain's cabin, with Mateo clinging to her, both emotionally exhausted from their respective ordeals. Captain De Poincy had slept in a hammock on the quarter deck to give the siblings his quarters and some privacy. Maria bedded down in a corner of the great cabin, mothering them all. Only Stefano had ventured out to see them sail, relieved to have his brother back safely, but keen to move on with life.

The morning land breeze helped them out of the harbour and as the sun rose in the sky, a steady westerly wind allowing them to make a steady speed, in otherwise calm conditions.

Between the captain's steward and Maria, the siblings were fussed over. The steward wanting them to eat a hearty breakfast and Maria trying to give Agata privacy to make herself presentable. She was conscious they were surrounded by all these worldly men, but Agata seemed to be in a daze with her little brother not wanting to leave her side.

After breakfasting with his guests on the quarter deck and ensuring the crew had settled into their sea routines, De Poincy went down to see how Agata was doing.

'Are you ready for a visitor?' De Poincy enquired from the open cabin door.

'Yes, yes, please come in Captain,' Agata insisted, 'thank you so much for giving us your cabin last night,' putting on her refined demeanour so well.

She was now all cleaned up, with a light blue silk summer dress, that hugged her trim figure, her hair up neatly showing off her elegant long neck and unblemished skin. De Poincy stared at her for a moment.

'She is truly a most beautiful creature,' he mused. However, he also noted that spark of enthusiasm for life, she had in her eyes before, was somewhat diminished which made him sad.

'Please have your cabin back, captain,' she insisted, 'I think we have put everything in order,' looking around the space, while she tried to hold back tears.

'Oh, you have not yet met Mateo,' she continued, taking his hand, and gently raising his downcast face with her dainty fingers.

'This is Captain De Poincy, who is a good friend and commands this ship,' she explained. Mateo, who showed little emotion, held her hand tightly.

The moment was awkward, De Poincy recognising the pain they were going through but feeling ill-equipped to help them. Distraction he thought might lighten the mood, so he decided to host a lunch that would help his guests mingle.

'There are quite a few guests onboard for this short passage to Livorno. So, I will have my steward prepare a tasty lunch for us all to eat together and there is someone particular I would like you to meet,' De Poincy announced.

Agata smiled but did not seem enthusiastic.

San Giovanni hugged the coast most of the morning. With little swell, the vessel had been steady, allowing everyone to build an appetite for lunch. So, after he confirmed the noon day position, the captain retreated to his cabin to socialise with his guests. There was much chatter in the low-ceilinged great cabin when he arrived. He was glad to see Agata smiling, even if he still detected it was an unenthusiastic performance.

After grabbing something to eat, he approached her, pulling her away from listening to Signior Beniamino's stories, as he noted a new guest arrive.

'Please let me introduce you to Commandeur Robert Blundell,' he ventured, 'Robert, let me introduce you to Agata Conti, whom you have already heard so much about.'

'It is an honour Signorina,' Blundell said with a short, stiff bow and serious face.

'So, you have an advantage over me, Signior, as you know about me, but I know nothing about you.' Agata replied coolly.

'Commandeur Blundell is a fellow Knight of St John but serves as a diplomat representing us at the Vatican and other Royal courts,' De Poincy interjected, 'he is also English, but still a friend,' he smiled, slapping Blundell on the back.

De Poincy left Blundell to elaborate and joined his other guests.

'English eh,' Agata responded, showing more interest as De Poincy had hoped she would. 'I did not know there were any Englishmen in the Order.'

'There are not many but unlike most of my countrymen I am Catholic and generally not welcome in my place of birth. So, I have found a home within the

Order, while many of my family have emigrated to the new world to seek religious freedom there,' Blundell explained, with a sad tone to his voice.

'The English are mysteries to me, but I guess many people are,' Agata responded rapidly losing interest.

Blundell caught her mood and thought of what she had said to her maid on deck the night before. He had seen her, but she did not notice him in the shadows.

"All the world's a stage and all the men and women merely players; they have their exits and their entrances, and one man in his time plays many parts…"
Blundell recited.

Now he had Agata's attention, and she was intrigued. 'That is by an English playwright I greatly admire,' Blundell explained.

'That is a play I think I would like to see.' She stared at Blundell with renewed interest, wondering where she could see a play like that, having never seen a play.

De Poincy came back over to join them with Orlando in tow, looking animated.

'Good to see you two getting on,' he interjected, 'if I may Robert, I would like you to explain again what you have found out and how you have become involved. It will help us all to put you in context and lay out what is still to be discovered.'

Blundell looked at those that were listening and quickly calculated how much to reveal.

'Recently I have been serving as part of the Order's diplomatic mission to the Vatican. There I received a message from the Grand Master about your report of the Gela attack and suspicions,' Blundell started, looking straight at De Poincy. 'You would have not long arrived back in Malta then, but your suspicions did not surprise me. Following the clue that these generous merchants where on route from Genoa to Valencia, I travelled to Madrid to take the Orders' greetings there via Valencia and speaking to contacts along the way. It became clear that there were some forces determined to disrupt the flow of payments from Spain to Genoa, whose purpose seemed to be to destabilise Spanish or Genoese commerce or both. I learned that the date and departure port for the treasury vessels had changed, although not the details, I figured this information was for sale!' then looking at Orlando, 'When I heard that Archbishop Stefanu was sailing to Rome via Genoa, just after the treasury vessels left, I decided to follow. I have long had my suspicions about him and feel he would have been more suited to an assignment in Paris than Madrid.'

He paused to let the others take in what he had just disclosed and to think about how much more to tell them.

'I arrived in Genoa only the day before yesterday to find the Archbishop had already left and spotting *San Giovanni* in port, called on Captain De Poincy.' Blundell took a breath.

'How extensive do you think this conspiracy is?' Orlando asked, with concern.

'Well, clearly a complex international network, but my task is to find out the identity of those behind it and what their ultimate goal is,' Blundell replied.

'Well, the Turks and pirates seem obvious,' De Poincy suggested innocuously.

'They are clearly involved; however, they have to at least have major assistance from others within the international establishment in Europe and…' Blundell paused for effect, 'I believe, whereas making money is the objective for the pirates, damage to Spain and Genoa are the main objectives of other, unknown parties.'

He eased himself into a chair next to Signior Beniamino, who had been quietly listening to the conversation while sipping some wine. He thought the wine was really good and he wondered if it was Maltese. The others stood around, deep in their own thoughts with the implications of what Blundell had said.

Agata leaned back on the captain's desk and had a momentary flashback to her struggle with the pirate on that spot. To take her mind away from the shiver of fear that ran up her spine, she looked over at her brothers. They both sat on the cabin deck, Stefano amusing Mateo by teaching him some knots the sailors had taught him. It was good to see Mateo focusing on something positive and seeming to enjoy the lesson. Hopefully, his mind was beginning to heal; he had still said nothing since the rescue. Bernardo remained deep in thought, standing near the boys. He looked as if he was torn between joining Blundell's conversation or the boys on the deck tying knots.

'What will you do now, Bernardo,' she thought to herself, 'and where should we go?'

Although she had intimated that they would return to Malta after this trip, she had actually, not given it much thought, being totally focused on rescuing her brother. Now she needed to think what was best for him, despite her feelings being all over the place.

Beniamino and Blundell were quietly talking to each other when Agata turned back to refocus on them.

'May I ask,' she interrupted, 'how do you go about finding out about this network?'

All eyes turned to Blundell, similar questions rolling about everyone's minds. He paused and smiled up at her.

'You ask around!' Blundell replied, as if it were so obvious. However, with the blank stares that greeted him, it was clearly not obvious to all his listeners.

'Archbishop Stefanu left Genoa on route to Rome and will travel via Livorno and Siena, where I have some contacts…after that, I will probably follow him to Rome,'

Blundell explained. 'People talk…it is just about following that talk and seeing where it leads.' There was general credulity, but Blundell sounded confident and now all would have to choose their own path.

This was not the sort of task De Poincy desired, so he was pleased to hear Blundell would continue to pursue the issue. He was also pleased the Grand Master had taken his concerns seriously and passed the investigation on. Now his mission was completed, so unless something else came up, returning to Malta was probably the next move for him.

'Once we safely deliver you to Livorno, we should probably not stay long, but continue on back to Malta.' De Poincy declared to all generally, but unenthusiastically.

'Although I would have liked to have pursued this further, I think I need to return to my duties in Palermo soon,' Orlando interjected, 'and although I will keep my ears open for any useful information about this network, I doubt we will hear much in Sicily.'

His thoughts were already turning towards how much he should report to the Inquisition on his return.

Agata looked over to Bernardo to hear about his plans, but he remained silent.

'When do you think we will arrive in Livorno, captain?' Signior Beniamino asked.

'If the wind continues to be favourable, between four or five hours from now. Well before sunset,' De Poincy confirmed.

'Excellent,' Beniamino declared happily, 'plenty of time to make arrangements,' he continued thoughtfully. 'Soon after we arrive, I will run my errand for the Doge and speak to some old friends from the Jewish community there. I will see if they have heard any useful information from the merchants that come and go. We can also find lodging for anyone who needs it for the night,' he concluded, addressing the group, but particularly looking at Agata.

She thought for a moment, but remained unsure of her next step, realising Mateo needed somewhere he would feel safe to heal.

'My family has an estate in the Livorno hills, near Monte Nero,' Beniamino continued, 'my youngest sister and aunt, both widowed, live there with some of their grown children and their families,' and looking at Agata and the boys, almost reading her mind, 'you will be welcome to stay there until you decide where you want to go next.'

'Monte Nero,' Bernardo suddenly pitched it, 'the Sanctuary of Montenero is there, is it not?' he asked.

'Certainly, it is, we could pass it on our way to my estate and could drop you off if you like?' Beniamino offered.

'Thank you that would be helpful, I need time to pray about either going onto Rome with the commentaries or back to medical training in Malta,' Bernardo commented.

Then, not looking at Agata, fell silent again. Beniamino gave a questioning look to Agata.

'Thank you, Signior Beniamino, your hospitality would be useful, while we too consider if we are to return to Malta right away or not.' Agata gratefully agreed.

'Our sabbath begins tomorrow night, so I will complete as much business as I can tonight, travel to my estate tomorrow, then we can all rest, while both of us observe our holy days,' Beniamino addressed the group, 'so, may I suggest we all meet up on Monday night at my estate and compare findings, then decide our individual next steps?'

There were some thoughtful nods.

'I too have to decide if I wait in Livorno for the Doge's task to be completed, or return later, but by Monday that should become clear…can you stay that long captain?'

'I do not see why not,' De Poincy replied.

So, with relieved smiles all around, it was agreed.

As the sun became low in the sky, Signior Beniamino's carriage drew up alongside *San Giovanni* at their berth in Livorno. De Poincy and Orlando accompanied him to the jewellers in the Jewish quarter of the city, as pre-arranged. Orlando waited by the carriage with the driver as De Poincy accompanied Signior Beniamino and the flat box to meet with a jeweller who he knew well. Once that delicate task was completed, they all sighed with relief, as they headed back to the ship to collect Agata and the boys. Later they dined in a nearby Inn where they had secured lodgings for the night.

Following that, Blundell and Beniamino had both arranged meetings that evening with local acquaintances. Agata decided she and her brothers would keep a low profile and ate in their room, this would shelter Mateo from having to interact with strangers.

Hopefully, it would also give her a chance to think through what the best course of action would be for them. Rescuing Mateo had dominated her mind so much, she had not considered what would happen after that. Fully considering the consequences of both saving him or failing to do so had been too much for her. Now she had to think what was best for Mateo, who had not yet uttered a word.

Chapter 73

The sunlight was almost gone as Blundell left the busy waterfront and walked briskly along a narrow, deserted alleyway. He knocked on an unadorned wooden door in an unassuming building with no windows. A small hatch at eye level opened sharply and an ear could just be seen through a metal grill.

'For lack of fruit, the tree was cursed,' he whispered into the grill which then shut abruptly. He waited patiently.

With a creek, the heavy door opened, and an arm beckoned him into a lightless void.

As the door closed behind him, he stood, motionless in complete darkness. A thin hand took his arm, and he allowed himself to be led across a stone floor, the tap of his leather boots echoing into a cavern-like space. The guide was silent and directed slowly in the darkness' allowing him to carefully place each foot down on the smooth surface.

They must have turned a corner, as a faint glow of a lamp could now be seen ahead, and he was led towards that spot. Reaching out old hands, feeling the heat from the light, the unseen guide took the lamp from its hook. Turning a screw to extend the wick, it illuminated the room. Handing the lamp to Blundell, the guide turned to leave. At that moment, Blundell caught sight of his lifeless eyes, as he disappeared back towards the entrance.

Blundell lifted the lamp and looked at a series of simple wooden cubicles in a long dark, unadorned corridor. Some cubicles had closed curtains, others open. Knowing the routine well, he went into an open one and removed his boots, sword, and outer clothing. On a hook was a long, white silk robe, plain, except for a black Grail symbol on the breast. A cross, cut out of the middle of the black challis shape, allowed the white silk to show through.

In additionally, there was a long, pointed hat, also made of the same white silk, except stiffened with something. Attached to the hat was a long veil, which when allowed to drop from the rim of the hat, covered his face. Two eye holes were cut to allow the wearer to see, but once on, the covered head was anonymous.

Exiting the changing space and, leaving the curtain closed, he could hear the entrance door creaking open. Without hesitation, he picked up a large white candle. It was attached to a sword like wooden handle complete with hand guard, which was lying on a low bench in the hall. He lit the candle with the lamp flame. Then, turning the wick back down to save the oil, he returned it to the hook on the wall where he had first seen it.

With the candle held in front of him, lighting his way, Blundell carefully walked down the dark corridor passing more curtained cubicles, towards the sound of low chanting.

He descended a short flight of spiralling stone steps, emerging into a spacious subterranean area with large pillars, supporting the foundations of the building above. The pillars had wall-mounted, inward facing metal brackets holding torches. Together with the candles of the many shrouded figures, they brightly illuminated the space in marked contrast to the gloom in the changing area. Unsurprisingly this place was smoky. The air was filled with the smell from the candle wax and increasingly from incense as he entered the almost bare chamber.

All present were gathered round a simple stone altar in the centre of this enormous basement, rhythmically reciting Bible verses.

'…For they have shed the blood of saints and prophets, and thou hast given then blood to drink; for they are worthy…' repeated like a mantra.

As Blundell approached the group, some turned to make room for him in the circle, greeting him with raised left hands, palm exposed, showing a white scar in the centre of their hand. Blundell did, likewise, revealing a similar scar.

In the centre, three initiates, their identities hidden with the same silk robes and hoods as the assembly, held their left palms out over a bowl on the alter. A tall figure, dressed in a similar styled robe and hood, but in scarlet silk moved forward. He raised a heavily bejewelled, short-bladed dagger and cut each hand, allowing the blood to drip into the bowl.

The hands stretched out over the bowl trembled as did Blundell's, remembering the pain of his initiation.

Afterwards another white clad figure reached out to each bleeding hand, pushing a cloth into it, to staunch the bleeding and expertly bound the wound. Meanwhile, the scarlet clad figure raised the bowl above his head and said a prayer. He then handed the bowl in turn to the three inductees. Each drank from the bowl, and as they did so, there was stamping of bare feet on the stone floor, while hands kept hold of the long candles. Pronouncements of faith and oaths of secrecy followed.

After a final prayer, the crowd started to disperse into small groups with quiet chatter. Blundell hung back, watching the three newcomers, and listening to whispered conversations around him. It had been a year since he last attended a brotherhood meeting in Livorno, but the ceremonies were all the same. It would be in a tavern later that discussions would happen. So, he quietly redressed, exited the building, and headed back out into the now dark alley.

It looked as if he was the first to leave and he found a dark doorway along the alley.

There he could observe unnoticed both those leaving the gathering and any carriages picking participants up from the main harbour road. He was well accustomed with waiting and watching from the shadows, so settled himself down to be patient, observant, and alert.

With little sun light, it was hard to see faces of those who departed in twos and threes mostly. However, Blundell looked out for distinctive clothes or walks, so he could identify the person later, and possibly follow them to the nearby tavern or the harbour area.

The sun had gone down completely when Blundell walked to the tavern in almost complete darkness. However, he had only to retrace his steps along the alleyway and turn right onto the waterfront. It was his usual meeting place and was already busy when he tried to find a spare table and stool. On entry, he spotted a group of four who he had seen leave the assembly and go to the tavern, huddled together talking. Unfortunately, he could not sit close enough to hear what they talked about, but he watched them discreetly. He had not long sat down when two heavily bearded men, probably in their early thirties slumped down opposite him. They were already guzzling tankages of watered-down red wine to quench their thirst.

They sweated profusely in loose fitting cotton shirts, showing off muscular chests. He did not greet them or even look up.

'It has been a while since we last saw you,' burped Rodrigo, the larger of the two, slamming his tankard clumsily onto the rough wooden table and spilling some of the content.

Enrico, the smaller of the two, but equally as gassy, came around to sit beside Blundell.

'Do you not like us anymore, amigo?' he slurred.

Blundell looked up with a menacing stare at these two overtly jolly men. A sly smile came over his face, as he reached out and clapped Enrico on the shoulder boisterously.

'So, what have you two reprobates been up to since our paths crossed last?' he asked them smiling.

'What do Spanish traders do—buy, sell, and look for good deals, amigo?' Rodrigo replied, '…and you have always been good at pointing us towards a good deal.'

A large breasted matron with a sour face, came by their table and put a jug of wine down with another tankard. She scooped up some coins Blundell had left ready for her.

'Mmm…' Blundell responded thoughtfully. His new companions poured him some wine and helped themselves to some more.

'…not sure I know of any ripe deals for you to pluck right now though a treasury vessel arrived in Genoa recently, so their banks have plenty of silver to re-invest.' Rodrigo looked at Enrico, nodding as if planning their next move.

'Have you heard anything interesting during your travels…anyone causing trouble?' Blundell enquired. 'Anything outside of Rome about the Knights of the Apocalypse since they locked up Agostino Gabrino in the madhouse?'

'No…' Rodrigo replied scornfully, 'that mob are not widespread and will just be a nuisance to any they consider the antichrist.'

A small, stooping cleric came into the tavern and went straight to the table of the four men Blundell was keeping an eye on. He did not sit down, but leaned in, seeming to give instructions, then left. The four men followed close behind. Blundell had to find out who they were meeting so excused himself and followed them out of the tavern, staying away from any lights. By the time Blundell reached the street, he could see another man with a lantern guiding the five towards a carriage nearby. The door opened and the cleric got inside, but the other four and lantern holder waited by the carriage door, looking in. Blundell edged closer hoping to overhear the conversation. It looked like the four men he was following, were listening intently to whoever was inside the carriage. Unfortunately, if he went any closer he would give his presence away, so he stayed close to the less well-lit side of the tavern.

Suddenly the conversation was clearly over, as the carriage door closed. The lantern holder climbed up by the driver and the carriage pulled away. The four men were left in almost complete darkness save from the harbour lights.

'So, what are you up to this time?' whispered a voice behind Blundell.

He recognised the voice but was annoyed with himself that he had not noticed anyone approaching in the darkness.

'I must be losing my edge,' he thought.

'Can we help?' Enrico asked enthusiastically and in far too loud a whisper.

Blundell pushed him back towards the tavern, while keeping one eye on the four men.

The four did not seem to notice them and started to walk along the harbour road, deep in conversation.

'Come on, amigo,' Rodrigo pleaded, 'you know we are good at following people.'

Blundell thought for a moment but was keen not to lose sight of the four men in the darkness. He remembered how helpful these two Spaniards had been in the past. Reasoning he might need help following these men and need not disclose any sensitive information to his helpers.

'Alright, be quiet and follow me,' he whispered, as he started to move out into the street, 'I will explain later…for now, we must not lose sight of these four.'

In truth, it was easier with three pairs of eyes and ears. If spotted, they would just pretend to be a group of slightly inebriated friends walking home from the tavern. The four men employed a boy with a torch to light their way and guide them. This made it even easier to follow them. Soon, it was evident where they were going too. Across one of the many canals in the city, linking the harbour to the warehouses, were inns that provided accommodation and food.

Blundell, Rodrigo, and Enrico waited outside the chosen inn for a while, to ensure this was where the men were going to stay for the night, rather than just eat and drink.

Blundell thought about these two "amigos" and how much he could trust them. He had first worked with them a couple of years before, when investigating what was happening to silver, being sent to pay troops, that was repeatedly going missing. At that time, both these men were experienced soldiers serving in the Spanish army.

'As it looks like they will be staying here overnight, we will take shifts at watching the place. Enrico, you go first and Rodrigo you relieve him before dawn. We will go and find some accommodation at another inn,' Blundell instructed, '…be discrete—no interaction.'

'Don't worry, we know the routine,' Enrico dismissively replied, 'so who are they?'

'To be honest, I don't know, but they are my only, very tentative leads and I can't tell you much more.'

Blundell paused in his explanation and thought for a moment, how much to tell these two who had loyally served him before.

'They are part of a secret society I infiltrated not long after we last saw each other. The theft of the silver we located before and what is going on now, may all be connected. We recovered much of the troop's pay then and punished some villains but did not fully get to the bottom of who was behind the whole thing. After we parted, I continued to follow leads.'

'We are with you, amigo,' Enrico declared, clapping him on the back and smiling broadly, though in the dark, he could not see that.

'Much appreciated,' Blundell responded, 'I hope I am not drawing you away from any good business.'

'Naw, we have nothing on right now…to be honest we were better soldiers than we are merchants,' Rodrigo admitted sheepishly.

'And the King rewarded us well when we helped recover all that silver,' Enrico added.

'So, what is this group you have infiltrated?' Rodrigo asked quietly, as they left Enrico and retraced their steps along the main harbour road.

'They call themselves the Knights of the Holy Blood, or Blood Brothers for short,' Blundell explained, 'and they appear to have meeting houses in many capitals and major port cities. So, far they seem harmless, but it is their widespread network and secrecy that has drawn me to look into them. For now, we just need to observe with little interaction.'

Chapter 74

The next day dawned with a bright, cloudless, blue, summer sky that did nothing to hide the burning sun. It was just as well *San Giovanni* was not trying to sail, as there was not a breath of wind available to help them move. Agata and the boys sweated as they bumped along with Signior Beniamino in his carriage to his family estate in the hills. Thanks to investments by the Medici Duke of Tuscany, there was a good road from the port city of Livorno and into the hills of Monte Nero. Nevertheless, it was not a comfortable journey though the countryside was beautiful to look at. They all remained silent, deep in their own thoughts.

They dropped Bernardo off at the religious complex that surrounded the Shire of Our Lady of Grace, who was the patron saint of Tuscany. The Vallumbrosan monks, similar to Bernardo's Benedictine order, maintained it. They would give him sanctuary while he contemplated his future and provide a father confessor. He was pleased to spend a few days immersed in the rhythm of prayer and worship which would hopefully settle his mind.

Meanwhile, it was a long, hot, and boring day for Blundell and his team, as they kept watch on the four men. They observed them leave the inn late morning and enjoy a long leisurely lunch near the harbour. Returning to the inn for a siesta in the heat of the afternoon. As the sun began to disappear over the horizon, the team wondered if this was a waste of time. On a hunch, Blundell started keeping a watch on the meeting place of the "Knights of the Holy Blood", where he had been the previous night. Just before sunset, he noticed two men, one clearly senior clergy, going into the same door he had the night before.

'Would the four men they were following, join them?' he wondered.

He decided he needed a closer look, so he told Rodrigo, still observing the inn, that he was going into the meeting house, and they should continue to follow the four wherever they went. Using the "For lack of fruit the tree was cursed" passphrase, he once again entered the darkened building, led by the blind man.

This time he did not leave his clothes, boots, and sword in the changing cubical, but still put the white, sink robe and hood on.

Neither did he take the large candle that was provided, in case they were counted. Instead, he used a small one of his own to navigate the dark winding stone steps, blowing the flame out just before he reached the basement level. He felt his way around the outer wall. He tried to find an alcove or hiding place behind a pillar, using only the dim light from the candles on the altar and held by the two men who had entered before him. He tried to remember the layout of the space from the night before, and finally found a shadowed recess on the outer perimeter where a large bulbous pillar connected to the wall. He slid himself in as tightly as he could behind it. Although now unable to see the altar or those around it, he could hear most of what the two men were saying.

'The others should be here soon...' one said, '...you do not need to do anything more to the altar, we will just talk...'

Meanwhile back outside the Inn, Enrico returned for his shift watching the four men.

'Rodrigo, I am here,' Enrico whispered, 'do you want me to relieve you while you grab some food or...?'

'Shu, they are coming out,' Rodrigo, interrupted, 'let's both follow them...Blundell has gone back to the place he was last night, and he thinks these fellows will go there too.'

Keeping their distance, they trailed the four back to the alleyway near the tavern and to the unassuming door which they entered after speaking through a hatch.

'So, he was right.' Rodrigo whispered, mostly to himself, as they tucked themselves into a siding behind the tavern and off the alleyway. The place was good for hiding at night being unlit and just storing the waste from the tavern. However, it stank, and rats scurried over their feet as they stood there.

'Well, I guess this will take a while, so I may as well grab some food in the tavern...' Rodrigo whispered, '...let me know if you see them leave.'

Enrico grunted agreement, not so pleased about the hiding place behind the tavern. It smelled bad and he squirmed as he felt a rat running over his feet in the darkness. Looking around, he could see the shapes of more rats running around the back ally. He kicked them when he could but did not want to make much noise or draw attention to himself.

Chapter 75

Blundell noted the new arrivals more by the dancing shadows on the ceiling of the cellar than the bare footsteps. There was brief murmured greeting, followed by a prayer with the recital of the same Bible passage as the night before. Then clearly, they turned to pressing business.

'So, the latest payment still arrived in Genoa, after all our efforts and having to be involved with that distasteful Corsican,' stated the same voice who said the prayers, 'We will have to find another way to de-stabilise Genoa's economy and put some money into Louis's treasury…things are becoming critical.'

'But we win every battle…' another voice interjected, '…at least here in Europe… and Charles is getting weaker all the time…soon he will die and with no heir…'

'It is not just about winning battles,' the first voice interrupted, 'Louis is running out of money fast!' There was a general disapproving murmur.

'Our failure to intercept the silver from the Spanish colonies and the payments to Genoa means they can keep funding their failures, but we can't! Nor will Charles' demise necessarily change things, not financially anyway. We need to weaken Spain, even before the contest for that throne erupts into more war.'

'So, what now?' asked another voice.

There was a pause, Blundell held his breath.

'There is a priceless gift being commissioned by the Doge of Genoa, destined for Queen Marie Anne of Spain, as Charles tries to appease her into trying for another child,' the original voice was explaining, 'we believe this gift is to be made by Livorno jewellers, but when the stones will arrive and which jewellers, we do not know. If we could intercept this, it would not only cause great embarrassment, but it would also restore Louis's faith in us and bring in a tidy sum.' Murmuring of approval was evident.

'Squeeze every contact you have…we must find how and when this delivery will take place.'

More murmuring stopped Blundell hearing the rest of the conversation, but it was clear the meeting was coming to an end and at least one person was leaving.

Blundell had no idea of the expensive gift they were talking about. However, he was now convinced these conspirators were working on behalf of France. It was evident they were from the same group as the ones who had both collaborated with the pirates and probably tried to steal the Spanish army pay before. He had to find a way to expose them.

For now, he made himself as small as he could, praying the shadows continued to hide him as the gang began to leave. He could see the light of one disappear around the stone stair, then a group of four departed together. Finally, the last one put out the altar candles and followed them up the stair. No one noticed him. He sighed with relief but continued to wait, allowing them to clear the building before emerging.

Enrico saw the door open, and one person leave, being picked up by a carriage at the end of the alley on the harbour road. He slipped quietly into the tavern and waved at Rodrigo, who came out to their hiding place behind the tavern and watched for more to leave. Within minutes, a group of four emerged, chattering to each other near the door.

'So far, someone on their own quickly disappeared in a carriage and that looks like the four we have been following…they do not look like they are in a hurry to leave…maybe they are waiting for someone else?' Enrico whispered.

Inside the meeting place, the Master of the house slipped some coins to the blind guide, as he was leaving.

'Grazie Salvatore, I am the last one, you can lock up now and go home.'

'No master, there is one more person,' Salvatore replied, 'I guided seven persons in, but only six of you have left.'

The master froze for a moment, then stuck his head out of the door.

'Nico, come back here with your men,' he shouted out, '…we may have an unwanted visitor.'

The four immediately turned and re-entered the building, the door slamming behind them.

'Holy mother of God…what do we do now?' Enrico asked Rodrigo, as they heard what had just been said.

'No idea, amigo, we will just have to pray they bring Blundell out alive, as we two can't storm the place...' Rodrigo replied, fingering the hilt of his sword, frustrated by their helplessness.

In the dark entrance, Salvatore guided the House Master, Nico and the other three to the chamber with the cubicles. There they each picked up long candles and drew swords and daggers, then looked in all the cubicles. As they were all empty, they carefully descended the stone staircase, assembling at the bottom and looking around. The basement looked empty, but they started to walk around the perimeter and look behind the large pillars. They were beginning to think Salvatore was getting senile and miscounted, when, Nico spotted the edge of a leather boot protruding from the base of one of the pillars that was attached to the outer wall. He signalled silently to his compatriots, and they gathered around the pillar, weapons ready. They pounced on Blundell together—he did not stand a chance.

'Don't kill him...we need to know what he heard, and what others might know,' the Master cried. Just in time, as Nico's blade hovered above Blundell's throat.

They dragged him out of his hiding place and in front of the Master, who was carefully calculating outcomes.

'So, do we question him here?' Nico asked, keeping his blade at Blundell's throat as two others held his arms and the third held the candles.

'No, I know an ideal place,' the Master answered with a sly smile. 'There is an abandoned macello (abattoir) nearby that used to belong to a Jew before the last purge. We can hang him from a meat hook there and no one will hear him scream, we can leave the body handing, crucifixion like, there and blame the Jews. The jeweller we will be looking for is bound to be a Jew and we can use the uproar that will create to allow us to flush out the jeweller.'

He smiled at the prospect.

'We also need to let the Archbishop know...he might want to interrogate him too.'

They marched Blundell up the staircase at the point of several swords.

Meanwhile Blundell prayed Enrico and Rodrigo were keeping a close watch on the proceedings and would follow with help. He was thinking this would also expose the Archbishop if they could rescue him at the right time. He breathed deeply to calm his nerves and slow his heart that felt like it was going to explode.

Outside, Enrico and Rodrigo watched one person leave. They were not sure if this was a good or bad sign. However, when that person returned with a carriage, stopping right outside the door they were watching, they knew it was not good. Several people left the building in a group, and they thought they could see someone being bundled into the carriage.

It was hard to see from their hiding place with the carriage in the way, but they decided to take the risk and follow. It was easy to follow the carriage, as it had to travel slowly on the cobbled streets. It did not go far, stopping by a large, abandoned looking building a short distance from the harbour. They waited until the gang, now clearly dragging someone, went around the back, then followed, keeping to the shadows until they found somewhere to observe without being seen.

Chapter 76

The boarded up macello, a couple of streets and a canal away from the harbour was surrounded by a low wall and had entrances in the front and back. Live animals would be brought through the back entrance and butchered carcasses would leave by the front. This was all a good distance from other buildings and a scrawny, unkept hedge ran around the perimeter of the property. Blundell was dragged in via the back door, straight into the slaughter room. With hands tied by leather thongs, he was hung from a meat hook over a metal vat for draining the blood of butchered animals, to ensure it was Kosha.

'Leave him hanging there,' the Master of the house instructed, 'it should make him more cooperative when we interrogate him…I will take a message to the Archbishop and see if he wants to question him personally.'

There were wicked smiles all around, as a heavy metal door was slammed shut.

Blundell was in pain and dazed from the beating he had received since being captured. The place was as silent as a tomb, except for a drip, drip from a mixture of blood and sweat running off his chin and into the metal vat his feet dangled in.

In the rear courtyard, there was a broken cart, leaning heavily to one side, as a wheel was missing. It was behind this, that Rodrigo and Enrico hid to watch for an opportunity to rescue Blundell. They had not been in position to see the gang take him into the rear entrance but did see the one they assumed was in charge leave, confirming to them that this was the only door not boarded up.

'This is where they will interrogate and perhaps kill him.' Rodrigo whispered to Enrico, while they hid behind the cart.

'Should we try to break in and rescue him…there are probably only four guarding him right now?' Enrico asked.

Rodrigo did not reply right away as he thought about their options.

'Not unless we can figure out a way to get in without them realising who we are until we have our daggers at their throats. Right now, I can't think of how we can do that.'

There was another silence. Enrico stared at the rear door from behind the wooden cart, Listening to the cockroaches scurrying around the rotting wood and the soil under their feet.

A slight breeze brought the whiff of rotten flesh up his nose and he wondered what this place had been. He was keen to try to rescue his friend, remembering how Blundell had fought so hard beside them when they were almost overwhelmed by attackers. However, he realised they could not just smash the door down and expect to fight off four armed, prepared men in this abandoned building.

Rodrigo put his hand on Enrico's arm and leaned in towards him, 'The man that just left,' he whispered, 'from what we have seen, he looks like being in charge. So, with him gone, the other four are probably holding Blundell for now…if they had killed him, they would have all left.'

'Mmm,' Enrico responded nodding.

'I bet he has gone to tell their boss, probably the one who left in the carriage, that they captured a spy and to see if he wants to interrogate him.'

Rodrigo squeezed Enrico's arm so he would not interrupt his train of thought, as he verbally processed the situation.

'It is unlikely he will return before dawn, so Blundell will be kept alive until then at least, which gives us this night to organise a rescue which needs to be ready when that door opens on his return.'

'Makes sense, though by then we will have at least six to contend with…the odds are getting worse!' Enrico was sounding despondent.

'Yes, but we can get some help.' He waited while Enrico caught up with his thinking, but there was silence.

'Blundell mentioned there was a Knights of Malta ship in the harbour that he had arrived on…what was it…*San Giovanni*…if I can find it and convince a few knights to help us, we could sort this lot out.'

Rodrigo was pleased he had reasoned that all out, but now wondered how he would find *San Giovanni* in the dark and convince anyone to help.

'Keep watch here, I should be back before dawn, and we will need to know if anything has changed.' Rodrigo whispered, patting his friend on the back, and slipping out from behind the cart, along the side of the building and towards the harbour.

Chapter 77

It took much longer than Rodrigo had assumed to find *San Giovanni* in a large harbour in the dark, and to re-find the abandoned macello. The pre-dawn light made everything look weirdly different and the previously empty, quiet streets were starting to come alive for the day. By the time Rodrigo returned with Captain De Poincy and six other knights, there was a black carriage sitting outside the front of the building. A sleepy driver was leaning up against the carriage and seemed to be alone. They had to ensure he didn't raise the alarm, so Rodrigo whispered an idea into the captain's ear. He nodded his agreement and Rodrigo set off down the street. He put on a wobbly gait as he passed the carriage, as if returning from a heavy night of drinking. To attract attention, he mumbled an old Spanish army song. He couldn't remember all the words but that didn't matter.

The driver became alert, watching him carefully. It wasn't the best of diversions, but it allowed Pierre, one of De Poincy's senior knights, to sneak up beside the driver. By the time he realised he was there, Pierre struck him hard on the temple. He collapsed to the ground unconscious.

Rodrigo signalled them all to be quiet, then led them around the side of the building to the broken cart, where Enrico was still on watch. Brief nods of greetings were exchanged, but Enrico looked agitated.

'You took a while,' he moaned to Rodrigo, '...three men just arrived...the one we saw leave, a small cleric, and a bigger fellow, probably guarding the cleric...now we have an army...' looking at all the knights huddled beside them, '...do we just storm the place?'

De Poincy had been looking carefully at the building while he listened to Enrico.

Dawn's light was making the structure clearer. It had two levels and at the back had a lower building extending out from the rear of the main section. On the second story, above the extension, there were some windows that were not boarded up. De Poincy nudged Pierre and Rodrigo with his arm, pointing to one of these windows above the lower building.

'If we give you a leg up, do you think you two could get up to that window and sneak in?' he whispered.

They looked at the window, then each other, and nodded. Orders were whispered around the knights. Two knights left their swords behind, holding onto their daggers to stop them clinking. They had no armour on, to limit any noise, so crept silently over to the lower building and knelt down by the outer wall.

Pierre and Rodrigo did likewise and with these knights acting as steps, clambered on top of the lower building, tiptoeing across the roof to the window which was now at shoulder height. They looked in but could not see anything in the darkness. With their daggers, they prised the window half open, sticking their heads inside, and listened. Voices could be faintly heard from down below. Pierre helped Rodrigo ease himself through the window and into the room, then Rodrigo returned the favour—they stood for a moment and listened. There were louder voices now and a cry of pain, this could be enough distraction for them to sneak in closer.

In the slaughter room, Blundell had passed out, so Nico punched him awake and drew his dagger over his bare chest, making him cry out in pain. The Archbishop stood in front of Blundell and looked at his face intently.

'I have seen you somewhere before…now where was it?' he half asked himself.

'Who are you?' the Master shouted at Blundell, signalling to the other men, who struck him on the chest with old chains they had found hanging in the slaughter room.

'You better tell us who you are and what you know, or we will drain you like an old goat,' Nico threatened.

Blundell's eyes were swollen from the previous beating, but he spat blood in Nico's general direction defiantly. The general commotion allowed Pierre to signal to his comrades, and two more knights had joined him above the slaughter room.

The Archbishop noted the first rays of sun light starting to peak in through the boards on the windows and signalled to the Master of the house to follow him out of the slaughter room towards the back door.

'Day has arrived, and I can't be seen here…this is going to take a while, but you know the information we need, then dispose of the body as you suggested.'

As he finished speaking his bodyguard opened the back door and all three walked into the rear courtyard.

'Come to me after dark tonight and report,' he concluded, and with this, he, and his guard disappeared around the side of the building.

As the Master turned to go back into the rear door, he was struck on the back of the head by one of the knights that had been crouching close by after helping his brothers onto the lower building's roof. Without another word, De Poincy, Enrico and remaining knights rushed through the back door. Shouts from Blundell's interrogators and clashing of steel alerted Rodrigo, Pierre and the other two knights that their brothers were attacking. They swooped down the short staircase from the room above and joined the affray.

Nico and his three accomplices, despite their surprise at the sudden arrival of the knights, put up a strong fight and managed to injure several rescuers. However, they paid with their lives for that. Enrico and Rodrigo carefully took Blundell down from the hook he was hanging from while the other knights looked around the building for anyone else—friend or foe. By the time they looked outside, both the Archbishop's carriage and the House Master, left unconscious by the back door, were gone.

Blundell was in a sorry state, unable to walk and weak from loss of blood. The knights made a simple litter from one of the inside doors and carried his barely conscience body back to their ship in the nearby harbour. He felt relieved at being rescued and grateful to be in the *San Giovanni* Hospitaller's care, though he could not express this.

Back onboard, Rodrigo and Enrico were sitting in the captain's cabin, giving a report of what had happened when Antonio came in with his report on Blundell's condition.

'How is he?' De Poincy asked concerned.

Antonio wiped his blood-soaked hands and looked worried.

'Well, I have just about finished cleaning him up and examining him,' Antonio said, 'he is in a bad state…several broken ribs and he has lost a lot of blood…not sure if there are any internal injuries…I will monitor him over the next twenty-four hours. If he does not deteriorate, I think he will live, but he will take a long time to heal and needs to be somewhere he can rest and regain his strength.'

'Thank you, Antonio, I know he is in good hands, and we will keep him in our prayers over the next few days.' De Poincy assured.

The Hospitaller left and the captain paced his cabin deep in thought for a few minutes.

Rodrigo and Enrico waited patiently for him to continue their report, appreciating the goblet of wine, he had given them.

'So, it is clear Blundell suspected this group and he may well have information about them we should hear, but you do not know what went on before he was captured…am I understanding you correctly?'

'Yes, Capitano,' Rodrigo replied, feeling he was back in the army, 'he told us something was going on, but he was not exactly sure what. He was trying to discover who was master-minding things…these men being his only lead.'

De Poincy stared at these two Spaniards, strangers to him, but clearly trusted allies of Blundell, who he did know and trust.

'Are you two prepared to continue to help us?' De Poincy asked point blank.

'Yes, sir,' they both chorused. 'We have fought with Roberto before and will not abandon him now,' Rodrigo added.

'Good,' De Poincy continued to pace, 'I will furnish you with some money to pay for accommodation ashore and you can clean yourselves up here before you go there. Go back to where we found Blundell and dispose of the bodies. Then, discretely, keep an eye on the place to see if those that escaped return. Can you do that?'

'Certainly,' Rodrigo continued to be the spokesman, but they both nodded. 'We will watch the place and as soon as it is dark, we will dispose of the bodies. When do you sail?'

'Probably Tuesday morning…I have a meeting Monday night. Report back to me at sun-up on Monday.'

With that, the captain concluded the meeting and called his steward. This was all so much more Blundell's world than his. However, he was glad they were able to help and now they needed more information to figure out what was going on.

Chapter 78

The harbour was a hive of activity on the bright Monday morning, with stores and cargo being loaded onto the various vessels all around. Rodrigo and Enrico had dressed as smartly as they could in order to report to Captain De Poincy. They felt more than a little intimidated by him, yet keen to check up on their old friend's condition.

The captain's steward knocked on the cabin door, where De Poincy and Antonio were in conversation.

'Those two men to see you, capt'n, shall I bring them in or tell them to wait?'

'Send them in now…this is good timing,' the captain responded rising to greet the two Spaniards.

'Gentlemen, we have good news about our brother…' De Poincy announced, as Rodrigo and Enrico came into his cabin. '…please sit down and Antonio will explain.'

The captain's demeanour was very different to the night they rescued Blundell and he oozed with friendly charm, making them feel much more relaxed than their last encounter.

All eyes turned to Antonio.

'I am pleased to say, Commandeur Blundell is recovering well. I do not think he had any injuries to his internal organs, though his broken ribs are causing him much pain and the loss of blood makes him very weak. However, with rest, I believe he will make a good recovery.'

Antonio smiled as he finished, as did everyone else and there was a general sigh of relief mixed in with other emotions.

'However,' Antonio continued, 'I have just recommended to the captain, that the Commandeur does not sail with us tomorrow, as such a voyage would cause him much pain, even if the weather is fine.'

All eyes turned now to the captain for his reaction.

'This morning, a friend of ours will travel from his estate in the hills to the city for a meeting. Once that is concluded, he will pick me up and take me to his villa to meet with those that we have been working with lately.' The captain's intensity had returned, and they all listened carefully.

'I will ask him if we can leave Commandeur Blundell to recover at his villa…from what friar Antonio tells me this could take many weeks.' The captain started to pace in front of the aft window, trying to think things through.

'Antonio, a carriage ride to the Livorno hills with broken ribs is going to be painful. However, if we send the carriage back for you after siesta, could you accompany him and make him as comfortable as possible?' the captain asked.

Antonio looking concerned, nodded.

'I am sure he will be well cared for once there.'

The captain sat back down, and Antonio asked if he could go back to his duties. He nodded to the two Spaniards as he left.

'I am sure the Commandeur will be please if you visit him before you leave,' he said.

'We would like to see him,' they both responded, smiling broadly.

Watching Captain De Poincy, sitting back behind his large desk looking stern, Rodrigo and Enrico waited to give their report.

'Did you dispose of the bodies?' the captain asked first, watching them intently.

'Yes, we buried them in the rear courtyard…even said a prayer over them and dragged the broken cart over the freshly dug soil to stop it looking obviously a recently dug grave.'

The captain nodded approval.

'And has there been any sign of the others returning?'

'No sign of anyone near the place,' Rodrigo confirmed, shaking his head. 'Nor any sign of them in that part of the town…has Roberto told you what happened?'

The captain shook his head as he continued the dialogue.

'When he eventually woke up, his face was badly swollen, and it was hard for him to speak or concentrate, but let's all go and see him now…Antonio said he had managed to take some broth for breakfast this morning.'

As he said this, he stood up and started to walk out of his cabin, the two Spaniards followed, supposing that was what they were to do.

They found Blundell propped up in a make-shift cot at the aft-end of the gun deck.

It was quite cool, as a light breeze came through the open gun ports on either side. Antonio was helping him drink some water, much of which he spilled from his swollen lips. Neither his swollen, almost closed eyes, nor mouth, could smile when he saw his visitors, but he grasped Enrico's hand firmly as he sat by his bed, with the others standing around.

'We are glad to see you alive, amigo,' Enrico said, 'we were very worried about you…the state you were in.'

Surprisingly for an old solider, Enrico felt quite teary.

'Unfortunately, those that seemed in charge got away, but the other four are now facing their heavenly judge,' Rodrigo added.

'Antonio assures us you will recover, but it is going to take time, so I will ask Signior Beniamino if you can recuperate at his villa in the hills.' De Poincy tried to sound reassuring but was unsure if this pleased Blundell or not.

'Can you tell us anything about what happened…if you found anything out?' De Poincy asked, as he felt he should, even if uncertain Blundell would be able to answer.

After a short time, Blundell seemed to try to answer the captain's questions, but it came out as a hard to recognise, raspy whisper.

'Steel gift…made for Queen Mar…An… made here…Arch…Stefanu involved…with Knights of Holy Blood…'

Even these few words seemed to exhaust him and that was as much as he could say, before he seemed to drift off to sleep.

Rodrigo and Enrico asked if they could stay with Blundell in case he woke up again and both Antonio and De Poincy thought that was a good idea, so left them by his bedside.

De Poincy returned to his cabin, thinking about what Blundell had whispered.

'The jewels they had secretly brought to Livorno. "A gift for an important lady", the Doge had said. Was this gift for the Queen Marie Anne of Spain?' De Poincy pondered, '…and if so, was the whereabouts of the jewels known already to this group? How did the Archbishop fit into all this and had they managed to disrupt, delay, or accelerate plans to steal the jewels?'

There were so many questions and he needed to warn Beniamino but did not think he could help much more. It was important that Blundell was allowed to recover as quickly as possible, somewhere safe, then he could pick up where he left off. In the meantime, the location of the jewels had to be kept secret.

Chapter 79

De Poincy spent the rest of the morning ensuring they would be able to sail the next day, weather permitting. Just before noon a smiling Signior Beniamino arrived in his carriage to pick him up. Medici Duke of Tuscany's investments had made the road out of the city and into the hills around Livorno better. Still, they bumped along in the carriage as De Poincy updated Beniamino on what had happened to Blundell and what he whispered to them that morning. Beniamino looked concerned.

'Things are proceeding well with the jeweller and only a very few trusted people know who is doing the work and where. We had already agreed the design and purchased the gold for the setting beforehand. Nevertheless, this is not a quick job,' Beniamino explained.

'However, the presentation is on the queen's birthday which is not until October...though, of course, we have to get it safely to Madrid by then!' He frowned, acknowledging the safe delivery was no small task.

On the way to Signior Beniamino's villa, they picked up Bernardo who was looking much more peaceful now, as was Agata and the boys when they arrived at the villa, surrounded by beautiful orchards and vineyards that produced a steady income for the estate.

De Poincy breathed in the rejuvenating scent of blossom, even sweeter than the sea air he loved and much better than the smelly, musty port smells. It was good to see them all looking refreshed. Agata's eyes lit up when she saw Bernardo, as did his, seeing her pretty face.

After dinner, they all enjoyed a cool evening breeze, as they were served drinks on a large veranda at the back of the villa, overlooking the orchards. The low sun illuminated the fruit trees like some master artist's oil painting. Bird song entertained them, allowing them to feel far from the mad world of political intrigue they inhabited.

Agata watched with pleasure Mateo running around with other children from the estate, playing tag and laughing freely. She was so pleased he was starting to relax.

'Returning to Malta and nursing him back to full strength of mind, might be the best thing, though he seems happy here,' she thought to herself.

Later, as she walked with Bernardo through the orchard, she was reminded of their journey across Sicily, even though that now seemed a lifetime ago now.

'Stefano, Mateo and I should return to Malta soon...we will be safe there and I will make sure they are both educated properly,' she said as she walked close by Bernardo, 'have you decided what you will do next?'

'Almost,' Bernardo conceded. 'I have decided to send the commentaries to Rome from here, to fulfil Father Aiello's wishes, but I do not know if I will go with them.' He paused as he considered his words. 'I too wish to return to Malta and continue my medical training, however, I am not completely sure I want to join the Order of Saint John, so I do not know how that will work.'

Agata was delighted to hear he wanted to return to Malta too, as well as not being sure about his calling to be a monk but realised she could not rush him into any decisions.

'Did you know Captain Orlando left a few days ago on a vessel back to Sicily?' Bernardo asked Agata and she nodded, having been informed over dinner.

'Well, Captain De Poincy passed me a letter from Orlando he wrote before he left *San Giovanni.*' Agata listened intrigued.

'He suggests I let him know where I can be reached, so he can keep in touch with me as he investigates into what happened to my father.'

Agata stopped walking and looked at Bernardo, puzzled.

'But I thought everyone said your father was killed, probably by the Inquisition?' Agata asked.

'Well, that is what everyone assumed...that he was captured by the Inquisition and died under interrogation or was killed in a fight with the Inquisition guards during the period he had sent William, on Orlando's ship, to Genoa. That is what William and Orlando were told on their return and they just accepted it. However, Orlando has been puzzling over why the Inquisition is still looking for him if they killed him. If they didn't, who did, or where did he go?' Bernardo said with a shrug.

Agata did not know what to say and stared at Bernardo, who looked equally confused.

Turning back the way they had walked, they noticed friar Antonio on the veranda talking to the group sipping their drinks there. Seeing him, they were both curious why he had come all the way from the ship. Bernardo was keen to speak with him about future training, so they walked back to join the others. On seeing them, Antonio greeted them warmly.

'I have brought Commandeur Blundell to convalesce at the villa while we sail back to Malta tomorrow,' he explained.

Overhearing them, De Poincy stood up in front of all gathered there, feeling he should explain some of what was going on, yet without revealing too much that would break confidences with the Doge.

'Let me explain what has transpired since we parted,' he began. 'Commandeur Blundell was following a lead to track down who is behind the conspiracy we have all been, to different degrees, involved in.'

He paused as everyone sat down and took in the gravity of what he was saying.

'He followed some men…even spied on a secret society meeting but ended up being captured and tortured. Fortunately, he had met some old friends in Livorno who alerted us, and together we rescued him. The main person he already suspected got away, however, it has not been all for nothing. He has confirmed his suspect's involvement and something of what they might have been planning.' He looked over at Signior Beniamino and hoped he had not disclosed anything he should not have.

'Antonio reassures us that he will make a full recovery, unfortunately this will take some weeks, so Signior Beniamino agreed he can recuperate here at this villa. Antonio has just settled him in a bed now.' De Poincy finished and looked over to Antonio as he sat down feeling he should not say anymore.

Antonio, enjoying a plate for food that had been brought to him, stood to reassure them all.

'He has several broken ribs which make movement painful, and he has lost a lot of blood which has weakened him, so I am afraid the journey here has exhausted him. I left him asleep in a fine, clean, soft bed in an airy room. We are grateful for your hospitality,' Antonio explained, nodding over at Signior Beniamino and his sister, Rachael, sitting next to him, 'I am confident he will make a speedy recovery and be at full strength in a few weeks.'

He sat down as he finished his report and continued eating eagerly.

Although they all had questions, they could tell by the atmosphere generated by the stiffness of the reports, that the conversation was over, and they would not get any more explanation. So, they contented themselves with asking if they could visit Blundell when he was able to receive visitors.

'So, captain,' Signior Beniamino said loudly to break the awkward silence that had crept into their pleasant evening, 'will you sail back to Malta tomorrow?'

'If the winds allows,' De Poincy replied, looking around at the sky, slowly turning red, 'and continue patrolling the seas for pirates as were my instructions.'

'My understanding is that Signorina Agata will also return to Malta with her brothers,' Beniamino said, turning to Agata, 'but is not in a hurry, which has so pleased my sister,' looking at his smiling sister Rachael, 'who has so enjoyed having them staying here.'

Agata smiled sweetly and nodded towards Rachael aware that she was growing rapidly fond of her.

'So, what are your plans Bernardo...' focusing now on Bernardo, '...did the sanctuary help you come to a conclusion?'

'Yes, thank you, I feel I have cleared my head a bit and although I too will probably return to Malta, if you would not mind, I am not in a hurry either...' Bernardo looked at Beniamino and his sister hopefully.

'...I have to arrange for two large Bible commentaries written by my late mentor, Father Aiello, to be sent to the Vatican library in Rome, as was his wish. Before he goes,' he continued, looking over at Antonio, 'I will talk to Antonio about continuing my training with the Hospitallers in the future.'

Antonio smiled broadly on hearing that.

'Well, I am glad you are not rushing off like the captain,' Beniamino asserted, 'you are welcome here as long as you need but let's have some more wine and watch the sunset. Let us pause from the worries of the day and enjoy God's creation and hopefully a good night's sleep after that.'

Glasses were filled, raised and all agreed the red sky over the orchards made for a wonderful sight.

Chapter 80

As the sun began to rise the next morning, Captain De Poincy stood on the veranda they had been on the night before. He looked up at puffy, cumulus clouds forming in the purple sky.

Feeling the northerly breeze on his face, he smiled. After days of clear blue skies and no wind, the weather was changing, he prayed for fair winds to speed them on their way. He went back into the villa to visit Blundell before they left and found him propped up in bed, surrounded by carers. Antonio was watching Beniamino's sister Rachael and Agata's maid Maria change a large bandage around Blundell's chest, carefully easing him up to wind the white cloth around his back. He nodded a greeting as he saw his captain.

'Our patient is in good hands here,' Antonio declared, smiling and nodding. As the ladies finished and put a pillow behind Blundell's back. De Poincy sat beside his bed.

'We need to leave soon brother, but I am confident you will be looked after well here,' De Poincy assured him, patting his arm gently.

Blundell, still finding it hard to move his facial muscles, took De Poincy's hand in his and squeezed it.

'Thank you, brother, I am grateful to be alive and here,' Blundell said in a raspy whisper.

Rachael and her maid left to give the friends some privacy to say goodbye, followed by Antonio, looking to say good-bye to Bernardo. As they left, Signior Beniamino looked in.

'The carriage is ready to go, and I will come with you so I can book myself on a ship sailing to Genoa,' Beniamino said as he sat at the bottom of Blundell's bed.

'So, it will take a while for the gift to be finished?' De Poincy enquired.

'Several weeks the jeweller estimated…it is detailed work,' Beniamino replied, 'We will keep in contact via coded messages. His identity and his work must be kept secret.'

De Poincy thought for a moment and then looked intently at Blundell.

'I have these two Spanish friends of yours keeping an eye out for your interrogators,' De Poincy said, 'they already know a little about what is going on, so are you confident about their reliability?'

Blundell nodded and squeezed De Poincy's hand which he was still holding.

'In that case,' De Poincy continued, looking now at Beniamino, 'I suggest you take them into your employment. They can keep an eye on the jeweller's workplace and what is going on in the city in case the ones that got away return! Then they can report to the Commandeur here via your staff, who can meet with them discreetly.'

Beniamino nodded, but remained silent as he could see the captain, who stood and started pacing by the bed, was in mid-thought.

'It strikes me, that this gift will have to be delivered secretly too,' De Poincy paused looking intently at Blundell. 'Once the Commandeur is fit again, he and these two Spaniards might be unnoticed couriers,' De Poincy continued, looking at Beniamino and hoping he followed his reasoning.

'As they are supposed to be Spanish traders, perhaps you could arrange for them to trade some items from here to Spain which would give them a legitimate reason to stay around and then travel to Spain? Perhaps also explaining why they are in contact with a local business agent of yours if they are observed?'

'This sounds a good plan,' Beniamino responded, 'I had something similar arranged for the delivery. However, now we know that the gift is known of by this group, who are trying to disrupt relations between Spain and Genoa, another means of delivery would be wise.' Beniamino stood up ready to go but paused to address Blundell. 'The captain and I can talk more during the carriage ride, but do you agree so far, Commandeur Blundell?'

Blundell nodded and through swollen lips, rasped, 'Good idea…'

Satisfied that things were in place for Blundell's recovery and fulfilling the Doge's instructions, De Poincy said goodbye, keen to get back to his ship and sail.

'Not sure how long we will be here, but there is a fine library to explore.' Bernardo was saying to Antonio as De Poincy, and Beniamino arrived at the carriage waiting for them.

'Goodbye captain, thank you for your patience with us,' Bernardo said, while Agata stood close by his side looking unusually shy.

'It has been an honour to serve with you and I remain grateful to Mademoiselle Agata,' De Poincy replied with a polite, formal bow to them both.

They stood at the entrance to the villa's main house, as the sunlight started to illuminate the courtyard, and waved De Poincy and Antonio off, feeling they had come to an end, but not sure of what.

Chapter 81

Livorno, Italy 5 September 1693

Several peaceful weeks had passed while Blundell slowly recovered his strength at Signior Beniamino's estate in the Monte Nero hills. Rodrigo and Enrico carefully watched what went on down in Livorno, and reported regularly to Blundell, as they prepared to secretly escort the gift to Queen Marie Anne of Spain.

'Careful now, do not push your bruised body too much,' Rachael remarked, as she saw Blundell gingerly hopping along on the crutches they had made for him.

'Good morning, Madonna,' Blundell tried to cover the pain he felt with a weak smile, as he looked up at Rachael's gentle face, 'you have made me very comfortable while I heal, but I must exercise my limbs to regain some strength. It will not be long before I must be on my way.' He pushed himself up to near full height which towered over Rachael's petite frame. He was growing fond of her and was very grateful for her generous hospitality.

'Can I help you…where were you hoping to go during your exercise?' She said, reaching out to steady him, as he wobbled a bit.

'No, no,' Blundell replied, steadying himself with the crutches, 'I just want to wander and regain my balance myself.'

'Very well,' Rachael conceded, leaving him to waddle around on his own.

In truth, the effort was tiring him out quickly, as each movement caused shooting pain along his bruised sides. However, he persevered, pausing at the open door of the library where he stopped to watch and listen to Bernardo teaching the Conti siblings.

Bernardo had taken to teaching all three Conti's each morning in the library. Agata was determined they would have an education while enjoying the calm of the house and estate which she hoped would aid Mateo's emotional recovery. Blundell leaned on his crutches in the doorway of the library, quietly keeping out of sight of the class. He had listened in before when Bernardo gave them history, geography, and mythology lessons.

He thought Bernardo was a good storyteller and a natural teacher.

'Can you check my sums,' Stephano asked, his fingers covered in ink from the figures he had been tabulating on a sheet of paper. He was engrossed with his work, taking great satisfaction from correctly completing the tasks Bernardo set him.

'Just a minute,' Bernardo replied, picking two books from the well-stocked library shelves. He took the books over to Mateo, showing him the pictures of birds and animals in one and flowers in the other.

'Perhaps you could copy some of these out, Mateo,' he suggested, as he tried to distract the boy's mind onto positive imagery. It was clear he had a natural gift for recording on paper what he saw in front of him or in his mind. However, many of the pictures he drew had disturbing images. Mateo looked through the pages enthusiastically, though he still remained silent, his emotions locked inside.

'Well done, Stephano,' Bernardo congratulated his beaming pupil, 'now subtract this total from the first column of figures and see what the result is.'

Agata looked up from her writing and over at her brothers with pleasure, hoping they would become men of consequence, well-educated and living in safety. She was writing a formal letter and although she wrote slowly, her script was elegant, and Bernardo was pleased with how well she had picked up the skill.

'How is it coming along?' Bernardo asked Agata, as he moved on from Stephano's sums.

'Slowly,' Agata signed. 'It is important I phrase this explanation well. The Baron and Baroness Castellietti were so kind to us, and I need to update them on our situation…yet ensure they understand we are all well, want to return to them, but why we have delayed returning to Malta. At the same time, I am not sure I want to share all the details of our adventures…' She tailed off, thinking about what not to mention in the letter.

Agata was so grateful for their kindness towards her and Stephano. She was fairly confident that returning to live as part of their household would be a good thing for all of them. However, she also thought the fewer moves that Mateo made, the more chance he had to recover from his ordeal. Therefore, she was also grateful that Rachael and her family had made them so welcome at this estate, providing for them, while giving them space to remould a family unit that could protect Mateo.

'That is beautiful, Mateo,' Bernardo encouraged, as he looked over what Mateo had been copying, 'you have managed to grasp the idea of perspective and form already,' he smiled happily, while Mateo was intensely lost in his drawing. It was approaching midday, and the heat was building, although there in the hills it was cooler than in the city, September in Italy is still hot.

'You have all done well this morning,' Bernardo congratulated them. 'Please finish up your tasks, as I think it's time for some food. After eating, and just before siesta I will, again, read you a little more from the book of Samuel. Remember David has just been anointed King of Judah.'

Stephano smiled broadly. He loved hearing of David's adventures, as Bernardo thought he would, and this was a good way to get him into reading the Bible. The rest of the household, being Jewish, also loved hearing stories of King David and would listen in to Bernardo's narration which he would translate from the Latin text to a common vernacular.

Blundell slipped away from his vantage spot before the class ended, returning slowly to his room. These young people intrigued him, especially the more he got to know of their past experiences. Bernardo's family was particularly interesting. Over the past weeks, he and Bernardo had time to talk about the politics of the last couple of decades. Bernardo was well educated and knew a lot of facts, but little of what was behind many of the events in history he had read or been told about. However, he was keen to learn and had found in Blundell an experienced political observer, well-travelled and astute.

'Stephano,' Bernardo called as they cleared their things from the library, 'as part of your education and as a hopeful distraction for Mateo, Rachael has arranged for you both to go with the estate manager tomorrow, to see how he organises the grape harvest. We thought it would be good for you to learn how this was managed here, so you could compare it with what you had been show in Malta, earlier in the year. Agata will want to finish the letter to the Count and Countess and send it off, so we hope Mateo will be alright with just you.'

Stephano beamed delight, and Bernardo prayed it would be another small step for Mateo, out of his protective emotional shell.

The following day, after settling Agata in the library to finish her letter, Bernardo carried the box, Beniamino has given him, and a letter to Blundell's room. He caught him at his bedroom door about to go for his now frequent daily exercises.

'Can I walk with you,' Bernardo asked, while Blundell steady himself on his crutches, 'I have something confidential I would like to discuss with you?'

'Certainly,' Blundell replied, noting the old box under Bernardo's arm. They walked slowly towards the rear of the villa, where they hoped not to be overheard.

'Yesterday I received a letter from Captain Orlando in Sicily,' Bernardo began, 'I explained to you before that he is following up on the details of my father's demise.'

Blundell nodded but remained silent.

'He is now not sure that my father died while he and William where in Genoa and there is a possibility he left for Spain, during that time, which would be just before Inquisitor Diego was recalled to Spain. There is a suggestion that it was not just letters that convinced King Carlos to recall Diego, but my father's personal appeal via the King's mother, Queen Mariana, who had made him a Knight of the Golden Fleece while she was regent.'

Blundell looked intently at Bernardo, as he reflected on what he had said. They paused on the veranda and breathed in the sweet, but the already humid air.

'Your father is someone I wish I had known…what you have said is plausible for a man, like him.'

'Yes,' Bernardo agreed, 'however, this only raises further questions. Why did he not return, and if he did return to Sicily, why did none of his friends know about it?' Bernardo looked agitated. 'We still do not know what happened to him, however, the last place we think he was, before he seems to have disappeared, seems to be Spain.'

'And you want to look for him, or evidence of what happened to him in Spain…am I right?' Blundell suggested, recognising Bernardo's distress.

'I struggle to be at peace while I do not know his fate, and if he abandoned my mother and I,' Bernardo looked distraught, '…so I wonder if I could come with you to the Spanish court and seek information about him. My understanding is Queen Mariana is still alive.'

Blundell stared out over the orchard as he thought for a moment, considering the ramifications of adding Bernardo to the group taking the gift for Queen Marie Anne. Over the days in recovery, he had been thinking through the best way to get the gift to the King, without the conspirators noticing. Help and distractions were going to be needed, yet he also felt compassion for this young man, especially now he knew his story. Could both tasks be combined?

'Yes, I think you could join us on this trip; however, you would have to follow my instructions carefully, as this mission is very sensitive, possibly dangerous, and extremely secret.'

Blundell and Bernardo stared intensely at each other in silence for quite some time, as both thought through the implications of going to Spain together. In an attempt to alleviate what turned into an awkward moment, Blundell looked down at the old box Bernardo now held in his hand.

'What's in the box?' Blundell enquired, which successfully brought Bernardo out of his deep introspection. He had almost forgotten he wanted to show Blundell the inscription to get his opinion of it.

'Oh yes!' Bernardo said, handing the box to Blundell, balancing on one crutch to examine it carefully.

'This was a box left with Signior Beniamino by my grandfather many years ago. We guess it originally housed the knife now inside it, or something similar. The knife once had jewels in the hilt, which my mother sold to support us. The knife came to us from my father via William the Archer, who brought word of my father's death, as I told you before.'

Blundell stared at the inscription and rubbed his finger over the strange letters. He could not read the language, though he had a vague feeling he had seen it somewhere before.

'It is Aramaic,' Bernardo explained as he watched Blundell's fascination, 'it reads, "For lack of fruit, the tree was cursed". Signior Beniamino thinks the box is very old—probably originating in the Holy Land.'

Blundell's heart skipped a beat and his mind started to race as soon as he heard the inscription translated. Then he recognised the knife, even without the jewels, as similar to the one used by the Knights of the Holy Blood in their initiation ceremonies. He gave Bernardo a puzzled look.

'In Orlando's letter, he also says my father appears to have been aided by another group to travel to Spain, which is why the Beati Paoli members did not know anything about it. It maybe that my father was part of another secret society, may have been for a long time, and this knife and box may give us some clues to that organisation,' Bernardo took a deep breath, he knew this was a long shot. 'I thought, with your extensive investigations into this sort of thing, you might be able to shed some light.'

Blundell didn't answer him for a while. He eased himself down onto a seat on the veranda and stared at the box. Pieces of a puzzle were coming together in his mind, however, they didn't all make sense. The idea that Cavaliere Mateo di Boscogrande was a member of the Knights of the Holy Blood was not necessarily a surprise. The group had been around for a long time, probably since shortly after the Templars were disbanded, and had many nobles within its ranks. Archbishop Stefanu and his cronies were probably using the network for their political ends, without that being the policy of the whole organisation.

After all, Blundell's own investigations had found that there were chapters of the Knight of the Holy Blood in France, Spain and throughout most of Europe. The idea that the whole organisation favoured one country over another seemed unlikely. From what Bernardo was saying now, and his father's story he had shared earlier, there was a reasonable possibility that the Blood Brothers from Spain and Sicily had helped Bernardo's father to secretly travel to Spain so he could appeal to the King's mother for help if he were indeed one of them.

'May I keep this for a while?' Blundell asked. Bernardo hesitated, surprised by the request.

'I may indeed be able to shed some light on what this knife and box represents and something of your father's past, however, I want to think about it some, perhaps investigate a little, before I say anything. I do not want to mislead you with an uninformed guess.'

Bernardo considered this. Although slightly reluctant to part with the box and knife, for reasons even he was not clear, this seemed a sensible thing to do. Long awaited answers could wait a little longer. He nodded agreement, still trying to understand what he was feeling.

'Although I am healing well and my next mission needs to begin soon, it is clear I am not yet ready for a voyage to Spain,' Blundell reasoned, 'Let's talk of this again in a day or so. Signior Beniamino is due back tomorrow and we will make the final arrangements for our journey then. We will talk after we see how things are working out.' He smiled at Bernardo in an attempt to be reassuring and sought Bernardo's strong arms to lift him upright so he could balance on the crutches.

Back in his room alone, Blundell sat on the edge of his bed and stared at the inscription on the box.

"For lack of fruit, the tree was cursed." The phase he had used to gain entry to the Blood brothers' meeting houses.

He also stared intently at the ceremonial dagger in the box. This looked similar to the dagger that was used to cut the left palm of initiates to the brotherhood. He ran his fingers along the sharp edge of the blade, it was good quality steel. He remembered his own initiation and the pain of the cut, expertly made. Deep enough to leave a clear scar, but not deep enough to damage the tendons in the hand. If this had been the property of a Chapter House Master, it would have been guarded with his life.

How had it come into the house of Boscogrande? Could there be an advantage in using this, and the Boscogrande family to expose the Archbishop's schemes to the brotherhood? Or was that path just too winding to dare go down? He would not know which of the Blood brothers sympathised with the Archbishop and which did not. He lay back on his bed and thought through the many ramifications of using these emblems and possibly using Bernardo to flush out the Archbishop's supporters.

Chapter 82

The Genoese cargo ship began its approach to Livorno harbour, furling most of it sails and letting the afternoon sea breeze push it slowly along. Rodrigo and Enrico observed the vessels from a discrete corner of the quay, enjoying the breeze on their faces, after another hot day.

There was much activity in the port today. A vessel unloading cargo on one side of the main quay, while another loaded the crates stacked in front of it. The place was noisy and congested, with shouted orders, clattering crates and chatter of men working together.

Amongst the movement of crew and stevedores, Enrico noted a group of men observing the approaching vessel from behind a large stack of crates. He nudged Rodrigo on his shoulder.

'What do you think of them?' he asked, indicating the group, 'They don't look like they're doing any loading or discharging, but maybe meeting the Genoese vessel like us?'

'Mmmm,' was Rodrigo's only reaction, 'we may have company.'

No sooner had the Genoese vessel been secured on the quay, and the gangplank put out, Signior Beniamino appeared at the top of the gangway. He looked along the quay for his carriage which had been arranged to meet him as the vessel berthed. From his vantage point, he could see his carriage trying to wind its way through the busy port. He wondered if it would make it all the way to alongside his vessel with so much cargo being moved around on carts.

'Perhaps,' he thought, 'I'll just walk along the quay to meet the carriage and we can pick up my bags later.'

As he stepped on to the quay, and started to walk along it, carrying just a small leather satchel, he passed stacks of boxes taller than him waiting to be loaded onto a vessel.

'These are going to be in the way of the carriage,' he thought. They also obscured his view as he weaved in and out of the busy stevedores.

Suddenly a group of men, he initially assumed were dockworkers, were standing right in front of him. He noted in their hands cargo hooks and knives, but the way they stared at him he was quickly alerted that they were more interested in him than any cargo.

'Welcome back Signior,' sneered one of the men, 'we've been waiting for you. Perhaps you'd be good enough to come with us,' indicating a path through the men.

Although this invitation was polite, nevertheless Beniamino detected a level of threat. These were no friends of his.

'Where exactly are we going?' Beniamino asked defiantly.

'Just for a little chat,' was the reply, 'my master would like to have a word with you.'

The group of three closed in on Beniamino, and he wondered if he should cry out, but noting the amount of shouting on the quay, he reasoned this was probably futile. Just then there were distinctive clicks of muskets being cocked, and the three men turned around simultaneously. They were greeted by Rodrigo and Enrico with cocked pistols in their left hands and daggers in their right.

'I don't think our friend wants to go with you to see anybody,' Rodrigo asserted, 'perhaps another time. For now, I think it would be best you just leave.' His voice was steady, but playfully intimidating.

For a moment, there was a standoff, both groups staring at each other in silence.

Then the three men looked at each other and in unison decided they would not risk a fight against two pistols and men clearly willing to use them. Without a word they slinked off.

Signior Beniamino exhaled—he'd been holding his breath.

'Thank you, I'm grateful you came to meet me. If we can help my carriage driver through this throng, we can collect my things from the ship and be on our way.'

Chapter 83

The Conti sibling's time at Signior Beniamino's estate had been peaceful and allowed everyone to feel safe. They felt hopeful for their futures, even though some emotional wounds were buried, rather than healed. Now, with Signior Beniamino's return, it was as if it was time to face the world again, and Agata, for one, was not sure she was ready for that yet.

'When will you go?' Agata asked Bernardo as they took their now regular after-dinner stroll between the veranda and orchard. His plan to go to Spain with the others disturbed her, raising fears, he may not return, despite his reassurances.

'That is being discussed now,' he replied, looking up at the group gathered on the Veranda. 'but I would guess soon.' They walked on in silence for a while, both lost in their own feelings.

'Will you return to Malta soon?' Bernardo asked, wishing he could say more to Agata, but not feeling he was free to commit to anything.

'Yes, soon…probably shortly after you leave. I will talk to Stephano, Mateo, and Maria about it and give Mateo time to…prepare himself.' She really did not know how Mateo was going to react to another sea voyage and new people, but knew they had to move on sometime.

'Once we settle Mateo in Malta, I am sure he will do well…we all will…' tears came to Agata's eyes, her bottled up emotions bubbling up to the surface. She buried her head in Bernardo's large chest and sobbed.

'I had hoped we could all stay together…I do not want to lose you.' Despite feeling awkward, Bernardo enveloped Agata in his powerful arms.

'I do not want to lose you either.' He had just about made up his mind that the key to his happiness was his relationship with Agata and possibly them all living in Malta together, yet still felt he could not be at peace until he found out the whole truth about his family's past. 'However, I do not think I can settle until I know what happened to my father and why family and friends were kept in the dark.' Bernardo eased Agata away from their embrace gently and stared into her eyes.

'Once this mystery is solved, I will return to you, and then we can think through a future together.' His words were reassuring and Agata wiped her tears, whilst simultaneously smiling up at him.

'Of course,' she replied, straightening herself into a lady-like demeanour. However, in her heart, she was not certain Bernardo would return. 'I will pray for you every day.'

On the veranda, Signior Beniamino, Blundell, Rodrigo and Enrico were enjoying the cooler evening air, with a glass of good wine and full stomachs. It was a satisfying feeling and they all felt quite relaxed. Each reported what they had observed or heard, so they could consider the timing of their next move.

'The gift is ready,' Beniamino announced, 'and preparations for your shipments to Spain completed. They will be loaded onto a suitable vessel as soon as you want. When and how do you propose we take the next step?' All eyes focused on Blundell.

'You Signior, should make a point of collecting something from the Jewish quarter of the city, then immediately getting on a Genoa bound vessel, preferably with a Genoese guard escort.' Blundell explained these ideas, while easing himself into a comfortable position for his bruised sides.

'This should convince those inevitably watching that the gift is on its way to Genoa. The actual gift should secretly be passed to us. It is vital no one notices you passing it off and no one connects any of us with what you are doing,' Blundell paused, looking over at Rodrigo and Enrico. 'Now you two have been seen by those watching the port and Signior Beniamino, you need to keep an even lower profile, to avoid a connection being made.' Blundell thought for a moment.

'This is where Bernardo may be of great help. No one has seen him yet, so he can help with receiving the gift from Signior Beniamino.' He looked intently at Rodrigo.

'Arrange for your shipments to be loaded and sail as soon as possible after Signior Beniamino leaves for Genoa. We will all board at the last minute, so we are gone before anyone watching realises, but hopefully their attention will have shifted to Genoa.' There were general nods of agreement. As Blundell eased himself up from his seat on the veranda, he thought through the details of how they could distract the attention of those watching.

'If anyone realises we have the gift and are sailing to Spain with it, we will be in great danger,' he thought, looking over at Bernardo and Agata walking towards the veranda.

He walked stiffly towards them, as Rodrigo and Enrico entered into deep conversation about which one of them would do what the next day.

'You make the final arrangements with the vessel we have chosen while I visit the warehouse and arrange for the loading,' Rodrigo was saying, 'and we need four bunks onboard now, instead of three…' Enrico listened carefully and nodded.

Blundell, quietly intercepted Bernardo as he climbed the veranda stairs, and Agata left him to find her brothers.

'Bernardo, please come with me to my room,' he had dispensed with his crutches, feeling they only hurt his sides, which was all that was notably left to heal. 'I will return your box, and now I have consulted with Signior Beniamino, I will venture an opinion.'

Blundell walked slowly from the veranda like an old man, slightly bent over, trying not to move the muscles in his side. He had healed well over the weeks, but still had his strength to rebuild.

The box with the dagger inside was sitting on a table by Blundell's bed. He picked it up as soon as he arrived in the room.

'Shut the door please Bernardo,' Blundell said, 'what I am going to disclose is for your ears only,' his eyes staring intently at Bernardo as if he could read his thoughts.

'Have this back, and I would suggest you keep it hidden.' Blundell handed the box back to Bernardo with both hands as if heavy. He perched himself on the end of the bed and looked up at Bernardo, who was staring at the dagger in the box, reflecting on his long-standing emotional attachment to it.

'From what Signior Beniamino has told me, together with information I have, we believe this box left Jerusalem several hundred years ago with a returning Templar Knight. Probably, it originally contained a relic, possibly an important relic, however its use to store the dagger was a later derivation. The once bejewelled dagger was for ceremonial use and may be from the same period, however, it may have no connection with the missing relic.'

He took a deep breath and lowered his voice, as if saying something he should not.

'Do you know what happened to the Templars?' Blundell asked Bernardo and waited patiently for him to sieve through the extensive history stored in his head.

'My understanding is they were denounced by King Phillip of France in 1307, excommunicated by the Pope shortly after, hunted down and many killed over the following years. Phillip confiscated their Paris treasury. Their extensive funds were also confiscated by the Pope and other Princes.' Bernardo thought for a moment. 'I do not know much more, though I remember Father Aiello saying he thought, "the satanic practises they were accused of, were probably concocted to justify their obliteration", if that makes sense.'

'Father Aiello is another person from your past I would have liked to have talked to. The more you tell me about him, the more astute I think he was.' Blundell smiled, imaging the old monk teaching Bernardo.

'The Templars had an extensive network throughout Europe, considerable wealth and influence' Blundell explained, 'No one quite knows how many supporters there were, or where all their treasures went. Over the years, those suspected of being knights or allied to them were hunted down, probably interrogated about where riches were hidden. I suspect a great number of unconnected scores were settled during that period too, as often happens in purges. However, much of their wealth and many members of the Order simply disappeared, probably given sanctuary by sympathetic nobles around Europe.'

Bernardo nodded, remembering a discussion he had about them with his mentor.

'Shortly after their fall from grace, a number of other secretive Orders sprang up, some of which gained official approval for a time, like the Knights of Christ in Portugal, while others remained in the shadows.' Blundell was considering carefully how much to reveal to Bernardo.

'Just over a year ago, I joined a secret society called "The Knights of the Holy Blood".'

He watched Bernardo's reaction to what he told him carefully.

'This was as part of my investigations into agents working for France and stealing funds from Spain. Clues led me to these "Blood brothers", as they call themselves, and I received their mark during initiation.' Blundell raised his left palm to reveal the scar.

'This cut was made with a knife like that one, though still bejewelled.' Bernardo stared at the dagger, looking at it in a different light that he had before.

'The secret pass phase to enter their meetings is, "For the lack of fruit the tree was cursed".'

Bernardo's mouth dropped open, his head starting to spin with questions. Blundell raised his hand as if to silence Bernardo and continued.

'It is my belief, that the "Knight of the Holy Blood", are remnants of the Templars, possibly one of many. Whoever started them, many years ago, had this box, possibly the relic within, probably had copies of the original ceremonial dagger made. The order is organised into houses located in major port cities, and some capital cities too. The head of each house was given one of the daggers, or possibly there is just one shared between several houses. That I am not sure about. However, the ceremonial knife looked very similar to your dagger. Of course, I only caught a glimpse of the knife when I was initiated, it could be just coincidentally similar, but not exactly the same.' Now Blundell thought for a moment. As an investigator, he did not believe in coincidences.

'Do you think my father was a member of this secret society?' Bernardo asked.

'Possibly,' Blundell hesitatingly replied, 'or just helped by them for their ends, or possibly they thought he was part of their brotherhood.'

Now Bernardo was completely confused, 'Because of the dagger?' he suggested.

'Well,' Blundell hypothesised, 'someone could have seen your father with the dagger. Signior Beniamino said he told your father of the box's inscription, though not much more about it, as he did not seem interested. However, what if, during a desperate period, your father hears the words and remembers the box? Who recruited who and to what end?'

'Also,' Blundell was on a roll, after thinking much about all Bernardo and Signior Beniamino had told him, 'what if the relic, that was once in this box, had just been taken when your grandfather came across the knight, with the empty box and the dagger? Or did your grandfather take the relic, separating it from the box to conceal it?'

Bernardo looked at the box and dagger now with very different eyes. He was not sure if he wanted to keep them, with such a potentially murky past. However, it was one of the few things he had from his family.

Blundell sensed Bernardo's distress, for him this was just following clues to an investigation. To Bernardo this was very personal and possibly very painful to hear.

'There is a lot of conjecture here, Bernardo. For now, just keep these things safe and hidden. They may just help us unpick what happened to your father, though I can't promise anything.' There was a distinct gloomy atmosphere in the room and Blundell wanted it to end, so abruptly changed the subject.

'You want to join us in going to Spain, yes?' he ventured. Bernardo nodded.

'Well, there is a task you can perform to help us, but I will explain the details tomorrow. I am going to have Signior Beniamino pass something to you in Livorno, but without any observers finding out.' Blundell winked and smiled.

Bernardo left him, rehearsing the revelations about the box and dagger in his mind, and with growing curiosity about the task Blundell had for him.

Chapter 84

As usual, the port of Livorno was a hive of activity, as was the Jewish quarter, a short distance from the harbour. Signior Beniamino had arranged to make the short voyage to Genoa, with some extra bodyguards. He would leave early that morning as soon as the ship's paperwork was completed. At first light, he had taken his carriage, accompanied by the bodyguards, to the Jewish quarter and picked up the necklace and some other items. Their assumption was that they would be observed.

'This is close enough,' Beniamino called to the driver, as his carriage reached halfway down the quay, 'we can walk the rest of the way, rather than weave our way through these crates.'

His bodyguards, in smart Genoese livery, jumped down from the rear of the carriage and beside the driver, alert to anyone approaching.

The sun had risen, but the sky was still red with the early morning rays. Nevertheless, the quay was full of activity. Stevedores pushing crates to be loaded onto vessels, seamen securing the last things on the Genevan vessel that they were to board. The old man seemed to struggle out of his carriage, carrying a non-descript leather satchel. His bodyguards tried to help him steady himself, when out of nowhere, a tall man, in dusty old pantaloons, a loose-fitting white shirt and floppy hat that hid his face, bumped into Beniamino.

'A thousand apologies Signior,' the tall man said, as he tried to hand back Beniamino's satchel which had slid off his shoulder. The bodyguards, embarrassed they had not seen what they presumed was a large sailor, pushed him away roughly.

'No need for that,' Beniamino insisted, as he stared into the tall man's deep blue eyes, 'no harm done.' They continued onto the ship, while the tall man, wobbling as if a bit worse for drink, staggered along the quay and out of sight, behind a building. There Rodrigo was waiting, as Enrico kept watch on the quay area from the doorway of an inn.

'Well done, amigo,' even those close by would not have noticed what just happened.

The Genoa bound ship will sail within the hour and our ship finishes loading today, ready for a sunrise sail tomorrow. Now we just need to keep out of sight till then.'

As Rodrigo talked, Bernardo slipped back into his Benedictine habit, discarding the floppy hat etc…into his travel bag, along with the flat box he had recovered from Beniamino.

'What now?' Bernardo asked.

'We split up…best not to be seen together, and board the vessel separately…just in case,' Rodrigo advised. 'You said you wanted to go for confession, so now you have all day,' Rodrigo smiled. 'The new Duomo Livorno in Piazza Grande, is dedicated to saint Francis, but I am sure they will not reject you,' he laughed, enjoying making fun of the young monk. Bernardo accepted the teasing with a board smile.

'Actually, that is a good idea,' Bernardo agreed, 'there is quite a bit of fine artwork I would like to see there, especially Angelico's painting of "Christ crowned with thorns". And…' Bernardo continued, his smile turning to a smirk, 'it will be cool in there.'

He sauntered off towards the city, thinking through his goodbye to Agata, Stephano and Mateo. There had been tears, but he promised to catch up with them in Malta, and their prayer was that would not be in the too distant future. He gave Stefano his long bow to look after for him, promising to teach him how to use it when they would next be together. To Agata he gave one of the three credit notes he had from Signior Beniamino, to keep safe for him. He thought these would be good tokens of his serious intentions to be reunited with them.

'I will ask the Franciscans for hospitality tonight,' he thought to himself. His step was light as he looked forward to looking at the artwork, as well as having time by himself to contemplate all Blundell had told him.

Chapter 85

Bernardo leaned over the railings, watching the sailors secure the vessel, as they arrived in Valencia. He clutched his bandaged hand, the scar on his left palm almost completely healed after the eight-day sail. Blundell had cut his palm to look like a Knight of the Holy Blood affiliate, in anticipation of what might come next. The cut was not deep. Made with a sharp blade, carefully cut, just through the epidermis, enough to leave a scar but not cutting into the muscle of the hand. Apart from that, it had been an uneventful passage, the boredom alleviated by Bernardo trying to learn Spanish—much to Rodrigo and Enrico's amusement.

With his accent, he was never going to pass for a regular Spaniard, but he now knew enough to get by.

'Ah, the sweet smell of Spain!' Enrico declared, throwing his arm around Bernardo's broad shoulders.

'What do you mean sweet,' Bernardo laughed, 'it smells as rotten as all busy ports!'

'Where is your romance, amigo, home always smells good,' they both laughed, as they caught sight of Rodrigo helping Blundell out of the accommodation. It had been a difficult voyage for him. Although he was healing well, and the voyage had been relatively smooth, he had found it uncomfortable in his tiny bunk, being tossed from side to side, thus hard to sleep.

'We will find an inn with a big soft bed for you tonight, then by tomorrow, you will be as strong as you were before,' Rodrigo assured him.

'Just remember our cover story,' Blundell whispered to them all as they watched the gangway being put out, 'you are merchants with cargo to sell, and we are independent passengers, that you just happened to have struck up a friendship with during the voyage. We must not arouse suspicion from anyone.'

As he finished, Bernardo noticed a small column of soldiers approaching. The vessel's master greeted them with papers in hand and Bernardo assumed this was for clearance by port officials. However, he wondered why the need for a military escort.

Rodrigo and Enrico collected documents from their cabin. They would need these soon to claim their cargo once it had been unloaded. There was nothing really for Bernardo to do, collecting his things would only take a moment, so he leant over the rail of the vessel and watched all that was going on. The soldiers with the poor looking officials loitered at the bottom of the gangway. As they were only a few feet away from Bernardo, he noted how badly worn their uniforms were. He would not have expected them to be in their best kit for a routine operation like clearing a vessel inbound with cargo. Nevertheless, a proud force like the Spanish army he thought would have been better turned out than the near rags these soldiers were wearing.

'Are things in Spain difficult?' Bernardo asked Blundell, indicating the uniforms.

'Very,' replied Blundell quietly, 'wealth is held by a small number of nobles and the vast population kept in poverty. The system here stinks—corruption is rife!'

'Let's go ashore and have some lunch,' Rodrigo said to them, 'we're not going to be able to claim our cargo until tomorrow, so we may as well stretch our legs, get some food and find somewhere to lodge for the night.'

'A walk would be a welcome change,' thought Bernardo, so he happily grabbed his already packed bag.

'Are you able to walk to an inn, amigo?' Enrico asked Blundell, collecting his bag for him.

'Yes, yes, the walk will do me good, I might just be a bit slow,' Blundell replied.

After checking with the ship's sailing master, the three of them almost skipped ashore, delighted to have arrived safely, with Blundell taking up the rear, trying to walk upright and keep up with them. The prospect of a steady bed for the night was encouraging him greatly.

Bernardo was impressed with the size of the port and the many impressive buildings.

Clearly a great deal of money had been spent relatively recently in making things look grand.

However, many of the working folk he saw, like the soldiers, seemed to be in rags, so despite the wealth of the city, there seemed much poverty too. There were also lots of clergy around, so Bernardo thought he would be just one more tree in a forest. He discussed this with Rodrigo as they walked along, while Enrico helped Blundell with his bag.

'Yes, brother, many young men go into the church…better to be poor there, uh!' Rodrigo explained. 'But there are also lots of inquisitors around, watching out for heretics and spies. There is much suspicion everywhere. People know their King is in ill health, he has been most of his life, he has no heir, and they know there will be another power struggle, but they are unsure of from where it will come. Inside or out?' he shrugged, despondently. In the end, they walked well away from the port, into the heart of the city to an inn that Rodrigo said he knew, that happened to be near to a contact he hoped to meet who could help them on the next part of their journey.

The inn turned out to be large and extremely noisy, boasting fine accommodation with available rooms. Once settled, Rodrigo and Enrico decided to leave the other two while they sought out their contact, elsewhere in the city. This would give the advantage of disconnecting their association should anyone be observing them.

'We will see you here for lunch tomorrow, by which time we hope to have secured unsuspicious transport to Madrid. Rest well amigos,' Rodrigo said, after a satisfying lunch together, then departed.

As promised, thanks mostly to Signior Beniamino's generosity for them being Genoese courtiers, Blundell could afford a large, soft bed to sleep in that night. After a good meal, and plenty of passible wine, they both quickly slipped into deep sleep.

Rodrigo and Enrico looked frazzled as they joined Blundell and Bernardo for lunch the next day.

'We trust you slept well, and agree with us that this is a fine place to stay?' Enrico enquired, as he and Rodrigo sat down opposite them.

'Yes, thank you, that was the best night's sleep I have had in a long time,' Blundell replied, 'but you two look hot and bothered…is everything alright?'

'Ah, we had some issues claiming our cargo this morning. Just officials looking for handouts, but it is all sorted now, and we have secured excellent transport, with armed escort to take our merchandise to Madrid.' Rodrigo reassured.

'This was helped by the consignment we brought for our old army friend that now runs a business transporting goods safely from this port to Madrid and elsewhere in Spain,' Enrico explained with a satisfied smile, 'We brought him a tierce of Mozzarella cheese in brine…it is his favourite. He got a taste for it when we were on campaign in Calabria together many years ago. It was good to catch up with him last night, though we were up late.' Enrico yawned.

'We need an armed escort?' Bernardo questioned.

'Oh, yes,' Rodrigo assured, 'it is about 66 leagues to Madrid, it will take us around five days through country that is not all friendly.' Rodrigo shrugged, as food was laid out in front of them. 'Unfortunately, wealth is not evenly spread in Spain…to say the least…there are some desperate people around.'

'But our friend and his men are used to transporting goods safely,' Enrico assured, 'he seems to be doing well on it, and they know the best places to stop along the way.'

'We trust our friend completely and for anyone else curious about us, we have explained we made two friends on the voyage,' Rodrigo interjected, pointing to them across the table, 'these friends happened to also be on their way to Madrid, and we all agree that travelling together will be the safest way.' He continued while they eagerly tucked into a generous lunch. 'Domingo, our friend, will be travelling with us…he has lots of good contacts in Madrid, and you are already his hero.' The old soldiers both smiled triumphantly at Blundell.

'How does he know me?' Blundell questioned, already concerned his identity had been revealed.

'He left the army just before we met you, and due to the army pay being stolen, he missed out on a great deal of back pay. After we recovered the silver, he eventually received all that was owed to him, and with that he started this thriving business he has now. So, he is very favourable to helping us, and yes, you are a hero to him,' Rodrigo concluded, raising a tankard to toast Blundell. 'A real hero,' echoed Enrico, joining in the toast.

'You will meet him tomorrow, as he is going to travel with us to Madrid.' They drank heartedly. Blundell scowled at them, thinking they were not being as discreet as he had instructed, though he recognised these old soldiers were loyal to each other.

Chapter 86

Domingo Ortega Sanchez was only five feet tall, with broad shoulders and burly legs. The light cotton shirt that hung off his muscular frame was open to the bottom of his sternum, showing off the physique of a clearly powerful man. He could have been mistaken for a well-built young boy, if it was not for the well-developed muscles, pointed beard and elaborate moustache that was waxed into points. His face seemed to be in a continuous grin, and he liked to talk!

'It is an honour to meet you, mi capitán, nuestros amigos have sung your praises, and rightly so. It will be my pleasure to accompany you on this journey, and see you have the best of everything, si?' His grin was shared with everyone as he looked around for agreement.

'We are grateful for all the arrangements you have made, señor Sanchez,' Blundell replied, studying the little man in front of him who seemed larger than life.

'My friends call me Dom and I hope we are friends,' Dom insisted, slapping Blundell on the arm with such force, he had to stifle a wince, but managed to force a smile.

Each of them were provided with fine horses for the journey and the cargo was carefully loaded into two well-covered wagons with two drivers and two hefty cart horses each. They set off early with plans to reach a treelined steam by mid-day, to water the horses and all rest in shade from the heat of the day. By the time they arrived at a suitable inn just before the sun set, Sanchez had things all worked out, and to Blundell's amazement, he had done this all the while talking during the whole journey.

On the forth night, over diner, their talk finally moved away from anecdotes of their army days to what should happen on arrival in Madrid.

'While you are dropping off the cargo to the merchants, I have to visit the Finance Ministry to deliver a letter and parcel,' Blundell was explaining, 'it is rather important, but we can rendezvous later if you can suggest a good place.'

'Si, I have a good place for us to stay tomorrow night, we can gather there and celebrate a successful delivery,' Sanchez assured, with a raised tankage and his usual grin.

As they retired that night, Blundell considered if he could ask the Minister of Finance's help with getting a note to Queen Mariana, the King's mother. That seemed to him the best place to enquire about Bernardo's father's movements seven years earlier.

Blundell looked over at Bernardo, who he was sharing a room with, rising from evening prayers by his bed. 'Bernardo,' he said, 'I think you should write a letter to Queen Mariana, asking about your father. I will help you compose it. If we can, I will ask the Finance Minister to have it delivered as a matter of urgency, along with delivery of the gift, which I am sure the Queen will want to know about. After the delivery, I would have thought he would be in a cooperative disposition.'

Bernardo nodded and got some paper, ink, and a quill out of his bag.

'Should I ask to speak to the Queen?' Bernardo asked, as he sat down to write.

'Offer it as an option, however, make it clear that any help locating your father would be appreciated,' Blundell advised, looking over his shoulder in order to help compose the letter.

He already had a formal letter to the Inquisitor General Emmanuel Garcia, written which he carried around with him discretely. In it, he warns of Archbishop Stefanu Buonaparte using the Knight of the Holy Blood and his suspicion of involvement in trying to damage Spain and Genoa's economic alliance. He was not sure how he was going to confidentially get that letter to Garcia but thought he should take on each task one at a time, prioritising them carefully and ensuring one did not compromise the other.

Chapter 87

Archbishop Stefanu paced his Madrid office in frustration after reading a report from his agents in Livorno. Since returning to Spain, he had tried to find out more details of the gift the Genevans were going to send to the King for the Queen's birthday, just over a month away. The King and his courtiers were being tight-lipped about it, even the regular blabber mouths. He heard rumours that the King's mother was behind the gift, it being her idea and her contacts had made the suggestion to the Doge in Genoa. However, that might be wild speculation. He considered what he knew:

'They had failed to kidnap that awful count Jew Beniamino in Livorno, finding no clues about what was being made or by whom. Beniamino had been seen collecting something from the Jewish quarter, then immediately sailing to Genoa. It must have been something valuable, as he had an armed escort. No more details!' He fumed and paced.

'Was this the elusive birthday gift?' Stefanu thought, 'was it going to be transhipped from Genoa to somewhere in Spain?' He tried to reason without information.

'It would have to be soon, but do I have to have all the ports watched for a Genoese vessel unloading cargo for Madrid? That would be ridiculous. Can I watch out for someone coming from Genoa to the Spanish court, then try to intercept them before they reached the King or his mother?' He looked out of his office window at the setting sun considering his options. 'Discretion was imperative…perhaps I should solicit the help of the Blood brothers, if I visit one of their meetings…? That was always risky. The Inquisition was sure to be watching out for signs of them, as they did for all secret societies which they did not approve of, but I might have to risk it. I could send word to the local Brother's House Master to meet me in their usual rendezvous spot in Torrejón de Velasco.'

He went to bed, thinking through what to say to the House Master to gain his co-operation without revealing his intentions.

Chapter 88

Blundell nervously sat in the Minister of Finance's office with Bernardo. He was glad they had been expecting him, having received coded messages from the Doge in Genoa, but disappointed to learn the previous minister, Fernando de Valenzuela, who he had worked with before, was dead.

'So sorry to keep you like this,' the minister's secretary gushed, 'your arrival is a relief to the minister, however, he has to have the royal jeweller verify the piece right away...ensure it is genuine.' The young man gave a weak smile, obviously feeling rather awkward. 'Can I get you some refreshment,' while you wait.

'No thank you,' Blundell replied, looking to Bernardo for confirmation. 'We have a favour to ask, though.' He looked at the secretary hopefully.

'We assume that Queen Marianna is going to be informed of the gift's safe arrival,' Blundell ventured, and the secretary nodded, 'I am sure she will.'

'Then, along with that message to Queen Marianna, could we send a private message on another matter?' Blundell and Bernardo looked hopefully at the secretary, who continued to look uncomfortable.

'I can't see why not, depending on the nature of the message...you do realise its contents would be read by others...not just Queen Marianna?' the young man warned.

'Although I do not know the present Finance Minister, or what he knows of persons that aided the crown in the past, I did know the previous minister well, and the person that is discussed in the communications is known by Queen Marianna, and possibly the previous minister. Therefore, I can't see that the present minister would object.' Blundell hoped he was making sense, while not being sure how much he should say to people he did not know.

'Very well,' the secretary replied, 'if you give me the letter, I will ensure it goes with this message of the gift's arrival.' He held out long, thin, ink-stained fingers.

They had deliberately arrived at the Finance Ministry early in the morning, concerned this was going to take a while to sort out. However, now the morning was disappearing, and the Finance Minister's office was getting hot. Blundell and Bernardo started to drift off to sleep, wishing they had accepted the refreshments when offered. Just as they were beginning to think they had been forgotten, the office door burst open. The minister, who they had only met momentarily before, rushed into the office with the box containing the necklace, followed by a large entourage.

'My dear fellows,' the minister began, 'I am so sorry to have kept you, however, you will understand the urgency in verifying what you have gallantly brought us.' He was all smiles, so they assumed all was well. 'I am about to go, under escort, to the palace at Aranjuez, where the King and his mother will both be able to see this magnificent gift.'

His attendants continued to smarten up his appearance, an effort Blundell thought a waste of time, as the carriage or horse ride to Aranjuez, in the late morning heat would certainly, mess him up. They stood patiently while aids came and went arranging details of this trip.

'It would be good if you two would accompany me, then if his Majesty wants to meet the deliverers that the Doge has praised so much, you will be at hand.' Bernardo felt nervous at meeting Royalty but tried not to show it. 'My secretary has shown me the letter you want passed to Queen Marianna, and if I have the opportunity, I will certainly pass it to her…shall we go.' Swinging around, the minister and entourage left, so Blundell and Bernardo followed, rather bemused by the performance.

It was well passed mid-day by the time they reached the palace in Aranjuez, accompanied by twenty mounted cavalry. Riding on their own mounts, right through the hottest time of the day, seemed ludicrous to Blundell. With one short stop to water and rest the horses, they were all soaked in sweat and exhausted by the time they reach the palace. Fortunately, the interior of the palace was cool, and their horses taken off to be watered and fed. Blundell and Bernardo dozed on a plush couch in a long hall, while they waited to possibly be summoned.

'Excuse us señor.' Blundell opened his eyes to an angelic vision. Two young courtiers, dressed in brilliant while cotton shirts with sliver coloured silk breaches and matching waistcoats, stood before them. In their hands were small trays with silver goblets and a jug, of what they assumed was wine, as well as dishes of cut-up fruit.

'We have brought refreshments for you,' the servant said, putting the trays down on small tables beside them. 'Queen Marinna sends her compliments, and when you are ready we will show you to her favourite part of the garden, where she is will shortly be taking her post siesta stroll and would like to thank you personally for your service to the crown.' The servants both smiled and took a pace backwards, with their hands behind their backs.

Blundell shook Bernardo, who was beginning to snore, and pointed to the food and drink.

'We are in luck, Queen Marinna wants to meet us,' he whispered to Bernardo, while gratefully drinking the fine wine.

The ornate gardens at Aranjuez palace were magnificent and huge. It took quite some time to navigate the straight rows of trees and plants to reach Queen Marinna's favourite spot, where there was a stone seat by a fountain.

'She looks incredible for an aging dowager,' Blundell thought to himself as he was presented to the Queen. She was dressed in an elaborate silk dress, hair hidden in a tall white wig and her face was white with powder. As he bowed before her, he was not sure if the heavy floral scent was from her or the plants in the garden. He guessed both.

'I understand this is not the first time you have served us, Comandante Blundell,' the Queen said, in a huskier voice than Blundell had expected, 'We are aware of the risks you took to deliver this gift from our friends in Genoa and are grateful for such devoted service.'

She looked over his shoulder at the shy Bernardo, standing a couple of paces behind him.

'This is the unmistakable son of Cavaliere Mateo di Boscogrande,' she observed, 'though I am surprised to see you in that habit. Your father was a warrior and son of a warrior, yet you have chosen another service.'

'Your majesty,' Bernardo stubbled in faltering Spanish, 'did you by chance read my letter about my father's last visit to Spain?'

'Yes, Fraile Bernardo, I read your letter,' the Queen replied, 'I can confirm your father did visit me some seven years ago. It was pleasant to see him after so long, I missed having our big handsome Sicilian around.' She paused to reminisce, and a small smile came to her face. 'Yes, I do recall helping him petition to have the Sicilian chief inquisitor recalled. However, I am most concerned that he did not make it home. We will have to find out what happened to him.'

Bernardo was elated. Could the whereabouts of his father be discovered, at last? Yet, to Bernardo's confusion, the audience ended there and the Queen, accompanied by her ladies-in-waiting returned to the palace. As they were led back to their horses, a courtier approached them. 'señor, where can you be reached?'

'Posada de los tres toros,' Blundell replied, 'in Torrejón de Velasco, near the castle.'

'Thank you señor, someone will be in contact with you soon, and here is Cavaliere Mateo di Boscogrande's honour parchment. The courtier handed over Boscogrande's induction to the Knights of the Golden Fleece, that they had sent with the letter to Queen Marinna in way of a reference and bowed. They rode back to the city with high hopes that Bernardo's father's movements would finally be revealed.'

Chapter 89

'We should celebrate,' Rodrigo declared, raising a tankard, 'this has been a most successful day.' They all smiled agreement and joined in the toast.

'Here is your share,' he said, as he handed a pouch of silver over to Bernardo.

Blundell raise his eyebrows in surprise, as Bernardo quickly looked in the pouch, then tied it to his belt under his scapular.

'In order to purchase the goods to sell here, Rodrigo and Enrico had to raise funds. Signior Beniamino invested and recommended I did too. So, I cashed one of the credit notes he had supplied me with, and now I have made a profit,' he explained. Bernardo looked thoughtful, 'I have been thinking a great deal since Genoa what to do with my inheritance.' There was a chorus of, 'well done,' from them all, as they tucked into the sumptuous meal set before them.

'Now our business is concluded here, I will be happy to help you safely back to Valencia,' Sanchez suggested, 'I have some cargo to take back to the port which I can collect as soon as tomorrow.'

'That is most helpful, unfortunately, I still have some business here, though I hope it will not take long,' Blundell informed them, 'can you hang on a couple of days?'

'Certainly,' Sanchez reassured, 'we are at your service.'

'I would not mind hanging around here for a few days,' Enrico said, smiling broadly at an attractive woman serving them more wine.

'Why did you tell the royal courtier you could be reached at Posada de los tres toros, rather than here?' Bernardo asked Blundell.

'That is where I arranged to meet a contact, and I will have to move there tomorrow to ensure I can complete the rest of my mission,' Blundell clarified.

'Posada de los tres toros,' Sanchez looked serious for once, 'now there is a viper's nest, if ever there was one.' He leaned into the table centre and dropped low his usual booming voice, 'You do realise it is right by the Inquisition regional headquarters…it is used by many of the castle guards.'

'Yes,' Burnell replied with a smile, 'which is one of the reasons I am going there.'

Sanchez straightened up and returned to his usual jolly self, shrugging.

'You know who the bar keeper there is?' he asked his bemused friends, who shook their heads. 'Fat Sargento Manuel that we served with in the Low country in '89.

Rodrigo and Enrico nodded, looking amused, while stuffing their faces with food.

'He left the army shortly after me, I think, and went into business with someone, to run that inn…I can't remember who,' Sanchez stroked his beard, trying to remember details.

'We will have to pop in and say hello,' Enrico suggested.

'Nay, I never really liked him,' Rodrigo said, shaking his head.

'He will like you though, amigo,' Rodrigo said, pointing to Blundell, 'if I remember right, he owes his life to you…when we were trapped recovering the army pay back from the French, you got us out of that fix.' He raised his tankard to Blundell and took a gulp.

'He helped you with that?' Sanchez asked, surprised.

'Not exactly helped,' Rodrigo explained, 'more got in the way, but we all escaped with the silver together.' Blundell listened to the story without comment.

'Actually, I would appreciate it if you do not visit los tres toros,' Blundell said, 'I do not want to draw any attention, so it would be best I stay there myself.'

'Amigo,' Sanchez exclaimed, 'that is not a good place to be without protection.'

'I did not say I would not appreciate assistance, only it will have to be discreet,' Blundell explained. 'Tomorrow I will speak to Manuel, arrange a room and have him take messages for me, then the following night, we will rendezvous in the stable behind the inn. If my meeting does not go well…perhaps you can…help me out?' They all looked puzzled. 'Sorry,' Blundell explained, 'I do not have a plan, as I do not know what is going to happen, or even who I am going to meet.' He shrugged and raised his tankard to his comrades. 'To friendship,' he toasted and smiled limply at them!

Chapter 90

His carriage sat in a shadowy area, opposite the inn in Madrid's autonomous region of Torrejón de Velasco. Looking out of the carriage window, Archbishop Stefanu could see the entrance to the inn well illuminated, and impatiently waited for his contact to appear. He scanned the street nervously at everyone that passed.

The regional office of the Inquisition was in the nearby castle. Emmanuel Garcia was Diego Sarmiento de Valladares, the Grand Inquisitor's, right-hand man, and his office was in this castle. He was an intimidatingly powerful cleric, as Valladares was getting so old he increasingly relied on Garcia. The castle was also a prison, but not your run of the mill prison. In its towers, it housed nobles, and men of note, being investigated or "chastised" by the church but living in relative comfort compared to those in the dungeons below the castle.

'If I am seen by an Inquisition agent, I need a plausible excuse why I am in this area.' Stefanu considered. 'I could say I was coming to see Inquisitor Garcia, but what would I be visiting him for…what would I have to talk to him about?' He did not like coming near the Inquisition, they were suspicious of everyone.

'Where is Juan?' he muttered to himself staring out of the carriage window. Then, to his surprise, a face came into view that he recognised.

'That is the intruder we were interrogating in Livorno, I am sure of it,' Stefanu thought, 'I wish I could remember where I had seen him before…could it have been the Vatican? Is he an agent of the Pope? What is he doing here? Could he be the Genoese gift courier?' Then an intriguing idea come to his mind which made him smile.

At that moment, Juan, the local House Master of the Knights of the Holy Blood, came out of the inn. He spotted the Archbishop's carriage in its usual rendezvous spot and walked over to it. As soon as he reached the carriage, the door swung open, and the Archbishop beckoned him inside.

'Did you see the tall man in the black jacket and long riding boots going into the inn as you left?' the Archbishop asked immediately without any greeting. Juan was taken aback but cast his mind back to people he just passed.

'Perhaps…vaguely,' Juan replied, rather confused.

'Go back and keep an eye on him,' the Archbishop ordered to Juan's surprise, 'I am sure, he is an intruder that spied on our brother's meeting in Livorno, and I fear he is trying to expose us here. I am going to try to get the Inquisition to arrest him, so I can find out who he is.'

At the mention of the Inquisition, Juan's eyes widened, and he looked visibly distressed.

'Don't worry,' the Archbishop reassured, 'you do not need to get involved,' just point him out to me when I return…now go,' he said shoving Juan out of the carriage door.

Leaning out of the carriage window, he ordered his driver to go to the castle. He would pay a visit to the Inquisition after all and solicit their help. Siting back in his carriage seat, he congratulated himself on his ingenuity but then realised he would have to explain the details to Garcia.

'He is no fool and will not necessarily trust what I say,' Stefanu thought, 'after all, I have hardly ever talked to him, keeping out of the way of the Inquisition being the best thing. I will have to have a plausible reason for being here to see this tall stranger, and reason for knowing his face in the first place.'

He concocted a story as he was driven into the castle grounds.

'Must keep this simple in case I am cross-questioned and let slip something I will regret. All I need is for them to question this fellow, so we find out who he is, and hopefully, flush out the gift courier at the same time.'

He continued to think through how he was going to present his suspicions to Garcia, as he was shown into the Inquisitor's office in Puñonrostro Castle.

Chapter 91

Monsignor Emmanuel Garcia's black, purple-trimmed cassock with its purple sash was immaculate, made of light cotton, though the trim and sash were silk. He was pious, wearing the uniform of his office without flamboyancy. The crucifix around his neck was of a simple design on a thin silver chain. A slight built man with piecing dark brown eyes and black hair, greying at the temples, he sat listening intently to Archbishop Stefanu Buonaparte's accusation.

In contrast, the small, round Archbishop, was dressed all in purple silk, including dainty gloves, with his gold ring of office over them. An elaborate gold chain and crucifix around his neck, displayed opulence. Garcia was surprised by his visit, however, he and his staff greeted Stefanu as a prince of the church, with due reverence. Now he focused on his elaborate story.

'It is imperative you act fast, or we might lose this man, and not stop his corrupting force,' the Archbishop was insisting.

Garcia signalled to one of the aids, standing behind the Archbishop. 'Take some guards, accompany the Archbishop to this inn, and apprehend this individual. Bring him to the cells below for questioning.'

Archbishop Stefanu ordered his carriage back to the dark corner opposite the inn of the three bulls (Posada de los tres toros). On arrival, he sent one of the four Inquisition guards into the inn to initially look for Juan, who he described to them, so Juan could point out the suspect.

'How will we know we have the right man?' the guards asked.

'Bring him...quietly...to me here, and I will identify him,' Stefanu instructed.

Juan was not hard to find from his description, though he was not enthusiastic about going out outside with the Inquisition guard. When he had been brought to the Archbishop in the carriage, the door opened, the other three guards stepped out, and Juan got in.

'Relax, Juan, you are not in any trouble,' Archbishop Stefanu assured the trembling man, before him.

'Take the four guards into the inn, point out clearly the man you have been watching and then you can go home.'

Juan nodded agreement and led the guards back into the inn.

Blundell had been waiting quite some time for his contact to arrive, and he was beginning to think he would not come that night. He spotted the Inquisition guards coming into the inn but realised there was no way he could slip out unnoticed. Initially he was uncertain the guards were after him, however, that became clear when they surrounded him. A rather large guard leaned his sizable truncheon on Blundell's table. It was close enough for him to see it must be made of hard wood, possibly mahogany, as the fine wood was well worn, yet not scratched or dented, an expensive item from South American he surmised.

'We would like you to come with us,' the large guard said.

Blundell was certain this was not a request, so he slowly stood. Quickly the other guards removed his sword and dagger, then shoved him towards the entrance to the inn. Blundell waved at Manuel as he passed the bar.

'See you later, amigo,' he said. Manuel nodded and carried on serving customers.

As Blundell came into the light at the entrance to the inn, Archbishop Stefanu indicated that he was the right man. He had his carriage go back to the castle, leaving the guards to march Blundell there. Stefanu went straight to Garcia's office on arrival at the castle. Blundell arrived shortly afterwards, whilst Garcia observed from a window in the Barbican.

'Have the suspect taken to the first cell in the interrogation level,' he instructed one of his assistant inquisitors. 'Have him searched, but not beaten or chained up, just locked in the cell. Report to me anything you find on him, anything he says and what he calls himself.'

'Yes sir,' responded the young Dominican, leaving to carry out the instructions.

'Brother Tomas,' Garcia said, calling the monk back, 'report to me out of earshot of the Archbishop, who is sitting in my office…is that understood?' Brother Tomas nodded.

Chapter 92

As instructed, Blundell was marched straight to the cells below the castle. These were in two levels. The upper level had holding and interrogation cells, and below that, dark, dank dungeons were prisoners rotted for extended periods. Like all these places, it stank of stale urine, faeces, and hopelessness. This all helped to loosen prisoner's tongues and have them betray their comrades or confess to whatever sins the inquisition accused them off. The last time Blundell had been to this castle, was when they handed over the surviving conspirators that were involved in stealing the Spanish army payroll. He knew then, they had not apprehended them all, and the ones they did, remained either loyal to their compatriots or didn't know their names, so could not betray them, even under sever torture.

He was led down some stones steps and a fat jailer unlocked the first cell they came to, lighting wall-mounted lanterns as soon as he entered. The cell was only about twelve feet square, with straw on the floor and no windows. A rough wooden table with two chairs on one side, was in the centre of the space, with a wooden bench pushed up against the opposite wall.

There were manacles attached to the wall by heavy chains alongside the bench and another set hanging from a hook in the ceiling. Blundell's heart missed a beat when he saw these, and he quickly prayed he would not be hung from them.

A young Dominican quietly gave the jailer some instruction, Blundell could not hear what was said. The cell door was closed with the guards, jailer, and inquisitor all inside.

Guards positioned themselves either side of Blundell, by the bench, while the young inquisitor and jailer stood on the opposite side of the table, staring at him. So far, although being pushed around, Blundell had not been beaten, and he hoped this would continue.

'Take off your clothes,' the young inquisitor ordered, 'lay the items on the table.'

Humiliating as that was, Blundell complied, and the jailer looked through his clothes carefully. He was clearly experienced in this, and although he almost missed the letter, concealed in the leather lining of his riding boots, the jailer eventually found the letter and handed it to the inquisitor.

By the time the young Dominican had read the letter, and the jailer searched through all his things, Blundell was naked, and felt extremely vulnerable. The inquisitor looked up from the letter at Blundell with puzzlement. He considered his instructions carefully.

'What is your name?' the inquisitor asked.

'Comandante Roberto Blundell De los Caballeros de San Juan,' he replied in perfect Spanish.

The young inquisitor stared at him, clearing thinking about what he should do next.

'You can put your clothes back on Comandante Blundell,' the inquisitor instructed, 'we will keep the rest of your things for now.' He nodded to the jailer to return his clothes.

'Shall we secure him?' the jailer asked, wondering who the prisoner was.

'No,' replied the inquisitor, 'take his things with you, but you can just leave him locked in here until we have further instructions.'

Without another word, they all left, and Blundell flopped onto the bench, incredibly relieved. The trouble with working in the shadows, he could not announce his presence to officials, never knowing who he could trust, or who would gossip to who. A risky business, but he had little choice.

'Now,' he prayed, 'get the letter to Garcia and please remember who I am.'

Chapter 93

Garcia reread the letter in his hand and considered the information provided. It had been found concealed in the prisoner's boot when he was searched. Brother Tomas had brought it to him without saying a word, as instructed.

He might have disregarded it as nonsense if it were not for the signature at the bottom and the seal of the Knights of St John. He remembered Blundell, an unusual operative, yet an effective and loyal one. The accusations against Archbishop Stefanu were both detailed and outlandish. However, he pondered the "proof" near the bottom of the note:

...the scar on the Archbishop's left palm...

Walking over to one of his aids, Garcia whispered in his ear. The aid nodded and left the room. Garcia turned his attention back to the purple cladded figure sitting in front of his desk, looking quite agitated. He stared at him for a moment in silence.

'Are you going to interrogate the prisoner now?' Stefanu enquired.

'Shortly,' Garcia replied, 'I find it best to leave prisoners in the cells for a while, before questioning them. It gives them time to contemplate their errors and makes them more ready to confess.'

'Sorry,' Archbishop Stefanu said, noting Garcia's gaze. 'I am not as used to apprehending suspects as you are, it made me quite nervous,' he said, emptying the goblet of wine he had been given.

'More wine?' Garcia asked, lifting the jug off the tray on his desk and offering its contents to the Archbishop.

'Thank you,' replied Stefanu, allowing Garcia to refill his goblet and gulping it down quickly to calm his nerves.

Just then two of Garcia's aids returned, one with a heavy canvas bag in his hands, and stood in front of the inquisitor's desk, where the Archbishop could see the bag.

'Do you recognise this man?' Garcia asked, nodding to the aid, who removed a bleeding head from the bag and dropped it into the Archbishop's glove covered hands. The Archbishop squealed and pushed the head onto the floor.

'Idiot,' Garcia shouted, 'the Archbishop does not want that in his lap!'

The aid picked up the head, put it back in the bag and left. The second aid brought a basin of water and towel over to the Archbishop, while Garcia came over beside the Archbishop apologising profusely.

'A thousand apologies, your Excellency, please let us help you clean up.'

Stefanu took his blood-soaked gloves off and discarded them on the floor, then placed his hands in the basin of water, gratefully cleaning off the blood from his hands. Garcia watched carefully, observing the scar on the Archbishop's left palm.

'Let me leave you to clean yourself up,' Garcia said, 'the brother here will tend to your needs,' he then left without waiting for comment from Stefanu.

Garcia rapidly crossed the bailey to the dungeon entrance. The guard at the door acknowledged him and opened the heavy door, revealing a dimly lit stairway. Immediately the whiff of stale urine assaulted Garcia's nose. As he descended the stairs to the interrogation level, he passed the room with the jailor and three guards playing cards.

'Cruz,' he called to the jailor, 'bring your keys.'

All four stood up to join him.

'No, I only need Cruz and the keys,' Garcia insisted.

At the bottom of the stair, a heavy door was opened, and then the door to the first cell on the interrogation level.

Blundell recognised Garcia immediately, though Garcia had to beckon Blundell into the light before he recognised the now dishevelled knight and fellow investigator.

'That will be all, you can leave us now,' Garcia ordered the jailor, 'close the door behind you.' He stared at Blundell intently and in silence, considering the circumstances.

'Well, Comandante Blundell, I did not expect to meet you again under these circumstances,' Garcia teased.

'Did you get my letter?' Blundell replied calmly, 'I was wondering how to get it to you discretely, and this was not an option I had considered.'

'Yes...' replied Garcia, perching himself on the wooden bench in the centre of the room, continuing to stare at Blundell. '...and I noted the scar on the Archbishop's palm. This is quite an outlandish accusation against the Pope's nuncio to the Spanish Court...I need more evidence before I move on him,' Garcia insisted, 'do you have a plan?'

Blundell smiled, not needing to ask Garcia if he believed him, which was a relief. He sat down on the bench opposite Garcia, hoping they could come up with something workable fast. 'You need to catch him red-handed, don't you,' Blundell ventured.

'Anything less, would put us in a difficult position with the Royal court and possibly His Holiness the Pope,' Garcia confirmed.

'Then we have to convince Stefanu that the Queen's gift has not been delivered yet, and he still has the opportunity to intercept it,' Blundell suggested, 'and we will have to work together on this.'

'And has the gift been delivered?' Garcia asked. Blundell nodded. 'So, we have no need to fear it will be compromised...that helps.'

'I believe the inn that I was arrested in, has a connection with the Knights of the Holy Blood, probably they meet in one of the cellars beneath it. If we can convince the Archbishop that the gift courier is meeting someone in the inn, he will most likely try to use the blood brothers to apprehend the courier and get a hold of the gift. I do not think he knows exactly what it is yet, but he is bound to realise it will be in Spain by now,' Blundell suggested.

'Mmmm,' Garcia replied, thinking though Blundell's suggestion, 'I think I need to be careless and leave some information on my desk for the Archbishop to read, not much, yet enough to have him keep a watch on the inn.'

'Tomorrow night I was supposed to rendezvous with my comrades that helped me get the gift to the King,' Blundell continued, 'among them is a rather tall, well-built Benedictine monk. If I do not meet them in the stables as arranged, it will be him who ventures into the inn to talk to the inn keeper. He could be the bait, however, we will have to watch carefully and discretely to move in as soon as they apprehend him, as he will be in great danger. I have already experienced their hospitality and it near killed me!' Garcia nodded, then put his head out of the door.

He called to the jailor, who was loitering in the hallway, waiting for what he thought, was initial questioning to be over.

'Fetch me a quill, ink and a piece of paper,' Garcia ordered, and the jailor immediately scurried off.

'Let's compose something that we will have found on your person, a clue to the rendezvous in the inn,' Garcia suggested.

They started composing a cryptic clue.

Archbishop Stefanu sat in the Inquisition office impatiently. He had already spent half the night either there or outside the inn and he was getting fed up. He slurped another goblet of wine, which was now starting to go to his head, but nevertheless it was calming his nerves.

He heard muffled talk outside of the office door, and Garcia burst in looking agitated, carrying a scrap of paper.

Garcia did not greet the Archbishop, or even acknowledge his presence, rather staring transfixed at the paper he had brought in with him. He wrote something on another sheet, sat back and stared at it with a frustrated frown on his head. An aid knocked and came into the office. Walking around to Garcia, the aid whispered in his ear and Garcia angerly rushed out of the office, leaving the papers and quill behind.

The Archbishop sat watching all of this with great interest. As soon as Garcia had left the office and he was on his own again, he crept around the other side of the desk and looked at a thin scrap of paper and another newer sheet of paper on the desk.

On the thin scrap of paper, there were rows of letters that did not make sense:

MULGIN ANGAM MERTARF SERTARF ENIUGNAS NI MAIVBO IRUAT AUQ NI

On the newer sheet of paper, there were words that looked similar to that on the scrap paper but in reverse, now legible as Latin, with a translation into Spanish under that, a scribbled note below that could be what Garcia just wrote:

> *Fratrem magna nigrum in qua tauri obviam in sanguine fratres*
>
> *Gran hermano negro donde los toros se encuentran con los hermanos de sangre*
>
> **Large black brother…where three bulls meet the blood brothers.**
>
> **A negro monk will meet someone in the matador's bullring.**

Archbishop Stefanu stared at the writing, then quickly sat down in front of the desk, sipping his wine, before inquisitor Garcia returned. He thought carefully about what he had read and what it meant. It looked like the scrap of paper came from the suspect. A simple code perhaps. On the newer paper were notes from Garcia or an assistant, trying to decipher the message.

If this person in the cells below is connected to the courier of the gift from Genoa, which he was now certain he was, and this information came from him, then this could be a clue as to a meeting of the courier and those helping him. Clearly Garcia's interpretation of the message was wrong, as he did not know about the blood brothers. As far as the Archbishop was concerned this message suggested a large or tall Benedictine monk (commonly referred to as Black Frailes as their habit was black) would meet someone in the inn of the three bulls where the blood brothers also meet. He had to get that inn under surveillance as soon as possible. While the Inquisition were looking in bullrings, he could then catch the courier with the gift.

He was feeling smug about working that out, despite the wine starting to fog his mind, when an angry looking Garcia returned.

'How is the interrogation going?' Stefanu ask Garcia, as he sat down at his desk.

'Not well,' Garcia replied, 'those fools use too much force, now we will be lucky to get anything more out of him.' He stared at the papers on his desk, clearly puzzled.

'Oh well,' exclaimed the yawning Archbishop, 'I think I will retire for the night. I pray you have more success in the morning,' he stood to go.

'Thank you for your assistance, your Excellency, my apologies again for the clumsiness of my staff.' Respectfully Garcia stood to say goodbye, 'Hopefully, the blood stains will come out of your cassock.'

'I am sure my valet will be able to do something, God bless you,' the Archbishop said calmly, making a sign of the cross over Garcia as a blessing and leaving as rapidly as he could.

The Archbishop raced down to his carriage, hoping his driver was awake. 'I need to get a note to Juan right away. We need the brothers help to watch for the tall Benedictine.'

Meanwhile Garcia, sat in his office, pleased with the performance that night, and thought through his own surveillance of the inn. They would have to be very discreet to not frighten off this group the Archbishop was sure to involve.

'Now,' he thought, 'should I move Blundell into better accommodation or leave him where he is for the night?' He walked back down to the cells with a smirk on his face to speak to him.

Chapter 94

Bernardo was particularly agitated, as they all waited in the stables for Blundell. If there were any messages about his father from the Queen, they would be delivered to this inn, and he was anxious for any news.

'If I do not make the stable rendezvous, you go into the inn, ask for Manuel the innkeeper and ask him—only him—if there are any messages for brother Bernardo or Comandante Blundell. If I am delayed or have to go elsewhere…I will try to leave you a message with Manuel,' Blundell had instructed him. Now Blundell was already late.

'I will go and speak to your friend Manuel,' Bernardo suggested, 'perhaps there are fresh instructions for us?' Enrico nodded agreement, but Rodrigo was a lot more hesitant.

The inn was crowded and noisy as Bernardo entered with Rodrigo following him from a distance, feeling uneasy about what Bernardo was going to encounter.

'So, who am I looking for,' Bernardo thought to himself, as he entered the busy inn.

'Manuel was described as a fat man and must be as old, or older than the other ex-soldiers I have been traveling with.'

There were lots of men in the inn that fitted that description, but none behind the bar.

He asked a passing girl serving drinks if he could speak to Manuel the innkeeper. She looked around but could not see him.

'I can't see him right now. Take a seat and I will tell him you are looking for him,' she said smiling and walked off back to the bar with empty tankards.

Bernardo perched himself on an empty bench, looking around for someone who looked like the innkeeper. Within minutes, the girl had returned and placed a tankard of wine in front of him, then moved onto other customers. The wine was of poor quality and watered down, but Bernardo sipped it anyway, grateful for something to drink.

It was not long before a muscular looking man stood in front of him, backed by two other similarly menacing figures behind him. In his peripheral vision, Bernardo noted another man standing close beside him.

'We would like a quiet word with you brother,' the first man said. Bernardo caught himself feeling the dagger beneath his scapular.

'Do you think you will fight your way out of this situation?' he chastised himself, as he stood up and towered above the men.

'Yes,' said the first man to his companions, 'this looks like the large Benedictine we we're looking for,' and the group closed in tighter to Bernardo, who kept his hand loose by his sides, to show no resistance. Bernardo stepped towards the entrance, assuming that was the way they wanted him to go, but they blocked that path.

'This way,' the first man indicated, pointing towards the back of the bar area.

Bernardo swung around with the man at his side now leading the way, and the other three taking up the rear. They approached a curtained-off area, and the lead man pulled the curtain aside to reveal a heavy-built door with a hatch at eye level. He knocked on the door and the hatch slid open, allowing him to say something through a metal grill. Bernardo could not make out what he was saying for the noise in the bar and trying to listen to what the first man was saying to one of the other men behind him. It sounded like, '…tell the Archbishop we have him…' but again, words were blurred by the general noise in the inn.

The heavy door opened, and they all walked into an area lit only by the lantern carried by the person opening the door. The door was closed behind them, and they followed the lantern holder along a short corridor to another door. Once that was opened they stepped into a better lit room with curtained cubicles along one wall and a hatch in the wooden floor with the top of a staircase just visible.

A tall figure, because of the peeked hat he wore, dressed in a crimson silk robe, stood in front of them. On the robe was the Grail symbol which Bernardo recognised from the box Signior Beniamino had given him. The crimson-clad figure raised his left palm, as did the rest of the group, showing white scars on their palms. Bernardo did, likewise, revealing his scar. On seeing Bernardo's scar, the crimson clad figure rocked notably backwards.

'Are you a blood brother?' he asked, with incredulity.

'Why would I not be?' Bernardo asked, trying hard to remain calm and remembering all he had learned of this organisation from Blundell.

'Then do you have something for us?' the crimson clad figure asked, realising how unclear he was of the Archbishop's intentions and his rushed instructions.

'Yes,' Bernardo answered, trying to sound confident, 'I have it nearby and safe, my instructions were to wait to be contacted.'

Now the crimson clad figure, who was the House Master, was totally confused. He was trying to go over in his mind what the Archbishop had said, and if he had got things completely wrong.

'Didn't he say they were trying to expose us,' the Master thought, 'or was that just the other fellow that the Inquisition arrested?'

Meanwhile, Rodrigo had been keeping an eye on Bernardo and had seen him being taken to the back of the bar area. He spotted Manuel heading towards the bar and moved through the crowd towards him.

'Hello Manuel, it has been a long time,' Rodrigo said once in speaking distance.

Manuel looked initially surprised then smiled broadly, 'Well, well,' he exclaimed, 'it has been a long time since I was shouting at your lot to move your arses.' There was no warmth between the two old soldiers.

'Quite a place you have here,' Rodrigo observed, 'but would you like to tell me what is beyond the curtains at the back.' Rodrigo watched Manuel carefully, noting he moved behind the bar and had his hands under the bar top.

'He will have a weapon under there,' Rodrigo thought, putting his hand on his sword hilt.

'You are going to have some extra visitors tonight, Manuel, I am sure you will make them welcome,' a familiar voice said behind Rodrigo.

He swung around to see Blundell, staring intently at Manuel, who responded with a wide grin stepping away from the bar.

'Comandante,' Manuel smiled broadly, 'it is good to see you.'

Manual gulped as he recognised inquisitor Garcia arriving beside Blundell, but tried to keep grinning.

'You are all welcome, of course.'

'Behind the curtain at the back of this room,' Rodrigo pointed with relief at seeing Blundell, 'that is where they took Bernardo.'

Blundell wasted no time in discussion, rushing towards the back of the bar area.

Garcia also did not hesitate, signalling his men to follow. Arriving at the curtain, Blundell pulled it back to reveal the heavy door with the hatch at eye level. He knocked on the door and as it opened, he put his mouth close to the hatch, so his words could be heard, but those inside could not see anything outside.

'For lack of fruit, the tree was cursed,' he whispered.

The hatch closed, bolts were heard moving and the door opened. As soon as it was ajar Blundell and the Inquisition guards burst in. He pushed the old man carrying the lantern forward the short distance to the next room. That door was still open, and a group of men could be seen inside a lit room. By the time they all turned around to see what was happening, the Inquisition guards had surrounded them.

Blundell was relieved to see Bernardo in one piece. Rather than acknowledge him, Bernardo was concentrating on the House Master, who was disappearing down the floor hatch. As Blundell reached out to greet him, Bernardo rushed towards the hatch, calling over his shoulder.

'He is getting away.'

Bernardo and Blundell both now disappeared down the floor hatch stair, and Garcia quickly divided his men, some to arrest those apprehended in this space and others to follow him down the stairs.

Their mad rush down to the basement slowed rapidly as they found themselves in darkness, Bernardo already bumping into the altar in the middle of the room. They fleetingly caught sight of a candle flame disappearing ahead. They paused and called from some lanterns to be brought down.

In the stables, Enrico was brushing the chestnut mare Sanchez had lent him and talking to her.

'You are a lovely creature, but not the type of beautiful female I had intended to spend my evening with.'

The floor beneath his feet moved, and looking down, Enrico realised he was standing on a hatch. He stepped to one side and just in front of the horse. As he did this, the hatch came flying open in a cloud of dust and straw. A rather flustered looking man in a crimson silk robe, carrying a large candle and some more silk, came up some stairs. He did not see Enrico, his view obscured by the startled horse, so started to run out of the horse's stall.

Enrico was not quite sure what he was seeing, however, guessing he was up to no good, he stretched out his right leg in front of the fleeing man. He tripped over the extended leg, tumbling onto the straw covered, dung splattered floor, with a crash.

Enrico cautiously approached the man, to get a better look. The man swung around, holding an ornate dagger in his hand. However, Enrico had picked up the long wooden fork, used to clean the dung and urine-soaked straw from the stable. He pointed the sturdy prongs towards the prone man's throat.

'Drop it, or I will skewer you,' Enrico demanded.

The crimson clad man dropped the dagger on the floor, and Enrico scooped it up, just as he heard familiar voices from beneath the hatch. Bernardo and Blundell appeared from below, pausing to take in what they saw, Enrico standing over the man in the crimson rope. By this time, he had quietly pocketed the bejewelled dagger.

'Well done, Enrico,' Blundell exclaimed, 'so this is where that tunnel leads.' Just then Garcia appeared, and after taking in the situation, he ordered his men to arrest the groaning figure on the stable floor. The rest of them caught their breath.

'As I was being taken behind the curtain, one of the assailants was dispatched to collect the Archbishop,' Bernardo announced. 'I am guessing that is Stefanu.'

'Then he could be here any minute now,' Garcia reasoned, 'we need to get out of sight. He must be lured into revealing himself, or he could claim to be helping flush out this group, rather than being part of it.'

With nods all around, they all descended back into the basement, except Enrico who closed the opening behind them, kicking the straw over the hatch to conceal its recent use.

No sooner had he completed that task and gone into the neighbouring stall to brush Rodrigo's horse than a carriage pulled up outside the stable.

The Archbishop's bodyguard jumped down from beside the driver and helped the rotund, purple clad figure out of the carriage. The other blood brother with them, went into the stable and straight to the horse stall with the hatch. He heard singing in the neighbouring stall and someone talking to a horse. Assuming it was a stable hand and of no consequence, he opened the hatch to let them descend. Picking up and lighting a lantern, hanging on a hook on the horse stall entrance, he led the way for the Archbishop into the basement.

'Stay here,' the Archbishop ordered his burly bodyguard, 'make sure our exit is kept clear.' The bodyguard nodded, closing the hatch behind the Archbishop.

On hearing the noises from the neighbouring stall, he crept out to see who was singing to the horses. As he exited the horse stall, he was struck full in the face with the handle of the stout wooden hay fork. He saw flashing lights for a moment, then passed out, crashing to the floor like a felled tree.

Enrico looked at the hay fork.

'Two in one night,' he told it, 'you are on a roll, amigo.'

In the basement, the only light was from the lantern they were carrying, so the Archbishop called out.

'Hello…Juan, are you there?'

A large shape, dressed in an indistinct silk robe and pointed hat, started to come into focus ahead of them, silhouetted by the glow of the light from the stairs leading down to the basement.

'You have disappointed us,' came a voice ahead of him.

'What,' Stefanu replied, 'who is this?'

'Your attempts to disrupt the Spanish army pay and payments to the Genoese have repeatedly failed,' said the same voice with an unusual accent, 'we are beginning to wonder exactly where your loyalties lie.' The voice sounded menacing.

'Who are you?' Stefanu pleaded, fear muddling his mind.

'Vous savez qui nous sommes *(You know who we are)*,' came the reply, and Stefanu's blood ran cold. Were his paymasters in France coming to eliminate him?

'Vous savez que j'ai toujours été fidèle à la France *(You know I've always been loyal to France)*,' Stefanu replied in perfect French.

During this strange conversation, other figures had been descending the stairs. Now lanterns began to light around then, and they soon realised they were surrounded by the Inquisition guards.

'Bonsoir, Archevêque *(Good evening, Archbishop)*,' Blundell greeted Stefanu, stepping from behind Bernardo's large, white-clad frame, and he realised this is who he had been speaking to.

Garcia stepped forward. 'So, your loyalties lie with France, do they, Archbishop?' he said, 'We need to have a talk about that,' and signalled his guards to arrest the now trembling cleric.

Chapter 95

After a day of taking statements, and as Archbishop Stefanu did not take much persuasion to tell all he knew; inquisitor Garcia was content to let Blundell and his group go.

'Stefanu is opening up so many more lines of inquiry, we are going to be busy for quite some time,' Garcia told Blundell.

'For me,' Blundell replied, 'this is the end of over two years of investigation. It would be good if I could disappear back into the shadows in order to be most effective.'

Garcia nodded agreement. 'Where next?' he enquired.

'Malta,' Blundell confirmed, putting down the wine he was sharing with Garcia.

'I should report the Grand Master of my Order, so we will take the first ship we can find out of Spain.'

He stood to leave.

'About that other matter,' Blundell enquired, 'did you find any records of Cavaliere Mateo di Boscogrande being arrested?'

Garcia shook his head. 'Tell the young Benedictine, we searched our records and found no mention of him. If he visited Queen Marianna, he managed to slip in and out of Spain without us knowing anything about it.' Garcia looked genuinely sad. 'I feel sorry for Fraile Bernardo, and I pray he can find what happened to his father, but he will have to look elsewhere.'

By the time Blundell met up with his compatriots, early the next morning, he found the three Spaniards in jovial spirits.

'Well, you all seem to be in good moods,' Blundell remarked when meeting them.

'It has been a profitable venture, amigo, and now we have a wagon full of goods to take to the port of Valencia to courier for a client,' Sanchez replied.

'This is a profitable business,' Rodrigo interjected, 'and we have decided to go into partnership with Domingo. This business has room to expand, and we are better at this than trading ourselves.'

Enrico smiled and nodded agreement.

The five-day ride to the coast was full of good cheer, talk of the future as well as of the past. However, most evenings, while they settled down to drinking and storytelling after dinner, Bernardo would retire to the room he most often shared with Blundell. Blundell did not stay up that late either and would often walk in on Bernardo while he knelt by his bed praying. Repeatedly he found his young friend just staring at his dagger and rosary, lying on the bed in front of him. If he did not find out what had happened to his father, he was not sure Bernardo would ever be free.

'Sorry brother, I do not know where else to look for evidence of your father's fate,' was all Blundell could say, and he knew it did not help.

By the time they reached Valencia and found a ship to sail in, Bernardo's frustration about his father seemed to be turning to anger, Blundell witnessed it eating away at the young man.

'Amigos, we will miss you,' the three Spaniards chorused, genuinely.

Bernardo embraced them all with big bear hugs, close to tears. Blundell too, embraced his old comrades, though perhaps with a little less emotion than the others.

Chapter 96

The Spanish ship they sailed on was a sturdy cargo vessel with an experienced sailing master, heavily loaded with cargo for several ports in the western Mediterranean. Initially they sailed due west to Palma in Mallorca in fine early October weather. Steady, nor westerly winds pushed them along but had a chill in them as it funnelled down from the Pyrenees. From there, they continued onto Cagliari in southern Sardinia, making good speeds in increasing northerly winds and choppy water.

Bernardo did not say much on the voyage, despite sharing a hammock space with Blundell, seemingly growing in anger over the mystery of his father's disappearance. Blundell did not know how to comfort him, so left him to seethe quietly, praying God would give him a revelation.

From Cagliari, they were to sail onto Trapani in eastern Sicily, before continuing on to Malta. From there, the vessel would sail back to eastern Sicily and onto further ports in Italy, eventually returning to Spain with, hopefully, full holds.

'This is usually a lucrative route,' the sailing master told them, 'that we repeat about three times per year.'

The day after they left Cagliari, a strong northly wind whipped down from the Alps and started throwing the ship around mercilessly. The crew had already battened down everything they could and shortened sail to reduce the excessive heel. However, the master warned them all he might have to hove-to and ride out the storm.

'These storms are not uncommon this time of year,' the master was explaining, as they tried to stay upright near the great wheel.

'Unfortunately, we seem to be getting a particularly bad one.'

The ship took another lurch and heeled more, taking on more water that they were desperately trying to pump out.

'I am not sure we will make Trapani,' the master warned Blundell, 'I may head for a sandy cove to the north of there and beach us. It is either that, risk breaking up on rocks or taking on too much water and sinking.'

It sounded rather ominous.

'That is, if I can find the beach.'

He stared ahead into the blackness before them, heavy clouds blocking moon and stars, as rain came down in sheets, forcing them to sail blindly. As morning came, there was a slight reprieve, as the clouds parted a little and the rain stopped. The sailing master thought he spotted the headland at San Vito Lo Capo, and he headed straight for it.

Looking out for the sandy cove he remembered, he prayed he could control the vessel enough to beach her safely. The crew were now exhausted from pumping water out of the bilges all night. Bernardo watched from the main deck, clinging onto the standing rigging, and praying they would survive the voyage. They could see the bay coming into view, and hope started to fill their hearts. Then the wind picked up again, and controlling the vessel became even more difficult. Bernardo and Blundell clung on for dear life, and frantic shouting at the crew could be heard. Suddenly the ship heeled over excessively and anyone or anything not tied down enough flew over the side into the boiling sea. There was a massive grinding noise, and the ship started to break up. It had grounded, but where exactly were they?

'Were they all doomed?' Bernardo thought as he clung onto the rigging.

As the sun rose higher, visibility improved, and Bernardo could see the beach ahead. Within the bay, the sea was rough, but not as bad as it had been. Perhaps he could make it ashore.

He looked aft, where others were clinging desperately to anything that was fixed down, and he caught sight of Blundell near the great wheel, now abandoned.

'Blundell,' he cried, though the wind seemed to sweep his voice away.

He scrambled aft, eventually making it to within clear sight and call of Blundell. He was cradling the sailing master, who was bleeding profusely from a head wound.

Out of the corner of his eye, he caught sight of movement and ducked down. A heavy wooden block that had broken free, swung by his head, but thankfully it was still attached to some of the running rigging. Something like that, he surmised, had struck the sailing master.

'Blundell,' he cried again, 'we have to go,' and this time Blundell looked up.

He felt for breath on the master's mouth, but it was clear he was dead. He lowered 390 his head gently to the deck and began to crawl over the heavily slopping deck towards Bernardo.

'Grab onto some of the flotsam,' Blundell shouted back to Bernardo, as he allowed himself to slide off the deck and into the sea.

Bernardo followed, then they both grabbed a hold of anything that was floating free, kicking off with their feet and willed themselves to get to the shore. Bernardo found it difficult to keep his head above water, and the beach did not seem to be getting any closer. He lost track of time as he became tired and began to lose consciousness. Is this how it was to end? So many plans, all now nonsense.

'Agata, I'm sorry,' he thought.

There were voices. Were they in his head…was he hallucinating? Suddenly many arms were dragging him out of the water, voices shouting.

'Here, another one,' he heard, 'a Frate here…heavy, we need a hand.'

Locals were rescuing survivors from the surf.

Bernardo lay on his back on the cool sand, looking up at blue sky peeking out from dispersing clouds. The wind had dropped considerably, and as he took deep breaths and thanked God, he was alive, his head cleared. He sat up on his elbows and looked around. Many bodies were scattered around him on the beach, some moving and others not. Groups, of what he assumed were locals, were running into the surf and dragging bodies out of the water. The ship did not seem as far away from the beach, as the beach had from the vessel. It was heeling over heavily, almost completely on its side, rigging a tangled mess.

'Praise God, you are alive,' said a voice he recognised.

He looked up into Blundell's smiling face.

'I have been looking for you,' Blundell said, offering him a hand to get up.

'I think I lost consciousness for a while,' Bernardo replied.

He noticed two Franciscans going from body to body, stopping to give last rites, or waving at locals to bring some assistance.

'I should help,' he thought, 'there is much to do.'

He walked towards the Franciscans, dripping wet and unsteady on his feet as a cart was being manoeuvred along the beach towards them.

'Can I help?' he said weakly, when within ear shot.

The younger of the two monks looked up at him with alarm.

'Are you alright, brother?' he asked, raising a rag to Bernardo's forehead.

Unbeknown to him, he was bleeding from a blow to the top of his skull. The young Franciscan pulled away the now bloody rag and peered at the wound.

'I think it is superficial, you were probably struck by some debris on your way ashore.' The older monk looked up at that moment.

'Bless you brother,' he said, 'praying for the dead and dying will be helpful, there are many, but if you feel dizzy, do not push yourself.'

He too looked at the scar on Bernardo's forehead. The bleeding had either stopped or was now very little.

'This cart will be taking the wounded to Santuario di San Vito nearby,' the older priest was saying, as he took Bernardo's arm. 'Go with them, if you feel dizzy, lay down there. If you are well enough, sit with those that are in distress. We will join you soon.'

He turned to continue checking the bodies on the beach.

The sun was low in the sky by the time the two, now very weary, Franciscans returned to their chapel. The sanctuary pews had been turned into makeshift beds and local women tended the injured. Bernardo had given the last rites to many that day, feeling guilty that he was not yet an ordained priest, but did it really matter he reasoned to himself if it comforted them.

'How are you doing, brother?' Blundell asked, coming in with the Franciscans and some other local men, carrying more bodies.

Bernardo looked mentally and emotionally exhausted. He looked down at the peaceful, pale face of a woman he had been praying for. Like so many others, she had not made it.

'Stop now, brother,' the older Franciscan ordered, 'we have some food and drink being prepared for us, come, and join us.'

He put his arm around Bernardo, his pastoral heart showing through his emotional control.

'Is this your first experience of having to pray for the dying?' he asked Bernardo.

'Unfortunately, not, Father, but so many...' Bernardo replied, near tears.

They gathered in a simple room behind the chapel, where a table with food and jugs of wine were laid out. Many locals were there, men and women, as well as the other younger monk. All looked exhausted, grateful for the energy the food was providing and stopping for a moment. There was little chatter at first but as the food and wine refreshed them, quiet conversations broke out around the group.

'We will never get the bodies all in the ground before dark,' an older man was saying to the older Franciscan in a low voice.

'No,' he replied in an almost whisper, 'you and your men dig as many graves as you can today…we will store the bodies in the sanctuary overnight, then start the burials in the morning. We need time to record the identities if we can figure that out.'

He walked away with the older man to talk to the younger monk and a group of other locals, clearly planning what was to happen next. The old Franciscan returned to where Blundell and Bernardo were sitting in silence.

'My apologies for not introducing myself, I am Father Samuel and that' pointing over at the younger Franciscan, 'is brother Nicolas.'

Blundell stood up in greeting and bowed. 'We understand, father,' Blundell reassured,

'I am Commandeur Blundell of the Knights of St John, and this is my good friend Brother Bernardo, both heading back to Malta. We are grateful for your efforts here and we are at your service.'

'Do you think you could help us identify any of your fellow passengers and crew? Father Samuel asked, 'Only we want to avoid burying them without recording who they are.'

'We will certainly try,' Blundell replied, glancing down at Bernardo, still looking frail.

'You seem quite experienced in such tragedies, has this happened here before?' Blundell asked.

Bernardo suddenly took more interest in the conversation.

'This coastline can be dangerous, especially at this time of year, when the wind picks up suddenly. We must bury a fisherman or two, lost to the sea, every other year and every few years, deal with a shipwreck,' the old priest replied. 'Though we have not had a wreck as bad as yours for many years, I have served here a long time and seen too many souls lost to the sea.'

'Can you remember a bad storm about seven years ago, that might have caused a wreck?' Bernardo enquired.

'Without a doubt,' Father Samuel replied, 'although a long time ago, that night is etched in my memory, as it was such a bad storm, seventeenth October.

It came over suddenly and drove a ship like yours up on our beach. We tried our best with the injured, but we ended up burying many in our cemetery.'

'And you keep a record of the names of those you bury?' Bernardo asked and Blundell realised what he was thinking.

'As best we can,' Samuel answered, 'by asking the injured their names, looking at documents of the dead and having survivors helping us identify those already passed away. As you can hopefully help us now with identification.'

'We will do what we can, Father,' Blundell assured, 'and record the names carefully.'

By sunset, the day following the storm, they were all physically exhausted and emotionally numb. Bernardo had spent the day helping to bury the dead and saying prayers. While he was walking back from the cemetery with Father Samuel, Blundell was watching for them to return to Santuario di San Vito, having completed the investigation into the identities of the dead bodies.

'Father, we have the lists of the dead almost completed, do you want me to write these into your records for you?'

'That would be very helpful, my son, I have much more still to do,' Samuel replied, 'I will show you where our records are kept. Good work, both of you,' said the old monk, as he led them into his vestry.

Taking a key from his belt and opening a cupboard in there. He removed an enormous, clearly old, leather-bound ledger.

'Record the names and date into this ledger, there is room for short notes too,' Samuel explained, 'please follow the pattern as previous entries.'

The priest locked the cupboard and left them. While Blundell fetched ink and a fresh quill, Bernardo set the large ledger on the table in the vestry, lit a candle and stared at it.

Shortly afterwards, Blundell returned and as he looked at Bernardo, he realised they were both thinking the same thing—they could not wait. They opened the ledger and found the entries for 17 October 1686. There, under "Wreck caused by storm" was a list of persons buried in the cemetery. Some had comments beside their names, such as: "dragged from sea, badly injured, died on 18th,19th, 20th etc…" But one such entry stood out for them. Written in a neat hand:

"Boscogrande, Mateo—died of head injuries sustained during wreck— Next of Kin unknown—buried in San Vito cemetery—18 October 1686."

Bernardo sat back on the chair in the vestry and stared at the entry. So now he knew what had become of his father. Although he did not feel happy by the confirmation that his father was dead, and the tragic circumstances of his death, he felt a great weight lift from his shoulders. He was coming back for them.

Blundell closed the ledger and put his arm around Bernardo, who now wept uncontrollably. Grieving for both his father, and his mother, who would be dead within a year of his father. He wept for the happy life they could have had if his father had made it back to them, perhaps returning to Palermo or settling in the country at his manor. He would never know, but years of pent-up grief poured out of him, and Blundell just let him weep, without trying to comfort him with useless words.

Later, Blundell collected some food, while Bernardo tried to understand what he was feeling. That night they both slept soundly, quite exhausted in every way.

Chapter 97

Two days after reading the ledger, the task of recording all the names of those recently buried was completed. Bernardo and Blundell planned to get a lift on a cart, going early in the morning to Trapani market. There they hoped to catch a ship for Malta, or a port for another ship bound for Valletta.

Blundell woke on a bright morning; he noticed Bernardo's sleeping area was empty. Initially he thought he had gone to Lauds prayer, then noticed a note by his riding boots:

"After talking to locals about Trapani port and the coast road, I decided to walk the 6 leagues. As the sun sets, tomorrow night, I can meet you on the sea wall opposite Ligny tower. It is apparently very obvious. Sorry I did not discuss this with you. I came to the decision in the night and need some time on my own to think. Please say my goodbyes for me."

Bernardo Blundell thought for a few moments after reading the note. He was not entirely surprised by Bernardo's decision. The young man had reached one of those critical moments in life. A fork in the road of destiny, where you have to decide which way to go, realising your decision will have major implications. He too had reached that point when he decided to leave England, probably for good.

Bernardo was perceptibly growing up in front of him. Even over this trip to Spain and back, his hair had changed from a straw-coloured mop to longer, darker locks. His youthful whiskers were taking over his hardening jaw line. While inside, there was a hardening too. It was inevitable, yet Blundell regretted the passing of innocence, knowing it never returns.

As requested, he said goodbye on behalf of them both and joined the cart going to market, in the early morning light. The market was not actually in Trapani port, but in a neighbouring village before the port. So, after some lunch and a snooze under a convenient tree, Blundell walked another 2 leagues to the actual port. He found lodgings for the night in a waterfront tavern that evening, enjoyed the local seafood, while making enquiries about ships bound for Malta.

A bright blue sky welcomed him the following day after a restful night in a passable bed. It was going to be a hot day, with little wind to cool the air, so he purposefully set out after some breakfast to find the harbour master's office.

It seemed his wrecked vessel was the main one that made the Trapani to Malta trip three times a year. The best he could do was catch a vessel going to Gela, or even Messina, then seek a ship going south to Malta. He felt quite despondent as he wandered around the port.

As the sun began to set, there were fine cirrus clouds dotting the otherwise clear skies.

'Another weather system coming over.' Blundell's experienced eye told him, 'The wind will change again. Wish we could predict what it will do.'

He could clearly see the newly built Ligny tower, to the southwest of the port, as expected.

Approaching the sea wall, he observed lots of men fishing but no black clad Benedictine. He walked along towards a point just opposite the tower, now framed by the reddening sky. He breathed in the salty air, mixed with the aroma unique to fishing harbours. There was a large, Scandinavian-looking seaman, sitting on the wall, tying knots in a piece of line. He sat near him and looked at his light locks, tied back in a short ponytail.

'Bernardo?' Blundell asked with surprise, recognising the figure.

He was greeted with a faint smile under those deep blue eyes.

'Are you a sailor now?' he asked, half in jest.

'Perhaps for a while,' Bernardo replied, looking down at the line in his hands. 'I am trying to practise the knots and hitches the sailors have taught me during our voyages. It might help me get a berth on a Maltese-bound vessel.'

'And your calling to the church?' Blundell enquired, realising it was time Bernardo talked about such things.

Bernardo paused and sighed. He looked at the sky changing colour, enjoying the slight sea breeze on his sun-baked face.

'I am no longer sure I ever had a calling, just a dedication to the Rule of Saint Benedict. The discipline of the church was all I knew and what made me feel safe,' he replied.

They sat in silence for a moment.

'You lost your father to a storm and mother to a fever; I could see how you would be angry with God.' Blundell ventured. Recollecting his own family's misfortunes.

To his surprise Bernardo smiled, while still admiring the changing colours in the sky.

'Have you ever read the book of Job?' Bernardo asked, sounding philosophical.

'Many years ago, I had a priest teacher who read it to our class,' Blundell answered, surprised by the question.

'Father Aiello and I debated it for a long time,' Bernardo recalled, 'as he encouraged me to think it through, I ended up challenging how unfair it was of God to let Satan take away everything from such a good man.'

He laughed as he remembered the heated discussion he had with his old tutor. Then a tear came to his eyes, as he pictured Aiello in his mind. There had been genuine love between them, but it was never expressed.

'What was the old academic's conclusion?' Blundell asked intrigued.

'As I remember it, he did not really have a definitive answer...'

Blundell was surprised how disappointed he was with this response but listened carefully.

'In fact, he accused me of arrogance...' Bernardo looked over to Blundell with amusement, as Blundell looked puzzled. '...would I dare put myself in judgement over the creator of all things? "Where were you when I laid the foundations of the earth", God challenged Job.'

Bernardo looked as if he would cry, his words choking him, as he continued. 'The idea that God allowed our apparently previous happy family life to be disrupted by the Inquisition, my father's death through a storm at sea and mother's subsequent death through fever, saddens me deeply.'

Tears rolled down Bernardo's cheeks. 'I needed this time on my own to process all of this and grieve. Yet...' he brushed the tears from his cheeks, '...in all of this, I see I have always been loved and cared for. I have someone now, who loves me, and I love her, and I want to embrace that love, not push it away. Our lives remain in God's hands, they can be snuffed out at any moment, but I trust Him. Despite it all, I believe He is caring for us.' Bernardo smiled and his eyes brightened.

'So much mystery. Yet Saint Paul says, in the end "only hope and love remain".'

The two friends watched the sun descend into the azure, blue sea. All sorts of emotions, many long buried, crashed together in their minds, like waves crashing onto rocks, then immediately retreating again. Finally, as it was getting dark, Blundell broke the mesmerising silence.

'I could not find a ship going to Malta. We will have to find something sailing to another port, then change for a vessel sailing south,' he stated despondently.

'See that gaff-rigged sloop over there?' Bernardo said, pointing back into the port. Blundell nodded.

'The master has agreed to take on two temporary apprentices, for no pay, for a trip along the coast, as far Gela. I said you were with the Knights of St John, and he thinks you are all pirate hunters and that I was still learning after several voyages.' Bernardo grinned, pleased with his fortuitous meeting earlier that day.

'They sail at first light tomorrow and we can sleep on board tonight, ready to rise before dawn.'

Bernardo stood up, picking up a sailor's canvas bag he had purchased along with the cotton shirt and leather breaches he was wearing. He had his Benedictine habit, rosary, and dagger in the bag, which he tossed over his shoulder. His money pouch, with the profits from the Spanish trip, was tied to his waist-belt but discreetly tucked inside his breaches.

'Let's eat, then I will introduce you,' Bernardo suggested.

He felt more at ease with himself than he could remember, as they walked along towards a nearby tavern where he knew the sloop master would be drinking.

'I lost the box,' Bernardo said, out of the blue, 'coming ashore after the wreck.'

'Does that bother you?' asked Blundell, noticing Bernardo's change in demeanour.

Not really,' he answered, 'though I have wondered what became of the relic it once housed.'

'What do you think it was—a saint's bone perhaps?' Blundell ventured.

'No,' Bernardo thoughtfully replied, 'I think it was something far more significant.'

'Like what?' Blundell was curious now. 'Like a fragment of a gnostic gospel or ancient Hebrew text. Something worth stealing and hiding all this time,' Bernardo mused.

'Something that may turn up one of these days and upset some people. Of course, we have no clue how to find it now.'

'Father Aiello and I talked about such things, some people, he said, put much faith in such things,' he shrugged and smiled.

Chapter 98

San Giovanni tacked laboriously as it tried to make headway towards Sicily in the freshening north wind. Her patrol had been uneventful, no pirate attacks being reported in weeks. Captain De Poincy was hoping he could be released to escort some Genoese vessels to and from the Levant, after so many victories against the barbary corsairs around these waters.

'Sail starboard bow,' the lookout cried, and both the captain and sailing master eagerly took up their telescopes to have a look.

'Xebec, but one of ours, I think capt'n,' the sailing master, said.

'Yes,' a disappointed De Policy replied, 'I can see her flag, but we will keep an eye on her anyway in case it is a rouse.'

'Another sail to larboard,' called the lookout, and they could see a sloop making good speed along the Sicilian coast on a broad reach.

'Wonder where she is going,' De Poincy asked out loud, but mainly talking to himself.

'Gela, I would guess,' the sailing master replied, hearing his captain's verbal musings.

'Let's close her and see if she has any news, seen any other vessels and keep between her and the xebec,' the captain ordered.

Instructions were shouted, and they changed tack to close the sloop while continuing generally, to the north, fulfilling their patrol mandate.

On the sloop, the strengthening northly wind was keeping them all busy on board, though allowing them to make great speed. Their proximity to the coast had helped reduce the swell and fetch, while the cooler north wind and building clouds, helped keep an otherwise hot day quite pleasant.

Bernardo was happily using his strength to pull on sheets, and was taking instructions from the bosun on what to look out for in the rigging. Meanwhile, Blundell was talking to the vessel's master about the xebec he had spotted.

'What do you make of her,' the master was asking, pointing to the xebec, two points on their starboard bow, 'that's the sort of vessel these er pirates use?'

'Yes, however she seems to be on her own and they usually hunt in packs,' replied Blundell, 'also I think I see a Knights of Malta flag on her,' looking through the master's telescope.

'Hope you are right,' the master said despondently, 'all we have is some muskets to defend ourselves.' The master walked forward.

'Enzo,' he shouted, 'break out the muskets, powder and shot.'

The bosun looked worried but immediately walked aft to the gun locker. The rest of the crew looked forward for what was worrying the master, praying they were not under attack. As they closed the xebec, she seemed to be turning away from them and Blundell continued to get a better look at her flag. Then he spotted another, larger vessel. At first, this concerned him.

'Was this the rest of the pirate flotilla coming into view,' he thought, his heart starting to thump, as Bernardo came to join him.

'Could I borrow the glass,' Bernardo asked, the other vessel closing in on them rapidly.

He lifted the telescope, looking over at the larger of the vessels and smiled.

'It's *San Giovanni*,' he announced, 'De Poincy's command,' with much relief onboard.

As the vessels closed each other, there was much waving and cheering, and not just from Bernardo and Blundell. The whole crew were relieved they had the protection of the Knights of Malta. De Poincy recognised Bernardo and Blundell and had *San Giovanni* turn to parallel the sloop's course, his sailing master approaching as close as he dared.

As they came within 200 feet, De Poincy leaned over the railing on his quarter deck. Cupping his hands over his mouth, he shouted, 'Good to see you in one piece,' though the wind made it hard to hear.

The sailing master on *San Giovanni* carefully watched his helm. If the wind caught them and they suddenly turned into the wind, they would slice the sloop in two! The sloop master was also nervous for the same reason.

'They like to chance their arm, do these knights,' he remarked to Blundell, as he tried to ensure a steady course.

'Don't worry, they are good seamen. You just stay steady on this heading, and they will be gone soon,' Blundell reassured.

'Where are you bound now?' De Poincy called, glancing up at the sails, starting to spill.

'Gela then Malta,' Bernardo replied, 'if we can find a ship going there.'

'Happy to give you a lift…see you in Gela,' De Poincy shouted, but his words tailed off, as the sailing master brought the helm slightly around to starboard to maintain distance from the sloop. The wind, now more on the quarter, pushed *San Giovanni* ahead, and away from the sloop, with far more sail area giving her greater speed.

'Well, now we know how we will get to Malta,' Blundell said to Bernardo, clapping him on the back, happy to be almost reunited with their old friends.

Chapter 99

Gela harbour was quiet when the sloop arrived the next morning, perhaps because it was October. Passing through the small breakwater, they could see *San Giovanni*, already secured alongside. Bernardo and Blundell quickly gathered their things and said their goodbyes. The sloop master gave them a day's wage after all, pleased with their service. So, in good spirits, they near skipped along the quay to *San Giovanni*.

On arrival, Bernardo ran up the gangway and was immediately greeted by some of the crew he knew, surprised to see him out of his habit, they teased him about looking like a sailor. Blundell smiled, turning aft towards the captain's cabin, where he bumped into De Poincy coming onto the deck.

'Good to see you well, brother,' De Poincy exclaimed, throwing his arms around Blundell.

Then over his shoulder he caught sight of Bernardo.

Well,' De Poincy bellowed, 'what have we here?' He scowled, hands on hips over dramatically. 'What happened to our young Benedictine brother?' a broad smile coming to his face. 'Has the salt got into your blood…it does for most of us?'

Bernardo sheepishly turned to face De Poincy and just shrugged. The crew that knew Bernardo were laughing but with much affection. New crew looked on, rather confused. With Bernardo and Blundell now standing beside each other in front of De Poincy, he dropped his voice and looked momentarily serious.

'Was the mission a success?' De Poincy asked.

Uncharacteristically, Blundell paused and looked to Bernardo to reply, knowing his experiences had been life changing.

'Completely,' Bernardo assured, realising Blundell was waiting for him to respond. De Poincy smiled broadly again.

'And have you changed professions and wanting a berth as a seaman?' he asked, looking Bernardo over.

'For now,' Bernardo replied, 'if that is acceptable…I am learning new skills which I thought would come in handy.'

De Poincy nodded, noting the sailing master was now standing beside him.

'Master Cardona, do you think we have room for another apprentice?' he asked.

'I am sure we have a spare hammock on the gun deck, and I already know this fellow comes with good references,' Cardona agreed and winked at Bernardo.

He took Bernardo off to see the bosun.

'I am about to call on the harbour master,' De Poincy said, 'do you want to walk with me, then we can talk?'

Blundell nodded and dropped a small bag off in the captain's cabin. Walking along the quay, into the town, the two old comrades conferred quietly, and seriously.

'Have you fully recovered?' De Poincy enquired with concern.

'Almost completely…' Blundell replied, stretching his right arm up and wincing a little, 'just the odd pang in my sides.'

'And the mission?' De Poincy enquired. 'The gift for the Queen was delivered, Archbishop Stefanu arrested by the Inquisition and a two-year-old case came to a final conclusion. As Stefanu sings like a bird, I think the Inquisition will mop others up and close that network…for the time being!' Blundell replied, raising his eyebrows.

'We also found Bernardo's father,' Blundell added and De Poincy gasped.

'You found Mateo in Spain?' De Poincy exclaimed in surprise.

'We found his burial spot in San Vito Lo Capo near Trapani. He was shipwrecked on his way home from persuading Queen Marianna to use her influence to recall the Sicilian chief inquisitor.'

De Poincy stopped on hearing this and took a moment to control his rising feelings.

'He was a great man and a dear brother,' De Poincy said, staring at Blundell, a lump in his throat. 'Is this why Bernardo has given up his calling to the church?'

'Sort of,' Blundell explained, 'he says he now believes he did not actually have a calling to enter the church, just all he knew—what he felt comfortable with,' they continued walking.

'So, does he really want to be a sailor now?' De Poincy asked, in semi disbelief.

'He wants to spread his wings and be free,' Blundell suggested, 'I do not really think he knows exactly what that will look like, however, being united with Agata and her younger brothers is the next step.'

De Poincy nodded thoughtfully, as they walked towards the harbour master's office. Now he would give his men the night off in Gela and sail back to Malta in the morning, hoping for a more interesting assignment next.

Chapter 100

Once secure alongside their usual moorings in Birgu, overlooked by Fort Saint Angelo in Valletta, Captain De Poincy and Commandeur Blundell went ashore to report to their Grand Master. Bernardo sent a note to Agata to let her know he had returned, then he went to the Sacra Infermeria to find Brother Antonio. He wanted to talk things through with Antonio, before he saw Agata, realising he had some big decisions to make, and believing Antonio's level-headedness would help.

'Continuing my studies here would bring me great joy,' Bernardo explained, while walking with Antonio around the hospital grounds, 'as would travelling to other seats of great learning. There are many places I would like to visit. However, first I need time to sort out my relationship with Agata, free from clerical restrictions.'

'Well, you have not been ordained yet, nor made any commitments. You certainly have the financial means, so you are free to do and go as you feel led. It is best you sort out exactly what you want…how you feel called, before taking any oaths,' Antonio confirmed.

'It was easy for me,' he continued, 'I always wanted to focus on healing the sick, and this has been a great place to train.'

They sat down together on a stone bench, both reflecting on their experiences.

'Being part of the Hospitallers here in Malta, has allowed me to learn, and to sail with the fleet,' Antonio was clearly content with his situation, 'also my friendship with Captain De Poincy has allowed me to go on some adventures, which now you too have experienced!'

The two friends laughed together, though Bernardo had mixed feelings about some of the recent adventures he had been part of.

'Although I have little experience of these things, it is clear to all that Agata loves you and you love her. You both have to decide if this love is as brother and sister, or something more, before you commit to anything.' Antonio looked carefully into Bernardo's eyes, as a big brother would his dearly loved younger sibling.

'Thank you, brother,' Bernardo said, embracing Antonio as they stood together, 'I pray our friendship will remain, no matter what.'

'I am confident it will,' Antonio reassured, 'now I must get back to my duties and you to yours.' The two friends parted, with Bernardo looking forward to seeing Agata and her brothers.

The next morning, Bernardo was helping to load some supplies onto *San Giovanni* when a carriage rolled up and all three Conti siblings clambered out.

Agata was dressed in a fine light green silk dress and looked every part the prosperous young lady. Both Stefano and Mateo were dressed in fine navy-blue silk breaches, cotton white shirts and matching jackets. Bernardo, who had been keeping an eye out for them, hoping they would visit soon, immediately came down the gangway waving. The boys waved back and called out, 'Bernardo,' while Agata studied his appearance, without his Benedictine habit.

Her mind was full of questions and possible answers she almost dared not hope for.

'Bernardo does not look injured,' she thought with relief, 'but why is he not wearing his habit? Has he stopped being a Benedictine?'

By the time Bernardo was on the quay, striding towards them, the brothers had both run up beside him.

'Bernardo, Bernardo,' shouted Mateo, hugging Bernardo's tree-trunk sized thigh. Bernardo looked down at him with surprise and joy.

'Yes,' Stefano said, smiling broadly, 'he has found his voice again, and the whole Castellietti household have made him feel safe and loved. All of us in fact. We are truly blessed.'

Now, despite her lady-like appearance, Agata could not contain her emotions anymore, breaking into a run towards him. She jumped up, throwing her arms around his neck, kissing him full on the lips. He returned her embrace enthusiastically, holding her up in his muscular arms.

'Well,' Stefano exclaimed, standing, and smiling in front of them, now looking much taller than his sister, 'I guess you are not a monk anymore.'

Bernardo gently put Agata's feet back on the quay, looking adoringly down at her. Agata returned the gaze, her eyes tearing up. They both laughed and arm-in arm, walked along the quay.

Epilogue

Tuscany, May 1733

It had been a week since the funeral, and only now did Agata feel she could face going through the papers in her late husband's study. Sitting at Bernardo's desk, facing the large open window that looked out onto a shaded part of the garden, she could hear her grandchildren happily playing. She smiled to herself, reflecting on the delight they gave her and had given Bernardo. She would much rather be playing with them than sorting through Bernardo's things, however, his life's work was recorded in the journals scattered around, and they needed to be carefully stored away. She would also have to make a start to writing to friends with the news of Bernardo's demise, and many contact addresses would be in his papers. The fever that took him, caught them all by surprise, friends needed to be told.

Agata looked at the ubiquitous pile of books on the desk that so reminded her of the intelligent, yet big, strong, and gentle man she had so loved. She missed him. Falling in love with him in her mid-teens, they had been happily married for nearly forty years. Forty years of travel and adventures in turbulent times. Forty years of bringing up a family, developing a successful business, and creating this comfortable family home in the Tuscan hills, while trying to shield them from the violent conflicts raging all around.

As Agata looked out of the window, the sky turning orange as the sun began to set, she worried about the continuing wars so close by and how she would protect her family.

Even in quiet Tuscany, the Medici's power was waning, the rulers of this region may change soon too. How would that affect them? They had served the now "old" authorities and been honoured for their help. Now the new powers around may view them in a very different light.

'God protect us,' she whispered under her breath, as she refocused on the task at hand.

Three large, leather-bound volumes of Bernardo's journals, describing key events in their families life and some of the research he had done into the mysteries of the secret societies he had become aware of during their adventures. She open a volume randomly and came across some of her younger brother's sketches that he had discarded, and Bernardo had retrieved, storing them between the covers of his journals.

These were sketches of her, Bernardo, and her other brother Stefano when they lived together in Malta. Mateo had been such a gifted artist, but a troubled soul. A tear came to her eyes as she remember her brother and his early death in Florence. Trying to look out for Mateo was one of the reasons they initially settled in Tuscany.

She glanced over at a wooden trunk that sat on the floor under one of the many bookshelves. She pulled it out and looked through the drawings and half-done paintings within.

Her temperamental artist brother Mateo had been so quick to throw things out that did not reach his exacting standards, but Bernardo always kept them. Treasuring everything Mateo did.

They had been so close, right from the beginning. Bernardo so patiently trying to reach the troubled youth, who buried his emotions and found it so hard to express himself.

Bernardo was one of the few people he really felt safe enough around to reveal his deepest fears, needs, hurts. Mateo always called him "Brother Bernardo", both as when he first knew him he was a trainee Benedictine monk, and as they became a family, though Bernardo was more like a father to him.

She took out preliminary sketches Mateo had made of their family, that later he would use when creating the large oil paintings, they had hanging around their spacious villa. These all brought back happy memories, even when they were brief interludes, between their adventures in often dangerous times.

As the light faded, she lit some lamps, engrossed in the material that brought back such vivid memories and helped her review her life with Bernardo. There were ghosts she had to face before she could finally say "goodbye". Joys and pains, and although she had trusted Bernardo completely, there were things that had remained unsaid between them which she regretted.

The study door opened, and a tall elegant young woman entered. Her long dark hair, running down her back in a delicately braided, single tail. Bernadette was her oldest daughter and mother of three of the children she had happily listen to playing earlier. She joined her mother on the polished wooden floor, surrounded by old parchments and drawings.

'Are you alright?' Bernadette asked with much concern in her voice, 'we have put the children to bed and wondered if you wanted some supper.'

'No, I am fine,' Agata replied, admiring once again the beauty in her daughters face.

The late Captain De Poincy said she so reminded him of Bernardo's mother, Abriana.

'I am not hungry, just lost in old memories,' Agata said, reaching out and gently taking her daughter's hand, '...putting to rest in my mind, many who are not with us anymore.'

Bernadette picked up a sketch she recognised of her uncle Stefano and his family, she held it to the desk lamp, sitting on the floor beside them.

'This looks like the painting Uncle Stefano has in the manor in Malta, it must be one of the sketches Uncle Mateo made to create the oil painting,' Bernadette exclaimed with delight.

'Yes,' Agata agreed, 'it was your uncle Stefano who helped us build up our vineyard here. He became such a skilled wine maker and businessman.'

'It is such a pity he could not make it to father's funeral,' Bernadette said, looking downcast.

'Yes, unfortunately his poor health limits him and your father's death was so sudden and unexpected,' Agata dropped her hands into her lap and looked like she would cry.

The study door opened again and Luciano, Agata's oldest son came in. He was as tall and broad as his father, with his same blue eyes, but short, curly dark hair. Whenever he entered a room, he seemed to fill it with his presence, and he stood over them with his large hands on his hips.

'What is all this?' he asked in a semi-disapprovingly voice. Unlike his intellectual father, Luciano, named after Agata's brother that was killed by pirates, was a man of the land.

He managed their family estate—the commercial vineyards and small farm—working hard and focusing on practicalities.

Agata looked up at his towering figure unintimidated. He might be a powerful man now, but she had wiped his bottom when he was a baby. She had comforted him when he cried, and it had been her that had made the critical business decisions as they settled in this region. She studied his features for a moment and considered him. In some ways, he looked like his father, but in others he was completely different, even to the rest of the family. He had rarely been interested in Bernardo's studies, though relished the bow practice that had so broaden his chest muscles. She remembered Stefano trying to teach him to fence, but his uncle despaired at his lack of balance, pose and grace.

'No, no,' Stefano would shout, 'this is a rapier, not an axe. Stand up straight, breath steadily. Fencing is like dancing; it is a graceful activity.'

Stefano had been a fine dancer as well as a master swordsman, but Luciano mastered neither skills. However, he did learn well about wine making from his uncle, and about managing his employees. He was always first to arrive at work and last to leave, and his management of the estate had been exemplary.

'We are looking through our father's things,' Bernadette replied, annoyed at her brother's abruptness, 'some will have to go into storage...'

'What is this?' Luciano asked, ignoring his younger sister, as he often did. He was looking through pages in one of the journals on his father's desk. There were sketches of an old box with other drawings at the side, of the symbols on the box. There was also writing in languages he did not recognise.

Agata got up from the floor and came over to the desk to stand by Luciano, towering above her. She was trying not to get annoyed at his abruptness, knowing he did not mean to be insensitive.

'This was one of the main mysteries your father has spent many years trying to solve,' Agata explained, pointing at the sketches and strange writing, 'This was a box, supposedly found by your great grandfather in France. Your father thought it had originally contained a receptacle with a holy relic inside. He was sure the relic was important...important enough for people to kill for it, but never figured out what happened to the relic. These sketches are clues to what it was, and the writing is Aramaic, the language of Christ and his disciples.

The words say, "For lack of fruit, the tree was cursed", and that turned out to be the passphrase for entry to the Knight of the Holy Blood's meetings.'

'Oh, one of those secret societies father was investigating,' Luciano said.

'So, you were paying attention to the stories father told us,' Bernadette commented sarcastically, as she joined them at the desk.

'Your father did a great deal of research into holy relics that came from the middle east, many with the Templars,' Agata explained, 'and his findings are in these journals. If it was not for these incessant conflicts, I think we would have travelled around more looking for them. One day, someone may be able to pick up where he left off.'

Luciano shrugged, 'Well we need to store them somewhere dry and protected them from rodents,' ever practically thinking.

'Our family history is contained within these volumes,' Agata explained, 'please add to it but keep the journals for future generations.'

'We will,' chorused her children, and she knew they would.

End of The Dagger and Rosary

Glossary of Terms Mentioned in Story

Amīr al-baḥr

(Lord of the sea) Admiral in English.

Capuce

The capuce is one of the three parts of the white Dominican habit and has a short shoulder cape attached to it. It is worn over the scapular, which is worn over the tunic.

Scapular

The scapular is a short monastic cloak, bare at the arms, covering the shoulders like a long apron.

Cavaliere

Italian for Knight, so Cavaliere Mateo is similar to Sir Matthew in English.

Larboard

The old name for port. The left-hand side of a vessel when looking forward. You can guess why it was changed.

Canna

Derived from the Latin for Reed, equals two metres.

Xebecs

Xebecs were Mediterranean sailing vessel, similar but smaller than galleys which had both lateen sails and oars. Used extensively by Barbary pirates. Early xebecs had two masts, later three. They had a distinctive hull with pronounced overhanding bow and stern, and rarely displaced more than 200 tons.

Pied du roi

A pre-revolution French length measurement which equals 1.066 feet or 32.48

Langue

Or tongue, is the administrative divisions of the Knights of St John (e.g., French, German).

Bali

Title for the head of each Langue.

Levant

Geographical area covering eastern the Mediterranean part of western Asia.

Ducat

This was a gold or silver coin used to trade in Europe from the late Middle ages until early 20th century.

Qubtan

Arabic for captain. Qubtan albahr means captain of the Sea.

Conditierre

Conditierre was an Italian captain in command of mercenary companies during the Middle Ages, made up of multinational armies. They served European monarchs, city states and Popes during the Italian Wars of the Renaissance and European Wars of Religion.

Leagues

Unit of measurement approximately three and a half miles.

Kosha

Name for something, usually food, that meets Jewish dietary laws. In the case of meat, it has to be completely drained of blood.

Sloop

A sloop is a sailboat with a single mast, typically having one sail in front of the mast and one aft of (behind) the mast.

Teniete de Navio

Spanish for Naval Lieutenant.

Macello

Italian slaughterhouse or abattoir.

Coenobite

Coenobite is a member of a monastic community.

Note on text, *For lack of fruit the tree was cursed*:

In Genoese, it would be: *Pe mancansa de fruti l'erbu u l'stetu malediu.*
(Italian did not exist at the time, so the different states spoke local dialects.
The text in Italian today would be *Per mancanza di frutti, l'albero fu maledetto*).

Times of prayers (offices) in religious orders:

Matins (or Vigil) about 2 AM

Lauds (or Dawn Prayer) about 5 AM (Just before monks workday begins)

Prime (or Early Morning Prayer) about 6 AM

Terce (or Mi-Morning Prayer) about 9 AM

Sext (or Midday Prayers) about 12 noon

None (or Mid-Afternoon Prayer) about 3 PM

Vespers (or Evening Prayer) about 6 PM

Compline (or Night Prayer) about 7 PM (Before monks would retire for the night)